# THE CLEWSEY CLASSICS

HE SMILED. "DON'T YOU RECOGNISE ME, WATSON?"

# 1ST CULPRIT

## A CRIME WRITERS' ASSOCIATION ANNUAL

### edited by

## LIZA CODY AND MICHAEL Z LEWIN

WORLDWIDE®

TORONTO • NEW YORK • LONDON
AMSTERDAM • PARIS • SYDNEY • HAMBURG
STOCKHOLM • ATHENS • TOKYO • MILAN
MADRID • WARSAW • BUDAPEST • AUCKLAND

## 1ST CULPRIT: A CRIME WRITERS' ASSOCIATION ANNUAL

A Worldwide Mystery/December 1994

First published by St. Martin's Press, Incorporated.

ISBN 0-373-15275-2

# CONTENTS

## THE ANNUAL ANTHOLOGY OF THE CRIME WRITERS' ASSOCIATION

# 1ST CULPRIT

# THE MOUSE IN THE CORNER

★

## RUTH RENDELL

'I THINK YOU KNOW who killed your stepfather,' said Wexford.

It was a throwaway line, uttered on parting and over his shoulder as he reached the door. A swift exit was, however, impossible. He had to bend almost double. The girl he spoke to was a small woman, the boyfriend she lived with no more than five foot six. Life in the caravan, he thought, would otherwise have been insupportable.

Stuck in the doorway, he said when she made no reply, 'You won't mind if I come back in a day or two and we'll have another talk. All the same if I do, isn't it?

'You don't have to talk to me, Miss Heddon. It's open to you to say no.' It would all have been more dignified if he could have stood up and faced her, but Wexford wasn't much concerned with dignity. He spoke rather gravely but with gentleness. 'But if you've no objection we'll continue this conversation on Monday. I've a feeling you know a lot more than you've told me.'

She said it, one of those phrases that invariably means its opposite. 'I don't know what you're talking about.'

'That's unworthy of someone of your intelligence,' he said and he had meant it.

He opened the door and climbed out. She followed him and stood there, holding the door, a pretty young woman of twenty who looked even younger than her age because her blonde hair was waist-length and her white blouse school-girlish.

'Monday, then,' Wexford said. 'Shall we say three-ish?'

'Suit yourself.' With one of her flashes of humour, she said, 'You must feel like a Rottweiler in a rabbit hutch in here.'

He smiled. 'You may be right. It's true my bite is worse than my bark.'

Possibly digesting this, she closed the door without another word. He picked his way back to the car where Donaldson waited at the wheel. A path of cinders made a just usable track across the corner of a muddy field. In the cold haze the shape of a cottage converted from a railway carriage could just be seen against a grey tangle of wilderness. Two inches of rain had fallen in the week since Tom Peterlee's death and the sky of massive grey cumulus was loaded with more.

'Go by way of Feverel's, will you Steve?' said Wexford. 'I don't want to stop, just take a look.'

The farm shop remained close, though a wood board offering for sale apples, pears, plums and walnuts for picking still stood by the gate. Wexford told Donaldson to stop the car and park for a few moments. Let Heather Peterlee see him. That sort of thing did no harm. He looked, for the dozenth time, at the shack that had been a shop, the huddle of wooden buildings, the house itself and the inevitable caravan.

The house was a Victorian building, rendered in a pale stone colour that the rain had turned to khaki. The shallow roof was of dull grey slate. Some ten yards of bleak ground, part gravel and part scrubby grass, separated the house from the shop. In between and a little distance behind, the caravan stood on a concrete slab, and beyond it stretched the market gardens.

The shop, its double doors closed and padlocked, its windows boarded up, seemed a dilapidated hut. A sheet of the corrugated iron that roofed it had come loose and clanged up and down rhythmically in the increasing wind. It was a dreary place. No visitor would have difficulty in believing a man had been clubbed to death there.

As Donaldson started the engine a black spaniel came out from the back of the house and began barking inside the gate. Wexford had felt its teeth through his jacket sleeve, though blood had not been drawn.

'That the dog, is it, sir?'

They all knew the story, even those only remotely involved. Wexford confirmed that this indeed was the dog, this was Scamp.

Wexford spared a glance for the neighbours. Joseph Peterlee had a plant hire business and a customer was in the act of returning a mechanical digger. In conversation with her husband and the digger driver on the concrete entrance, an area much cracked, pitted and now puddled, was Mrs Monica Peterlee in her unvarying uniform of rubber boots and floral cross-over overall. And those are the characters in this drama, he thought, with the exception of one who (to paraphrase Kipling) has gone to the husband of her bosom the same as she ought to go, and one who has gone heaven only knows where.

Why was he so sure Arlene Heddon had the answer? Mike Burden, his second-in-command at Kingsmarkham CID, said with contempt that at any rate she was more attractive than the wife and the widow. With his usual distaste for those whose lives failed to approximate fairly closely to his own, he spoke scathingly of 'the Peterlee girl' as if having no job and no proper roof over one's head directly conduced to homicide.

'Her name,' Wexford said rather dourly, 'is Heddon. It was her father's name. Heather Peterlee, if you remember, was a Mrs Heddon before she remarried.' He added, wondering as he did so, why he bothered to indulge Burden's absurd prejudices, 'a widow, incidentally'.

Quick as a flash, Burden came back with, 'What did her first husband die of?'

'Oh God, Mike, some bone disease. We went into all that. But back to Arlene Heddon, she's a very intelligent young woman, you know.'

'No, I don't know. You must be joking. Intelligent girls don't live on benefit in caravans with unemployed welders.'

'What a snob you are.'

'*Married* welders. I'm not just a snob, I'm a moralist. Intelligent girls do well at school, go on to further education, get suitable well-paid jobs and buy themselves homes on mortgages.'

'Somehow and somewhere along the line Arlene Heddon missed out on that. In any case, I didn't say she was academically inclined. She's sharp, she's clever, she's got a good brain.'

'And her mother, the two-times widow, is she the genius Arlene inherited her IQ from?'

This was neither the time nor the place to be discussing the murder, Wexford's house on a Saturday evening, but Burden had come round for a drink and whatever the topic of conversation, things had a way of coming back to the Peterlees. Wexford suggested they go over the sequence of events again. Dora, his wife, was present, but sitting on the window-seat, reading tranquilly.

'You can set me right on the details,' Wexford began, 'but I think you'll agree it was broadly like this. On Thursday, October 10, Heather Peterlee opened the farm shop at Feverel's as usual at nine in the morning. Heather had her sister-in-law Mrs Monica Peterlee to help her, again as usual. Her husband, Tom, was working outside, and at lunchtime he brought up to the shop by tractor the vegetables he had lifted and picked during the morning.

'They ate their midday meal in the shop, keeping it open, and at three or thereabouts Joseph Peterlee arrived in his car to fetch his wife and take her shopping in Kingsmarkham. Tom and Heather served in the shop until closing time at five when they returned to the house and Heather began preparing a meal. Tom had brought in the shop's takings with him which he intended to put in the safe but in the meantime he left the notes on the kitchen dresser that faces the outside door. The sum was about £360. He put the money on the dresser shelf and placed on top of it his camera in its case, presumably to stop it blowing about when the door was opened. He then went to the caravan to discuss raising the rent with Carol Fox who had been living there since the summer.'

'Tom Peterlee was killed for £360,' said Burden.

'No, but various people would like us to think he was. It's a problem even guessing why he was killed. Everyone seems to have liked him. We have had...' Wexford hesitated, 'golden opinions from all sorts of people. He was something of a paragon by all accounts, an ideal husband, good, kind, undeniably handsome. He was even handsome on the slab—forgive me, Dora.

'But I'll go on. They ate their meal at five-thirty. During the course of it, according to her statement, Tom said to his wife that they had fixed up the matter of the rent amicably. Carol wanted to stay on and understood the rent she was paying was inadequate...'

Dora interrupted him. 'Is that the woman who'd left her husband and Heather Peterlee said she could have their caravan because she'd nowhere to live?'

'A friend of Heather's from way back, apparently. According to Heather, she told Tom she'd be round in an hour to accompany her on a dog walk. Heather always took the

dog out after supper and Carol had got into the habit of
going with her. Heather washed up their dishes and Tom
dried. As I've said, he was an ideal husband. At some point
he went out to the woodshed and fetched in a basket of logs
to feed the wood-burning stoves, of which there was one in
the kitchen and another in the living-room.

'Carol knocked on the door and came into the kitchen at
twenty past six. It wasn't raining but it looked like rain and
Carol was wearing only a cardigan. Heather suggested she
put on one of the rainproof jackets hanging behind the back
door and Carol took a fawn-coloured one.'

'Strange, wasn't it,' Burden put in, 'that she didn't fetch
a coat of her own from the caravan? Especially a woman
like that. Very conscious of her appearance, I'd say. But
perhaps she wouldn't care, out on her own with another
woman. It was a dull evening and they weren't likely to meet
anyone.'

Dora gave him a look, enigmatic, half-smiling, but said
nothing. Her husband went on, 'If you remember, when the
caravan was searched as the house was, the fact was remarked on that Carol Fox had no raincoat among her
clothes. She has said and Heather has confirmed it that she
always used one of Heather's. They took the dog and went
for a walk through the Feverel's land, across the meadows
by the public footpath and down to the river. It was sometime between six-twenty and six-thirty that they left. It was
still light and would be for another half-hour. What Tom
did in their absence we don't know and probably never shall
know, except that putting that money into the safe wasn't
among his activities.

'At about ten to seven Arlene Heddon arrived at Feverel's, brought in her boyfriend's van.' Wexford raised an
eyebrow at Burden. 'The unemployed, married welder, Gary
Wyatt. Arlene and Gary have no phone and Arlene got the
message from grandma on whose land she lives. She's not

really her grandmother, of course, but she calls her grandma.'

'The old witch,' said Dora. 'That's what people call her. She's well known.'

'I don't think she's as old as she looks and she's definitely not a witch, though she cultivates that appearance. To be the mother of Joseph and Tom she need be no more than sixty-five and I dare say she's not. The message Arlene got from Mrs Peterlee Senior was that mum had finished her jumper and if she wanted it for the Friday, could she come and pick it up? The time suggested was about eight. Grandma said she'd drive Arlene herself on account of she was going to her Conservative Association meeting in Kingsmarkham—I kid you not, Dora—but she said, no, Gary and she would still be eating their tea. Gary would take her in the van a bit later on.

'In fact, Gary wanted to go out at half-past six. He dropped her off at Feverel's, thus getting her there more than an hour earlier than her mother had suggested, and went on to have a drink with his pals in the Red Rose at Edenwick. Not that anyone has confirmed this. Neither the licensee nor the girl behind the bar remembers him being there. Which is in direct contrast to the evidence of the old witch's witnesses. Strange as her presence there might seem, every Tory in Kingsmarkham seems to remember her in the Seminar Room of the Olive and Dove Hotel that night. Not until seven-thirty, however, when the meeting started. Where had she been in that lost hour and a half?

'Gary promised to come back for Arlene in an hour. Arlene went round the back of the house and entered by the kitchen door, which was unlocked. As a daughter of the house, she didn't knock or call out, but walked straight in.

'There, in the kitchen, on the floor, she found the body of her stepfather, Tom Peterlee, lying face downwards, with a wound in the back of the head. She knelt down and touched his face. It was still faintly warm. She knew there was a phone in the sitting-room but, fearing whoever had done this might still be in the house, she didn't go in there but ran back outside in the hope Gary had not yet gone. When she saw that he had, she ran the hundred yards or so to Mr and Mrs Joe Peterlee's where she used their phone and dialed 999.

'Joe Peterlee was out, according to his wife. Arlene—all this is Arlene's evidence, partly confirmed by Monica Peterlee—Arlene asked her to come back with her and wait for the police but she said she was too frightened to do that, so Arlene went back alone. Within a very few minutes—it was now five past seven—her mother and Carol Fox returned from their walk with the dog. She was waiting outside the back door.

'She prepared them for what they would see and Heather cried out, pushed open the door and rushed into the kitchen. She threw herself on the body and when Arlene and Carol pulled her off and lifted her up, she began banging her head and face against the kitchen wall.'

Burden nodded. 'These two—what do we call them? Hysterical acts? Manifestations of grief?—account for the blood on the front of her jacket and the extensive bruising to her face. Or at least are possible explanations for them.'

'The police came and everyone was questioned on the spot. Of course no one had seen any suspicious characters hanging about Feverel's. No one ever has. Joe Peterlee has never been able to give a satisfactory account of his movements between six-twenty and six-fifty. Nor have Gary Wyatt and Grandma Peterlee.

'The money was gone. There was no weapon. No prints, other than those of Tom, Heather, Carol Fox and Arlene, were found. The pathologist says Tom died between six-fifteen and seven-fifteen, a time which can be much narrowed down if Arlene is to be believed. Remember, she says he felt warm when she touched him at six-fifty.

'I think she's lying. I think she's lying all along the line, she's protecting someone, and that's why I'm going to keep on talking to her until I find out who. Grandma or her boyfriend or her Uncle Joe—or her mother.'

Dora wrinkled up her nose. 'Isn't it a bit distasteful, Reg, getting a girl to betray her own mother? It's like the KGB.'

'And we know what happened to them,' said Burden.

Wexford smiled. 'I may only be getting her to betray her step-aunt by marriage, or isn't that allowed either?'

Burden left them at about ten to ten. He was on foot, for he and Wexford lived less than a mile apart. His route home was to take him past the big new shopping mall, the York Crest Centre. He deplored the name and the place, all a far cry from what Kingsmarkham had been when first he came.

Then there was life in the town at night, people entering or emerging from pubs and restaurants, cinema visitors, walkers strolling, in those days before the ubiquitous car. Television, the effects of recession and the fear of street violence had all combined to keep the townsfolk indoors and the place was deserted. It was silent, empty but brightly lit, and therefore slightly uncanny.

His footfalls made a faint hollow echo; he saw his solitary figure reflected in gleaming shop windows. Not a soul passed him as he entered York Street, not a single being waited on a corner or at the bus stop. He turned into the alley that ran along the side of the York Crest Centre, to cut a furlong or so off his journey.

Into his silent speculation burst the raiders. It took him about thirty seconds to realise what this was. He had seen it on television but thought it confined to the north. A ram raid. That was what someone had named this kind of heist. The Land Rover first, turning on the paved court, reversing at the highest speed it could make into the huge glass double doors that shut off the centre by night. The noise of crashing glass was enormous, like a bomb.

It vanished inside, followed by two cars, a Volvo and a Volvo Estate, rattling over the broken glass, the wreckage of the doors. He didn't wait to see what happened. He had his cell-phone in his hand and switched on before the second car's tail lights had disappeared. 'No service' came up on its screen and 'No service' when he shook it and pulled the aerial out. It had gone wrong. Never before had that happened but it had to happen tonight when he was in the right place at the right time.

Burden raced down the alley to the phones on the post office wall, four of them under plastic hoods. The first he tried had been vandalised, the second worked. If he could get them there within five minutes, within ten even ... He pounded back, remembered it would be advisable not to be heard, and crept the rest of the way. They were leaving, the Land Rover—stolen of course—with all its glass shattered, the two Volvos hard on its rear, and were gone God knew where by the time the Mid-Sussex Constabulary cars arrived.

THE PURPOSE OF THE RAID had been to remove as much electronic equipment as the thieves could shift in five minutes from Nixon's in the Centre. It had been a tremendous haul and had probably taken twelve men to accomplish it.

The phone on the post office wall was repaired and on the following day vandalised again along with all the others in the row. That was on a Monday, the date of Wexford's second conversation with Arlene Heddon. He went along to the caravan on old Mrs Peterlee's land in the late afternoon. Arlene sometimes had a cleaning job but she was always in during the afternoons. He tapped on the door and she called out to him to come in.

The television was on and she was watching, lounging on the seat that ran the length of the opposite wall. She looked so relaxed, even somnolent, that Wexford thought she would switch off by means of the channel changer which lay on top of the partition that divided living/bedroom from kitchen, but she got up and pressed the switch. They faced each other, and this time she seemed anxious to talk. He began to take her through a series of new enquiries and all the old ones.

He noticed, then, that what she said differed very slightly from what she had said the first time, if in minor details. Her mother had not thrown herself on the body but knelt down and cradled the dead man's head in her arms. It was on one of the counters, not against the wall, that Heather had beaten her head.

The dog had howled at the sight of its dead master. The first time she said she thought she had heard a noise upstairs when first she arrived. This time she said she denied it, all had been silent. She had not noticed if the money was there or not when she first arrived. Now she said the money was there with the camera on top of the notes. When she came back from making her phone call she had not gone back into the house but had waited outside for her mother to return. That was what she said the first time. Now she said she had gone briefly into the kitchen once more. The camera was there but the money gone.

Wexford pointed out these discrepancies in a casual way. She made no comment. He asked, with apparent indifference, 'Just as a matter of interest, how did you know your mother was out with the dog?'

'The dog wasn't there and she wasn't.'

'You were afraid to use the phone in the house in case your stepfather's killer might still be there. You never considered the possibility that your mother might have been dead in some other part of the house? That Carol Fox might

have taken the dog out on her own, as perhaps she sometimes did?'

'I didn't know Carol very well,' said Arlene Heddon.

It was hardly an answer. 'But she was a close friend of
your mother's, an old friend, wasn't she? You might say
your mother offered her sanctuary when she left her husband. That's the action of a close friend, isn't it?'

'I haven't lived at home since I was seventeen. I don't
know all the friends my mother's got. I didn't know whether
Carol took the dog out or what. Tom sometimes took him
out and my mother did. I never heard of Carol going with
my mother, but I wouldn't. I wasn't interested in Carol.'

'Yet you waited for them both to come back from their
walk, Miss Heddon?'

'I waited for my mother,' she said.

Wexford left her, promising to come back for another talk
on Thursday. Grandma was nowhere to be seen but as he
approached his car hers swept in, bumping over the rough
ground, lurching through a trough or two, skidding with a
scream of brakes on the ice and, describing a swift half-
circle round the railway carriage, juddering to a stop. Florrie Peterlee, getting on for seventy and looking eighty, drove
like an eighteen-year-old madbrain at the wheel of his first
jalopy.

She gave the impression of clawing her way out. Her white
hair was as long and straight as Arlene's and she was always dressed in trailing black that sometimes had a curiously fashionable look. On a teenager it would have been
trendy. She had a hooky nose and prominent chin, and
bright black eyes. So far she had shown no grief whatever
at the death of her son.

'You're too old for her,' said the old witch.

'Too old for what?' said Wexford, refusing to be out-
faced.

'Ooh, hark at him! That's a nice question to ask a senior citizen. Mind I don't put a spell on you. Why don't you leave her alone, poor lamb.'

'She's going to tell me who killed your son Tom.'

'Get away. She don't know. Maybe I did.' She stared at him with a bold defiance. 'I all but killed his dad once. I said, you've knocked me about once too often, Arthur Peterlee, and I picked up the kitchen knife and come at him with it. I won't say he never touched me again, human nature never worked that way, but he dropped dead with his heart soon after, poor old sod. I was so glad to see the back of him I danced on his grave. People say that, I know, it's just a way of talking, but me, I really did it. Went up the cemetery with a half-bottle of gin and danced on the bugger's grave.'

Wexford could see her, hair flying, black draperies blowing, the bottle in one hand, her wrinkled face dabbled with gin, dancing under the rugged ilexes and the yew tree's shade. He put up his eyebrows. Before she had more chances to shock him, or try to, he asked her if she had thought any more about telling him where she had been in that lost hour on the evening of her son's death.

'You'd be surprised.'

She said it, not as a figure of speech, but as a genuine undertaking that she could astonish him. He had no doubt she could. She grinned, showing even white teeth, not dentures. The thought came to him that if she had a good bath, put her copious hair up and dressed in something more appropriate for a rural matriarch, she might look rather wonderful. He wasn't too worried about her alibi or lack of one, for he doubted if she had the strength to wield the 'blunt instrument' that had killed Tom Peterlee.

He was very certain he knew what that instrument was and what had become of it. Arriving at Feverel's within the hour, he had seen the wood splinters in Tom Peterlee's head

wound before the pathologist arrived. With a sinking heart
he had taken in the implications of a basket full of logs just
inside the back door and the big wood-burning stove in an
embrasure of the wall facing the door into the house. They
would never find the weapon. Without being able to prove
it, he knew from the first that it had been an iron-hard log
of oak, maybe a foot long and three or four inches in di-
ameter, a log used to strike again and again, then pushed in
among the blazing embers in that stove.

He had even looked. The stove had been allowed to go
out. Could you imagine anyone making up the fire at a time
like that? A pale grey powdery dust glowed red still in one
patch at the heart of it and as he watched, died. Later on,
he had those ashes analysed. All the time he was up there the
dog howled. Someone shut it up in a distant room but its
long drawn-out cries pursued him up the road on his way to
see Joseph and Monica Peterlee.

He remembered wondering, not relevantly, if she dressed
like that to sit down at table, to watch television. At nine
o'clock at night she was still in her cross-over overall, her
black wellies. Her husband was a bigger and heavier version of his brother, three or four years older, his hair iron-
grey where Tom's had been brown, his belly fat and slack
where Tom's had been flat. They alibied each other, use-
lessly, and Joe had no alibi for the relevant time. He had
been out shooting rabbits, he said, producing his shotgun
and shotgun license.

'They done Tom in for the money,' he told Wexford
sagely. He spoke as if, without his proffered information,
such a solution would never have occurred to the police. 'I
told him. I said to him time and again I said, you don't want
to leave that laying about, not even for an hour, not even in
daylight. What you got a safe for if you don't use it? I said
that, didn't I, girl?'

His wife confirmed that he had indeed said it. Over and over. Wexford had the impression she would have confirmed anything he said. For peace, for a quiet life. It was two days later that, interviewing them again, he asked about the relationship between Tom and Heather Peterlee.

'They was a very happy couple,' Joe said. 'Never a cross word in all the ten years they was married.'

Wexford, later, wondered what Dora would have said if he had made such a remark about relatives of his. Or Burden's wife Jenny if he had. Something dry, surely. There would have been some quick intervention, some, 'Oh, come on, how would you know?' But Monica said nothing. She smiled nervously. Her husband looked at her and she stopped smiling.

THE RAM RAIDERS were expected to have another go the following Saturday night. Instead they came on Friday, late shopping night at Stowerton Brook Buyers' Heaven, less than an hour after the shops closed. Another stolen Land Rover burst through the entrance doors, followed by a stolen Range Rover and a BMW. This time the haul was from Electronic World but was similar to that taken the previous time. The men in those three vehicles got away with an astonishing £35,000 worth of equipment.

This time Burden had not been nearby, on his way home. No one had, since the Stowerton Brook industrial site where Buyers' Heaven lay totally deserted by night, emptier by far than Kingsmarkham town centre. The two guard dogs that kept watch over the neighbouring builders' supplies yard had been destroyed a month before in the purge on dangerous breeds.

Burden had been five miles away, talking to Carol Fox and her husband Raymond. To Burden, who never much noticed any woman's appearance but his wife's, she was simply rather above average good-looking. In her mid-

thirties, ten years younger than Heather, she was brightly
dressed and vivacious. It was Wexford who described her as
one of that group or category that seems to have more natural colour than most women with her pure red hair, glowing, luminous skin, ivory and pink, and her eyes of gentian
blue. He said nothing about the unnatural colour that dec-
orated Mrs Fox's lips, nails and eyelids to excess. Burden
assessed her as 'just a cockney with an awful voice'. Privately, he thought of her as common. She was loud and
coarse, a strange friend for the quiet, reserved and mousy
Heather.

The husband she had returned to after a six-month separation was thin and toothy with hag-ridden eyes, some sort
of salesman. He seemed proud of her and exaggeratedly
pleased to have her back. On that particular evening, the
case not much more than a week old, he was anxious to assure Burden and anyone else who would listen that his and
his wife's parting had been no more than a 'trial', an exper-
imental living apart to refresh their relationship. They were
together again now for good. Their separation hadn't been
a success but a source of misery to both of them.

Carol said nothing. Asked by Burden to go over with him
once more the events of 10 October, she reaffirmed six-
twenty as the time she and Heather had gone out. Yes, there
had been a basket of logs just inside the back door. She
hadn't seen any money on the counter or the dresser. Tom
had been drying dishes when she came in. He was alive and
well when they left, putting the dishes away in the cupboard.

'I should be so lucky,' said Carol with a not very affectionate glance at her husband.

'Did you like Tom Peterlee, Mrs Fox?'

Was it his imagination or had Raymond Fox's expression changed minutely? It would be too much to say that he
had winced. Burden repeated his question.

'He was always pleasant,' she said. 'I never saw much of him.'

The results came from the lab disclosing that a piece of animal bone had been among the stove ashes. Burden had found out, that first evening, what the Peterlees had had for their evening meal: lamb chops with potatoes and cabbage Tom had grown himself. The remains were put into the bin for the compost heap, never into the stove. Bones, cooked or otherwise, the Peterlees weren't particular, were put on the back doorstep for the dog.

What had become of the missing money? They searched the house a second time, observing the empty safe, the absence of any jewellery, the absence of books, any kind of reading matter or any sign of the generally accepted contributions to gracious living.

Heather Peterlee shut herself up in the house and when approached, said nothing. Questioned, she stared dumbly and remained dumb. Everyone explained her silence as due to her grief. Wexford, without much hope of anything coming of it, asked to remove the film from the camera that had weighted down the missing notes. She shrugged, muttered that he could have it, he was welcome, and turned her face to the wall. But when he came to look, he found no film in the camera.

Burden said Wexford's continued visits to Arlene Heddon were an obsession, the Chief Constable that they were a waste of time. Since his second visit she had given precisely the same answers to all the questions he asked—the same, that is, as on that second occasion. He wondered how she did it. Either it was the transparent truth or she had total recall. In that case, why did it differ from what she had said the first time he questioned her? Now all was perfect consistency.

If she made a personal comment there might be something new, but she rarely did. Every time he referred to Tom

Peterlee as her stepfather she corrected him by saying, 'I called him Tom,' and if he spoke of Joseph and Monica as her uncle and aunt she told him they weren't her uncle and aunt. Carol Fox was her mother's great friend; Heather had known her for years, but she, Arlene, knew Carol scarcely at all.

'I never heard of Carol walking the dog with my mother but I wouldn't. I wasn't interested in Carol.'

Sometimes Gary Wyatt was there. When Wexford came he always left. He always had a muttered excuse about having to see someone about something and being late already. One Monday—it was usually Mondays and Thursdays that Wexford went to the caravan—he asked Gary to wait a moment. Had he thought any more about giving details of where he was between six forty-five and seven-thirty that evening? Gary hadn't. He had been in the pub, the Red Rose at Edenwick.

'No one remembers seeing you.'

'That's their problem.'

'It may become yours, Gary. You didn't like Tom Peterlee, did you? Isn't it a fact that Tom refused to let you and Arlene have the caravan Mrs Fox lived in because you'd left your wife and children?'

'That was the pot calling the kettle,' said Gary.

'And what does that mean?'

Nothing, they said. It meant nothing. He hadn't been referring to Tom. A small smile crossed Arlene's face and was gone. Gary went out to see someone about something, an appointment for which he was already late, and Wexford began asking about Heather's behaviour when she came home after her walk.

'She didn't throw herself at him,' Arlene said glibly, without, it seemed, a vestige of feeling. 'She knelt down and sort of held his head and cuddled it. She got his blood on her. Carol and me, we made her get up and then she started banging her face on that counter.'

It was the same as last time, always the same.

THERE HAD BEEN no appeals to the public for witnesses to come forward. Witnesses to what? Heather Peterlee's alibi was supplied by Carol Fox and Wexford couldn't see why she should have lied or the two of them have been in cahoots. Friend she might be, but not such a friend as to perjure herself to save a woman who had motivelessly murdered an ideal husband.

He wondered about the bone fragment. But they had a dog. It was hardly too far-fetched to imagine a dog's bone getting in among the logs for the stove. Awkward, yes, but awkward inexplicable things do happen. It was still hard for him to accept that Arlene had simply taken it for granted her mother was out walking the dog with Carol Fox when she scarcely seemed to know that Carol lived there. And he had never really been able to swallow that business about Heather banging her face against the counter. Carol had only said, 'Oh, yes, she did,' and Heather herself put her hands over her mouth and turned her face to the wall.

Then a curious thing happened that began to change everything. An elderly man who had been a regular customer at the farm shop asked to speak to Wexford. He was a widower who shopped and cooked for himself, living on the state pension and a pension from the Mid-Sussex Water Authority.

Frank Waterton began by apologising, he was sure it was nothing, he shouldn't really be troubling Wexford, but this was a matter which had haunted him. He had always meant to do something about it, though he was never sure what. That was why he had, in the event, done nothing.

'What is it, Mr Waterton? Why not tell me and I'll decide if it's nothing.' The old man looked at him almost

wistfully. 'No one will blame you if it's nothing. You'll still
have been public-spirited and done your duty.'

Wexford didn't even know then that it was connected with
the Peterlee case. Because he was due to pay one of his
twice-weekly calls on Arlene Heddon, he was impatient and
did his best not to let his impatience show.

'It's to do with what I noticed once or twice when I went
shopping for my bits and pieces at Feverel's,' he said and
then Wexford ceased to feel exasperated or to worry about
getting to Arlene on time. 'It must have been back in June
the first time, I know it was June on account of the strawberries were in. I can see her now looking through the
strawberries to get me a nice punnet and when she lifted her
face up—well, I was shocked. I was really shocked. She was
bruised like someone had been knocking her about. She'd
a black eye and a cut on her cheek. I said, you've been in the
wars, Mrs Peterlee, and she said she'd had a fall and hit
herself on the sink.'

'You say that was the first time?'

'That's right. I sort of half-believed her when she said that
but not the next time. Not when I went in there again when
the Cox's apples first came in—must have been late September—and her face was black and blue all over again.
And she'd got her wrist strapped up—well, bandaged. I
didn't comment, not that time. I reckoned it wouldn't be—
well, tactful.

'I just thought I ought to come and tell someone. It's been
preying on my mind ever since I heard about Tom Peterlee
getting done in. I sort of hesitated and hummed and hawed.
If it had been *her* found killed I'd have been in like a shot, I
can tell you.'

He made it to Arlene's only a quarter of an hour late.
Because it fascinated him, hearing her give all those same
answers, parrot-like, except that the voice this parrot mim-
icked was her own, he asked her all the same things over

again. The question about her mother's bruised face he left till last, to have the effect of a bombshell.

First of all, he got the same stuff. 'She knelt down and took hold of his head and sort of cuddled it. That's how she got his blood on her. Me and Carol pulled her off him and lifted her up and she started banging her face on the counter.'

'Was she banging her face on the counter in June, Miss Heddon? Was she doing the same thing in September? And how about her bandaged wrist?'

Arlene Heddon didn't know. She looked him straight in the eye, both her eyes into both his, and said she didn't know.

'I never saw her wrist bandaged.'

He turned deliberately from her hypnotic gaze and looked round the caravan. They had acquired a microwave since he was last there. An electric jug kettle had replaced the old chrome one. Presents from Grandma? The old witch was reputed to be well-off. It was said that none of the money she had made from selling off acres of her land in building lots had found its way into her son's pockets. He had noticed a new car parked outside the railway carriage cottage and wouldn't have been surprised to learn that she replaced hers every couple of years.

'It'll be Tuesday next week not Monday, Miss Heddon,' he said as he left.

'Suit yourself.'

'Gary found himself a job yet?'

'What job? You must be joking.'

'Perhaps I am. Perhaps there's something hilarious in the idea of either of you working. I mean, have you ever given it a thought? Earning your living is what I'm talking about.'

She shut the door hard between them.

After that, enquiries among the people who had known them elicited plenty of descriptions of Mrs Peterlee's visible injuries. Regular customers at the farm shop remembered her bandaged arm. One spoke of a black eye so bad that it had closed up and on the following day Heather Peterlee had covered it with a shade. She explained a scab on her upper lip as a cold sore but the customer to whom she had told this story hadn't believed her.

The myth of the ideal husband was fading. Only the Peterlees themselves continued to support it and Monica Peterlee, when Burden asked her about it, seemed stricken dumb with fear. It was as if he had put his finger on the sorest part of a trauma and reawakened everything that caused the wound.

'I don't want to talk about it. You can't make me. I don't want to know.'

Joseph treated the suggestion as a monstrous calumny on his dead brother. He blustered. 'You want to be very careful what you're insinuating. Tom's dead and he can't defend himself, so you lot think you can say anything. The police aren't gods any more, you want to remember that. There's not an evening goes by when you don't see it on the telly, another lot of coppers up in court for making things up they'd write down and saying things what never happened.'

His wife was looking at him the way a mouse in a corner looks at a cat that has temporarily mislaid it. Burden wasn't going to question Heather. They left her severely alone as they began to build up a case against her.

THE DAY AFTER the third ram raid—this time on the Kingsbrook Centre itself in the middle of Kingsmarkham—Wexford was back in Arlene Heddon's caravan and Arlene was saying, 'I never saw her wrist bandaged.'

'Miss Heddon, you know your stepfather repeatedly assaulted your mother. He knocked her about, gave her black eyes, cut her cheek. His brother Joseph doubtless hands out the same treatment to his wife. What have you got to gain by pretending you knew nothing about it?'

'She knelt on the floor and lifted up his head and sort of cuddled it. That's how she got blood on her. Me and Carol sort of pulled her off him and then she started banging...'

Wexford stopped her. 'No. She got those bruises because Tom hit her in the face. I don't know why. Do you know why? Maybe it was over money, the shop takings he left on the dresser. Or maybe she'd protested about him asking for more rent from Carol Fox. If your mother argued with him he reacted by hitting her. That was his way.'

'If you say so.'

'No, Miss Heddon. It's not what I say, it's what you say.'

He waited for her to rejoin with, 'I never saw her wrist bandaged,' but she lifted her eyes and he could have sworn there was amusement in them, a flash of it that came and went. She astounded him by what she said. It was the last thing he expected. She fidgeted for a moment or two with the channel changer on the divider between them, lifted her eyes and said slowly, 'Carol Fox was Tom's girlfriend.'

He digested this, saw fleetingly a host of possible implications, then said, 'What, precisely, do you mean by that term?'

She was almost contemptuous. 'What everyone means. His girlfriend. His lover. What me and Gary are.'

'NOT MUCH POINT in denying it, is there?' said Carol Fox.

'I'm surprised you didn't give us this piece of information, Mr Fox,' Wexford said.

When her husband said nothing, Carol broke in impatiently, 'Oh, he's ashamed. Thinks it's a reflection on his manhood or whatever. I told him, you can't keep a thing like that dark, so why bother?'

'You kept it dark from us deliberately for a month.'

She shrugged, unrepentant. 'I felt a bit bad about Heather, to be honest with you. It was like Tom said I could live in this caravan on his land. He never said it was right next door. Still, there was another girl he'd had four or five years back he actually brought to live in the house. He called her the au pair, as if those Peterlees weren't one generation from gypsies when all's said and done.'

'Then I take it his visit to you that evening had nothing to do with raising the rent?'

The husband got up and left the room. Wexford didn't try to stop him. His presence hadn't much inhibited his wife but his absence freed her further. She smiled just a little. 'It's not what you're thinking. We had a drink.'

'A bit odd, wasn't it, you going out for a walk with his wife? Or didn't she know? That's pretty hard to believe, Mrs Fox.'

'Of course she knew. She hated me. And I can't say I was too keen on her. That wasn't true about us often going out together. That walk, that night, I fixed it up because I wanted to talk to her. I wanted to tell her I was leaving, it was all over between me and Tom, and I was going back to Ray.' She drew in a long breath. 'I'll be honest with you, it was a physical thing. The way he looked—well, between you and me, I couldn't get enough of it. Maybe it's all worked out for the best. But the fact is, it'd have been different if Tom'd have said he'd leave her, but he wouldn't and I'd had it.'

Wexford said, when he and Burden were out in the car, 'I was beginning to see Heather's alibi going down the drain. Her best friend lying for her. Not now. I can't see Tom's girlfriend alibiing the wife she wanted out of the way.'

'Well, no. Especially not alibiing the woman who'd killed the man she loved or once had loved. It looks as if we start again.'

'Does anyone but Heather have a motive? What was in it for Arlene or Gary Wyatt? The man's own mother's capable of anything her strength allows her but I don't think her strength would have allowed her this. Joseph had nothing to gain by Tom's death—the farm becomes Heather's—and it's evident all Monica wants is a quiet life. So we're left with the marauder who goes about the countryside murdering smallholders for three hundred and sixty quid.'

Next morning an envelope arrived addressed to him. It contained nothing but a photographic film processor's chit which was also a receipt for one pound. The receipt was on paper headed with the name of a pharmacist in the York Crest Centre. Wexford guessed the origin of the film before he had Sergeant Martin collect the processed shots. Arlene, at home to him on Tuesday, was back at her parrot game.

'I haven't lived at home since I was seventeen. I don't know all the friends my mother's got. I didn't know whether Carol took the dog out or what. Tom sometimes took him out and my mother did. I never heard of Carol going with my mother, but I wouldn't. I wasn't interested in Carol.'

'This is reaching the proportions of a psychosis, Miss Heddon.'

She knew what he meant. He didn't have to explain. He could see comprehension in her eyes and her small satisfied smile. Others would have asked when all this was going to stop, when would he leave it alone. Not she. She would give all the same answers to his questions indefinitely, and every few weeks throw in a bombshell, as she had when she told him of Carol Fox's place in the Peterlees' lives. Always supposing, of course, that she had more bombshells to throw.

He knocked on the old witch's door. After rather a long time she came. Wexford wasn't invited in and he could see she already had company. An elderly man with a white beard, but wearing jeans and red leather cowboy boots, was standing by the fireplace pouring wine from a half-empty bottle into two glasses.

She gave him the grin that cracked her face into a thousand wrinkles and showed her remarkable teeth.

'I had half an hour going spare, Mrs Peterlee, so I thought I'd use it asking you where you were between six and seven-thirty on the evening your son was killed.'

She put her head on one side. 'I reckoned I'd keep you all guessing.'

'And now you're going to tell me,' he said patiently.

'Why not?' She turned and shouted over her shoulder at a pitch absurdly loud for the distance. 'If that one's finished, Eric, you can go and open another. It's on the kitchen table.' Wexford was favoured with a wink. 'I was with my boyfriend. *Him.* At his place. I always drop in for a quick one before the meeting.' She very nearly made him blush. 'A quick *drink*,' she said. 'You can ask him when he comes back. Rude bunch of buggers you cops are. It's written all over your face what you're thinking. Well, he'd marry me tomorrow if I said the word, but I'm shy, I've been bitten once. He may be nice as pie now and all lovey-dovey but it's another story when they've got the ring on your finger. Don't want another one knocking me to kingdom come when his tea's five minutes late on the table.'

'Is that why Tom beat up Heather, because his meal was late?'

If she was taken aback she didn't show it. 'Come on, they don't need a reason, not when the drink's in them. It's just you being there and not as strong as them and scared too, that's enough for them. You needn't look like that. I don't suppose you do like the sound of it. You want to've been on the receiving end. OK, Eric, I'm coming.'

Now that he no longer suspected her, after he had left her alone for a month, he went to Feverel's and saw Heather Peterlee. It was the night of the third ram raid and they knew it was coming when a Volvo Estate and a Land Rover were reported stolen during the day. But that was still three or four hours off.

Abused women have a look in common. Wexford castigated himself for not having seen it when he first came to the house. It had nothing to do with bruises and not much to do with a cowed beaten way of holding themselves. That washed-out, tired, drained appearance told it all, if you knew what you were looking for.

She was very thin but not with the young vigorous slimness of her daughter or the wiriness of her mother-in-law. Her leanness showed slack muscles in her arms and stringy tendons at her wrists. There were hollows under her cheekbones and her mouth was already sunken. The benefit of weeks without Tom had not yet begun to show. Heather Peterlee had neglected herself and her home, had perhaps spent her time of widowhood in silent brooding here in this ugly dark house with only the spaniel for company.

The dog barked and snarled when Wexford came. To silence it she struck it too brutally across the muzzle. Violence begets violence, he thought. You receive it and store it up and then you transmit it—on to whoever or whatever is feebler than you.

Even now she denied it. Sitting opposite him in a drab cotton dress with a thick knitted cardigan dragged shawl-like around her, she repudiated any suggestion that Tom had been less than good and gentle. As for Carol, yes it was true Tom had offered her the caravan and not she. Tom had been told by a friend she wanted a place to live. What friend? She didn't know the name. And the 'au pair'?

'You've been talking to my daughter.'

Wexford admitted that this was indeed the case, though not to what weary extent it was true.

'Arlene imagines things. She's got too much imagination.' A spark of vitality made a small change in her when she spoke of her daughter. Her voice became a fraction more animated. 'She's brainy, is Arlene, she's a bright one. Wanted to go in for the police, you know.'

'I'm sorry?'

'Get to be a policewoman or whatever they call them now.'

'A police officer,' said Wexford. 'Did she really? What stopped that, then?'

'Took up with that Gary, didn't she?'

It was hardly an answer but Wexford didn't pursue it. He didn't ask about her husband's involvement with Carol Fox either. He had proof of that, not only in Carol's own admission but in the film from Tom Peterlee's camera. All the shots were of Carol, three nudes taken with a flash inside the Feverel's caravan. They were decorous enough, for Carol had been coy in her posing.

Wexford studied the three photographs again that evening. Their setting, not their voluptuous subject, made them pathetic. Sordidness of background, a window with a sagging net curtain, a coat hanging up, a glimpse of an encrusted pot on a hotplate, gave an air of attempts at creating pornography in some makeshift studio.

The identity of the sender of the processor's chit wasn't a problem. He had known that, if not from the moment he took it from its envelope, at least long before forensics matched with an existing set the fingerprints on the paper. He knew who had handed over the counter the film and the pound deposit. It was not even the subject of the shots that predominantly concerned him now. His slight depression vanished and he was suddenly alert. From those pictures he suddenly knew who had killed Tom Peterlee and why.

THE POLICE WERE WAITING, virtually encircling the Kingsbrook Centre, when the ram raiders arrived. This time there were only four of them, all inside the stolen Land Rover. If others were following through the narrow streets of the town centre, some prior warning turned them back. The same warning perhaps, maybe no more than feeling or intuition, which halted the Land Rover on the big paved forecourt from which the centre's entrance doors opened.

At first the watchers thought only that the Land Rover was reversing, prior to performing its backwards ramming of the doors. It was a few seconds before it became clear that this was a three-point turn, forwards up to the fifteen-foot-high brick wall, reverse towards the doors, then, while they braced themselves for the crash of the doors going down and the Land Rover backing through it, it shot forward again and was away through the alley into the High Street.

But it never entered the wider road. Its occupants left it to block the exit, flung all four doors open, and leapt out. The police, there in thirty seconds, found an empty vehicle, with no trace of any occupancy but its owner's and not a print to be found.

HE SAID TO BURDEN, before they made the arrest, 'You see, she told us she didn't possess a raincoat and we didn't find one, but in this photo a raincoat is hanging up inside the caravan.'

Burden took the magnifying lens from him and looked. 'Bright emerald green and the buttons that sort of bone that is part white, part brown.'

'She came into the kitchen when she said she did or maybe five minutes earlier. I think it was true she'd finished with Tom but that she meant to go for a long walk with Heather in order to tell her so, that was a fiction. She wore the raincoat because it was already drizzling and maybe because she knew she looked nice in it. She came to tell Heather she'd be leaving and no doubt that Heather could have him and welcome.

'Did she know Tom beat his wife? Maybe and maybe not. No doubt, she thought that if Tom and she had ever got together permanently he wouldn't beat *her*. But that's by the way. She came into the kitchen and saw Heather crouched against the counter and Tom hitting her in the face.

'It's said that a woman can't really defend herself against a brutal man, but another woman can defend her. What happened to Carol Fox, Mike? Pure anger? Total disillusionment with Tom Peterlee? Some pull of the great sisterhood of women? Perhaps we shall find out. She snatched up a log out of that basket, a strong oak log, and struck him over the back of the head with it. And again and again. Once she'd started she went on in a frenzy—until he was dead.'

'One of them,' said Burden, '—and I'd say Carol, wouldn't you?—acted with great presence of mind then, organising what they must do. Carol took off the raincoat that was covered with blood and thrust it along with the weapon into the stove. In the hour or so before we got there everything was consumed but part of one of the buttons.'

'Carol washed her hands, put on one of Heather's jackets, they took the dog and went out down to the river. It was never, as we thought, Carol providing an alibi for Heather. It was Heather alibiing Carol. They would stay out for three-quarters of an hour, come back and "find" the body, or even try to get rid of the body, clean up the kitchen, pretend that Tom had gone away. What they didn't foresee was Arlene's arrival.'

'But Arlene came an hour early,' Burden said.

'Arlene assumed that her mother had done it and she would think she knew why. The mouse in the corner attacked when the cat's attention was diverted. The worm turned as grandma turned when her husband struck her once too often.'

He said much the same to Arlene Heddon next day after Carol Fox had been charged with murder. 'You only told me she was Tom's girlfriend when you thought things were looking bad for your mother. You reasoned that if a man's mistress gave a man's wife an alibi it was bound to seem genuine. In case I didn't believe you and she denied it, you sent me the receipt when you took the film you'd removed from Tom Peterlee's camera along to the York Crest Centre to be processed. I suppose your mother told you the kind of pictures he took.'

She shrugged, said rather spitefully, 'You weren't so clever. All that about me knowing who'd killed Tom. I didn't know, I thought it was my mother.'

He glanced round the caravan, took in the radio and tape player, microwave oven, video, and his eye fell on the small black rectangle he had in the past, without a closer look, taken for a remote control channel changer. Now he thought how lazy you would have to be, how incapacitated almost, to need to change channels by this means. Almost anywhere in here you were within an arm's length of the television set. He picked it up.

It was a tape recorder, five inches long, two inches wide, flat, black. The end with the red 'on' light was and always had been turned towards the kitchen area.

So confident had she been in her control of things and perhaps in her superior intelligence that she had not even stripped the tiny label off its underside. Nixon's, York Crest, £54.99—he was certain Arlene hadn't paid £55 for it.

'You can't have that!' She was no longer cool.

'I'll give you a receipt for it,' he said, and then, 'Gary, no doubt, was with his pals that evening planning the first ram raid. I don't know where but I know it wasn't the Red Rose at Edenwick.'

She was quite silent, staring at him. He fancied she would have liked to snatch the recorder from him but did not quite dare. Serendipity or a long experience in reading faces and drawing conclusions made him say, 'Let's hear what you've been taping on here, Miss Heddon.'

He heard his own voice, then hers. As clear as a phone conversation. It was a good tape recorder. He thought, yes, Gary Wyatt was involved in the first ram raid, the one that took place after the murder and after the first time I came here to talk to her. From then on, from the second time...

'I didn't know Carol very well.'

'But she was a close friend of your mother's...' His voice tailed away into cracklings.

'I haven't lived at home since I was seventeen. I don't know all the friends my mother's got...'

'So that was how you did it,' he said. 'You recorded our conversations and learnt your replies off by heart. That was a way to guarantee your answers would never vary.'

In a stiff wooden voice she said, 'If you say so.'

He got up. 'I don't think Gary's going to be with you much longer, Miss Heddon. You'll be visiting him once a month, if you're so inclined. Some say there's a very thin line dividing the cop from the criminal, they've the same kind of intelligence. Your mother tells me you once had ambitions to be a police officer. You've got off to a bad start but maybe it's not too late.'

With the recorder in his pocket, stooping as he made his way out of the caravan, he turned back and said, 'If you like the idea, give me a ring.'

He closed the door behind him and descended the steps on to the muddy field and the cinder path.

# AS MY WIMSEY TAKES ME

★

## TERENCE FAHERTY

───────────────────────────

DOROTHY HAD JUST REACHED the top of the stairs when she remembered the cat. Leaving the light on, she made her way slowly down again, the stairs protesting softly as she passed. So much to do, it was little wonder she had forgotten to feed Beatrice. 'It's the time of year,' she thought to herself, 'and not you, old girl. You're not slipping yet.' She was immensely tired, but consoled by a feeling of accomplishment. The Christmas shopping was all but done after a single day's heroic effort. Now she could get back to serious work. That thought carried her instantly to Dante and the last lines she had translated from the *Paradiso*. She picked up the rhyme effortlessly, like some piece of knitting from the war years, and fussed with the unravelled end. 'If I was naught,' she recited aloud, 'O Love that rules the Heights, save that of me which Thou didst last create...'

A voice from the dark study beyond her took up the line: 'Thou know'st, that didst uplift me with Thy light.'

The voice coming from out of the darkness in a house where she was quite alone startled her, and she nearly missed the last step. It was a voice she knew but couldn't place. One she felt she hadn't heard for ages. 'Who is it?' she challenged loudly.

In answer, a desk lamp deep in the study was switched on. There, in her leather wing chair, sat a man of about forty with sleek blond hair and a narrow face dominated by a large, high-arched nose and a monocle. His blue eyes were laughing at her, she thought, but the thin lips were still. The figure was dressed in a dated style of evening attire, and Beatrice, the cat, was curled comfortably in his lap. His long fingers stroked her absentmindedly.

'Wimsey, by God!' the old woman exclaimed.

'Right,' said the figure in the chair. 'Lord Peter Death Bredon Wimsey, if you want all the king's horses.'

The old woman squinted through her glasses and pressed her hand against her forehead. 'Granted,' she said, uncertainly, 'it is the time of year for Dickens, but I don't know that I care to be addressed by "an undigested bit of beef".'

'Pâté de foie gras, more likely,' said the other.

Dorothy squared her shoulders and took a step towards the light. 'I thought I had done with you years ago,' she said.

'So you had. Reichenbached me something awful, marrying me off like that and moving me out to the country. That was a master stroke, by the by. We fictional detectives can withstand anything but domesticity. Nothing like it for showing up the greasepaint and the trick wires, don't you know. Still, a sleuth-hound is a devilishly hard creature to kill off, Harriet.'

'Whatever do you mean by calling me that?' the old woman demanded. She marched confidently into the room and stood next to the desk, her arms folded before her. 'You may call me Miss Sayers, if you must address me at all.'

'I say! Rather formal considering our relationship, don't you think? I mean—not to be indelicate—considering that I've been supporting you and yours for thirty years now.'

'You supporting me? I like that!'

'I'll never forget the first time I saw you. You were a thin, sickly thing. No real job, no prospects, no decent digs. I've often thought that was why you made me so beastly rich. So you could enjoy throwing my money about, I mean. Lord knows you've run through enough of it since.'

The old woman brought an open hand down on her desk top, scattering manuscript pages and causing an old jam pot to leap into the air. 'I beg your pardon,' she said, 'but nothing and no one has supported me these thirty years but my own industry.'

'Your industry? That's a nice thing to say to the Johnny who flew the Atlantic before Lindbergh, who's been shot, half buried in a bog, and concussed by demon bells. Not to mention—the memory makes my blood run cold—all the bad driving you had me do.'

'I had you do. Precisely. I made you out of whole cloth because, as you say, I needed the money. And you jumped through my hoops until I had money to spare.'

His Lordship did not appear to be listening. He gently nudged Beatrice from his lap and checked the black broadcloth of his impeccably pressed trousers for a stray bit of fur. Remarkably, there was none.

'I don't mean to sound ungrateful,' Dorothy said in a more conciliatory tone. 'I remember those early days myself. I came very close to failing then. Very close to despair.'

Lord Peter looked up and smiled. 'Then I entered in my usual role: hero *ex machina.*'

'Yes. All teeth and spats and beautiful neckties. You were a silly ass in those days, Wimsey.'

'Call me Peter, won't you? Seems only fitting as you christened me. Good name, Peter. A solid cornerstone for an otherwise airy persona. I only wish you'd given me a good solid face to go with it, instead of this Algernony affair I was blessed with. Dashed weary-making, you can't imagine, to have one's intelligence always undersold on the evidence of one's profile.'

'And how you could talk piffle. Half a book of you just prattling on and on. How I loved the sound of it.'

'Well, we're all silly when we're young, if we do it right. I lost some of my blather as the years went by.'

'Yes, you grew. Indeed you did. I'm grateful for that, too, Peter. I don't know if I could have carried on with you so long if you'd stayed that flat, gaudy caricature. Your growth from detective to man gave me a chance to grow as a writer. It pointed me towards my more important works, the things that took your place, the religious plays and, of course, Dante. The things for which I'll be remembered.'

'You sound just like a doctor chappie I ran into the other day. Conan Doyle, I think the name was. He'd written a book that will live for ever, too. *The White Company.* Ever heard of it?'

'We'll see who laughs last, Peter Wimsey.'

'I hope we all laugh together at the last, dear Harriet.'

'Why do you insist on calling me that?'

'It's the only name I've ever called you.'

'I am not Harriet Vane.'

'I shall be very disappointed if that proves to be true. But we're getting ahead of ourselves. I've postulated that you made me rich because you were poor. But what of my other sterling qualities? My erudition, my high sense of honour, my wit, my seemingly inexhaustible knowledge of wine, food, women, et cetera. Stop me if I begin to sound immodest.'

'You were born to be a thriller hero,' the old woman said patiently. 'Someone to entertain bank clerks and typists in their quiet hours. The qualities you've named and your various accoutrements, from your man Bunter to your primrose dressing gowns, I created with an eye to that single purpose.'

'All my qualities? Forgive me for pressing the point—you made me damned inquisitive, too, don't forget—but what of my sensitivity? My recognition of a woman's right to her own life and work, I mean, and the blubbing I used to do when the murderer got his deserts. Rather ahead of the times in those respects, wasn't I?'

'I said before that you grew.'

'Yes, but why? The caricature was good enough to pay the bills. Why flesh me out, so to speak? It's all very well to say that you grew as a writer, but why did you grow with me? Why not a more plausible hero? For, when you come right down to it, I'm not that plausible, am I? You don't meet Peter Wimseys on the street every day.'

Dorothy sat down on the bare wooden desk chair. 'That is a sad fact I had learned just before I turned my hand to you,' she said. 'In those years of struggle after Oxford I searched for a man of spirit, of an intellectual breadth and courage sufficient to accept a woman as an equal, to stimulate her not just physically but mentally. A man able to accept the challenge of knowing another person fully, of exploring a soul. I found that men like that are as rare as unicorns. Perhaps as mythical.'

'So you created one, just as you created imaginary playmates as a child.'

'Yes.'

'The perfect lover.'

'Ah. I see your game, Peter Wimsey.' She leaned forward on her elbows, her head thrust more forward still. 'Now I understand your insistence on calling me Harriet Vane. It's the old charge that I fell in love with my own creation. That I wrote myself into the books in the guise of the Vane woman so I could consummate that love. Well, it won't wash.'

'Won't it?'

'Harriet Vane was a means of introducing my ideas into the novels, not my person. My ideas on women's education and careers, the radical notion that a good job of work and a life of intellectual commitment are goals as valid for a woman as a husband and a house full of babies.'

'And yet Harriet and I managed to have babies, as I re-call. Quite a cottage full, in fact.'

'Just another part of your impossible perfection, Peter. You could respect a will as strong as your own. You could see that there is more beauty and more heaven in a counter-point of two strong voices than in a harmony that subju-gates one voice to the other.'

She paused for a moment and smiled. 'Who am I quot-ing now, I wonder?'

'Yourself, I think,' Wimsey said. 'Your once-upon-a-time self.'

Dorothy took off her glasses and tossed them on to the desk, settling back in her chair with half-closed eyes. 'Per-haps you're right in a way. Perhaps I did create in you the man I couldn't find in this life. But it was not for some sub-liminal and sordid satisfaction. It was to show the world the type of man required for the satisfaction of a modern, un-fettered, educated woman. The awful, unattainable goal to be achieved.'

'And yet, if I may be allowed one more immodest obser-vation, you achieved it,' Wimsey said softly.

'In art, Peter.'

'It is no less of an achievement for that. It is no common soul that can shape the world to its own ideals, no matter that the world it masters is a fiction. And no common re-ward awaits the creators of this life. However modest their creations, each echoes the larger work.

"The glory of Him who moves all things soe'er
Impenetrates the universe, and bright
The splendour burns, more here and lesser there."'

'Dante,' she said. 'I'd almost forgotten him. It's time I was at work. That is, if I may be excused from the remainder of this dream. I will admit it's been a delightful dream. I feel most refreshed.'

'You've awakened from the dream without knowing it,' Wimsey said. 'And you've finished with my Italian rival, too, I'm afraid.' He held out a pale hand across the desk to her.

She hesitated for a moment and then reached to grasp it. To her surprise, the hand was as warm and solid as her own. Confused, she asked, 'What do you want?'

His Lordship, too, looked uncertain for a moment. 'My business brings to mind that unfortunate second name of mine, which timid souls mispronounce so as to rhyme with teeth.'

'Death,' she said, pronouncing it correctly and clearly. She looked back towards the hallway. There, in the shadow at the foot of the stairs, she saw the dim outline of a body, sadly shapeless and still.

At her sharp intake of breath, his grip on her hand tightened. 'No fear for us in one more body, is there? Not after all the soldiering we've done together.'

'No,' she said.

'That's right. It's not death but life that sent me. I'm here to bring you home. The Daimler awaits.' He rose, still holding her hand, and she rose with him.

The familiar room around her had acquired a soft haze that made the desk lamp look like a street light in a fog. But for his hand, she would have fallen. 'Peter, I'm confused. I can't think...'

'Shock, I expect. It'll pass. All things made clear shortly, and all that. You've only a little journey ahead of you. Then you'll be rid of me for good and all.'

There was a note of despair in his voice that she felt echo within her. 'I should regret that,' she said.

He paused and considered her for a moment, his head cocked to one side like a bird's. He had grown more substantial somehow, against the swirling room. 'Can't be helped, I'm afraid, except perhaps . . .'

'Perhaps?'

'Well,' he said, 'if you don't mind a stop on the way, I've heard of a murder down at Charing Cross station. Man discovered in the lost and found room. Wearing nothing but an overcoat and a pair of new galoshes. On the wrong feet. Cause of death, drowning. Don't want to overstay my welcome and so on, but I thought we might take a crack at it. For old times' sake, I mean.' He finished his speech as awkwardly as a schoolboy asking for his first kiss.

'Splendid, Peter,' she said, slipping her arm around his.

'And would you mind awfully much if I called you Harriet?'

'I should love it.'

'Right-ho! We're off!'

# PROGRAMMED FOR MURDER

★

## JAMES MELVILLE

---

...HAVE LOST IT within a week, I dare say. Probably a complete waste of money. Worth a try, all the same.'

Henry Gibson wondered vaguely what Nicholas was talking about as he opened the door to the sitting-room and the sound of his son's voice floated out. Then almost at once he realised that the fresh bottle of sherry he had gone to the cupboard under the stairs to fetch was not in fact in his hands; and retreated again.

Having replaced in the refrigerator the jar of tomato chutney he had unaccountably been carrying, Henry set out once more to join Nicholas and his charming girlfriend. Jane, or was it Jennifer? He had no idea why they'd turned up out of the blue at eleven on a Saturday morning, but was pleased that they had. His younger son William, coming from the other direction, grinned as he edged past his father in the passageway.

'And William too? What a pleasant surprise! Nicholas and, er, Janet are here, you know. Or have you said hello to them already?'

The expression of bafflement on William's cheerful face was fleeting: he was inured to his father's chronic inability to remember names, and was indeed mildly gratified that the old boy had got his own right.

'The loo's upstairs, my dear boy,' Henry went on. 'Surely, you haven't forgotten?'

'No, Dad. In fact I've been staying with you for the past few days. During the vac, you know. I'll just get the sherry.'

'But I already...oh. No, I haven't, have I?'

During this exchange, Nicholas and Jemima, with whom he had been sharing a flat for two and a half years, were continuing the discussion in the sitting-room.

'I do worry about him,' Nicholas said. 'I mean, he might harm himself in some way. Turn the oven on and forget to light it. That sort of thing. I wish I could persuade him to go and see a doctor.'

At twenty-four, Nicholas was a fledgling barrister who prided himself on his photographic memory and saw himself as a potential Lord Chancellor. He did and yet he didn't want his father to seek medical advice. Hang it all, Dad had always had a head like a sieve. Amazing that he'd ever been able to remember enough history to get a fellowship in the first place. On the other hand, he did seem to have been getting worse since Ma left. Couldn't be the early stages of Alzheimer's, surely? God, what a prospect. At least Alzheimer's wasn't hereditary. Or was it?

'He's an old sweetie really,' Jemima said. 'And he seems to bumble along well enough on his own. You fuss too much. I mean, he doesn't leave his zipper undone or anything like that; and the garden's a picture. All the same, I must say I do rather see your mother's point of view. He must have been maddening to live with. It's hardly surprising she fell for a well-organised man like Marshall Wentworth when he made a pass at her.'

Wentworth was head of department; at fifty he was six years younger than Henry, and wore expensive suits and well-polished shoes in sharp contrast to Henry's ancient, baggy jacket, drooping trousers and down-at-heel Hush Puppies. A masterful committee man, he often expressed his views on higher education on Channel 4, and as pro-vice-chancellor was a strong candidate for promotion in due course to the top job in the university. Miranda Gibson had gone to live with Professor Wentworth two years earlier when William had gone up to university, and had just asked Henry to agree to a divorce.

Nicholas scowled. 'It's her life, I suppose, but I think he's a creep and a pseud. He's a sadist, too. I went over there for dinner a couple of months ago and he kept making snide remarks about poor old Dad, you know, implying that he was useless to a red-blooded woman like Ma.'

'*You're* not useless,' Jemima purred, and seizing his hand bit the back of it briefly. Nicholas looked gratified, but pressed on.

'No, really. I thought it was disgusting. And all that pompous Marshall business. It's his middle name, you know. He's really called Rupert...ah, there you are, Dad! All OK?'

'Splendid, splendid! How very kind of you all to come to see me!' Henry blinked and beamed amiably at the young people while William refilled their glasses before raising his own in a toast.

'Happy birthday, Dad!'

'Oh, that's why you're all here, is it? I should have guessed. Dear, dear. Well, thank you...'

Nicholas and Jemima stood, they all sipped their sherry, and Jemima went over, kissed Henry on the cheek and squeezed his arm. 'I do believe you'd forgotten!' she said. 'Well, you won't next time. Where is it, Nick?'

It was William who crossed to the corner table and returned with a neat rectangular package, which he passed to his brother who offered it to Henry with something of a flourish.

'From all of us, with our love.'

Henry accepted the package shyly. 'For me? No, really, you shouldn't have...may I open it?' As the others clustered round him he clumsily tore off the gaily coloured wrapping paper, revealing a leather case, which he opened with a puzzled expression on his face.

William glanced at his wristwatch with satisfaction. He'd timed it perfectly. His father withdrew the elegant electronic personal organiser from its case and, even as he stared in dismay at its array of buttons it emitted a delicate bleep. Henry started.

'Oh dear, have I broken it?'

'Of course not,' William said. 'Look at the screen. No, on the other side.'

Henry obediently turned the little machine over and put his glasses on. When she left him, his wife had advised him to wear them on a cord round his neck, since she would no longer be available to find them for him several times a day. She had even bought him the cord, and Henry did indeed find it convenient.

What he saw when he finally focused on the tiny screen was a four-line message:

> HAPPY BIRTHDAY DAD
> HOPING THIS WILL SORT YOU OUT
> LOVE FROM N, W & J
> NB DONT LOSE IT

Henry blinked, and then took his glasses off and dabbed at moist eyes. 'You really shouldn't have spent your money on me,' he said. 'Especially on this, um, calculator, is it?'

Nicholas shook his head. 'No, it's a personal organiser. It can do all sorts of things. Tell you the telephone dialling code from Bangkok and the time there, replace your address book, calculate sixty-seven to the power of seventeen—'

'Dear Nicholas.' Henry smiled as he interrupted his son. Then he looked down again at the buttons on the gadget in his hand. 'I'm quite sure it's the most ingenious contrivance imaginable, but—'

'But he doesn't want to know the dialling code from Bangkok or do astronomer's sums, twit,' Jemima put in, ruffling her lover's hair affectionately.

'Of course he doesn't. Stop confusing things, Nick.' William reached out and gently relieved his father of the organiser, which he was staring at with manifest unease. 'Don't be nervous, Dad. It's not really all that complicated to operate, but unless you want to you don't have to fiddle with it. I can't see you wanting to bother with any of the functions except the diary alarms; and I'll set those up for you while I'm staying here. I've entered some regular things already—your Wednesday gardening club meeting and so forth. During the next few days just let me know whenever anything pops into your head that you need to remember, however far ahead, and I'll see to the rest. And on the appropriate day the organiser will bleep to remind you in good time and explain on the display exactly what you have to do.'

'Good gracious. Will it?'

The next hour or so passed agreeably enough as they ate the delicious smoked salmon sandwiches Nicholas and Jemima had brought, and Nicholas played with Henry's new toy, announcing from time to time the cube root of some inordinately long number or the time of day in various exotic places. Henry, warmed by the sherry, the sandwiches and the awareness of affection, became less agitated as it sank in that none of the young people had supposed for a second that he would be able either to understand or to use the organiser in any active sense.

William even promised to renew the batteries for him every few months; and stressed again that Henry simply had to follow the instructions that would appear on the screen whenever the organiser bleeped. That sounded reasonably straightforward; and when after a while the little machine chirruped again and they urged him to see what it wanted, he read

TIME FOR A BIT OF PEACE
AND QUIET FOR YOU DAD
CHUCK THEM OUT

Touched and diverted, Henry joined in the general laughter and saw them off at the door. William said he'd be back quite late and not to wait up, and after they'd all turned to wave from the gate Henry was alone with his birthday present.

It really was a splendid, thoughtful little companion. At four o'clock it suggested that he might make himself a cup of tea, and at five to six reminded him to watch the television news. On each occasion Henry thanked the organiser gravely; and he said good morning to it when it woke him at eight the next day. How clever it was to know that he liked an extra half-hour in bed on Sundays!

DURING THE FOLLOWING WEEK Henry watched, fascinated and not a little jealous, as William's fingers flickered expertly over the control keys and entered more and more reminders in the diary section. As the days went by he became less wary of the complex array of controls. He even, under William's tutelage, timidly learned to operate the TIDY button and banish the organiser's memory of events of the past few days; in order, as William explained, to make room for future commitments in days, weeks, months and years to come.

The spring vacation ended and William duly departed, but the sleek little miracle went on speaking to Henry several times a day. It reminded him to go to his gardeners' club meeting, at which he arrived on time to general amazement even though it was a special occasion, since they were to be

addressed by no less a luminary than Ben Barrow of the
BBC's gardening quiz programme. Old Mr Bufton was
particularly pleased, because he had to leave early, and was
able to hand over to Henry a promised packet of laburnum
seeds before the great man began to speak.

The organiser told Henry when to take his thyroid tablets; and when to go to the doctor for another prescription.
It warned him not to mow over the old daffodils before the
end of June, reminded him once a week to check his petrol
gauge, and sent him to the bank to draw out cash from time
to time, as well as to the big Sainsbury's on the outskirts of
the town for a major shop every couple of weeks.

Within a month Henry was showing off his organiser to
his students at the university, referring jocularly to it as his
familiar, while—strictly in private—he spoke to it, calling it
Marjorie, the name of a girl he had been fond of in his own
student days.

Although naturally enough they did their best to avoid
each other, their professional relationship made it inevitable that Henry and his wife's lover should meet from time
to time. Some weeks after Henry had been given his birthday present, Professor Wentworth waylaid him in a corridor, mentioned that he was on his way to an important
meeting at the offices of the Committee of Vice-Chancellors
and Principals in London, but nevertheless engaged him in
a brief discussion about a postgraduate seminar planned for
the coming academic year. All at once Marjorie the organiser, snugly ensconced in Henry's pocket, bleeped. With a
murmured apology Henry took it out and consulted the
screen, which said

TIME FOR LUNCH, MY FRIEND
TELL HIM TO GET LOST

'What on earth have you got there, Henry?'

Henry blushed; partly because Marjorie hadn't addressed him as 'Friend' before, and partly because he was taken aback by the peremptory tone of her instruction. He strove for nonchalance while improvising furiously.

'Oh, it's just my personal organiser. Most useful. It can do all manner of things, you know. Should you wish to know the time in Bangkok, you can . . . that is to say, I keep a note, for example, of, um, all the Public Record Office call numbers I need for my current work . . . that sort of thing.'

Wentworth's glasses flashed as his head jerked in astonishment. 'You do? Well, I'm . . . that is, what a good idea! Wonders will never—' He coughed loudly. 'What I was going to say was, these computer chaps come up with some remarkable contrivances, don't they? I find my own new lap-top indispensable for train journeys, of course, but I should never have thought . . . well, I really must be off. Now you won't forget the VC's garden party, will you?'

Gazing after Wentworth's retreating figure and pleasantly conscious of having got the better of him for once, Henry couldn't recall whether or not he had mentioned the garden party to William during one of their programming sessions together. He certainly couldn't remember now when it was to be: merely that some business tycoon or other had been invited as the guest of honour in the hope that he would be moved to part with a cheque for a very large sum of money on the discreet understanding that an honorary doctorate would follow. Oh well, Henry concluded breezily, he'd leave it up to Marjorie. Maybe she'd remind him, maybe not. He patted his pocket. 'Well done, sweetie,' he whispered. 'Let's go and find some lunch.'

As DAY FOLLOWED DAY, Henry came to regard Marjorie as an old and trusted friend. She never let him down, and her messages began to take on a skittish, even slightly flirtatious tone. At first, the reminders had been severely factual, such as

FACULTY MEETING IN 20 MINS
IN DEANS ROOM COMPLAIN ABOUT
COMMONROOM COFFEE

or

LEAVE HOME IN HALF AN HOUR
PICK UP 2 BAGS COMPOST
AT GARDEN CENTRE ON WAY

After the encounter with Wentworth during which she had first spoken out, however, Marjorie increasingly revealed aspects of her personality. She would sometimes be constructively sympathetic, as in

YOU POOR DEAR YOU MUST BE
SICK OF CORRECTING PROOFS
YOUVE EARNED A DRINK

and occasionally quite rude about people, as when she reminded him that

BRIAN HANCOCK OWES YOU
FIFTEEN QUID DON'T LET THE
CHEAP SKATE ROB YOU, DEAR

That one was particularly disconcerting. 'Cheapskate' was such an outdated expression. Come to think of it, the real Marjorie used to call people that, all those years ago.

MARJORIE DID REMEMBER the vice-chancellor's garden party. In fact she first mentioned it a good week ahead, urging Henry to get his one good suit dry-cleaned, and adding with a touch of bitchiness

> WENTWORTH MIGHT HAVE THE GALL
> TO BRING MIRANDA SO SHOW HER
> WE CAN DO JUST FINE ON OUR OWN

On succeeding days she made him get a haircut, and buy a new shirt, tie and silk handkerchief for the occasion. When he picked up the suit from Sketchley's the woman in charge told him he'd left a packet of peppercorns in the pocket and Henry was quite baffled until she handed it to him and he saw that it was in fact Mr Bufton's laburnum seeds. He stuffed them into his capacious jacket pocket next to Marjorie, and thought no more about them.

Until, that is, the day of the garden party, when after arraying himself in his new finery Henry tried to transfer Marjorie from his everyday jacket to the suit and discovered that somehow the packet of seeds had become caught up in a crevice in her outer casing. It proved quite impossible to detach it without risking tearing the packet and spilling the contents all over the place. Marjorie bleeped, and when Henry read the message it said

> NO TIME NOW DO IT LATER

so he obediently stowed both organiser and seeds away in the inside breast pocket of his well-pressed suit, and set out for the Master's Lodge.

The grounds boasted a particularly fine yew tree, and since Henry was so rarely privileged to see it at close quarters he made an early opportunity to stroll over to look at it.

Marjorie bleeped, and he took her out, the paper packet of laburnum seeds still attached.

## LOVELY LEAVES WHY NOT PICK A FEW

It seemed an odd thing to do, but Henry had never yet questioned an instruction of Marjorie's, so he plucked half a dozen yew leaves and, finally succeeding in detaching the packet, popped them in with the laburnum seeds.

'Why, you look quite smart, Henry,' Miranda Gibson said in a surprised way when, having decided he might as well get it over with, Henry wandered over to her and Marshall Wentworth to say hello.

'Quite the fashion plate,' Wentworth commented sourly, putting his plate of smoked mackerel *au poivre* and green salad down on the nearest of the little tables scattered about the spacious lawn. 'I'll go and get you another glass of wine, Miranda. Don't let them take my plate away. I haven't finished.'

After his departure, Henry exchanged a few awkward remarks with his estranged wife, but was greatly relieved when Marjorie bleeped—rather urgently, it seemed to him—and he could apologise and turn aside to attend to her. Marjorie didn't slip out of his pocket as smoothly as usual, and he had to tug at her. Embarrassed, he didn't notice that when he did eventually manage to extricate her, a little shower of yew leaves and laburnum seeds flew out of his pocket at the same time, nor that several of each ended up on Marshall Wentworth's plate, blending perfectly with the food already on it.

## YOUVE DONE THE NECESSARY
## NOW MAKE YOUR EXCUSES

Marjorie suggested, and by the time Wentworth returned to Miranda's side and greedily scoffed the remainder of his generous helping of the vice-chancellor's bounty, Henry was some yards away, chatting affably to his hostess and to the wife of the business tycoon, who agreed after he moved on that he was a charming man.

WENTWORTH'S DOCTOR, who detested him and had long been convinced that he would die following a heart attack, made no attempt to discover what if any symptoms had preceded the professor's demise, and signed the death certificate that vindicated his prediction without a second thought.

Henry went to the funeral, of course, wearing a newly purchased black tie with his good suit. He felt sorry for Miranda who gave him a brave, hopeful little smile, but decided to let the divorce proceedings take their course. He was learning to enjoy his bachelor existence, with Marjorie for company.

Outside his solicitor's office, after he had signed the necessary papers—and accepted his lawyer's congratulations on having been promoted to the chair of history vacated so unexpectedly by Marshall Wentworth—Henry decided to drop into a pub and have a drink. On the way, Marjorie bleeped.

### WHY NOT? YOU'VE EARNED IT

she said, and then, when he was enjoying a large whisky and water,

### TIDY UP PAST MEMORY NOW DARLING

Henry knew how to do that, and he duly expunged every

past diary entry. Marjorie gave what sounded uncommonly like a contented bleep, and Henry returned to the bar to buy himself another whisky.

# THE CHRISTMAS CRIMES
## AT 'CINDERELLA'
### A PUZZLE IN FOUR PARTS
### PART ONE: CHRISTMAS EVE

★

## SIMON BRETT

THE CHRISTMAS EVE dress rehearsal for 'Cinderella' had really been murder.

Cinderella herself, played by declining pop singer Natalie Maine, had stumped off to her dressing-room because the pit orchestra's accompaniment didn't sound sufficiently like the backing track to her latest—so far unsuccessful—single.

One of the Ugly Sisters, Vaseline, played by outrageously camp comedian Danny Kino, had mistimed all his slapstick and blamed it on the other, less famous Ugly Sister, Glycerine.

The two ends of the pantomime horse (transformed from a rat by the Fairy Godmother) had had an argument. Their comic dance ended with the Front Legs kicking the Back Legs in a flurry of muffled oaths.

Buttons, popular middleweight boxer Ricky Sturridge in his first acting role, forgot everything he'd learned in rehearsal, and lost all his scenes with Cinderella overwhelmingly on points.

Baron Hardup, played by the veteran Freddie Link, had a secret supply of liquor, to which he resorted with increasing frequency.

By the time the rehearsal reached the walkdown and finale, the director was looking understandably frazzled.

Jack Tarrant watched this chaos from the auditorium. The former Scotland Yard detective inspector was there because of his girlfriend. Maria Lethbury ran her own public relations company, and one of her clients was Ricky Sturridge. She was masterminding his progress from boxer to media personality—uphill work, which had not been helped by recent tabloid revelations of teenage convictions for mugging.

Jack looked around as the director sent yet another terrified underling to coax Natalie Maine out of her dressing-room. Maria was off on the telephone, cancelling a television chat-show appearance set up for Ricky that evening. The dress rehearsal, scheduled to start at two-thirty like an ordinary matinée, was already overrunning horribly. The cast would be lucky to get away before Christmas Eve became Christmas Day.

Jack grinned at one of the dancers who sat poring over the *Times* crossword nearby. A pretty, vivacious girl called Niki Grayes, she was energetically giving of herself as a Villager, Court Lady, Mouse, Snow Fairy and Equerry to Prince Charming. Catching Jack's eye, she grinned back.

'In for a long night,' he observed.

'Too right. Always the same when you have emotional discord in the company.'

Jack Tarrant raised an interrogative eyebrow.

'Ricky and Natalie,' she explained. 'Didn't you know?'

He shook his head.

'Oh yes. Been very steamy over the last couple of weeks. Though, from the way they're behaving this evening, I'd say the magic has gone.'

Onstage the director clapped his hands. 'We'll take a five-minute break. I'll go up and fetch Natalie. God, I can't wait to get back to working with real actors again.'

'What d'you mean by that?' asked Ricky Sturridge with the aggression that had cowed middleweights all over the world.

In spite of his red bellboy's costume, this muscle-bound Buttons looked pretty frightening. The scowl on his face was accentuated by stage soot from the slapstick chimney-sweeping scene he'd just done with the Ugly Sisters.

The director backpedalled. 'I didn't mean *you*, Ricky. It's just Natalie...'

'She's impossible,' the boxer agreed gloomily. 'God, she makes me so angry sometimes I could...' But he thought better of making the threat specific.

The back end of the pantomime horse slumped wearily into the seat next to Niki.

'What a farce,' the young man said petulantly. 'What a total farce! Three years at university, two years at drama school, and I end up playing a horse's bum.'

The dancer squeezed his hand. 'Things'll get better. Everyone's got to start somewhere.'

'Huh.'

'Sorry, you don't know Jack Tarrant,' said Niki. 'Jack, this is Wink Carter.'

'My real name's William.'

'But everyone calls you Wink.'

'You know I don't like—'

He was interrupted by the bustling arrival of Maria Lethbury. Even in her current state of frustration, she looked terrific, red hair glowing in the light that spilled off the stage.

'Cancelled everything,' she announced. 'And of course now there's no chance of getting him on the show again for months.'

'May be a good thing,' said Jack. 'Not sure that Ricky's at his sparkling conversational best tonight.'

'He was totally incoherent in the kitchen scene,' Wink Carter chipped in. 'Couldn't remember a single line. It does make me sick...' His voice was shrill with neurosis. 'It's hard enough for real actors to get work, without having to face competition from talentless sportsmen and pop stars.'

'And comedians?' asked a waspish voice.

Danny Kino, hugely inflated by Vaseline's diamante ball-dress, towered over them. His face, beneath its splodges of rouge, looked sour.

'I didn't say comedians.' Wink Carter flinched away from Kino's eye. 'Actors and comedians are at least in the same business. We're on the same side.'

'We were,' the comedian agreed acidly, 'but there are people who change sides, you know. They're called traitors.'

Further development of this conversation was prevented by the reappearance of the director, leading an extremely truculent Natalie Maine.

'Right.' He clapped his hands, eager to reinject some purpose into the proceedings. 'Let's just get this walkdown and finale sorted. Then we can all go home, have a lovely break for Christmas, and meet up revived for a smashing Boxing Day matinée. OK?'

His forced jollity didn't spark any answering enthusiasm from the company. Grudgingly, they moved back towards the stage.

All went well until the very end of the walkdown. The dancers had come on, singing the mindlessly cheerful finale, and taken their bows. The minor characters had done likewise. Baron Hardup and the Fairy Godmother had tottered out for their ovation, and then the Ugly Sisters had erupted onstage in all their mincing flamboyance. Only Buttons and Cinderella remained.

Ricky Sturridge, now dressed in a silver lamé bellboy's costume, came thundering down the steps as if entering the Albert Hall for a title bout.

'Great,' said the director. 'Now, after your bow, Ricky, I want you to go back up the steps, hands outstretched, and lead Natalie down to join Prince Charming...'

'No!' Cinderella appeared at the top of the steps, her mouth tight with displeasure. 'I'm going to come onstage alone! I'm what the audience has come to see, after all. I'm not going to share the climax of my show with that dumb ox!'

A chill moment of silence ensued, while Ricky Sturridge turned slowly on his heel and faced the singer.

'You ever call me anything like that again,' he growled, his voice clotted with emotion, 'and I'll kill you!'

IT WAS just after midnight. While Jack Tarrant waited for Maria, he chatted to Ken the stage doorman, who had spent a long life watching the theatre's comings and goings.

At last Maria appeared, her face shadowed with annoyance.

'Happy Christmas, darling,' said Jack. 'Did you find him?'

'No. Don't know where he's got to. I just felt I should have had a word, after everything that happened.'

'This Mr Sturridge you're after?' asked Ken.

'That's right.'

'You missed him. Went about ten minutes ago. Just rushed out—not even a "Goodnight" for me, leave alone a "Merry Christmas".'

'Everyone's had a pretty stressful evening,' Maria apologised for her client.

'Oh, sure. Well, if you're off, that'll just leave Miss Snooty-Drawers upstairs.'

'Natalie?' asked Jack.

'Yes. She rang through to me—what, about half-past eleven—to ask if anyone'd left any messages for her, and since then hasn't come down. Now she's left her phone off the hook.' Ken heaved himself creaking from his chair. 'I'd better go up and chivvy her.'

'Don't worry,' said Jack. 'We'll go.'

They moved in silence up the stairs to the No. 1 dressing-room. Above the door someone—perhaps seriously, perhaps in mockery—had pinned a four-pointed Christmas star.

Jack Tarrant pushed the dressing-room door open.

The lights around the mirror illuminated an ugly scene. Natalie Maine lay back in a chair, her head strangely angled. Staring, bloodshot eyes, tongue poking obscenely through painted lips, at the corners of which white froth had gathered. On her neck purple marks of bruising were shadowed by smudges of black.

An uneducated hand had scrawled on her mirror in lipstick the word BICH.

If Natalie Maine was destined to have any more chart hits, they would be posthumous ones.

WHILE MARIA WENT DOWN to the stage door to phone the police, Jack, taking care to touch nothing, did a quick inspection of the murder scene. Not for the first time, he regretted his amateur status and cursed the villain's bullet which had ended his Scotland Yard career.

But at least the old-boy network paid off. The scene-of-crime officer who appeared knew Jack Tarrant's formidable reputation and readily agreed to keep him up to date with the official investigation.

The call came through in the morning while Jack and Maria were in bed enjoying a leisurely Christmas breakfast (amongst other things). All the clues, the Scotland Yard man said, pointed in the same direction. The black marks on Natalie Maine's neck had been identified as stage soot. The misspelling of BITCH betrayed a lack of education. The strangling had required exceptional strength.

Add to all this the fact that the entire company of 'Cinderella' had witnessed the suspect threatening to kill his victim, and it was with no surprise Jack Tarrant heard that Ricky Sturridge had been arrested for the murder.

IT WAS the old-boy network again that won Jack permission to reinspect the scene of the crime.

'Ricky didn't do it,' Maria announced, as she strode into the dressing-room, now occupied, on Christmas afternoon.

'No...' Jack lingered thoughtfully in the doorway. Suddenly he looked up. 'I thought so.'

He detached the four-pointed star carefully from the doorframe and, turning it over, read out loud:

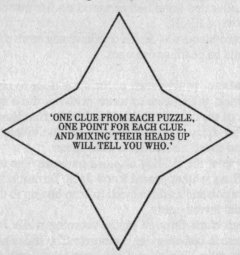

'ONE CLUE FROM EACH PUZZLE,
ONE POINT FOR EACH CLUE,
AND MIXING THEIR HEADS UP
WILL TELL YOU WHO.'

He looked into Maria's brown eyes. 'What a twisted mind,' he said grimly. 'We're up against a murderer with a warped sense of humour. Four puzzles will reveal his identity.'

'Or her identity,' Maria murmured softly.

'Yes.' He came into the dressing-room. 'So where's the first puzzle?'

'How about *this* . . . ?' Maria picked up an Advent calendar.

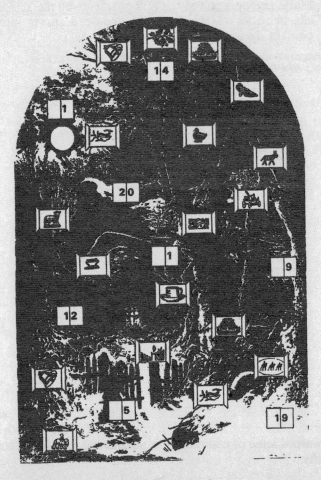

'Why?'

'Because, whereas most Advent calendars only have twenty-four little windows, this has twenty-six. And also the number "1" occurs twice.'

'Good thinking,' said Jack Tarrant, and together he and Maria Lethbury solved the first puzzle set by the 'Cinderella murderer'. Maria wrote the one-word answer into a point of the four-pointed star.

(*Continued on p. 107*)

# FAERY TALE

★

## CELIA DALE

---

I, EDWARD AUGUSTUS STEYNES, Associate of the Royal Academy of Arts, of Holland Park, London, wish to set down—yes, in hot blood while the events of the monstrous persecution of my ward are still fresh in my mind (not that they will ever fade but will remain branded on my memory)—the truth as I know it of the misfortunes which culminated in scenes worthy of a Roman circus rather than an English Coroner's Court, and the effects of which are only now, some five weeks later, beginning to recede into the nightmare past but from which, I fear, the delicate sensibilities of a young girl may never entirely recover.

To understand fully the sequence of events which led to this monstrous persecution it is necessary to go back many years—to 1868 it must have been, when my cousin Rollo Ogilvy brought his motherless daughter Blanche back to England from India where he had held a commission in a cavalry regiment. Although the atrocious Mutiny was in the past, the anxieties and rigours of army life, allied to a constitution always frail and further weakened by a second pregnancy, had been too much for Rollo's young wife Clara, to whom he was extravagantly attached, and she and the unborn babe had been laid to rest among, alas, so many of her compatriots in that alien land. Overwhelmed by grief, Rollo resigned his commission and returned to find refuge in the Oxfordshire home of his mother, Lady Ogilvy, my aunt, and widow for many years of a prosperous merchant knighted for his services to Industry and the Poor.

I was at that time establishing myself as a painter of classical subject pictures—my *Sweet Echo... within thy airy shell* attracted much critical commendation at the Royal Academy exhibition that year—and I did not visit Long Basing until the Christmas after their arrival there. My aunt was a formidable woman who kept great state and, although one's creature comforts were excellently catered for, I had always found her rules and regulations irksome (one was not allowed to smoke even in the billiard-room but must brave the elements on the terrace or, at best, the stables if in need of a cheroot). But Christmas was a Day of Obligation (as the Romans have it) and I always spent the two days of its festivities there, as much to honour my uncle's memory as my aunt's command.

My aunt had thought very little of Rollo's marriage. He was her only child and she had great ambitions for him, I presume. She had considered Clara to be weakly (and was correct), that to take her out to India would kill her (correct again), and that she was not of the stuff to breed good sturdy sons (once more, correct). But Rollo—a handsome fellow of great charm, whom many a duke's daughter might have looked on with favour—was head over heels in love, and duly bore his Clara off to those far reaches of our Sovereign's Might. Clara was only twenty-four when she passed away, and although I had met her only at her wedding I had always remembered her fragile gold-and-silver beauty, delicate as thistledown.

My first sight of Blanche that Christmas Eve made me catch my breath, for she was her mother in miniature. She was six years old at the time, brought to the drawing-room by her nurse to watch the candles being lit upon the Christmas tree. She could have graced the tree herself, for she was a faery child of pink and white, her long fair tresses falling down her little back to cover the wide sash at her waist, her full frilled petticoats rustling atop little feet shod in bronze slippers and drawn-thread socks.

Her nurse, a large slab-faced woman of fierce mien, held her fast, but she pulled her hand away and sped towards her father, love and gladness shining in her face. My aunt admonished her and bade her curtsy first to herself and then to me. 'This is your cousin Edward,' she declared, 'who paints famous pictures.'

The child gazed upon me earnestly and then, in the prettiest way possible, piped up, 'Will you paint a famous one of me?'

'Indeed I will, my dear,' I answered. And so indeed I did in the years to come.

THE PURITY OF CHILDHOOD is unique. Beside it men and women are as dross, heavy, brutish, tainted with the knowledge of sin. But a child is all innocence, all Creation, the wonder of the world in her eyes, her little body fresh and resilient as a flower. Gaze into a child's face and see with a painter's eye the marble eyeball, lustrous and fringed with curving lashes, the tender flush of cheek, the rosebud freshness of lip and the pearly teeth within. Every portion of a child is a miracle of God's work, pure and untouched by the dark forces that bedevil men and women. And so their minds are too, each day a wonder of discovery, each hour one in which they can bestow their artless love on His creations. Fears they may have, of witches and ogres perhaps: but fears of the desires and appetites that lurk within the adult human soul they have no knowledge of. They are as God made them, unstained, fresh from His hand.

This I have always tried to capture in my works. Not for me the haggard and unwholesome visions of the Rossettis and their ilk! Rather I try to capture on canvas the pearly radiance of young flesh and spirit—caught well. I think, in my *Not Angles but Angels* (now in Stopford art gallery) or *Attendant on Queen Mab* (Wenham town hall). I have had my struggles, my dark nights of the soul—all men have wrestled with the Devil, art students not least of all. Depravity and destruction are all too easy to embrace. But the Soul must rise above it and shall be as a little child.

I returned to London and my studio after Christmas, but my thoughts often turned to that faery child and her piping query. And I wondered how she would fare, torn from the sultry land of her birth, motherless at so tender an age, under the cold authority of Lady Ogilvy and that intimidating nurse.

The answer was—badly. For her father, unable to reconcile himself to the loss of his young wife or to apply himself either to country life or to the building of some new career, had disappeared into America. 'He intends to take up what is called "ranching",' my aunt wrote in her spiked calligraphy, 'although since he is ignorant of even the basic principles of home farming I am dubious of his success.' More than this, Blanche herself fell grievously ill, and my aunt intimated (it was not in her nature to beg) that I should visit them at Long Basing, as the child sorely missed the attentions of a father.

I found her stretched upon a sofa, not in the nursery but in Lady Ogilvy's sitting-room, the long windows open on to the rose garden. She was playing listlessly with her dolls and as she saw me advancing across the room her face lit up and she opened her little arms to me. 'Papa!' she cried: then, as the truth struck her, she fell back, her mouth trembling.

'It is Cousin Edward come all the way from London,' my aunt said.

The child brightened. 'To paint my famous picture?' she enquired.

'Very likely,' I said, sitting down on the couch beside her, 'if that is what you wish.'

'Oh yes!' she cried, and threw her arms about my neck. Her pale curls fell against my face and her little form trembled in my arms. She looked up, laughing. 'Oh, Cousin Edward, you have such silky whiskers!' she declared. And ever after, when we were alone, she would call me Silky. And I could call her Faery.

The facts of her illness emerged. She had been ill because, ignorant of the flora of our English countryside, she had wandered in the garden alone and espied what she took to be green pea pods lying on the path. Childlike, she had eaten some—but alas, they were not green peas but laburnum seeds and she was taken almost mortally ill.

Secondly, she was in my aunt's sitting-room and not the nursery because Nurse Hodge had been dismissed. Her negligence in allowing Blanche to wander unsupervised and so meet with an almost fatal accident had led Lady Ogilvy to dismiss her without a character, and she had packed her bags and taken herself off not to London but to the village inn, with whose widowed host she had, it appeared, been on somewhat familiar terms. My aunt had decided to care for the child herself, teaching her her letters and simple arithmetic, a nurserymaid being sufficient to see to her physical needs.

'With my son gone, Blanche is the only Ogilvy,' my aunt said with her cold smile. 'It is my duty—and my pleasure—to bring her up with due regard to her inheritance.'

I stayed the month of August. During that time my faery regained her strength and spirits and ran about the house and gardens of Long Basing like some merry sprite. She was somewhat in awe of Lady Ogilvy and worked studiously at their lessons together, learning with the quickness of a singular intelligence. But between this faery child and myself there grew up an intimacy, a confidence which took me into the magic world of childhood. Hand in hand we explored the woods and fields of the estate, looked at the animals on the Home Farm, rode together, I on Rollo's neglected hunter, she on her fat pony. On rainy days we would play dominoes or Happy Families, or, while she read the *Tales from Shakespeare* or Maria Edgeworth's stories, I would take my pad and charcoal and sketch her as she sat, her cheek upon her hand, lost to the world.

She told me all her secrets and once, when we sat one twilight in the nursery, she curled like a kitten on my lap, her little arms round my neck, she whispered, 'I'm so glad that Nurse has gone.'

'Was she unkind to you, dearest?'

'She was horrid. She pulled my hair and hurt my arms putting on my clothes. It was worth nearly dying to make her go away.'

'But,' I said, mystified, 'you didn't know those horrid seeds were poisonous?'

'No, I did not. I shall remember another time. They hurt me awfully, but it was worth it to make Nurse go away and you to come.'

I RETURNED TO LONDON. Time passed. It was some two years later that my aunt summoned me unexpectedly to Long Basing. Rollo was dead. A band of 'rustlers', as they are termed, had tried to drive away some of his cattle and in the fray Rollo had perished. My aunt, her face white marble in the cascading black of her mourning weeds, said stonily, 'Blanche is my heir. She will grow up different from her father. When I die, you shall be her guardian.'

THEREAFTER I WAS more often at Long Basing, and my faery was permitted to visit me in London several times a year, either with my aunt or, later on, with her maid Agnes.

These were joyous days indeed! Together we visited the Zoological Gardens, Madame Tussaud's, Maskelyne and Devants. At Christmas there was the pantomime, my faery entranced by the more tawdry fairies on the stage and by the drolleries of Dan Leno. I watched her grow from a chubby child into a slender ten-year-old, as white and gold as her mother had been but with a vitality that shone in the pulsing of the blood in her delicate veins and in the candid challenge of her eyes. She took an enchanting pleasure in pretty clothes, and it was my delight to buy her frills and flounces, little muffs, a bonnet or a small pelisse more frivolous than those allowed by my aunt, who kept her fairly strictly. She would throw her arms around my neck and shower kisses on me. 'Dearest Silky,' she would whisper, 'you are my best Papa.' And each time we parted, in the sunlit, stable-smelling caverns of Paddington station, she would say passionately, 'I wish that we could be together always.'

It was the following spring that Lady Ogilvy had a stroke. It had been planned that she and Blanche, accompanied by their maids, should join me for two months in Dieppe, a small watering-place on the French coast much patronised by English artists (although mostly of a more radical school than myself). This plan had, of course, to be abandoned, and instead I repaired to Long Basting and spent the summer there.

It was a strange time. On the one hand there was the sick-room where my aunt, bed-bound and able to do nothing for herself, lay day after day, cared for by the servants and the regular visits of the doctor, a room of shadows and drawn curtains, low voices and the cloying odours of medicines, to which my faery made twice daily visits, to read or prattle to my aunt as best she could while the maid took a brief respite—a sunbeam glancing into that drear room, in duty bound.

On the other, there were the fields and gardens, where Blanche and I wandered, she with her dolls, I with my sketching things, and the handsome, empty rooms of the

house of which she and I were now the sole monarchs. In the
morning-room, which faced north, I rigged up a studio, had
the carpet rolled up and put away, the curtains taken down.
And there, on many happy days, I made my pictures—
sketches, drawings, studies—my model my enchanting faery, content to sit as still as any eleven-year-old can be, art-
lessly prattling or sometimes falling silent, her eyes remote,
lost in who knows what thoughts. Some of my finest com-
positions grew from these sessions, worked up in my London studio at a later date—*Cupid and my Campaspe*,
Blanche half draped, a wreath of roses in her hair leaning
across a chequered board; and *Who shall be May Queen?*
(now in Storrington town hall). These were idyllic days, in
which beauty and innocence went hand in hand despite the
dark shadow of the sick-room.

When the time came near— 'I shall not be able to bear it
when you go back to London,' she whispered, her eyes luminous with tears. 'Why cannot I come and live with you?'

I smoothed her hair. 'Because you are all your grand-
mama has. Because you owe her duty in her last days.'

'I cannot bear it,' she repeated, and turned away from me
with that mutinous pout I loved so well.

She did not, poor child, have to bear it long, for a day or
two before I was due to depart Lady Ogilvy was taken mortally ill during the night. Unable to help herself, her atten-
dants sleeping, she succumbed to the ghastly symptoms of
an acute disorder and died before morning.

I WILL DRAW A VEIL over the next few weeks or months—the
grief, the condolences, the domestic and legal dispositions.
Suffice it to say that, my aunt having indeed appointed me
guardian of her grandchild and sole heir, I decided to
maintain Long Basing, the only home Blanche had ever
truly known, with the support of the excellent housekeeper
and staff. I myself would divide my time between that

household and my own in London, where the bulk of my clientele was to be found. The sketches and studies I made at Long Basing could be admirably worked up later in Holland Park. But the problem of my faery's education, hitherto undertaken by my aunt, remained. A series of governesses was the result.

I say a series for, alas, perfection was hard to find. Some were too strict, some not strict enough, some were true bluestockings, most were mere geese. My faery had the bright intelligence of unspoiled childhood, was quick to grasp a subject, had read widely in the books ranged on the library walls, was impatient of restraint. 'I don't need to learn French verbs like a parrot,' she would cry, curled on my lap in her old sweet way (although now, in her thirteenth year, she was no longer a kitten but, perhaps, a small, smooth, lissome cat). 'I will speak it well enough when we are in France together'—for I planned that holiday still. Or, 'Why do I need to know the water-table of Australia, I am never going to go there?'

Sometimes she came to me in tears. 'Miss X is cruel to me, she raps my knuckles,' or, with pretty disdain, 'Miss Y is so silly, she can only add up on her fingers.'

The governesses too were loud in their complaints, for few of them made allowances for the tragedies in my faery's short life; nor, when I was absent, could they readily accept the authority of the housekeeper and the sometime insolence of the servants, for a governess is neither fish nor fowl in the eyes of the lower orders.

Our most sunlit days were when she stayed with me in London, the faithful Agnes in attendance. Then, in her little ermine cape and muff, she would gaze wide-eyed at the wondrous displays in Regent Street or, in velvet and satin-sashed, clap her little hands at the antics of the clowns and harlequins. There were sunlit days too in Dieppe, the elegant, strolling crowds along the parade, the cakes and chocolate, the fellowship of brother artists gallantly curbing their sometimes raffish humour in deference to my young companion. Sunlit days indeed—in which the innocence of the child burgeoned into the radiance of the young girl, a child still but with the awareness of womanhood within her, half child, half woman, wholly mine.

MORE CHILD THAN WOMAN at first glance seemed Madeleine Fenton, daughter of an East Anglian rector and now cast upon the world at his death. But Miss Fenton's small and dainty person concealed a well-stocked mind and a character both pliable and firm. Barely a head taller than my faery (who had grown apace, as children will), she seemed more like an elder sister than a governess, and so it seemed that Blanche regarded her. A whimsical humour, a gentle but discerning tact, fitted Madeleine Fenton into our household as though she had been meant for it.

At last, it seemed, our troubles were done. Miss Fenton was only nineteen years of age, still close enough to childhood to feel and understand the innocent joys of simple country life, while her dainty stature, the fresh and laughing candour of her face, made her seem almost Blanche's twin. To watch them run together down the wide lawns of Basing, to see their two heads bent together in the lamplight as though two students, not mentor and pupil, was a joy inexpressible. It seemed that Blanche had given her her heart.

And so had I.

IT IS DIFFICULT FOR ME to write of subsequent events, for the agony is with me still. But I must do so, for my sole purpose in penning these lines is to vindicate and protect my faery, no matter what my own pain.

I began to care for Miss Fenton in a way which no woman my own age could ever evoke in me. Mature women, women wise in the ways of the world and of polite society, their beauty no longer with the bloom of innocence upon it, had never made appeal to me. I have seen too much of the world's dark side, of the shame and torment of our adult appetites, ever to feel true tenderness for those of my own age. But in Madeleine Fenton the bloom still glowed; fresh from the Suffolk rectory, she knew nothing of the evils of humankind, but saw the world still with the fresh vision of childhood. Her father had trained her mind but he had left her heart unsullied. I began to look at her with different eyes; to wonder if it might not be that we three could enter a faery world together, that these two bright spirits might not in fact become my child and wife...

I cannot dwell on it. The bare facts can be read in the scurrilous gutter-press of the day.

Madeleine Fenton was taken ill during the night of 27 July. Vomiting, pain unspeakable, fever, sweats. The doctor came, his potions eased her symptoms—but they returned. For three days she swung between life and death, and on the fourth day she died.

The doctor was mystified. He could not, he said, give out a death certificate. An inquest must be held.

IT WAS HELD in the parish hall in Basing village. The Coroner was a jumped-up local solicitor with whom the Ogilvys had never been on good terms; my aunt had never received him as she had, for instance, the rector or the doctor, and I believe he also nursed some resentment that he had never been put in charge of her affairs. These, which had been considerable, she had always deemed best to have handled by a London firm, a practice which I, as executor and Blanche's guardian, had continued. It was clear from the Coroner's opening remarks that he felt neither sympathy nor impartiality for the tragedy before him.

The acidulous—nay, malicious—tone of the proceedings soon captured the interest of the journalists sent by local newspapers. The Coroner's cross-questioning of Dr Pierce was not concluded by the end of the day, and when the inquest was resumed on the morrow the Grub Street jackals were there in abundance. TRAGIC EVENTS AT COUNTRY MANSION ran a headline in a London journal, MYSTERIOUS FATALITY AT FAMILY SEAT, DOCTOR QUIZZED ON HOUSE OF DOOM—for it had not taken the so-called Gentlemen of the Press long to discover and set out in paragraphs of lurid scurrility the sad facts in the family's past: the motherless child, the dramatic departure and subsequent death of the father, the sudden demise of Lady Ogilvy, and now that of Madeleine Fenton. In this sad catalogue the frail figure of the orphaned child stood out, a bright star in the midst of darkness, and on her the jackals fastened.

Only the doctor, myself and Mrs Poole, the housekeeper, had been required to attend the first day's proceedings. It was inconceivable to me that a child of tender years should be called on to do so, but when the doctor's evidence was at last concluded the Coroner ordered that Blanche should be called on the following day. I telegraphed Mr Forbes, our London lawyer, to be present, for at all costs I was determined to protect her by whatever means I could from the pain and confusion of what was fast becoming a raree-show. The Coroner also ordered that the domestic staff be called, and spent much time in questioning Mrs Burgess, the cook, as to the food served on those fatal days; also the housemaid who had attended Madeleine in her sickness, the under-housemaid who had served and removed the trays sent up to her room, the kitchenmaid who had washed up the utensils. For no matter how Dr Pierce had hedged his statements, trying nobly to protect his friends and patrons from the innuendoes of the court, he had been forced in the end to admit that Madeleine had expired from the ingestion of some noxious substance. What terrible mischance could have achieved so dread an outcome?

Everyone who had been in Long Basing that fatal day, or days, was summoned to the witness-box. My own ordeal had been quickly over, for I had been in London for some days when Madeleine first fell ill and, summoned by telegraph by Mrs Poole, the housekeeper, had arrived, alas, too late to bid my dearest friend farewell. Loyalties and resentments were revealed as one by one the servants gave their testimony—petty jealousies, for as I have said, a governess is often in uneasy relationship with the domestic staff: an under-gardener who had been too familiar, the housemaid who had not cared for extra duties, and, strangest of all, the unsuspected presence of Blanche's one-time nurse, now wife to the village innkeeper, who had, unbeknown to us or to Lady Ogilvy, been a familiar visitor to the servants' hall, having formed a friendship with Mrs Burgess. So little does the master know his man!

And then, despite the protests of Mr Forbes, our lawyer, my faery was summoned to the box.

I can scarce describe it. For four long hours she stood there, pale and steadfast as an altar candle, clad in deepest black, her fair curls hidden beneath a bonnet whose black veil she had thrown back, her little hands in their black gloves clasped on the wooden rail before her. Once she faltered and seemed like to faint; but against the protests of our lawyer, she remained in the box, sipping a glass of water, her gaze fixed on the Coroner. Had she visited the sick-room? Of course. Had she administered any substance? Of course not. What were her feelings for Miss Fenton? She loved her—and here her voice broke and her eyes filled with tears. Was Miss Fenton in the habit of taking patent medicines? She did not know—perhaps such as were in common use. Such as? Perhaps cough mixture or for headaches, or to help (her pale cheeks flushed here) elimination. Cascara, senna pods? Yes. Did Miss Fenton ever administer such things to her? Sometimes. But she came to no harm from them? Never.

Like terriers the Coroner and Mr Forbes fought out their battle, the one determined to intimidate the frail child in the box, the gist of his questioning ever more loathsomely clear, Mr Forbes striving with all the energy at his command to open the field of speculation, to show how possible it would have been for Madeleine's death to lie at several doors but, likeliest of all, at none. Disgruntled servants, even the long-nourished rancour of Nurse Hodge, dismissed, as she no doubt felt, unfairly and supplanted first by Lady Ogilvy (whose death, the Coroner dared to imply in his infamous summing-up, might also bear investigation) and then by a charming governess—all were possible. Most possible of all to any but his warped sensibilities, that Madeleine had accidentally dosed herself not with some common panacea such as senna pods but one which contained some unsuspected lethal substance.

The torture ended. Despite the Coroner's outrageous summing-up, the stalwart jurymen brought in an Open verdict. It was not what I hoped, but at least it stilled most tongues and lifted from us the foul burden of the public gaze. For five days we had lived in the ferocious glare of the yellow Press, our words and actions reported in every detail, our visages sketched and reproduced across the page—for the spectacle of a young girl, beautiful and gently bred, made the centre of what, in all but name, came near a trial for murder was for the Press a Roman holiday.

Half-fainting, she clung to me as we fought our way to the carriage. In tears she lay in my arms as I bore her up to her room, the servants whose characters had been so variously revealed flustering about us. At last she slept. And I, alone with my grief, could weep.

WE SHALL LEAVE Long Basing. It is entailed and cannot be sold, but tenants will be found and we shall never live here again. We shall live in my house in Holland Park, my faery and I, and put the past behind us. I have a faithful staff, my work goes well; the dreadful events of the past months have not harmed my professional reputation, which is, I believe, secure. The world shall wound us no more, for I shall keep my faery safe. As she grows to womanhood she will still pose for me; although she must lose the soft radiance of childhood, she will remain as sweet and winningly wilful as I have always known her. No doubt one day some handsome fellow will come to claim her from me. I dread that day, but pray I may be spared for many years to shield her from the fortune-hunters that I fear abound—for on my death, together with her Ogilvy inheritance, my faery will indeed be well endowed with this world's riches. But, as the Bard says, 'Beauty provoketh thieves sooner than gold,' and she is beautiful indeed, still with a childlike purity in her candid gaze.

I set all this down in the desperate hope of exorcising the dark memories of the past; to state the true facts as I understand them of that sad and singular sequence of events which resulted in so terrible an ordeal of suspicion and persecution; and to attest my deep and loving fidelity to my faery child, my Blanche.

EDWARD AUGUSTUS STEYNES

*These papers were among the effects of Edward Augustus Steynes, ARA, seen but not used by the Crown Prosecuting Counsel in the trial of Blanche Clarissa Ogilvy, aged seventeen years, for his murder by laburnum poisoning, for which she was sentenced to death by Mr Justice Talbot at the Old Bailey. The sentence was subsequently commuted to life imprisonment. It is thought she emigrated to Australia after her release.*

THE CLEWSEY CLASSICS

"PRAY CONTINUE," SAID HOLMES TO MISS HUNTRESS. "YOUR NARRATIVE PROMISES TO BE A MOST INTERESTING ONE."

# STEADY AS SHE GOES

★

## CATHERINE AIRD

---

'THE FACTS OF THE MATTER,' declared Superintendent Leeyes, 'are quite simple.'

Detective Inspector Sloan waited without saying anything. In fact, had there happened to have been a salt-cellar handy in the Superintendent's office in Berebury police station he might very well have taken a pinch from it. In his experience, open-and-shut cases seldom came his way anyway, and never if the superintendent had had a hand in matters to date.

'The deceased,' said Leeyes, 'died from poisoning by antimony.' He grunted and added, 'according to Dr Dabbe, that is.'

Sloan made a note. In his book, if not in the superintendent's, that constituted a solid fact. Dr Dabbe was the consultant pathologist for their half of the County of Calleshire and not a man to say antimony when he meant arsenic.

'The doctor,' swept on Leeyes, who was inclined to treat medical pronouncements as the starting point for discussion rather than the end of it, 'says in his report that the Reinsch test was positive for antimony.'

Detective Inspector Sloan made another note. By rights it was Detective Constable Crosby sitting by his side who should have been taking the notes but unfortunately as it happened the detective constable actually was a man to write alimony when he meant antimony and Sloan thought in a case of poisoning it was better to be on the safe side and do it himself.

'The deceased's sister,' growled the Superintendent, 'alleges that the poison was administered by the husband...'

'Most murderers are widowers,' remarked Detective Inspector Sloan, that most happily married of men. 'And certainly almost all male murderers are.'

The Superintendent rose effortlessly above the Home Office's statistics. 'And,' he continued with heavy irony, 'the husband is insisting that the sister did it.'

'Hasn't that got a funny name, sir?' Detective Constable Crosby's wayward attention seemed to have been engaged at last.

'Funny!' barked the Superintendent. 'Since when, may I ask, has there been anything funny about murder?'

'Not murder itself, sir' responded Crosby earnestly. 'I meant that I thought that the word for that sort of murder was a funny one.'

'Murder is always murder,' Leeyes was at his most majestic, 'whatever Defence Counsel chooses to call it at the trial.'

Detective Inspector Sloan's hobby was growing roses and he was just thinking about the parallel where they smelt as sweet by any other name when Crosby put his oar in again.

'They said so, sir,' persisted the detective constable with all the innocence of youth, 'at the training college.'

'Fratricide,' managed Leeyes between clenched teeth. Older and wiser men than Crosby knew better than to mention police training colleges to the Superintendent. Not only was the very concept anathema to him but there was nothing in his view better than the time-honoured walking the beat with a sergeant or 'sitting next to Nellie' way of learning.

'But that's when you kill your brother, isn't it, sir?' persisted Crosby. 'Shouldn't it be "sorocide" if it's your sister? Or is that satricide?'

'The word "homicide" will do, Crosby,' interposed Detective Inspector Sloan swiftly before either of the other two thought about the killing of satyrs—or kings, come to that. He enquired if such a thing as a motive for poisoning existed.

'According to the sister, yes. According to the husband, no.'

'Gain?' suggested Sloan, veteran of many a domestic murder. So far the case hadn't struck him as 'open and shut' in any way at all.

'The love of money is the root of all evil,' quoted the Superintendent sententiously.

This sentiment seemed to be the view, too, of Miss Kirsty McCormack, sister of the late Mrs Anna Macmillan.

She was a thin, rather dowdy woman, with thick glasses, living in a modest bungalow set in a very large garden on the outskirts of Berebury. Miss McCormack seemed only too anxious to talk to the two policemen.

'We came here about twelve years ago, Inspector, Mother and I,' she said, ushering them into a preternaturally neat and tidy sitting-room. 'Won't you sit over there, constable? On the settee. Inspector, I think you'd be more comfortable in Mother's old chair by the fire.'

'Thank you, miss.' Sloan could not think at first what it was that was so odd about the room and then it came to him. All the walls were bare. There was not a picture or a photograph to be seen.

'It was after her first heart attack that we moved. We thought she would be better not having to climb the stairs.'

'You've got rather a lot of land, though,' observed Sloan, no mean gardener.

'Indeed, yes, although as you can see I had to let it go.'
She sighed. 'The garden is part of the trouble.'

'Upkeep?' suggested Sloan, but unsympathetically. 'It
would be considerable.'

'Oh, no, Inspector. It's much too big even to try to keep
it up without help. Besides, I was too busy looking after
Mother, especially towards the end.'

'Quite so, miss.' He waited. 'And...'

'And then Mother died,' she said flatly.

Sloan coughed. 'She can't have been young.'

'She wasn't. I decided to move—there was a dear little flat
on the market in Calleford and I'd always wanted to live
over there.'

'A very pretty city,' said Sloan who would have found it
stifling himself.

'That's when the trouble started.'

'Trouble?' Sloan's head came up like that of an old war-
horse and even Crosby looked faintly interested.

'We found that this dreadful old garden was just what the
developers had been looking for.'

'I see, miss.' Detective Inspector Sloan, husband and father, who had to think carefully each autumn how many
new roses he could afford to add to his collection, wasn't
sure that he did.

'Anna and I suddenly became rather well off,' she said.

This time Sloan thought he was beginning to understand. 'You and your sister were co-heirs, I take it?'

'That's right, Inspector.' She looked him squarely in the
eye. 'So Paul had quite a lot to gain from killing Anna.'

'Her share of your mother's estate,' hazarded Sloan,
'would come to him in the ordinary way should his wife
die?'

'Exactly,' said Miss McCormack. A glint of amusement
crossed her flinty features.

'Unless she had willed it to you,' pointed out Sloan.

'She hadn't,' said Miss McCormack. 'If Paul outlived her it was to go to him.'

There was a small movement from the direction of the settee. 'And if he didn't?' asked Detective Constable Crosby.

'It came to me.' There was no mistaking the sardonic amusement in Miss McCormack's expression now. 'There are no children, you see.' She gave a wintry smile and said, 'Paul, of course, insists that the same argument about gain applies to me.'

'And does it?' enquired Sloan.

'Either Paul would have to be found guilty of Anna's murder or I would have had to kill them both to inherit.'

On the settee Detective Constable Crosby stirred. 'And did you try?'

All trace of amusement vanished from Miss McCormack's face and she looked merely sad and weary. 'No, Constable, I didn't. And I don't know either how Paul killed Anna but I can tell you one thing. He did it before my very eyes and I can't for the life of me think how.'

'Perhaps,' said Detective Inspector Sloan, falling back on formality, 'you would tell us about the day in question...'

'I'd gone over to their house after tea—not that they were tea drinkers—at about a quarter-past five. Paul was there but Anna hadn't come home from the hairdresser's—she was a bit later back than she expected. The traffic's always pretty bad then, you know.'

'We know,' said Sloan moderately.

'Paul said he'd only just got back from the office and he hadn't been home in the middle of the day because he'd had a business luncheon.'

'So there was no way that he could have given his wife any poison before you came?' said Crosby. 'Is that what you mean?'

They hadn't, apparently, taught the detective constable at the police training school anything about not accepting statements by interested parties at face value but Sloan let that pass for the time being.

'Exactly,' said Miss McCormack as if to a promising pupil. 'Anyway, Anna came in just then, very smart from the hairdresser's and with loads of shopping, and said she was dying for a drink.'

'And die she did,' said Crosby incorrigibly.

Sloan decided that there was perhaps something to be said for the 'sitting next to Nellie' school of learning after all. No self-respecting mentor would have let him get away with that.

'Paul asked me what I would have and I asked for a dry ginger ale...'

'You were driving, miss?' said Sloan. He would deal with Crosby in the privacy of the police car later.

'No, Inspector, I don't drive. I'm teetotal but,' again the steely glint of amusement, 'I think you could say that Paul and Anna weren't.'

'I see, miss. And then?'

'Paul asked Anna what she would like and she asked for a black cat.'

'A black cat?' Sloan wrote that down rather doubtfully.

'Paul said she wasn't to call it that. Its proper name was *pousse-café*. Naturally I asked what it was and Anna said it was a drink that Paul had been practising.'

Even the soi-disant detective sitting on the settee pricked up his ears at that.

'Paul,' continued Miss McCormack, 'said that he'd found the recipe in an old book of drinks and Anna and he rather liked it. In fact he said he'd have one too and was I sure I wouldn't change my mind about the ginger ale.'

'And did you, miss?'

'Certainly not, Inspector. I never touch alcohol and it's just as well I didn't because I'm sure that's how he killed her.'

'With the black cat?' Sloan sat back and thought hard. In his file were statements from the scene-of-crime officer and the forensic science people that none of the bottles in the Macmillans' drinks cabinet contained antimony.

'With the *pousse-café*. Anna said she liked the rainbow one best.' Miss McCormack pursed her lips and said, 'What I can't get over is that he must have poisoned her while I was watching him. He even told me what he was putting in it as he made it.'

'And can you remember, miss?'

'He started with grenadine syrup which is red and then maraschino... white.'

Sloan made a note. 'Then...'

'Crème de menthe.'

'That's green,' said Sloan confidently. 'After that?'

'Yellow Chartreuse. I remember that particularly because Paul couldn't find it to begin with and Anna said she was sure there was a full bottle of Chartreuse somewhere.'

'And was there?' Sloan had a list but he wasn't going to consult it. Not here and now. Nor his notes on the very high solubility of potassium antimony tartrate crystals.

'Yes but it was green Chartreuse and that wouldn't have done because of the crème de menthe, you see.'

'No, miss. I don't see. You'll have to tell me why it wouldn't have done.'

'The rainbow *pousse-café* is made up of drinks of all different colours,' said Miss McCormack. 'They're in the glass together but in layers.'

'Neapolitan,' said the overgrown schoolboy on the settee decisively.

'All you need is a steady hand,' she said, 'and you get a striped drink.'

'Did your brother-in-law find the yellow Chartreuse?' asked Sloan.

'Oh yes, in the end,' said Miss McCormack. 'And the orange curaçao and the cognac.'

'What colour is cognac?' enquired Crosby.

'Amber. That was last.' She looked up. 'I must say the two glasses looked quite pretty standing there.'

'Forever Amber,' said Crosby.

'And then?' said Sloan, taking no notice.

'And then they drank them.'

'Both of them?'

'That is the interesting thing,' agreed Miss McCormack. 'Yes, Paul drank his, too.'

'Like the dog that didn't bark in the night,' said Crosby. He was ignored.

'And you are quite sure, miss, that exactly the same—er—ingredients went into each drink?'

'Quite sure,' said Miss McCormack firmly. 'I tell you, I saw them made and the same amount came out of each bottle. Anyway, Paul let Anna choose the one she wanted herself.'

'Then what happened?' asked Sloan.

'We sat chatting while they drank their *pousse-cafés*. You obviously have to do it very slowly or the rainbow effect is spoilt.'

'Yes, miss.'

'We must have been sitting there for—oh, the best part of an hour, Inspector, when the phone went. Paul went to answer it—he hoped it would be the garage to say that his car was ready after servicing. He came back presently to say that it was and he was just slipping out to collect it before the garage closed at six.'

'And then?'

For the first time Miss McCormack's composure crumpled. 'Anna got up and took the empty glasses out to the kitchen and then I heard her start vomiting—just ordinarily at first and then really violently.'

Detective Inspector Sloan had all the information he needed about the lethal effects of antimony in his file too but he still listened to the woman in front of him.

'By the time Paul came back, poor Anna was in a pretty bad way with stomach cramps. He rang the doctor and they got her into hospital but she died that night in terrible pain.'

Sloan listened even more attentively to the distressed woman before him and then, policeman first and policeman second, said 'What happened to the empty glasses?'

'They were found on the draining board in the kitchen afterwards, washed and upside down. I think Anna must have done that before she started being ill.'

Sloan nodded. The police had gone to the house before Paul Macmillan had left the hospital and found no antimony anywhere, but he did not say so to the woman in front of him.

'And neither you nor your brother-in-law was taken ill as well?' asked Sloan, although he knew already that antimony wasn't one of those poisons to which you build up a tolerance with low doses.

'Right as ninepence, both of us,' responded Miss Mc-Cormack. 'I understand,' she went on spiritedly, 'that Paul is alleging that I poisoned Anna after he had left to pick up his car.'

'I haven't spoken to him yet,' said Sloan diplomatically. 'We're on our way there now...'

Once back in the police car, though, Sloan told Crosby to drive only as far as the nearest lay-by. The two policemen sat there for some time while Detective Inspector Sloan sat and thought and Detective Constable Crosby to all intents and purposes just sat.

Eventually Detective Inspector Sloan pulled out the list of the contents of the drinks cabinet *chez* Macmillan and studied it carefully.

'What was it you said about the dog that didn't bark in the night, Crosby?'

'That it was interesting,' said the constable. 'It's a quotation.'

'Would you say a bottle of grenadine that wasn't there was interesting, too?'

'Sir?'

'Never mind. Let's go and arrest Paul Macmillan for the murder of his wife, Anna.'

'How did he do it, then, sir?' Crosby let the clutch in at speed. If there was one thing in the world that he really liked it was driving fast cars fast.

'He put the antimony in the grenadine syrup beforehand and waited until his sister-in-law or some equally good witness came at drinks time. She was the best bet because she was both teetotal and short-sighted. Admirable characteristics, Crosby, if you propose murdering your wife by alcohol.'

'But Miss McCormack doesn't drink, sir.'

'Exactly. He knew she wouldn't accept a *pousse-café* or any other barbarically named alcoholic concoction. He could count on it.'

'What about the short sight?'

'I'm coming to that. He makes the cocktail up before her very eyes as the conjurors say, and lets his wife choose hers. It doesn't matter which glass she chooses because they've both got antimony in—'

'But, sir...'

'But remember, he knows there's antimony in his and his wife doesn't know that there's antimony in hers.'

'So...'

'So she drinks hers to the very last drop.'

'And he doesn't?'

'You can bet your life he doesn't, Crosby. He leaves the bottom layer.'

'The grenadine syrup?'

'Exactly. Put in first according to the recipe because it has got the highest specific gravity of all the constituents and thus stays at the bottom of the glass.'

'Where he leaves it?'

'Exactly. That was made much easier for him by the telephone ringing when it did—I dare say we shall find out when we ask that he arranged for the call from the garage as late in the day before they closed as possible. It gave him the excuse to leave the last of his drink untouched.'

'But what about the rest of the grenadine syrup?' asked Crosby, taking the corner at a speed that took insufficient account of centrifugal force.

'I think we shall find that went into his pocket while his back was to the two women and that it got lost on the way to or from the garage.'

'Like the Superintendent said, sir,' said Crosby, going through the gears, 'it was an open-and-shut case then after all.'

'Well,' said Sloan modestly, 'I think you might say it was really more a matter of knowing exactly where the rainbow ends.'

# SOLDIER, FROM THE WARS RETURNING

★

## ROBERT BARNARD

I HAVE A PHOTOGRAPH of my grandfather—my real grand-father—in the uniform of the King's Own Yorkshiremen, taken on leave in 1917, when he had finished his weeks of training and was about to be sent to France. He gazes out into the camera—young, confident, even cocky. I have been told that young soldiers were encouraged to have such pictures taken, ostensibly on the grounds that they encouraged smartness and pride in the regiment, in fact because their officers suspected that the photographs would soon be all that the family had to remember them by.

But this was not the case with my grandfather, Jimmy Larkins. He bucked the statistics. He served in France and Belgium for eighteen months and only sustained a minor wound in the final push of the autumn of 1918. He also survived the 'flu epidemic of 1919, that final dirty trick of the President of the Immortals. On his demob he got a job as a baker's roundsman in his home town of Armley, and he put the war behind him.

On the surface, at least. I do not believe that any nor-mally sensitive person could go through those hellish years entirely unchanged. He had not sunk, suffocating, into the mud, he had not been shot as he clambered over the ridge of his trench, but he had seen hundreds who had, had known them. What Jimmy Larkins would have been like if he had grown up normally in peacetime no one can now know. As it was he seems to have come home with an urge to make up for lost time, perhaps even to live a little for the lads who had not come home.

And there were plenty of women and girls in the Armley area who were willing to help him do it: women whose husbands had not come home, girls whose potential husbands were remembered collectively on Armistice Day, women whose husbands had come home crippled or haunted—and, indeed, women whose husbands followed the normal northern working-class tradition that the husband's leisure time was spent boozing with his mates while his wife stayed home to cook, clean and mind the children. There were lonely, unhappy, dissatisfied women a-plenty in Jimmy Larkins' Armley, and he did his best to bring a little joy into their lives. It was rumoured that at moments of climax he would cry 'That's one from Archie Hoddle!' or 'That's for you, Robbie Robson!'—all the names of mates of his who had never come home from France to sow their own wild oats.

This was a rumour, as I say, for this was not the sixties, when privacy and reticence were dirty words and happiness was thought to flow from endless talk about one's sexual proclivities and activities. This was the twenties, when you kept yourself to yourself, and all but the outcast families maintained a wall of respectability between them and the outside world.

But if the ladies did not discuss among themselves what Jimmy did or did not say when he was reaching climax with them, they did show their knowledge of his activities obliquely, in jokes. 'What she needs is a visit from Jimmy Larkins,' they would say of a sour spinster, or 'Serve your man right if you started asking Jimmy Larkins in,' they would tell a neglected wife. After a time they started hinting that they could see his features in the babies that were born. 'I don't like the look of that snub nose,' they would say, or

'Who does that high forehead remind me of?' Thus, in ritual jokes, did the women of Armley reveal their awareness of my grandfather's doings in the neighbourhood without their ever acknowledging that he had brought to them personally, along with the bread, that other staff of life.

The women, as I say, could joke about it. Some, no doubt, wanted more from the relationship and became emotional and demanding, but Jimmy had his ways of avoiding commitment. When asked why he had never married he always said briefly, 'It wouldn't be fair.' I take him to have been good-hearted and promiscuous, fleeing mentally from the blackness of those months in France. For a time, perhaps, even the men of Armley understood.

But the men never treated it as a joke, and as the twenties turned into the thirties they found that the whole business was becoming very sour indeed. These men had a pride in paternity as fierce as that of any aristocrat, and they added a sense of *possession*—exclusive possession—of a wife that boded ill both for the wives themselves and for Jimmy. The fact that they spent their evenings and weekends in pubs gave no sort of leeway to the wives they left cooped up with a brood within four walls. Their suspicion and anger found its own form, and it was not jocular. 'Someone should take a knife to that randy bastard,' they would mutter into their pint mugs, or 'I'd like to get that bugger up a back alley some dark night—I'd know what to do to him.'

Their rage and frustration was dynastic too: they looked at their children, and particularly their sons, and they wondered if they were the fathers. They studied features, even pondered their characters and tastes, and wondered 'where they got that from', as if that were a scientific study and could give them certainty one way or the other. In the end they usually subsided into a boiling uncertainty which found

occasional outlets in violence to their wives or their offspring.

Usually, but not always. They were simple men with
strong, not always rational, feelings and a fierce pride. Their
manhood was their most precious possession, and if they
felt it impugned they became enraged. They loved certain-
ties and feared doubt. To live in uncertainty, permanently,
was to them barely tolerable. Some of them, discussing the
matter over the years, first in hints and ambiguities, later
with angry directness, determined to do something about it.
There were six of them: Walter Abbot, Fred Walmsley, Bill
Hoggett, Mickey Turner, Harry Colton and Peter Huggins.
They are names that still crop up in conversations in Armley pubs and clubs, because the crime was a local sensation, something much more than a nine-days' wonder, and
the men—and, inevitably, their wives—became the objects
of finger-pointing that lasted the rest of their lives.

In spite of the violent prognostications of the Armley men
they decided not to castrate Jimmy. Something in them
shrank from that, as it did not shrink from murder. They
decided to kill him in such a way that all of them must be
under suspicion but no one would be able to decide which
had done it.

What may seem odd, even ironic, today is the game they
chose as a cover for the murder. Bowls has nowadays a
gentle, middle-class, elderly image: it is a game that is played
when physical powers have declined and all passions are
spent. But many working men in the thirties played bowls:
a relaxing game after a day of hard, physical work. Four of
the men were good players, and the pub where Jimmy Larkins had his pint or two after work was only a hundred yards
or so from the Armley Bowling Club. So one autumn evening the six of them turned up, casually and separately, in
the Waggon of Hay, bought Jimmy an extra pint, and finally set out for a game of bowls with Jimmy as umpire.

Whether Jimmy, as he rolled off with them, was secretly cock-a-hoop that he had cuckolded every one of them I do not know. I hope not—hope he regarded his relations with their womenfolk in a different light from that. But we shouldn't try to endow the people of a past age with our own ideological baggage.

The facts of the case were always simple. They played, in the failing light, a game of bowls. At some point in the game Jimmy went off, as he was bound to do, to go to the small public lavatory by the green. The other men claimed they had not noticed when he left, nor who had gone to the lavatory immediately afterwards. They had all relieved themselves at some stage of the game, but they had not gone into the cubicle. They had finished playing without Jimmy—it was a friendly game, and an umpire was not necessary—and had then gone home. Jimmy's body was found next morning in the cubicle. He had been stabbed, and the old raincoat which had been used to protect his murderer from blood had then been thrown over him.

Those were the facts, and no one ever got very far behind or beyond them. The next day the police began a series of interrogations of the men—and, to a buzz of local gossip, their wives. The men stuck doggedly to their story; they didn't remember when Jimmy had left the green, and they didn't remember who had gone to the lavatory after him. They had assumed he had gone home, and had gone on with the game without thinking any more of him. They never pretended to have seen other men or women on or around the green, for, though they were hard men, even brutal, they were fair. At one point, three weeks after the murder, the police charged them all with conspiracy to murder, but they could find no evidence that the men had conspired so, fearing a fiasco in court, they soon dropped the charge. And so there it was: six men, all with the opportunity and the identical motive for murder. The police, and everyone in Armley, knew that one of the men had done the deed, but no one knew which.

I must be one of the few people alive who does know. I was told by my grandmother, Florrie Abbot, sitting in her little kitchen in Armley, while upstairs, in the bedroom they had shared, the man I called my grandfather was dying painfully of cancer. She told me the story in low, angry tones, interrupted by tears, none of them for the dying man upstairs.

# GOODBYE JENNY

★

## PENELOPE WALLACE

---

'GOODBYE, JENNY. Goodbye, Baby Mary.'

'Goodbye, Ian. Have a good term.'

'Ian, have you got your glasses?'

'Yes, Mother.'

'Jenny, I'll catch the train from Reading so I'll be in London by seven-thirty if anyone rings.'

'Yes, Mrs Rayne.'

'I'll be back by seven.'

'Yes, Mr Rayne.'

'Get in the car, Ian.'

'Yes, Father.'

'Donna, don't forget your seat-belt.'

'I won't forget. Wave to Jenny, Ian.'

OF COURSE I SHALL WAVE to Jenny. Dear Jenny. I shall miss her. I hate going back to school. Why can't it always be the holidays?

POOR LITTLE SOD, he's nearly crying. Why doesn't he have more guts. Of course he's no good at games: no team spirit. Doesn't make for popularity. When I was at school...

WHEN FATHER WAS AT SCHOOL he was terrific at games: captain of cricket; played rugger for the school; rowed in the first eight. I wish I could do something to make him proud of me. I don't even do well at lessons. And I get bullied.

I DON'T DOUBT he gets bullied. Should fight back. Tried to teach him boxing but he doesn't seem interested. I should hide my disappointment in him, and Donna doesn't seem to care.

THANK GOD rehearsals start next week and I shan't have to be down in the dreary country. John at the typewriter all day and Ian...Ian's such a dull child. Maybe Mary will be brighter—even if she was an accident. And I'm not too sure she's John's. She might be Bruce's. Then she'd be bound to go on the stage, with an actress for a mother and an actor for a father. Bruce. Witty, wonderful Bruce. I'll see him this evening.

MOTHER'S SMILING. I think she's quite glad I'm going back. She doesn't really like me much. She's very beautiful—and famous. Father's famous, too. Sometimes he's mentioned in the papers: 'Famous Author'.

DONNA LOOKS PLEASED with herself—thinking about the new play, I suppose. I know she can't wait to get up to London but I'm glad I persuaded her to come with Ian today.

I REALLY DO HATE SCHOOL. I wish they understood. I do try. I suppose I'll be sharing with Brown again and he'll laugh at me and say Father writes trash and Mother gets her parts through the casting couch. I get so angry, and then he laughs more. I wish I could be like Masters. His mother hugs him and it makes him go pink, but he doesn't mind when everyone laughs at him. I like Masters's mother. She really seems pleased to see him and she writes him long letters and sends him chocolate biscuits in padded bags. Why does there have to be school? Why can't it all be holidays and living at home with Father and Jenny and Baby Mary—and Mother at weekends?

JOHN'S DRIVING SO SLOWLY. School by five-thirty. He'll help Ian with his trunk and I suppose I shall have to go up too—smiling at all those dreary mothers. Hope he won't want me to chat to the housemaster. I'll miss my train.

HE HASN'T SAID A WORD. I think I'll have to talk to his housemaster, see whether he recommends holiday coaching. Plenty of tutors in London. He could stay at the flat with Donna. He's old enough to be left alone when she goes to the theatre. Or she can get another girl like Jenny.

But no one's like Jenny.

Dear, sweet, warm Jenny.

And in a few hours she'll be in my arms.

IT'S A ROTTEN JOB being a policeman. That car—overtaking on a corner.

Driver must have been dreaming. They didn't stand a chance. All dead. Taking the boy back to school from the look of the trunk.

Just an ordinary happy family.

# THE CHRISTMAS CRIMES
## AT 'CINDERELLA'
## PART TWO: BOXING DAY

★

### SIMON BRETT

THE NUMBERS on the Advent calendar corresponded to the
letters of the alphabet. Maria Lethbury wrote the one-word
answer to the first puzzle into a point of the four-pointed
star:

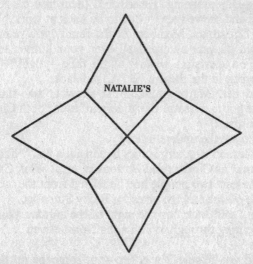

NATALIE'S

She then turned the paper over. 'I'm sure there's more
information in the rhyme—

> "ONE CLUE FROM EACH PUZZLE, ONE POINT
> FOR EACH CLUE,
> AND MIXING THEIR HEADS UP WILL TELL
> YOU WHO"...

*Who* killed Natalie Maine, presumably.'

'"Mixing their heads up"?' said Jack. 'Hm... That could refer to the initial letters...of the answers to each puzzle—'

Maria caught on quickly. 'So you mix up the four letters and that gives you the murderer's name!'

'Exactly. And all we've got so far is an "N"...'

'So what do we do next, Jack?'

'We go and talk to Ken.'

THE STAGE DOORMAN seemed delighted to see them early on Boxing Day morning. He ushered them into his tiny cubbyhole and brewed tea. 'Glad to be back at work,' he said. 'Hate Christmas. Members of the family you've managed to avoid all year slumped all over your house. All those people on television, *smiling* all the time—yugh!'

'Anyone in the theatre yet?' asked Jack.

'You bet. Major panic. First show at two-thirty and they've got to rehearse the understudies for both Cinderella and Buttons!'

'Who are the understudies?'

Ken leaned wheezily across to consult a list. 'Niki Grayes takes over as Cinders and Buttons is, er... Wink Carter.'

So at least two people had benefited from the murder of Natalie Maine and the arrest of Ricky Sturridge.

'Ken,' said Jack, 'on the night of the murder, you told us Natalie rang through to you at half-past eleven...'

'Yes.'

'And you're sure it was her—not someone putting on a voice?'

'It was her all right.'

'So she was certainly still alive then. Ricky Sturridge rushed out of the theatre at . . . what time?'

'Ten to twelve.'

'Were any other members of the company still here then?'

'No. Just Natalie. Been a long day. Everyone wanted to get back to their families.'

'And did anyone leave the theatre between eleven-thirty and ten to twelve?'

Ken, who'd already been through this with the police, had his answers ready. 'Niki Grayes, Wink Carter and Freddie Link—they all left together about a quarter to. Then, just before Ricky, someone else rushed out in one hell of a hurry.'

'Who?' Maria demanded urgently.

'Danny Kino.'

THERE WAS AN AIR OF PANIC about that morning's rehearsal, but it was controlled panic. The two understudies knew their lines and moves. Wink Carter made a workmanlike if somewhat subdued Buttons, but Niki Grayes showed real brilliance as Cinderella. The tabloids would be able to follow up their Boxing Day splashes about the murder with a good 'Star is Born' story the following day.

In fact, without the temperament of Natalie Maine and the incompetence of Ricky Sturridge, 'Cinderella' ran a lot more smoothly than it had on Christmas Eve.

Jack and Maria, watching the rehearsal from the back of the auditorium, were joined by Freddie Link. Even at that time in the morning, the actor moved in a mist of Scotch whisky.

Niki Grayes was just singing her big number. Natalie Maine's latest release. And she was singing it rather better than Natalie Maine had done.

'Clever little thing,' Freddie Link observed in a slurred voice. 'Very keen to learn, too.'

'Oh yes?'

'Mm. Other night after the dress rehearsal she was asking me about comic timing.'

'What time would this be?' asked Jack.

'Just before I left. Half-past eleven, I suppose. Talked for... I don't know, quarter of an hour...?'

'Was Wink Carter with you then?'

'No. He joined us just as we got to the stage door. We all left together.'

Jack and Maria exchanged looks. Unless there was some kind of conspiracy going on, their list of suspects was getting smaller.

Freddie Link lumbered to his feet. 'Better get onstage. Sing-along with Buttons next. God, I hate that scene,' he said as he swayed off down the aisle.

'I think he was telling the truth,' Maria murmured.

'I don't know. Why should he make such a point of giving himself an alibi?'

'You can't suspect him, Jack. He's too drunk all the time to work out puzzles.'

'*Appears* too drunk. Remember he's an actor.'

Onstage the sing-along scene had started. It was the inevitable pantomime moment when the words of a song were lowered from the flies and everyone was urged to join in. Difficult to rehearse without an audience.

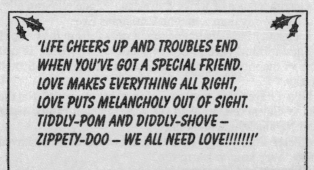

'LIFE CHEERS UP AND TROUBLES END
WHEN YOU'VE GOT A SPECIAL FRIEND.
LOVE MAKES EVERYTHING ALL RIGHT,
LOVE PUTS MELANCHOLY OUT OF SIGHT.
TIDDLY-POM AND DIDDLY-SHOVE –
ZIPPETY-DOO – WE ALL NEED LOVE!!!!!!!'

Still, Wink Carter and Freddie Link did their best, belting out the nonsense on the sheet behind them.

As they sang, Jack murmured, 'I think Freddie Link's a liar.'

'Oh no, he isn't,' Maria whispered back.

'Oh yes, he is.'

'Oh no, he isn't...'

FREDDIE LINK'S truthfulness was, however, confirmed. On their way out to grab a sandwich at lunchtime, they stopped again at Ken's cubbyhole and Maria casually mentioned what the actor had said.

'That's right,' the stage doorman wheezed. 'Freddie and Niki was in his dressing-room all the time from half-past eleven till they left.'

'How do you know?'

''Cause I seen them, haven't I?' The old man gestured across the corridor to a closed door. 'Freddie's dressing-room, that is. He had the door open last night and I seen young Niki go in and I seen them chatting...ooh, a good twenty minutes.'

'And was Freddie drinking at the time?'

'Course he was. When isn't he?'

'What about Niki?' asked Jack.

'No, she didn't have nothing. Dedicated professional, that girl. Got a lot of talent and not going to let the booze nor nothing stop her getting right to the top of the business. No, she's—'

He was interrupted by the sound of shouting from the stairs leading down to the stage door.

'I suppose I should say "Break a leg", but I actually hope you break something that does more permanent damage!' The voice, shrill with affront, was Danny Kino's. 'I trusted you!'

'I know, and I'm sorry, but—'

Wink Carter's pleading was cut short as the comedian continued furiously, 'And what thanks do I get for all I've given you? You go off chasing tarts!'

'Danny—'

'Well, at least one of them's out of the way now. Don't think you'll be lusting after Natalie Maine again in a hurry, will you—you *traitor*!'

As he spat the word out, Danny Kino appeared at the bottom of the stairs. Taking no notice of Jack and Maria, he stormed out of the stage door.

THEIR LIST OF SUSPECTS had now lost the names of Niki Grayes and Freddie Link. They were not surprised to find the latter in the pub at lunchtime, and it took only the purchase of a large Scotch to loosen his tongue.

'It was obvious from first day of rehearsal that Danny had taken a shine to young Wink. Boy didn't quite know how to react. Think he's a pretty confused kid...you know, uncertain about his identity...highly intelligent—too intelligent for his own good, probably—got a history of mental breakdowns, I gather...'

'Oh,' Jack reacted evenly.

'Anyway, I think he found it hard to cope with—two of them coming on strong to him.'

'Two?'

'Yes. Danny, of course. And...Natalie.'

'Really?'

'She came on to every man. That's what made Ricky Sturridge so mad. But she was doing it to Wink too. I mean, he's an attractive boy and Natalie was the kind who regarded every good-looking man as a challenge.'

'What about Danny Kino?' asked Maria. 'What's he really like?'

'Well, at his best, very good company. Great practical joker, old Danny, but...he's always had this really vicious streak.'

'Oh,' said Jack Tarrant diffidently. 'Has he?'

GIVEN THE SUDDEN cast changes, the first matinée of 'Cinderella' went exceptionally well. Wink Carter's Buttons gained confidence as he began to feel the audience's affection. And from her first entrance it was clear that Niki Grayes was destined to be a major star.

The only upset came in the sing-along scene. The words of the song that descended from the flies were totally different to the ones Baron Hardup and Buttons had rehearsed.

Jack Tarrant felt his hand urgently squeezed as Maria breathed in his ear, 'There it is—the second puzzle! The second word!'

'Yes!' Jack murmured excitedly. 'And there's a clue in the verse, isn't there?'

They were quickly able to fill in the second point of the star from the puzzle hidden in this sing-along doggerel:

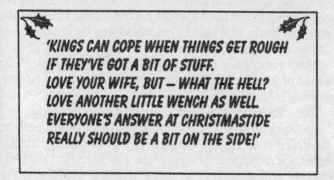

'KINGS CAN COPE WHEN THINGS GET ROUGH
IF THEY'VE GOT A BIT OF STUFF.
LOVE YOUR WIFE, BUT — WHAT THE HELL?
LOVE ANOTHER LITTLE WENCH AS WELL.
EVERYONE'S ANSWER AT CHRISTMASTIDE
REALLY SHOULD BE A BIT ON THE SIDE!'

(Continued on p. 215)

# BOOTS

## ★

## ANTONIA FRASER

HER MOTHER used to call her Little Red Riding Boots, and eventually by degrees of use (and affection) just Boots. And now that Emily was no longer quite so little—the smart red plastic boots which had given rise to the joke were beginning to pinch—she still liked being called the pet name by her mother. It was a private matter between them.

Emily's mother, Cora, was a widow: a pretty, slight young woman, not yet thirty, but still a widow. When Emily was a baby, her father had gone away to somewhere hot on an engineering project and had got himself killed. That at least was how Emily had heard Cora describing the situation on the occasion of her first date with Mr Inch.

'And not a penny after all these years,' Cora added. 'Just a load of luggage months later. Including the clothes he was *wearing*! Still covered in his blood...'

Then Mr Inch—not Cora—got up and shut the door.

Listening from her little bedroom, which was just next to the sitting-room, Emily imagined her father getting himself killed. Or rather she thought of the nasty accident she had recently witnessed on the zebra crossing opposite their house. Blood everywhere. Rather as if the old woman had been exploded, like you sometimes saw on the news on television. The old woman had been hit by one of the nasty long lorries which were always rumbling down their particular high street. Cora felt very strongly about the lorries, and often spoke to Emily about them, complaining about them, warning her about the crossing.

Perhaps that was why Cora had let Emily go on watching the scene out of the window when the old woman was hit, for quite a long time, in spite of all the blood.

Later Cora explained her views on this kind of thing to Mr Inch, and Emily listened.

'You see, you can't protect a child from life. From the first I never hid anything from Boots—Emily. It's all around us, isn't it? I mean, I want Emily to grow up knowing all about life: that's the best kind of protection, isn't it?'

'She is awfully young.' Mr Inch sounded rather doubtful. 'Perhaps it's just because she looks so tiny and delicate. Such a little doll. And pretty too. One wants to protect her. Pretty like her mother—'

On this occasion also, Mr Inch got up and shut the door. He was always shutting the door, thought Emily, shutting her out as if he did not like her. And yet when Mr Inch was alone with her, if her mother was cooking something smelly with the door shut, even more if Cora dashed down to the shops, Mr Inch used to take the opportunity to say that he liked Emily, that he liked Emily very much. And perhaps one day, who could say, perhaps Mr Inch might come to live with Emily and her mother all the time—would Emily like that?

At this point Mr Inch generally touched Emily's long thick curly hair, not gold but brown, otherwise hair just like a princess's in a fairy story (so Cora sometimes said, brushing it). Mr Inch also touched Emily's mother's hair in the same way: that was of course much shorter, which made it even curlier. But while Mr Inch touched Cora's hair in front of Emily, he never, Emily noticed, touched her own hair when Cora was present.

Emily paused to imagine what it would be like if Mr Inch got himself killed, like Emily's father. Would he explode like

the old woman at the crossing? Sometimes Emily watched
out of the window and saw Mr Inch approaching the house:
he was supposed to cross by the zebra too (although sometimes he did not bother). Sometimes Emily would watch Mr
Inch just running towards the house, galloping really, on his
long legs. When Mr Inch visited Cora he always brought
flowers, sweets for Emily, and sometimes a bottle of wine as
well. He still managed to run towards their house, even carrying all these things.

When Mr Inch ran, he looked like a big dog. A big old
dog. Or perhaps a wolf.

By now Emily had really grown out of fairy stories, including that story which her mother fondly imagined to be
her steady favourite, Little Red Riding Boots. To tell the
truth, she much preferred grown-up television; even if she
did not understand it all, she found she understood more
and more. Besides, Cora did not object.

That too, said Cora, was a form of protection.

'The news helps you to adjust painlessly... A child picks
and chooses,' she told Mr Inch. 'Knowledge is safety...'

'But Cora, darling, there are some things you wouldn't
want your sweet little Boots to know—I mean, what have
you told her about us?'

Because this time neither Cora nor Mr Inch shut the door,
Emily was left to reflect scornfully that there was no need
for her mother to tell her about Mr Inch, since she saw him
for herself, now almost every day, kissing her mother,
touching her curly hair. And hadn't Mr Inch himself, while
touching her hair, Emily's much longer hair, told Emily he
hoped to come and live with them one day?

All the same, there was a resemblance between Mr Inch
and a wolf. His big teeth. The way he smiled when alone
with Emily, for example.

'All the better to eat you with—' Emily could remember
the story even if she could no longer be bothered to read it.

Once, in spite of herself, she got out the old book and looked at her favourite picture—or rather, what had once been her favourite picture—of Grandmother in her frilly cap, Grandmother with big teeth, smiling.

Little Red Riding Boots stood in front of Grandmother, and though you could see the boots all right, all red and shiny, just like Emily's own, standing in the corner of her bedroom, you could not see the expression on the little girl's face. Nevertheless Emily could imagine that expression perfectly well. Definitely the little girl would not be looking afraid, in spite of everything, in spite of Grandmother's big teeth, in spite of being alone with her in the house.

This was because Emily herself was not afraid of Mr Inch, even when she was alone with him in the flat, and he called her his little girl, his little Boots (which Emily firmly ignored) and talked about all the treats he would give her 'one day', a day Mr Inch strongly hoped would come soon.

The girl in the picture was standing quite still. She knew that soon the woodcutter would come rushing in, as he did in the next picture, and save her. Then he would kill the wicked wolf, and in some books (not the version which was supposed to be her favourite) the woodcutter made a great cut in the wolf's stomach and out came tumbling all the other people the wolf had eaten. No blood, though, which was rather silly, because everyone knew that if you cut people open or knocked them or anything like that, there was masses of blood everywhere.

You saw it all the time in films when you were allowed to sit with your supper and hold your mother's hand during the frightening bits: 'Squeeze me, Boots, squeeze my hand.'

Emily loved sitting with Cora like this, to watch the films on television, and it was one of the things she really did not like about Mr Inch that when he arrived, Emily had to stop doing it.

Mr Inch watched the films with Cora instead and he held her hand; he probably squeezed it too. Sometimes he did other things. Once Emily had a bad dream and she came into the sitting-room. The television was still on but Mr Inch and Emily's mother were not watching it. Emily's mother lay on the floor all untidy and horrid, not pretty and tidy like she generally was and Mr Inch was bending over her. His trousers were lying on the floor between Emily and the television, and Emily saw his long white hairy legs, and his white shirt tails flapping when he hastily got up from the floor.

Now that *was* frightening, not like a film or the news, and Emily did not really like to think about the incident afterwards. Instead she began to imagine, in greater detail, how Mr Inch might get himself killed, like the wolf, like her father. She did not hold out much hope of Mr Inch going somewhere hot, because he never seemed to go anywhere, and also Mr Inch had plenty of money; lack of money was the reason that Emily's father had gone somewhere hot in the first place. Nor was he likely to be killed crossing the road, like the old woman, if only because Mr Inch was always warning Cora (and Emily) to take care; even when Emily watched Mr Inch running in their direction, she noticed that he always stopped for the lorries, and allowed plenty of time for them to pass. As for the woodcutter— which was a silly idea, anyway, because where would you find a woodcutter in a city?—even if you took it seriously, you would not expect a woodcutter to rush into their flat, because Cora saw so few people.

She was far too busy caring for her little girl, Cora explained to Mr Inch when they first met. Babysitters were expensive, and in any case unreliable.

'I shouldn't dream of trying to take you away from this dear little person,' Mr Inch had remarked on this occasion, flashing his big white teeth at Emily. 'It was always one of my great regrets that I never had a daughter of my own.'

No, Emily did not see how a woodcutter could be brought into the story. She wished that Mr Inch would be famous, and then he would go on television and maybe be killed. But Cora said that Mr Inch was not famous: 'Just a very good kind man, Boots, who wants to look after us.'

'Now I've got two little girls to look after,' said Mr Inch one day. For a moment Emily was mystified by his remark: she had a sudden hope that Mr Inch had found another little girl to look after somewhere else. It was only when Mr Inch took first Cora's hand, then Emily's, that she realised with a certain indignation that Mr Inch's other little girl was supposed to be her mother.

After that, the caring and looking-after by Mr Inch of Cora and Emily grew stronger all the time.

'I'll take very good care of her,' said Mr Inch, when Cora asked him to go down to the supermarket with Emily. 'And I'm sure you won't object on the way back if there's just one ice-cream.'

'Run along, Boots,' called Cora from the kitchen, 'and hold Mr Inch's hand very tightly. Specially crossing the road.'

Actually there was no need for Cora to mention crossing the road to Mr Inch, because he held Emily's hand so terribly tight on the way to the shops that she had to stop herself squeaking. Then Mr Inch cheated. He bought Emily not one but two ice-creams. He took her to the new ice-cream parlour: Emily had never been inside before because Cora said it was too expensive.

Emily ate her ice-creams in silence. She was imagining cutting open Mr Inch with the woodcutter's axe: she did not think the things inside Mr Inch would be very nice to see (certainly no exciting people had been swallowed by Mr Inch). But there would be plenty of blood.

Even when Mr Inch asked Emily to come and sit on his lap and said that he had something very exciting to tell her, that he was going to be her new Daddy, Emily still did not say anything. She let Mr Inch touch her long hair, and after a bit she laid her head on Mr Inch's chest, which is what he seemed to want, but still she was very quiet.

'Poor little Boots is tired,' said Mr Inch. 'We'd better go home to Mummy.'

So Emily and Mr Inch walked along the crowded street, the short way back to their flat from the shops. Emily did not say anything and she did not listen to what Mr Inch was saying either. When Emily and Mr Inch got to the crossing, they paused and Emily—as well as Mr Inch—looked left, right and left again, just as Cora had taught her. This time Mr Inch was not holding Emily's hand nearly so tight, so it was Emily who squeezed Mr Inch's hand, his big hairy hand, and Emily who smiled at Mr Inch, with her little white pearly teeth.

It was when one of the really big lorries was approaching, the sort that Cora said shouldn't be allowed down their street, the sort which were rumbling their flat to bits, that the little red boots, shiny red plastic boots, suddenly went twinkling and skipping and flashing out into the road.

Fast, fast, went the little red boots, shining. Quick, quick, went the wicked wolf after the little red boots.

Afterwards somebody said that the child had actually cried out: 'Catch me! Catch me! I bet you can't catch me!' But Cora, even in her distress, said that couldn't possibly be true because Emily would never be so careless and silly on a zebra crossing. Hadn't Emily crossed it every day, sometimes twice a day, all her life? In spite of what the lorry driver said about the little girl dashing out and the man running after her, Cora still blamed the driver for the accident.

As for poor Mr Inch—well, he had died trying to save Emily, save her from the dreadful heavy lorry, hadn't he? He was a hero. Even if he was now a sad sodden lump of a hero, like an old dog which had been run over on the road.

Emily said nothing. Now Boots expected to live happily ever after with her mother, watching television, as in a fairy story.

# A DISTANT AFFRAY

★

## ROGER ORMEROD

THE PRINCIPLE

DEAR SIR,

Please accept my most abject apologies for having missed most of the lectures in our weekend seminar. I am myself disappointed, this being the only course you conduct yourself, and as I have a keen interest in its subject: The Road to Success. The fact is that I have been beset, recently, by domestic problems, that much I can put forward as an excuse. But—as you so often say—excuses are empty, only reasons carry weight. I therefore offer the following explanation.

I do not think you have met my wife, as she has always refused to join me on our weekend courses. I have put forward every possible persuasion. But no. She has resolutely refused, and has always disapproved of my own weekend breaks. What, she kept asking, was the attraction? I believe she thought I was meeting another woman, which is not so. But now, more recently, she has changed. You will understand that this worried me, as the change was abrupt, and dates from two months ago. At that time she began actively to encourage me, even going as far as to comb your brochure for other weekend courses I might attend, such as Macramé for Beginners and Welsh for Seasoned Travellers. For this latest particular weekend she couldn't get rid of me quickly enough, with the result that I was on the road before the mist lifted on Friday, and had to spend half the day exploring remote corners of Wales, where the Welsh-speaking course would have been useful, in order to sign in promptly at five-thirty.

You may appreciate, sir, that her strange behaviour caused me concern, as I couldn't help wondering whether it had any connection with our new neighbour, Colin, who moved in about two months ago. Coincidence, of course, though he is younger than me, and unattached, as they say. Well, he doesn't need to be—he's one of those smooth and fascinating city types who only has to raise an eyebrow. The ladies around the avenue positively fall over each other for his smile. He's not much good in the garden, though. You should *see* his lawn.

You may not have observed that I spoke not a word during dinner that Friday evening. Immediately afterwards I went along to the pay-phone on the lower landing and called home. Or rather, I phoned next door, my intention being to tell Colin that I was worried about my wife's behaviour, and to ask him whether he would mind keeping an eye on her for me. Unfortunately there was no reply, so I phoned my wife.

I should explain that there's no reason for delay in answering, as we have extensions all over the house. But it rang on and on, and I was really worried when she eventually answered.

She sounded short of breath. I asked whether she was all right. She said she was, rather shortly, I thought. I said I didn't like the sound of her breathing, and she ought to ask the doctor to look at her chest, but she claimed there was nothing wrong with her chest and I had to agree with that, so she demanded to know what I wanted. I said that I had forgotten to tell her that when I did the shopping I'd had to bring Woof for our dog, Jason, instead of his usual Growl, and would she hide the label from him when she opened his tins. She said she would do that. He watches all the adverts, you see. She asked was that all, and I had to admit it was, but she didn't hear the last bit because she'd rung off.

That, sir, was why I missed part of your opening lecture on Accomplishment and Endurance, and the subsequent debate, which carried over into the bar, I understand. In fact, I went to my room early, so immersed was I in all that worrying.

Naturally, I couldn't sleep. You will understand that, as you no doubt covered this aspect in your Saturday-morning exposition on Concentration and Distraction. At around two in the morning—I cannot be certain of the exact time— I got up and went along to the phone, and called my wife again. Just to hear her voice.

Her breathing was much better, I was glad to hear, though her temper was somewhat short. She didn't seem pleased to hear my voice. No tit-for-tat in our marriage, that I think has been the trouble. I said I'd forgotten to remind her that she ought to take Jason for his walk, last thing. She assured me she'd done that, but in the distance I could hear him howling. Great Danes have a mellow voice, you know. I suggested she should look behind the settee in the morning, as Woof often upsets his stomach. She promised she would and asked whether I minded if she got back to sleep. It didn't sound to me as though she'd *been* asleep, but I agreed she could, not mentioning that I was certain I wouldn't be able to, and returned to my lonely room.

I'm sure, sir, that you know how it can be in the small, chill hours of the night. Reality goes all to pot, panic sets in, and you imagine all sorts of things. She has never failed to sleep very soundly when I am lying beside her, so perhaps my absence was in some way disturbing her sleep pattern. I found this thought flattering. But there was a possibility, remote perhaps but quite valid to me at the time—my agony of concern being a very real one—that she had started taking sleeping tablets. And that, finding one ineffective, she had maybe taken another. Or more. Would that explain her previous shortness of breath? Would it explain her definite shortness of patience with me?

This possibility occurred to me at about four in the morning. In a minor panic I stumbled along the corridor to the phone. I dialled our number. There was no reply. The phone is right by the bed. What was I to think? My panic was rapidly taking control. I'm sure you have a word, sir, for this behavioural pattern, and will understand when I admit that I could think of no other course but to phone our friend Colin, next door. I was, by then, prepared to take extreme measures.

Perhaps the pollen count in our district was high, but when he answered, without a second's delay, he too wasn't breathing very easily.

I told him about my worry, and the basis of it: that she had perhaps taken sleeping tablets, and maybe had even taken an overdose. He conceded that it was a possibility, no more, but otherwise didn't interrupt. I asked him, tentatively you understand because of the time, whether he would see if she was all right. He said it was no trouble at all to do that, see she was all right, he meant. I had to get him to promise to call back as soon as he had. He assured me it shouldn't take long.

I paced that stretch of landing by the phone for half an hour. Did you know, sir, that the heating goes off completely in the early morning? I felt I did not dare to leave the phone long enough to fetch my dressing gown. He didn't call back. I tried his number again, and got the engaged tone. Five times I got it, and had to tell myself that there are people who fumble when replacing a handset, especially when their minds aren't on it. In desperation, I tried to get my wife again. No reply.

You will have discovered by now, sir, that there is a chip out of the phone on the lower landing, where I hammered it against the wall. On receipt of the repair bill I will hon-our it at once. (Likewise with the wall, of course, sir.)

On Saturday morning, you will understand, I felt terri-ble. Maybe I'd had an hour's sleep. Certainly I cannot re-call breakfast. After the meal, assuming I ate any, I was forced once again to forgo a lecture, as it seemed critically important to speak to my wife. I phoned home. No answer. So I phoned my mate Colin next door. Line engaged. So I went for a walk round the college grounds in order to cool off. Visions of my wife in a coma came to haunt me. Vi-sions of Jason not getting his breakfast. Worse still, not getting his morning walk. The space behind the settee is limited, and he's a big dog.

I returned inside, having made a decision, and phoned the RSPCA. You don't like to worry the police, do you, though they suggested I ought to do that, but after ten minutes they agreed to send an Inspector round. He would call me back, they promised. There's a phone booth right opposite our front door. More waiting... I paced the lower landing. Half an hour later the clown called back to tell me there was no sound from the house. I asked if he'd shouted the magic word Jason through the letter-box. He said he hadn't known the animal's name, so he went back to try that.

Ten minutes later he called me again. Ten minutes—just to shout Jason! Nothing had happened. Surely she couldn't have given Jason sleeping tablets, too!

I admit to a certain amount of hysteria entering into the situation at that point. I said he had to get in there, and he told me he would have to get permission to use force, and I said he had it, but he wanted it in writing, at which time I think I shouted a little and said he could have a retrospec-tive deposition in writing...but the long words floored him. I thought we had reached an impasse, but at that point an-other voice, calm and assured, interrupted. The police had arrived. I shouted for them to smash down the door—smash it down! He made soothing noises, and hung up on me.

Some time later—I was way beyond counting—he rang back to say they'd gained access, as he called it, and the house was empty. There was no sign of my wife's car, nor of Jason.

But I'd had time, you see. I had realised, during that waiting period, what must have happened. I asked whether the house next door on the right was also empty, and when he said it was I said Ah! He asked me what Ah meant, and I had to admit that I'd made a stupid mistake in trusting our neighbour. Colin Something, I said his name was, and I'd told this Colin that she was alone in the house and I'd asked him to keep an eye on her. And he's always seemed a bit strange to me, now I came to think about it, sort of over-sexed, if the constable knew what I meant. He said he'd heard about it, cleared his throat, and suggested I should make such a serious charge as this—when I hadn't made one—to his Inspector. He gave me the number and I tried it.

Patient chap, that Inspector. I told him everything, and he expressed an opinion that it didn't have to mean anything as serious as assault. I asked him what else it could be, so he told me, and I said don't be stupid, she's not like that.

At this point there was a short pause, then he asked whether I was suggesting physical violence. He sounded a little cool. I said I wouldn't put it past her if my friend Colin tried anything, and maybe in the struggle...you know... He thought about it again, taking precious time and my precious money, I thought, then he said that, as both houses were empty, perhaps I might have a suggestion as to where they might be. Where Colin might have taken her, that is.

I thought his interest had perked up at the thought that there might be a body to be found.

Really, it didn't take much thought, as dear Colin had spoken proudly and often about it. He had a weekend cottage on the river somewhere in Shropshire. I didn't know exactly where, but Madge would know. Madge at No. 17, that was, and if not her try Edna at No. 24 or Jessie at No. 3—oh, pretty well any of the ladies in the avenue. He sounded dubious, but promised he would give it a try. He would, he promised, phone back.

You will appreciate, sir, that this was going to take a little time. But I didn't dare to desert the lower landing for long. I snatched a bit of lunch, but unfortunately had to miss your lecture on Desperation and Persistence. But the waiting time extended itself, and with the passage of it my nerves settled down, if not my fears, and I realised that it was, indeed, Saturday. And Saturday has always been my wife's day to tour the shops in town, including lunch there. She always took Jason along to scowl from inside the car. Better than those alarm bleepers, I always think.

I decided that the Inspector ought to know this, in case it affected his actions. As my hand reached for the phone, it rang. It was for me. It was him.

I never did get to telling him, he spoke so rapidly and with a kind of suppressed tone. It appeared that the local force in Shropshire had located the cottage, and discovered Colin there, in bed with Madge from No. 17. They had reported back, so that my Inspector had gone along to our place to check the situation. Yes, my wife was at home. She was, in fact, at that time standing in the drive and staring at the front door, which was flat on its back. So of course he had had to explain. In detail. Apparently, she had been quite violent and vocal, especially when she heard about Madge from No. 17. When she let Jason out of the car the Inspector had retired from the scene, rapidly I believe. She was still shouting outside his side window when he drove away.

He asked, then, where I was calling from. I explained that it was a weekend course at an adult residential college. He asked how far away and I told him just over a hundred miles, and he said just as well but he didn't blame me, and was it a dirty weekend? I said it hadn't worked out like that, so far, but there was still time. One has to pretend to a certain amount of nonchalance in these situations. Don't you think? But really, I was too exhausted. We hung up as friends.

This was not the end of it, but fortunately no more phoning was involved, as I was running out of change. I don't know whether you noticed, sir, but I was missing for a large part of Saturday evening. The local police sent a car for me, and they ran me down to the station. Another inspector. Wales has some very pleasant policemen, I find. We chatted. He explained that my wife was at that moment in custody, charged with grievous bodily harm inflicted with a deadly weapon, to wit, one shotgun. I had to admit that I'd forgotten to mention I owned such a weapon. He tutted a little, shaking his head, then told me that Madge was expected to recover, but the word was, from the hospital, that Colin would have no future practical use for his cottage. He raised his eyebrows at me and asked me whether she was usually that violent.

I shook my head. My opinion, which I expressed, was that something must have provoked her, though I couldn't imagine what that might have been, but the circumstances hadn't been normal, had they?

He cleared his throat and said no, they weren't normal for Wales—men shooting one woman out of their bed just in time to take another woman to their cottage. Not in Wales. I detected a certain amount of envy in his voice.

I asked after Jason. He was being cared for by the lady next door, on the left, I was assured. That would be Tina, a most attractive widow with a sense of humour.

My wife phoned this morning. She is out on bail, and staying at a quiet hotel, for her nerves. Tina is taking some of her things along, and will tell her I've quite recovered from the experience. My wife tells me she has seen a solicitor about divorce proceedings, and doesn't expect me to contest it. She sounded doubtful and tentative, but I'm sure Tina will encourage her to accept that divorce is the best solution. I'm to have custody of Jason.

Sir...one small point. Has anyone handed in a small drawstring pigskin bag, which I left on the shelf beneath the phone on the lower landing? I am not concerned about the small amount of coins in it, which you could count towards repair of the phone—and the wall—and there couldn't be more than £2 left from the £5 I brought with me. But the bag is a keepsake. I used to keep my marbles in it, as a child. I still have all my marbles, so I really need the bag.

# TRIP TRAP
## *A JOHN REBUS STORY*

★

## IAN RANKIN

---

BLAME IT ON PATIENCE.

Patience, coincidence, or fate. Whatever, Grace Gallagher came downstairs that morning and found herself sitting at the dining table with a cup of strong brown tea (there was just milk enough in the fridge for one other cup), staring at the pack of cards. She sucked cigarette smoke into her lungs, feeling her heart beat the faster for it. This cigarette she enjoyed. George did not allow her to smoke in his presence, and in his presence she was for the best part of each and every day. The smoke upset him, he said. It tasted his mouth, so that food took on a funny flavour. It irritated his nostrils, made him sneeze and cough. Made him giddy. George had written the book on hypochondria.

So the house became a no-smoking zone when George was up and about. Which was precisely why Grace relished this small moment by herself, a moment lasting from seven-fifteen until seven forty-five. For the forty years of their married life, Grace had always managed to wake up thirty clear minutes before her husband. She would sit at the table with a cigarette and tea until his feet forced a creak from the bedroom floorboard on his side of the bed. That floorboard had creaked from the day they'd moved into 26 Gillan Drive, thirty-odd years ago. George had promised to fix it; now he wasn't even fit to fix himself tea and toast.

Grace finished the cigarette and stared at the pack of cards. They'd played whist and rummy the previous eve-

ning, playing for stakes of a penny a game. And she'd lost
as usual. George hated losing, defeat bringing on a sulk
which could last the whole of the following day, so to make
her life a little easier Grace now allowed him to win, purposely throwing away useful cards, frittering her trumps.
George would sometimes notice and mock her for her stupidity. But more often he just clapped his hands together
after another win, his puffy fingers stroking the winnings
from the table top.

Grace now found herself opening the pack, shuffling, and
laying out the cards for a hand of patience, a hand which she
won without effort. She shuffled again, played again, won
again. This, it seemed, was her morning. She tried a third
game, and again the cards fell right, until four neat piles
stared back at her, black on red on black on red, all the way
from king to ace. She was halfway through a fourth hand,
and confident of success, when the floorboard creaked, her
name was called, and the day—her real day—began. She
made tea (that was the end of the milk) and toast, and took
it to George in bed. He'd been to the bathroom, and slipped
slowly back between the sheets.

'Leg's giving me gyp today,' he said. Grace was silent,
having no new replies to add to this statement. She placed
his tray on the bed and pulled open the curtains. The room
was stuffy, but even in summer he didn't like the windows
open. He blamed the pollution, the acid rain, the exhaust
fumes. They played merry hell with his lungs, making him
wheezy, breathless. Grace peered out on to the street. Across
the road, houses just like hers seemed already to be wilting
from the day's ordinariness. Yet inside her, despite everything, despite the sour smell of the room, the heavy breath
of her unshaven husband, the slurping of tea, the grey heat
of the morning, Grace could feel something extraordinary.
Hadn't she won at patience? Won time and time again?
Paths seemed to be opening up in front of her.

'I'll go fetch you your paper,' she said.

GEORGE GALLAGHER liked to study racing form. He would pore over the newspaper, sneering at the tipsters' choices, and would come up with a 'yankee'—five horses which, should they all romp home as winners, would make them their fortune. Grace would take his betting slip to the bookie's on the High Street, would hand across the stake money—less than £1.50 per day—and would go home to listen on the radio as horse after horse failed in its mission, the tipsters' choices meantime bringing in a fair return. But George had what he called 'inside knowledge', and besides, the tipsters were all crooked, weren't they? You couldn't trust them. Grace was a bloody fool if she thought she could. Often a choice of George's would come in second or third, but despite her efforts he refused to back any horse each way. All or nothing, that's what he wanted.

'You never win big by betting each way.'

Grace's smile was like a nail file: *we never win at all*.

George wondered sometimes why it took his wife so long to fetch the paper. After all, the shop was ten minutes' walk away at most, yet Grace would usually be out of the house for the best part of an hour. But there was always the story of a neighbour met, gossip exchanged, a queue in the shop, or the paper not having arrived, entailing a longer walk to the newsagent's further down the road . . .

In fact, Grace took the newspaper to Lossie Park, where, weather permitting, she sat on one of the benches and, taking a ballpoint pen (free with a woman's magazine, refilled twice since) from her handbag, proceeded to attempt the newspaper's crossword. At first, she'd filled in the 'quick' clues, but had grown more confident with the years so that she now did the 'cryptic', often finishing it, sometimes failing for want of one or two answers, which she would ponder over the rest of the day. George, his eyes fixed on the sports pages, never noticed that she'd been busy at the crossword. He got his news, so he said, from the TV and the radio, though in fact Grace had noticed that he normally slept through the television news, and seldom listened to the radio.

If the weather was dreich, Grace would sit on a sheltered bench, where one day a year or so back she had been joined by a gentleman of similar years (which was to say, eight or nine years younger than George). He was a local, a widower, and his name was Jim Malcolm. They talked, but spent most of the time just watching the park itself, studying mothers with prams, boys with their dogs, games of football, lovers' tiffs, and, even at that early hour, the occasional drunk. Every day they met at one bench or another, seeming to happen upon one another by accident, never seeing one another at any other time of the day, or any other location, other than those truly accidental meetings in a shop or on the pavement.

And then, a few weeks back, springtime, standing in the butcher's shop Grace had overheard the news of Jim Malcolm's death. When her turn came to be served, Grace asked for half a pound of steak mince, stead of the usual 'economy' stuff. The butcher raised an eyebrow.

'Something to celebrate, Mrs Gallagher?'

'Not really,' Grace had said quietly. That night, George had eaten the expensive mince without comment.

TODAY SHE COMPLETED the crossword in record time. It wasn't that the clues seemed easier than usual; it was more that her brain seemed to be working faster than ever before, catching that inference or this anagram. Anything, she decided, was possible on a day like this. Simply anything. The sun was appearing from behind a bank of cloud. She closed the newspaper, folded it into her bag alongside the pen, and stood up. She'd been in the park barely ten minutes. If she returned home so quickly, George might ask questions. So instead she walked a slow circuit of the playing fields, her thoughts on patience, and crosswords and creaking floorboards, and much more besides.

BLAME IT ON PATIENCE.

Detective Inspector John Rebus had known Dr Patience Aitken for several years, and not once during their working relationship had he been able to refuse her a favour. Patience seemed to Rebus the kind of woman his parents, if still alive, would have been trying to marry him off to, were he still single. Which, in a sense, he was, being divorced. On finding he *was* divorced, Patience had invited Rebus round to her surprisingly large house for what she had called 'dinner'. Halfway through a home-baked fruit pie, Patience had admitted to Rebus that she was wearing no underwear. Homely but smouldering: that was Patience. Who could deny such a woman a favour? Not John Rebus. And so it was that he found himself this evening standing on the doorstep of 26 Gillan Drive, and about to intrude on private grief.

Not that there was anything very private about a death, not in this part of Scotland, or in any part of Scotland come to that. Curtains twitched at neighbouring windows, people spoke in lowered voices across the divide of a garden fence, and fewer televisions than usual blared out the ubiquitous advertising jingles and even more ubiquitous game show applause.

Gillan Drive was part of an anonymous working-class district on the south-eastern outskirts of Edinburgh. The district had fallen on hard times, but there was still the smell of pride in the air. Gardens were kept tidy, the tiny lawns clipped like army haircuts, and the cars parked tight against the kerbs were old—W and X registrations predominated—but polished, showing no signs of rust. Rebus took it all in in a moment. In a neighbourhood like this, grief was for sharing. Everybody wanted their cut. Still something stopped him lifting the door knocker and letting it fall. Patience Aitken had been vague, wary, ambivalent: that was why she was asking him for a favour, and not for his professional help.

'I mean,' she had said over the telephone, 'I've been treating George Gallagher on and off—more *on* than off—for years. I think about the only complaints I've ever not known him to think he had are beri-beri and elephantiasis, and then only because you never read about them in the "Doc's Page" of the *Sunday Post*.'

Rebus smiled. GPs throughout Scotland feared their Monday morning surgeries, when people would suddenly appear in droves suffering from complaints read about the previous morning in the *Post*. No wonder people called the paper an 'institution'...

'And all the while,' Patience Aitken was saying, 'Grace has been by his bedside. Always patient with him, always looking after him. The woman's been an angel.'

'So what's the problem?' Rebus nursed not only the telephone, but a headache and a mug of black coffee as well. (Black coffee because he was dieting; a headache for not unconnected reasons.)

'The problem is that George fell downstairs this morning. He's dead.'

'I'm sorry to hear it.'

There was a silence at the other end of the line.

'I take it,' Rebus said, 'that you don't share my feelings.'

'George Gallagher was a cantankerous old man, grown from a bitter young man and most probably a fairly unsociable teenager. I don't think I ever heard him utter a civil word, never mind a "please" or a "thank you".'

'Fine,' said Rebus, 'so let's celebrate his demise.'

Silence again.

Rebus sighed and rubbed his temples. 'Out with it,' he ordered.

'He's supposed to have fallen downstairs,' Patience Aitken explained. 'He did go downstairs in the afternoon, sometimes to watch racing on the telly, sometimes just to stare at a different set of walls from the bedroom. But he fell at around eleven o'clock, which is a bit early for him...'

'And you think he was pushed?' Rebus tried not to sound cynical.

Her reply was blunt. 'Yes, I do.'

'By this angel who's managed to put up with him all these years?'

'That's right.'

'OK, Doc, so point me to the medical evidence.'

'Well, it's a narrow staircase, pretty steep, about eleven or twelve steps I'd say. If you weighed around thirteen stone, and happened to slip at the top, you'd sort of be bounced off the sides as you fell, wouldn't you?'

'Perhaps.'

'And you'd try to grab hold of something to stop your fall. There's a banister on one wall. They were waiting for the council to come and fit an extra banister on the other wall.'

'So you'd reach out to grab something, fair enough.' Rebus drained the sour black coffee and studied the pile of work in his in-tray.

'Well, you'd have bruising, wouldn't you?' said Patience Aitken. 'Grazes on your elbows or knees, there'd be marks where you'd clawed at the walls.'

Rebus knew that she was surmising, but could not disagree thus far. 'Go on,' he said.

'George Gallagher only has significant marks on his head, where he hit the floor at the bottom of the stairs, breaking his neck in the process. No real bruising or grazing to the body, no marks on the walls as far as I can see.'

'So you're saying he flew from the top landing with a fair bit of momentum, and the first thing he touched was the ground?'

'That's how it looks. Unless I'm imagining it.'

'So he either jumped, or he was pushed?'

'Yes.' She paused again. 'I know it sounds tenuous, John. And Christ knows I don't want to accuse Grace of anything...'

Rebus picked up a ballpoint pen from beside the tele
phone and scrabbled on the surface of his desk until he
found the back of an envelope upon which to write.

'You're only doing your job, Patience,' he said. 'Give me
the address and I'll go pay my respects.'

THE DOOR of 26 Gillan Road opened slowly, and a man
peered out at Rebus, then ushered him quickly inside, lay
ing a soft hand on his arm.

'In ye come, son. In ye come. The women are in the liv
ing-room. The kitchen's through here.' He nodded with his
head, then led Rebus through a narrow hallway past a closed
door, from behind which came tearful sounds, towards a
half-open door at the back of the house. Rebus had not even
glanced at the stairs as they'd passed them, the stairs which
had faced him at the open front door of the house. The
kitchen door was now opened from within, and Rebus saw
that seven or eight men had squeezed into the tiny back
room. There were stale smells of cooking fat and soup, stew
and fruit cake, but above them wafted a more recent smell:
whisky.

'Here ye are, son.' Someone was handing him a tumbler
with a good inch of amber liquid in it. Everyone else had
just such a glass nestling in their hand. They all shuffled
from one foot to another, awkward, hardly daring to speak.
They had nodded at Rebus's entrance, but now gave him
little heed. Glasses were replenished. Rebus noticed the Co-
Op price label on the bottle.

'You've just moved into Cashman Street, haven't you?'
someone was asking someone else.

'Aye, that's right. A couple of months ago. The wife used
to meet Mrs Gallagher at the shops, so we thought we'd
drop in.'

'See this estate, son, it was miners' rows once upon a time.
It used to be that you lived here and died here. But these
days there's that much coming and going . . .'

The conversation continued at the level of a murmur. Rebus was standing with his back to the sink's draining board, next to the back door. A figure appeared in front of him.

'Have another drop, son.' And the inch in his glass rose to an inch and a half. Rebus looked around him in vain, seeking out a relative of the deceased. But these men all looked like neighbours, like the sons of neighbours, the male half of the community's heart. Their wives, sisters, mothers would be in the living-room with Grace Gallagher. Closed curtains blocking out any light from what was left of the day; handkerchiefs and sweet sherry. The bereaved in an armchair, with someone else perched on an arm of the chair, offering a pat of the hand and well-meant words. Rebus had seen it all, seen it as a child with his own mother, and as a young man with his father, seen it with aunts and uncles, with the parents of friends and more recently with friends themselves. He wasn't so young now. The odd contemporary was already falling victim to the Big C or an unexpected heart attack. Today was the last day of April. Two days ago, he'd gone to Fife and laid flowers on his father's grave. Whether it was an act of remembrance or of simple contrition he couldn't have said...

His guide pulled him back to the present. 'Her daughter-in-law's already here. Come over from Falkirk this afternoon.'

Rebus nodded, trying to look wise. 'And the son?'

Eyes looked at him. 'Dead these past ten years. Don't you know that?'

There was suspicion now, and Rebus knew that he had either to reveal himself as a policeman, or else become more disingenuous still. These people, authentically mourning the loss of someone they had known, had taken him as a mourner too, had brought him in here to share with them, to be part of the remembering group.

'I'm just a friend of a friend,' he explained. 'They asked me to look in.'

It looked from his guide's face, however, as though an interrogation might be about to begin. But then somebody else spoke.

'Terrible crash it was. What was the name of the town again?'

'Methil. He'd been working on building a rig there.'

'That's right,' said the guide knowledgeably. 'Pay night it was. They'd been out for a few drinks, like. On their way to the dancing. Next thing...'

'Aye, terrible smash it was. The lad in the back seat had to have both legs taken off.'

Well, thought Rebus, I bet he didn't go to any more hops. Then he winced, trying to forgive himself for thinking such a thing. His guide saw the wince and laid the hand back on his arm.

'All right, son, all right.' And they were all looking at him again, perhaps expecting tears. Rebus was growing red in the face.

'I'll just...' he said, motioning towards the ceiling with his head.

'You know where it is?'

Rebus nodded. He'd seen all there was to see downstairs, and so knew the bathroom must lie upstairs, and upstairs was where he was heading. He closed the kitchen door behind him and breathed deeply. There was sweat beneath his shirt, and the headache was reasserting itself. That'll teach you, Rebus, it was saying. That'll teach you for taking a sip of whisky. That'll teach you for making cheap jokes to yourself. Take all the aspirin you like. They'll dissolve your stomach lining before they dissolve me.

Rebus called his headache two seven-letter words before beginning to climb the stairs.

He gave careful scrutiny to each stair as he climbed, and to the walls either side of each stair. The carpet itself was fairly new, with a thickish pile. The wallpaper was old, and showed a hunting scene, horse-riders and dogs with a fox panting and worried in the distance. As Patience Aitken had

said, there were no scrapes or claw-marks on the paper itself. What's more, there were no loose edges of carpet. The
whole thing had been tacked down with a professional's
skill. Nothing for George Gallagher to trip over, no threads
or untacked sections; and no smooth threadbare patches for
him to slip on.

He gave special attention to where the upstairs landing
met the stairs. George Gallagher probably fell from here,
from this height. Further down the stairs, his chances of
survival would have been much greater. Yes, it was a steep
and narrow staircase all right. A trip and a tumble would
certainly have caused bruising. Immediate death at the foot
of the stairs would doubtless have arrested much of the
bruising, the blood stilling in the veins and arteries, but
bruising there would have been. The postmortem would be
specific; so far Rebus was trading on speculation, and well
he knew it.

Four doors led off the landing: a large cupboard (what
Rebus as a child would have called a 'press'), filled with
sheets, blankets, two ancient suitcases, a black-and-white
television lying on its side; a musty spare bedroom, its single bed made up ready for the visitor who never came; the
bathroom, with a battery-operated razor lying on the cis-
tern, never to be used again by its owner; and the bedroom.
Nothing interested Rebus in either the spare bedroom or the
bathroom, so he slipped into the main bedroom closing the
door behind him, then opening it again, since to be discovered behind a closed door would be so much more suspicious than to be found inside an open one.

The sheets, blanket and quilt had been pulled back from
the bed, and three pillows had been placed on their ends
against the headboard, so that one person could sit up in
bed. He'd seen a breakfast tray in the kitchen, still boasting
the remnants of a morning meal: cups, toast crumbs on a
greasy plate, an old coffee jar now holding the remains of
some home-made jam. Beside the bed stood a walking-
frame. Patience Aitken had said that George Gallagher

usually wouldn't walk half a dozen steps without his walking-frame (a Zimmer she'd called it, but to Rebus Zimmer
was the German for 'room'...). Of course, if Grace were
helping him, he could walk without it, leaning on her the
way he'd lean his weight on a stick. Rebus visualised Grace
Gallagher coaxing her husband from his bed, telling him he
wouldn't be needing his walking-frame, she'd help him
down the stairs. He could lean on her...

On the bed rested a newspaper, dotted with tacky spots of
jam. It was today's paper, and it was open at the racing
pages. A blue pen had been used to ring some of the runners—Gypsy Pearl, Gazumpin, Lot's Wife, Castle Mallet,
Blondie—five in total, enough for a yankee. The blue pen
was sitting on a bedside table, beside a glass half filled with
water, some tablets (the label made out to Mr G. Gallagher), a pair of reading spectacles in their case, and a paperback cowboy novel—large print—borrowed from the
local library. Rebus sat on the edge of the bed and flipped
through the newspaper. His eyes came to rest on a particular page, the letters and cartoons page. At bottom right was
a crossword, a completed crossword at that. The pen used
to fill in the squares seemed different to that used for the
racing form further on in the paper, and the hand seemed
different too: more delicate, more feminine. Thin faint
marks rather than the robust lines used to circle the day's
favoured horses. Rebus enjoyed the occasional crossword,
and, impressed to find this one completed, was more impressed to find that the answers were those to the cryptic
clues rather than the quick clues most people favoured. He
began to read, until at some point in his reading his brow
furrowed, and he blinked a couple of times before closing
the paper, folding it twice, and rolling it into his jacket
pocket. A second or two's reflection later, he rose from the
bed and walked slowly to the bedroom door, out on to the
landing where, taking careful hold of the banister, he started
downstairs.

HE STOOD IN THE KITCHEN with his whisky, pondering the situation. Faces came and went. A man would finish his drink with a sigh or a clearing of the throat.

'Ay well,' he'd say, 'I suppose I'd better...' And with these words, and a bow of the head, he would move out of the kitchen, timidly opening the living-room door so as to say a few words to the widow before leaving. Rebus heard Grace Gallagher's voice, a high, wavering howl: 'Thanks for coming. It was good of you. Cheerio.'

The women came and went, too. Sandwiches appeared from somewhere and were shared out in the kitchen. Tongue, corned beef, salmon paste. White 'half-pan' bread sliced in halves. Despite his diet, Rebus ate his fill, saying nothing. Though he only half knew it, he was biding his time, not wishing to create a disturbance. He waited as the kitchen emptied. Once or twice someone had attempted to engage him in conversation, thinking they knew him from a neighbouring street or from the public bar of the local. Rebus just shook his head, the friend of a friend, and the enquiries usually ended there.

Even his guide left, again patting Rebus's arm and giving him a nod and a wink. It was a day for universal gestures, so Rebus winked back. Then, the kitchen vacant now, muggy with the smell of cheap cigarettes, whisky and body odour, Rebus rinsed out his glass and stood it end-up on the draining board. He walked into the hallway, paused, then knocked and pushed open the living-room door.

As he had suspected, Grace Gallagher, as frail-looking as he'd thought, dabbing behind her fifties-style spectacles, was seated in an armchair. On the arm of the chair sat a woman in her forties, heavy-bodied but not without presence. The other chairs were vacant. Teacups sat on a dining table, alongside an unfinished plate of sandwiches, empty sherry glasses, the bottle itself, and, curiously, a pack of playing cards, laid out as though someone had broken off halfway through a game of patience.

Opposite the television set sat another sunken armchair, looking as if it had not been sat in this whole afternoon. Rebus could guess why: the deceased's chair, the throne to his tiny kingdom. He smiled towards the two women. Grace Gallagher only half looked towards him.

'Thanks for dropping by,' she said, her voice slightly revived from earlier. 'It was good of you. Cheerio.'

'Actually, Mrs Gallagher,' said Rebus, stepping into the room, 'I'm a police officer, Detective Inspector Rebus. Doctor Aitken asked me to look in.'

'Oh.' Grace Gallagher looked at him now. Pretty eyes sinking into crinkly white skin. A dab of natural colour on each cheek. Her silvery hair hadn't seen a perm in quite a while, but someone had combed it, perhaps to enable her to face the rigours of the afternoon. The daughter-in-law—or so Rebus supposed the woman on the arm of the chair to be—was rising.

'Would you like me to...?'

Rebus nodded towards her. 'I don't think this'll take long. Just routine really, when there's been an accident.' He looked at Grace, then at the daughter-in-law. 'Maybe if you could go into the kitchen for five minutes or so?'

She nodded keenly, perhaps a little too keenly. Rebus hadn't seen her all evening, and so supposed she'd felt duty bound to stay cooped up in here with her mother-in-law. She seemed to relish the prospect of movement.

'I'll pop the kettle on,' she said, brushing past Rebus. He watched the door close, waited as she padded down the short hallway, listened until he heard water running, the sounds of dishes being tidied. Then he turned back to Grace Gallagher, took a deep breath, and walked over towards her, dragging a stiff-backed dining chair with him. This he sat on, only a foot or two from her. He could feel her growing uneasy. She writhed a little in the armchair, then tried to disguise the reaction by reaching for another paper hankie from a box on the floor beside her.

'This must be a very difficult time for you, Mrs Gallagher,' Rebus began. He wanted to keep things short and clear cut. He had no evidence, had nothing to play with but a little bit of psychology and the woman's own state of mind. It might not be enough; he wasn't sure whether or not he *wanted* it to be enough. He found himself shifting on the chair. His arm touched the newspaper in his pocket. It felt like a talisman.

'Dr Aitken told me,' he continued, 'that you'd looked after your husband for quite a few years. It can't have been easy.'

'I'd be lying if I said that it was.'

Rebus tried to find the requisite amount of iron in her words. Tried but failed.

'Yes,' he said, 'I believe your husband was, well, a bit *difficult* at times.'

'I won't deny that either. He could be a real bugger when he wanted to.' She smiled, as if in memory of the fact. 'But I'll miss him. Aye, I'll miss him.'

'I'm sure you will, Mrs Gallagher.'

He looked at her, and her eyes fixed on to his, challenging him. He cleared his throat again. 'There's something I'm not absolutely sure about, concerning the accident. I wonder if maybe you can help me?'

'I can try.'

Rebus smiled his appreciation. 'It's just this,' he said. 'Eleven o'clock was a bit early for your husband to be coming downstairs. What's more, he seemed to be trying to come down without his walking-frame, which is still beside the bed.' Rebus's voice was becoming firmer, his conviction growing. 'What's more, he seems to have fallen with a fair amount of force.'

She interrupted him with a snap. 'How do you mean?'

'I mean he fell straight down the stairs. He didn't just slip and fall, or stumble and roll down them. He went flying off the top step and didn't hit anything till he hit the ground.' Her eyes were filling again. Hating himself, Rebus pressed on. 'He didn't fall, Mrs Gallagher. He was helped to the top of the stairs, and then he was helped down them with a push in the back, a pretty vigorous push at that.' His voice grew less severe, less judgmental. 'I'm not saying you meant to kill him. Maybe you just wanted him hospitalised, so you could have a rest from looking after him. Was that it?'

She was blowing her nose, her small shoulders squeezed inwards towards a brittle neck. The shoulders twitched with sobs. 'I don't know what you're talking about. You think I... How could you? Why would you say anything like that? No, I don't believe you. Get out of my house.' But there was no power to any of her words, no real enthusiasm for the fight. Rebus reached into his pocket and brought out the newspaper.

'I notice you do crosswords, Mrs Gallagher.'

She glanced up at him, startled by this twist in the conversation. 'What?'

He motioned with the paper. 'I like crosswords myself. That's why I was interested when I saw you'd completed today's puzzle. Very impressive. When did you do that?'

'This morning,' she said through another handkerchief. 'In the park. I always do the crossword after I've bought the paper. Then I bring it home so George can look at his horses.'

Rebus nodded, and studied the crossword again. 'You must have been preoccupied with something this morning then,' he said.

'What do you mean?'

'It's quite an easy one, really. I mean, easy for someone who does crosswords like this and finishes them. Where is it now?' Rebus seemed to be searching the grid. 'Yes,' he said. 'Nineteen across. You've got the down solutions, so that means the answer to nineteen across must be something R something P. Now, what's the clue?' He looked for it, found it. 'Here it is, Mrs Gallagher. "Perhaps deadly in part." Four letters. Something R something P. Something deadly. Or deadly in part. And you've put TRIP. What were you thinking about, I wonder? I mean, when you wrote that? I wonder what your mind was on?'

'But it's the right answer,' said Grace Gallagher, her face creasing in puzzlement. Rebus was shaking his head.

'No,' he said. 'I don't think so. I think the "in part" means the letters of "part" make up the word you want. The answer's TRAP, Mrs Gallagher. "Perhaps deadly in part": TRAP. Do you see? But you were thinking of something else when you filled in the answer. You were thinking about how if your husband tripped down the stairs you might be rid of him. Isn't that right, Grace?'

She was silent for a moment, the silence broken only by the ticking of the mantelpiece clock and the clank of dishes being washed in the kitchen. Then she spoke, quite calmly.

'Myra's a good lass. It was terrible when Billy died. She's been like a daughter to me ever since.' Another pause, then her eyes met Rebus's again. He was thinking of his own mother, of how old she'd be today had she lived. Much the same age as this woman in front of him. He took another deep breath, but stayed silent, waiting.

'You know, son,' she said, 'if you look after an invalid, people think you're a martyr. I was a martyr all right, but only because I put up with him for forty years.' Her eyes strayed to the empty armchair, and focused on it as though her husband were sitting there and hearing the truth for the very first time. 'He was a sweet talker back then, and he had all the right moves. None of that once Billy came along. None of that ever again.' Her voice, which had been growing softer, now began hardening again. 'They shut the pit, so he got work at the bottle factory. Then they shut that, and all he could get was part-time chalking up the winners at the bookie's. A man gets gey bitter, Inspector. But he didn't have to take it out on me, did he?' She moved her eyes from the chair to Rebus. 'Will they lock me up?' She didn't sound particularly interested in his answer.

'That's not for me to say, Grace. Juries decide that sort of thing.'

She smiled. 'I thought I'd done the crossword in record time. Trust me to get one wrong.' And she shook her head slowly, the smile falling from her face as the tears came again, and her mouth opened in a near-silent bawl.

The door swung open, the daughter-in-law entering with a tray full of crockery.

'There now,' she called. 'We can all have a nice cup of—' She saw the look on Grace Gallagher's face, and she froze.

'What have you done?' she cried accusingly. Rebus stood up.

'Mrs Gallagher,' he said to her, 'I'm afraid I've got a bit of bad news...'

SHE HAD KNOWN of course. The daughter-in-law had known. Not that Grace had said anything, but there had been a special bond between them. Myra's parting words to Rebus's retreating back had been a vicious 'That bugger deserved all he got!' Net curtains had twitched; faces had appeared at darkened windows. Her words had echoed along the street and up into the smoking night air.

Maybe she was right at that. Rebus couldn't judge. All he could be was fair. So why was it that he felt so guilty? So ashamed? He could have shrugged it off, could have reported back to Patience that there was no substance to her fears. Grace Gallagher had suffered; would continue to suffer. Wasn't that enough? OK, so the law demanded more, but without Rebus there was no case, was there?

He felt right, felt vindicated, and at the same time felt a complete and utter bastard. More than that, he felt as though he'd just sentenced his own mother. He stopped at a late-night store and stocked up on beer and cigarettes. As an afterthought, he bought six assorted packets of crisps and a couple bars of chocolate. This was no time to diet. Back home, he could conduct his own post-mortem, could hold his own private wake. On his way out of the shop, he bought the final edition of the evening paper, and was reminded that this was 30 April. Tomorrow morning, before dawn, crowds of people would climb up Arthur's Seat and, at the hill's summit, would celebrate the rising of the sun and the coming of May. Some would dab their faces with dew, the old story being that it would make them more beautiful, more handsome. What exactly was it they were celebrating, all the hungover students and the druids and the curious? Rebus wasn't sure any more. Perhaps he had never known in the first place.

Later that night, much later, as he lay along his sofa, the hi-fi blaring some jazz music from the sixties, his eye caught the day's racing results on the paper's back page. Gypsy Pearl had come home first at three-to-one. In the very next race, Gazumpin had won at seven-to-two on. Two races further on, Lot's Wife had triumphed at a starting price of eight-to-one. At another meeting, Castle Mallet had won the two-thirty. Two-to-one joint favourite. That left only Blondie. Rebus tried to focus his eyes, and finally found the horse, its name misprinted to read 'Bloodie'. Though three-to-one favourite, it had come home third in a field of thirteen.

Rebus stared at the misspelling, wondering what had been going through the typist's mind when he or she had made that one small but no doubt meaningful slip...

# FREUD AT THIRTY PACES

★

## SARA PARETSKY

---

DR ULRICH VON HUTTEN saw patients in the back drawing-room of his Fifth Avenue house. Minor reconstruction of the ground floor had created a private hallway through which patients bypassed the front drawing-room and the stairway to the upper floors. In the back, a door led from the consulting room to a sidewalk connecting the house to 74th Street. A hedge separated this walk from the minuscule garden where Mrs von Hutten raised begonias and herbs.

This engineering separated the Von Hutten family from his patients. Indeed, some were never sure if the doctor was married. Others suspected the presence of a child (children?) from the faint sounds of piano practice seeping into the private hallway, or the rising smell of *sauce madère* on afternoons when the doctor was entertaining for dinner.

If they were punctual, patients never met one another, either—they left through a different door than the one they entered by. Von Hutten saw no need for a waiting room. He provided a small armchair outside the consulting room where the over-anxious could sit, waiting for the soft yellow light that showed the doctor was ready.

The meter began running precisely at the start of one analytical session and stopped exactly forty-five minutes later. Dr. von Hutten pressed a floor button which simultaneously unlocked the entrance, turned on the yellow light, and started the meter. The unpunctual patient, racing from a hairdresser at 60th and Madison, or a meeting in Wall Street, would find the doctor sitting expressionlessly in a leather armchair behind the shabby couch inherited from the great Dr L— in Berlin.

The flustered patient dropped parcels, coat, briefcase on a side table and scrambled on to the couch. Dr von Hutten remained ostentatiously silent. The only noise was the faint humming of the meter against the far wall. After forty-five minutes, the meter shut off, the street door automatically unlocked, and Dr von Hutten uttered his first words of the session: 'Our time is up. I will see you tomorrow at two.' Or Friday at nine-thirty, or whenever.

Dr von Hutten belonged to that strict class of analysts who believe they must say as little as possible to the patient. The patient should know nothing about the doctor— all transference should operate in one direction only. The doctor felt strongly about this. In addition to articles for the professional journals, he had written several impassioned columns for the *New York Times*, deploring the tendency of modern analysis to talk, to tell their patients of their love for Mozart, their hatred of begonias.

Dr von Hutten would not attack a fellow analyst in the popular press. Still, most of the New York psychoanalytic world knew that his remarks were not general. The specific object of his rage had an office across Central Park from him.

At 62nd and Central Park West, Dr Jacob Pfefferkorn saw patients in an untidy room whose curtained windows overlooked the park. A small room across the hall had been turned into a waiting area, where novels and magazines were jumbled in a stack on a side table.

The Pfefferkorn family correctly never went into the waiting room nor spoke to any patients. Still, the latter would often see Mrs Pfefferkorn sweep by with one or more of her noisy children *en route* to the ballet lessons, riding lessons, music lessons, or private school whose fees were covered by the massive bills generated by the meter ticking away on the analyst's wall.

In addition to these signs of life, the patients learned some things about Dr Pfefferkorn himself. For example, he loved Mozart and hated begonias. Whether this knowledge helped or hindered their therapies, no one could judge—except, perhaps Dr von Hutten. Other analysts wondered whether Pfefferkorn's well-known prejudices had inspired Mrs von Hutten to raise begonias at the Fifth Avenue house.

Besides their disagreement over silence in the consulting room, the doctors had a second rivalry. Both enjoyed doing literary psychoanalysis—analysing the personalities of writers based on their work. Dr Freud set the example. His brilliant deduction that Moses was an Egyptian, rather than a Hebrew, was based chiefly on biblical texts, with little corroborative historical evidence.

His disciples were inspired to undertake similar researches. Some studied figures like Virginia Woolf or Henry James, who left a large body of letters explaining their work. Others preferred to look at writers like Augustine, who left no external evidence other than his writings. With very little historical research, these literary analysts were able to perform astounding analytical *tours de force*, uncovering Oedipal relations, impotence, and other previously unknown traits of the fifth-century saint.

Dr Pfefferkorn had previously analysed Thomas à Kempis, Cardinal Newman and Emily Dickinson. Von Hutten's greatest prior efforts were devoted to the anonymous author of *The Cloud of Unknowing*. The two pointedly ignored each other's researches. Unfortunately, in 1980 both settled on the same writer as the passionate object of their research.

Saint Juliet of Cardiff (?1149—1203) had written numerous mystical works in a crabbed combination of Latin and Welsh. Little enough is known of the saint's life. She was canonised in 1560, in the great rash of pork-barrel canonisations following the Council of Trent, for miracles performed in connection with women haemorrhaging after childbirth.

Juliet's work in modern translation runs to some three volumes of meditations, ecstasies and prayers. From this effusion, the doctors were able to glean much about her life.

Dr Pfefferkorn recognised from her writings that Juliet had been a mistress of Henry II, taking the veil only after Eleanor of Aquitaine intervened in one of her rarely wifely moods. Juliet's mother had died in the saint's infancy. Her doting father, a man of substance, had her educated in a way open to few twelfth-century men and almost no women. He introduced her to court life. Dr Pfefferkorn speculated on an incestuous love between father and daughter, but felt the texts were ambiguous there. Juliet joined the Convent Of St Anne of Cardiff late in life. Her ecstasies were primarily eulogies of her liaison with Henry, disguised in theological language.

To Dr von Hutten, Juliet's work proved incontrovertibly that she had died a virgin. Dedicated to the Convent of Our Lady of the Sacred Heart of Cardiff at birth, she came from an impoverished family which could not provide a dowry. Juliet therefore performed manual labour for the convent, learning writing from cleaning the heavy bible chained to the altar in the convent chapel. Since she spoke no Latin, her own writing combined her native Welsh with what Latin she picked up from her secretive reading. Her ecstatic outpourings came from her sublimated, unrecognised sexuality. The fact that Welsh women believed she could stop post-partem bleeding was a folk testimony to her virginal state.

The bi-monthly *Psychoanalytical Review of Literature* published Dr Pfefferkorn and Dr von Hutten's articles side by side in their winter issue, and battle was fairly joined.

A mutual friend had warned Dr von Hutten that Dr Pfefferkorn had picked St Juliet as the subject of his research, but Dr von Hutten was staggered at the level of Pfefferkorn's stupidity. How could the man not recognise such a clear case of frigidity? How could he frivolously write of liaisons between a king and a commoner of demonstrably menial state?

Von Hutten fumed. With difficulty he listened to fears of impotence, fears of rejection, fears of frigidity from his own patients. He counted the minutes until the meter shut off for the day and he could settle down to attack Dr Pfefferkorn as he deserved. A man who told his patients he hated begonias was capable of anything, but this time he had *gone too far.* His letter to the editor covered the major defects in both Pfefferkorn's research and his medical practice.

Across the park on 62nd Street, Dr Pfefferkorn was equally enraged. Von Hutten's rigid attitudes—stemming doubtless from too early toilet-training and his morbid fears of castration—had led him into an utterly imbecilic account of Juliet's life. No man who had worked through his own neuroses could doubt that this was a woman whose physical life had been superbly fulfilled.

At the end of the workday, Pfefferkorn turned off the meter, told his wife to bring him sauerbraten and potatoes in his study, and settled down to a scathing attack on Von Hutten. His letter encompassed the doctor's inadequate analysis, his inability to separate his own fantasies from what he read, and then a line-by-line textual refutation of Von Hutten's major points.

Both letters appeared in the February issue of the *Psychoanalytical Review of Literature.* If Von Hutten was pleased at the accusations of impotence and projection, he gave no sign of it to his wife, who had also read the criticism.

As for Pfefferkorn, the charge that his analytical methods were as slovenly as his appearance provoked him to widen the circle of argument. He called on Walter Lederhosen, Professor of Middle English History at Columbia, and on Mark Antwerp at New York University.

As it turned out, neither was familiar with St Juliet. Neither could read the medieval Welsh-Latin in which she wrote. They both composed long treatises on twelfth-century England. Antwerp sidestepped the Juliet virginity issue. However, he proved that Henry was in Cardiff several times during what could be thought of as the relevant period. He also had a lot to say on Henry's love life and the stained relations between him and Eleanor.

Lederhosen concentrated on twelfth-century politics, especially Henry II's infrequent appearances in his English possessions, which did not please Pfefferkorn at all—how could he have inflamed the passions of the saint if he wasn't around to meet her? So he discarded the Columbia professor's remarks and produced a small pamphlet which contained the original articles, the rebutting letters, and Professor Antwerp's lengthy essay.

Pfefferkorn concluded the pamphlet with a summary in which he tied Antwerp's arguments back to his own. The whole thing was published in a little booklet entitled *The Mirror of the Eye*, and distributed at the summer meetings of the International Convention of Psychoanalysts. In the introduction, Pfefferkorn explained how in their writings psychoanalysts mirrored the distortions with which their own eyes presented the world to them. He then detailed his own diagnosis of Von Hutten's various psychosexual maladies and how Von Hutten had projected these on to the writing of St Juliet of Cardiff.

Von Hutten was speechless when he saw the pamphlet. He left the meeting a day early and flew back to Manhattan, where he consulted an old colleague now teaching history at

Yale. Like Lederhosen and Antwerp, Rudolph Narr had not read Juliet's works. However, he discoursed most learnedly for forty pages on analytical techniques applied to history, with a major subsection on frigidity and sublimation in the Middle Ages.

The essay delighted Von Hutten. He published it in a booklet called *The Mirror of the Hand,* along with his original essay from the *Psychoanalytical Review of Literature.* In a pithy introduction, he exposed Pfefferkorn's fraudulent analytical methods. Because Pfefferkorn's own internal neurotic problems were unresolved, he was unable to withdraw himself from centre stage in interacting with his patients. His needy ego took over from his patients: he projected his own desires and uncertainties on to what went on in the consulting room. Pfefferkorn's literary researches mirrored his intrusion into the patient's landscape—his hand, so to speak, covered the canvas.

The publication of *The Mirror of the Hand* coincided with the December meetings of the New York Psychoanalytical Association. While Pfefferkorn was furious—and made no secret of it—the other analysts were delighted. What a welcome change from the usual round of 'Undifferentiated Narcissism in Post-Adolescence Transference Neuroses' and other learned talks.

Partisans for both men sprang up among the New York analysts. Pfefferkorn's most vocal supporter was Everard Dirigible. Carlos McGillicutty soon led the Von Hutten group.

Dirigible scored a great coup early in the battle: he found a scholar at the University of Chicago who actually could read St Juliet's work in the original. Bernard Maledict leapt happily into the fray. Unacquainted with both the techniques and the language of psychoanalysis, he nonetheless had a great deal to say about Juliet's sexuality.

Maledict rejected Von Hutten's work: Juliet's writings could not possibly support a charge of frigidity. He was less clear in discussing an affair with Henry II—or any affairs with anyone. Instead, he described sexuality in the Middle Ages, explaining that the reasons for going into conventual life were often economic and had nothing to do with sexuality at all. In addition, virginity was not valued as highly in that era as it is today and while celibacy was expected in convents, no one was too shocked at lapses.

After Maledict's work appeared simultaneously in the *Psychoanalytical Review of Literature* and the *Journal of Medieval History*, Von Hutten and McGillicutty were almost foaming with rage. McGillicutty saw his duty clear: he unearthed a second St Juliet scholar at University College, Oxford. Robert Pferdlieber had devoted his life to translating and analysing *The Veil before the Temple*, Juliet's major opus. He welcomed a chance to present his views to a wider audience. Without commenting precisely on the original Pfefferkorn-Von Hutten debate, he roundly condemned all of Maledict's research. Von Hutten saw to it that his article—with an appropriate commentary—appeared in all the important European psychoanalytic publications, as well as those in America.

By now Pfefferkorn's energies were so consumed with this debate that he refused all new patients: he needed every hour he could grab to fight Von Hutten. He spent long evenings in the Freud archives, seeking evidence from the Master that his analytical techniques were correct.

Mrs Pfefferkorn became concerned: the eldest Pfefferkorn offspring was in his first year of Harvard Medical School; the youngest had embarked on some costly orthodonture; and in between lay three others with expensive needs. What did Pfefferkorn propose—that Ermine give up her horse? that Jodhpur sell his Ferrari? For those were the sacrifices she foresaw if the doctor's practice shrank. The

rivalry with Von Hutten she dismissed with a contemptuous wave of the hand—could he not be adult enough to take
a little criticism in his stride?

Across the park, Von Hutten had better self-control, at
least on the surface. He continued his usual sixty analytical
sessions a week. But his attention in the examining room
began to wander. When you are not speaking yourself, it is
hard to feel engaged in a dialogue: he found himself listening to Mrs J—'s sexual fantasies when he thought he was
hearing about Mr P—'s hatred of his mother.

For years Von Hutten had prided himself on his perfect
control and involvement in the consulting room. He could
only blame Pfefferkorn for his failure to maintain his own
rigid standards. His fury with Pfefferkorn turned into a
hatred which absorbed most of his waking moments and
quite a few of his sleeping ones as well. He was analyst
enough to know that a dream of his father lunging at him
with a baseball bat was a long-forgotten memory stirred to
life by Pfefferkorn's abuse, but the knowledge did not ease
his rage.

By lunch Von Hutten realised that the fantasy of murdering Pfefferkorn which had absorbed all his morning sessions was only a fantasy and would not solve his problem.
But his rage at the other analyst increased: Pfefferkorn had
caused him to contemplate his murder all morning, instead
of the more important needs of patients. Usually a self-
contained man who asked no one for help, Von Hutten
poured his anguish out to his wife.

Mrs von Hutten raised perfectly manicured eyebrows as
she served him a piece of poached salmon and some green
salad. 'I don't think his murder would help matters, Ulrich,' she pronounced majestically. 'You would still feel that
he had defeated you.'

'I know it!' Von Hutten almost screamed, pounding the table with his fist. 'And root out all those damned begonias after lunch. I never want to see another one of them.'

Mrs von Hutten ignored this with the same authority that she had ignored all her husband's greater and lesser pleas over the years. After lunch, however, she turned her own considerable intellect to the Von Hutten-Pfefferkorn debate. She pulled his Pfefferkorn files from the file cabinets in his study. By now, correspondence and articles filled a drawer and a half.

At five o'clock, she called down to the maid on the house phone that she would not be in for dinner: would Birgitta please inform the doctor. She took the remaining files to her dressing-room, locked the door, and continued reading until close to the following dawn.

Mrs von Hutten was one of those rigidly self-controlled people who set mental clocks for themselves and get up accordingly. She lay down for six hours' sleep and rose again at ten. Despite a heavy downpour, she walked across the park to 62nd Street, her pace brisk but not hurried. By noon she was back at the Fifth Avenue house, calmly serving her husband a small slice of chicken breast and some steamed vegetables.

## II

WHEN THE METER shut off for the day, Dr von Hutten dictated a few case notes. He stood frowning at the back window, staring at the drenched begonias with unseeing eyes for long minutes, until a firm knock roused him. Doubtless some patient had forgotten an umbrella, although he saw nothing on the side table. He went slowly to the door.

'You!' he hissed.

Dr Pfefferkorn shook his umbrella out on the mat and shed his bulky trench coat. 'Yes, Von Hutten. My wife persuaded me I ought to see you in person. Get this matter cleared up. We've become the laughing-stock of the New York analytical profession.'

'*You* may be,' Von Hutten said coldly. 'Your ideas are ridiculous and insupportable. I, however, notice no one laughing at me.'

'That, my dear Von Hutten, is because you are so self-centred that you notice nothing anyone else says.' Seeing that his host made no motion to invite him in, Pfefferkorn pushed past him and sat in an armchair facing the analyst's chair. 'So this is where it all takes place. Sterile atmosphere suitable for the sterile, outmoded ideas you profess.'

Von Hutten nearly ground his teeth. 'I have no need to see your consulting room—I am sure it is as sloppy as your thinking. As sloppy as your alleged research into Juliet of Cardiff.'

Pfefferkorn frowned. Mrs Pfefferkorn had persuaded him to make this trek, persuaded him against his better judgement, and now see what came of it: nothing but insults.

'Look, Von Hutten. Everyone knows your ideas on Juliet of Cardiff are as out of date as your so-called analytical methods. But let's agree to disagree. We can't keep escalating this scholarly battle. It takes too much time from my—our—practices.'

Von Hutten almost choked. 'That you dare call yourself an analyst is an insult to the memory of Freud. Agree to disagree! With you! I will not so demean the analytical profession.'

'Demean!' roared Pfefferkorn, springing to his feet. 'You should be decertified by the New York State Medical Society. Decertified? What am I saying! You should be certified as a lunatic and locked up where you can no longer hurt the innocent and vulnerable.'

Von Hutten jumped at him, grabbing his shoulders. 'You will eat those words, you miserable scum.'

Dr Pfefferkorn, equally enraged and seventy-five pounds heavier, wrenched Von Hutten's hands away and shoved him to the floor. 'You're welcome to try to make me do it, *Doctor* von Hutten. When and where you please, with weapons of your choosing. You'll live to regret this moment.'

He picked up his dripping trench coat and strode from the room, slamming the door behind him.

### III

THE MORNING OF THE DUEL was clear and sunny. At five-thirty, Dr von Hutten slid out of the Fifth Avenue house. A note to his wife lay on his study table, explaining everything in case he did not return home. He did not really expect to lose: he had practised all weekend and felt totally confident.

His second, McGillicutty, was waiting for him at the 72nd Street entrance to Central Park, carrying the weapons.

'Feeling fit, Doctor?' McGillicutty asked respectfully.

'Never better. We'll make short work of this charlatan.'

'Good. I've ordered breakfast at the Pierre for seven-thirty: we'll have a little champagne to celebrate.'

When they got to the trees behind the zoo, they found Pfefferkorn and Dirigible already waiting. Pfefferkorn was eating a ham sandwich and drinking from a thermos of coffee, arguing points with his mouth full. Disgusting, Von Hutten thought. It really was time to end the man's career.

The weapons were so heavy that the seconds violated the code of honour by each bringing the opponent's to the site. As soon as Dirigible saw McGillicutty, he excused himself to the wildly gesticulating Pfefferkorn and beckoned the other second to join him a little way away.

'You have brought all twenty-four volumes of the Standard Edition?'

McGillicutty nodded. He was as aware as Dirigible of the solemnity of the moment. They solemnly laid out two sets of the *Complete Works of Sigmund Freud* on the grass in front of them and counted each volume, fanning the pages to see if any were missing. This task completed, they returned again to the principals and called them together.

'Gentlemen—Doctors,' Dirigible cleared his throat nervously. 'The code of honour demands that we try one last time to reconcile you without a mortal blow being struck. Will you consider—for the sake of your wives, your patients, the honour of the entire psychoanalytical profession—will you bury your differences?'

Von Hutten said coldly, 'I came to see that this charlatan, this impostor, is unfrocked as he deserves.'

Pfefferkorn snorted, 'I would as soon touch an embalmed halibut as shake this man's hand. Sooner—the halibut would have more life to it.'

McGillicutty, too, tried a plea, with equally poor results. At last he said, 'Gentlemen: if it must be, let us begin. You understand the rules. Each of you may fire one shot. If the other does not fall, you may fire again.'

Dirigible and McGillicutty stood back to back. Each stepped forwards fifteen paces. Von Hutten and Pfefferkorn came to stand beside their seconds, who then moved to the centre of the field.

Dr Dirigible held up a white handkerchief. As it fluttered to the ground, Dr Pfefferkorn bellowed, 'You have a castration complex, Von Hutten, which interferes with your establishing any meaningful counter-transference!'

Von Hutten flinched but did not fall. 'You suffer from undifferentiated narcissism which leads to regression complexes and inability to distinguish between patients and your external speaking object.'

Without waiting for a nod from the seconds, Pfefferkorn shouted furiously, 'You are impotent both physically and psychologically. Your criticisms stem from your own inadequacies. They would be laughable if they didn't harm so many patients!'

A policeman patrolling the park strolled over, attracted by the shouting. He stood puzzled, not knowing whether to interfere.

'What's going on?' he finally asked the seconds.

'A duel,' McGillicutty said briefly. 'Freud at thirty paces.'

The policeman frowned uncertainly, not sure whether he was being laughed at. 'Who are these guys, anyway?'

'Psychoanalysts,' Dirigible replied, keeping his eyes on the action on the field. 'They're trying to resolve some underlying theoretical differences.'

'Oh, analysts,' the policeman nodded. 'You gotta expect strange behaviour from them.' He nodded again to himself several times to confirm this diagnosis and wandered off towards the reservoir to see if anyone had fallen in during the night.

Meanwhile, on the field of battle, argument was becoming more personal and less analytical. Dirigible and McGillicutty both tried to interrupt.

'Gentlemen, please. You're straying far from Freud.' Each went to reason with his own principal, but neither was willing to listen. Pfefferkorn, in fact, knocked Dirigible to the ground in his fury at being interrupted.

'And your mother! Oedipal fantasies about her? No wonder you're such a cold bastard. Imagine being in bed with that woman—enough to traumatise any child.'

'And you!' screamed Von Hutten. 'You never broke the tie with Mummy. You keep trying to recreate the experience with your patients—be Mummy for me—support me—love me!'

At this taunting, Pfefferkorn picked up *The Interpretation of Dreams* from the stack next to him and charged across the open space to Von Hutten. He flung the volume at his opponent. The book caught Von Hutten underneath the left eye. Blood poured down his face on to his immaculate shirt front. He ignored it. Snatching *The Psychopathology of Everyday Life* from the ground, he smashed it into Pfefferkorn's nose.

Pfefferkorn, too, began to bleed. *Jokes and their Relation to the Unconscious* lay close at hand. It landed on his opponent's left shoulder. Von Hutten was more successful with *Moses and Monotheism*—the book glanced off Pfefferkorn's ear.

In vain McGillicutty and Dirigible tried to separate the men. This failing, they quickly snatched all copies of Freud's works out of the way. The analysts promptly went for each other's throats.

'Blackguard! Impostor!' Von Hutten panted, trying to bite Pfefferkorn's ear.

'Charlatan! Imbecile!' hissed Pfefferkorn, sticking his knee in Von Hutten's stomach.

Pfefferkorn was by far the larger man, but Von Hutten's rage gave him superhuman strength. Neither could get close enough to the other to make a telling blow.

McGillicutty and Dirigible wrung their hands, anguished. How could they stop these giants of the New York Psychoanalytical Association from making fools of themselves? Worse, what if one of them really got in a solid blow and injured the other seriously? What if Pfefferkorn, already overheated and sweating, had a heart attack?

They debated nervously about whether to try to find the policeman again and get him to break up the fight. But what if he arrested the doctors? What harm would that publicity do the analytical world? As they talked agitatedly, Mrs von Hutten swept into the park. She quickly located her husband and walked up to the seconds, her golden hair shining magnificently in the morning sunlight.

'Why have you allowed this farce to continue so long?'

'Mrs von Hutten!' McGillicutty gasped. 'I—this is no sight for you. What are you doing here?'

'My husband left a note for me in his study. When he failed to show up for breakfast I naturally looked for him there and found his message. A duel in Central Park! I can't believe four adult men—so-called adults—could carry on in such a fashion.'

She moved to the heaving contestants. 'Ulrich! Dr Pfefferkorn! Please stop this at once. You are making a ridiculous spectacle.'

Her voice was low-pitched but penetrating. The two analysts pulled apart at once. Dr von Hutten tried to straighten his tie.

'Vera! What are you doing here?'

'More to the point, Ulrich, what are you doing here? What is the purpose of this duel with Dr Pfefferkorn? When Mrs Pfefferkorn and I spoke three weeks ago, it was in the hope that you two would resolve your problems, not that you would carry on like beasts in a side-show.'

'This—this man calls himself an analyst,' Von Hutten hissed through clenched teeth. 'But he makes a mockery of the teachings of Freud. There is no talking to him.'

Dr Pfefferkorn had moved to one side to clean off the blood caked around his nose and mouth. At that, he turned back. 'Your husband is a menace to the population of New York with his undifferentiated castration complex and fears of impotency.'

Mrs von Hutten raised a gloved hand. 'Please do not repeat your arguments: I have read the Juliet of Cardiff file and I am well aware of the names you have been calling each other for the past two years. I should point out—and Mrs Pfefferkorn is in total agreement with me—that you are jeopardising your practices by your obsession with this Juliet of Cardiff. Put her aside. Do no more literary criticism. For neither of you is skilled at it.'

Both men gasped. Dr Pfefferkorn saw his wife walking towards them through the park. He waited for her to come up, then exclaimed, 'Not understand literary criticism! Cordelia—don't tell me you have been discussing this serious intellectual matter with Mrs von Hutten here. Really, you should have better things to do with your time.'

'I do,' Mrs Pfefferkorn said drily. 'It was most annoying to have to spend that time looking at Juliet of Cardiff. But Vera and I have examined both your files on the subject. We have also looked at the saint's writings. And we discovered that neither of you—nor your learned colleagues in Chicago and Oxford—know what you're talking about. Please go back to analysis—about which you both know something, even if it is something different—and leave St Juliet to the experts.'

Von Hutten found his voice first. 'You don't know what you're talking about. My analysis conclusively proves—'

'Yes, dear,' Mrs von Hutten cut him off indulgently. 'You had some preconceptions, and you found answers to those in your analysis of *The Veil Before the Temple*. Dr Pfefferkorn, you did the same thing.'

'Yes, Jacob,' Mrs Pfefferkorn said. 'Vera and I have discovered that St Juliet never existed. The writings which are imputed to her are the composite literature of the Convent of the Blessed Virgin in Cardiff for a period of about a hundred years, beginning in 1203, long after Henry II died.'

The duellists were momentarily silent. Then Dr von Hutten said aloofly, 'Are you certain?'

'Positive,' his wife answered briskly. 'There are significant textual indicators for this, not just stylistic ones. You may have noted that the latter sections of the books are written entirely in Latin, the earlier in Welsh-Latin. The last parts were written in peacetime by women who had the leisure to learn scholarly Latin—the first were composed during the great upheaval surrounding John and the barons. There are numerous other pointers, of course—we can go over them when we get home if you'd like.'

'No, thank you,' Von Hutten responded coldly. 'I don't imagine I'll have the time.'

He and Pfefferkorn glowered at their wives. 'Improperly sublimated penis envy,' Von Hutten muttered.

'Separation from fathers never fully established; no proper internal integration,' Pfefferkorn added sullenly.

They looked at each other. Von Hutten said, 'How truly Freud spoke: women will never understand themselves, for they themselves are the problem.' Ignoring his swollen left eye, bloody shirt and torn jacket, he flicked back his cuff to look at his watch. 'Vera, will you please call my morning patients and reschedule their appointments? I'm going to breakfast at the Pierre. Coming, Pfefferkorn?'

The women watched their husbands stride from the park together, the seconds trailing behind them carrying Freud's works.

Mrs Pfefferkorn relaxed. 'An impressive performance, Vera. But what if—?'

'What if they ask for a point-by-point critique of St Juliet's writings to see how we know they were composed by a group? They won't: they're too embarrassed...speaking of breakfast, I haven't had any. Champagne at the Plaza?'

# POSITIVE VETTING

★

## STEPHEN MURRAY

---

DID HE KILL HER? I think so; and I think it happened like this.

Three years is a long time; a long time to be away from anyone you love, and a long time to be separated from someone to whom you want to be faithful.

And Bill Johnson had been faithful—that was part of his commitment to her. I don't think he was any sort of prude; if anything, the opposite. I had an assistant then, a lad called Ted Brand, seconded from I Corps. *He* reckoned Johnson was differently put together from the majority of men—must have been to have stayed faithful to Joyce all that time. He hadn't the instinct for men and women, hadn't Brand. It's the one thing you need to make a success of this game. Well, you don't need me to tell you that. No: I think Bill Johnson had all the usual quota of drives, and certainly he had all the opportunities for gratifying them that Cairo and Alexandria could offer. But like more than a few others, Bill Johnson chose not to take those opportunities. You see, he had in his mind's eye the image of Joyce, and that image was a dazzling one.

Joyce was worth saving himself for. Indeed, he lived (so far as his inner life was concerned, as opposed to the outward business of soldiering) for that night when he would return to Joyce in the flat in Maida Vale and when, after the meal, and the first shock and joy of seeing each other, they would go to bed, to seal in the full, mature physicality of their love the relief of being together once more.

Perhaps they wouldn't get as far as the bed. Bill Johnson's eye conjured up other endings: the discarded clothing on the sofa, the two locked bodies sleeping naked in front of the hissing gas fire. Or the shared bath, slippery flesh against flesh in wet delight. Or the discarded dishes, the drying-up cloth abandoned on the draining board, and two flickering shadows thrown against the white kitchen wall by the central bulb. He had plenty of time to dwell on these visions, and he did so happily, knowing that they were not fantasies but anticipations. The nocturnal fumblings his mates bragged of, and sometimes even managed, with Cairo tarts and 'colonels' daughters'; the frantic lip against lip of three-day sweethearts; and the trips to see the Pyramids where the girls came back with sand in their 'blackouts'—all these were pale compensations for the poor saps who didn't have a Joyce waiting for them at home.

I'm sure it crossed Bill Johnson's mind that Joyce might not have been totally faithful to him—he was an intelligent chap, and a realistic one, and humane, too. He didn't propose to ask too many questions too quickly when he went home, and he certainly planned to give her plenty of warning of his arrival. But never did he consider that Joyce might have done without him so long that he would be a stranger to her. And never for a moment did he imagine anything like the true reality.

Bill Johnson returned to England in January of 1944, a much leaner man than the one who had walked into Waterloo station with his kitbag on his shoulder three years ago, and darkly tanned. Three years of war had fined him down, toughened him up, brought out into the open all his latent competence, self-possession, maturity. He sensed something of this even as he descended the escalator to the Bakerloo line, seeing the pale, pinched faces, the war-weariness.

Nobody was interested in casting approving looks towards a soldier from foreign parts, who stood out even among the flood of multi-hued uniforms. On the contrary: he noted with a wry turn of the lips that everyone seemed concerned to show him just how uninterested they were. What did he expect—adulation? Didn't he know there was a war on?

I wonder whether perhaps Bill Johnson's thoughts grew more sober as the train wheezed endlessly from station to station. He was too intelligent a man to be completely blasé about the reunion that awaited him, only minutes away now after all those months. He had carefully written as planned to tell Joyce just when he hoped to return; and then wired from Birkenhead before he got on the train. But it was too late now to have doubts, and anyway, he had had faith in Joyce for three years, and he had faith still. It was himself, if anyone, he distrusted. He knew how much he had changed.

IT SEEMED UNBELIEVABLE to be climbing the stairs to No. 68. The real took on the character of a dream, and the cream-painted walls seemed far less substantial than when he had revisited them in night-time reveries under the desert stars.

He saw the note from the bottom of the last flight: a square of white pinned to the door. Despite his resolutions, his heart fell a little at this evidence that Joyce was out, even though he knew of her war work; and a little worm of bitterness asked whether she could not have taken one afternoon off, to meet him after so long.

Inside nothing much had changed; though there was one change which seemed universal, and that was the pall of dinginess which had descended over everything. All the way from Birkenhead, come to that, he had been unconsciously noticing the drab paintwork, the stumps where railings had been cut away, the grimy, leaking steam engines, the woodwork scored by servicemen's knives. The underground had taken him beneath bombed London, but not before the gaping canopy at Paddington, the roughly boarded-off areas, had told of blitz damage not repaired.

I don't know for sure, but I think at first Johnson went round touching things just to sort of establish that he really was at home. At any rate, though we never found any identifiable prints we found smudges everywhere, as if he had just touched pieces of furniture—a chest of drawers, an occasional table, the wireless set—not to open them, or use them, but in a ritual of homecoming—and later gone round carefully wiping everything he had touched. Some of the cupboards and drawers, of course, he did open. Joyce's lingerie drawer was one, and our searcher, who is very good (and a woman) reckoned he had lifted out some of Joyce's things, just to feel them, or hold them against his cheek—they were put back not quite right, she said, though she couldn't tell me what the 'not quite rightness' amounted to.

Joyce came back at seven. It was long dark by then, of course, daylight saving time notwithstanding. She brought with her their meal—what she could remember, and what she could obtain, of Bill's favourite.

I have often wondered what passed through the minds of men and women like Joyce and Bill as they heard the key scrape in the lock after months, or years, apart. The thrill of a dream realised? Fear at meeting a stranger? Guilt? Your guess is as good as mine here; but in Bill's case I think it was probably none of those things, but a calm gratitude that he had survived to enjoy this moment.

I don't know whether he thought her much changed, or not changed at all. Both were true. Joyce Johnson was twenty-five. She had been twenty-two when he left, a handsome, well-set-up young woman, with a sturdy frame carrying a slim but shapely body. She had never been one of these ethereal women with hand-span waists; she had everything a woman ought to have, and plenty of it. Not daintily feminine, but very female, if you see the difference. Strong, long legs. A definite waist, which masked the broadness of her hips. Breasts a man could weigh in his hands—and Bill had been doing so in his dreams for a long, long time.

And a broad, attractive, lively face with no beauty but plenty of character and good humour—that was how Bill remembered it. A face which could be split in a moment by a delightful, vulgar grin; or which could slacken and soften in the moment of love as he gazed down into it.

That was how Bill remembered her, anyway. I don't say she had changed for the worse in three years, but she had lived in London, she had worked ten hours a day fifty weeks in the year, she had organised the funerals of both her parents within six weeks of each other, she had seen the wreckage of her brother's handsome features after his tanker had been torpedoed—and she had done all that, from the sanctum of her flat in Maida Vale, alone, cooking for herself, mending and remending her clothes, coping; and lying awake through the raids, alone. No more than the lot of ten thousand young women in London, Liverpool, Coventry, any big city. But it must be expected to leave its mark.

Bill had been right to accept that she might have had affairs. She had had two: both early on, when his physical absence was keen and the need to be desired urgent. The first was the result of one of those frenetic nights out which people used to have in those days: when someone was home on leave, or passing through town in transit, and a gaggle of acquaintances would find themselves friends for one night. Joyce went along at the urging of one of her colleagues, who thought she needed taking out of herself, and anyway was at a loss how to make up the party. Three gunners were on embarkation leave—headed for the desert, like Bill. This was 1942, and the desert war was sucking in men and equipment in a number of futile pushes which came to an end with Montgomery's steamroller at Alamein.

Colin was older than the rest and seemed steadier. He was a sergeant, and had been a solicitor's clerk in Stafford until a few years before. In the course of the evening they found out quite a lot about each other, in a superficial way. Joyce enjoyed it, and certainly it was preferable to the spectacle of her friend growing increasingly drunk and embarrassingly crude. Women, I've often thought, have reserves of crudeness in them which even the most boorish men are hard pushed to match. When Daphne began putting her hand down her consort's battledress trousers and offering loud remarks about what she encountered there, Joyce's solicitor's clerk glanced at her quizzically and suggested he should walk her home. She gladly gathered her things together and took his arm as they went out into the black-out.

They were a long way from Maida Vale, and anyway Joyce made no moves towards inviting her escort back there, which she regarded as private territory, so they agreed that he would only walk her as far as the underground. But they ended up in the overgrown churchyard of a bombed-out church, and Joyce's solicitor's clerk proved very adept with his hands. Joyce was too startled or too intoxicated to resist when she found herself pressed against a wall with those efficient hands working skilfully away under her skirt. Colin's head was bent and the smell of his Brylcreemed hair was sharp in her nostrils as he concentrated on what he was trying to achieve, and then (her body treacherously assisting him) he had contrived his purpose. For a few moments she was banged rhythmically and painfully against the broken pillar. Then they were just two individuals again, he standing in the semi-darkness before her, buttoning his flies, she standing against the pillar with her knickers round her shins, the first trickle of damp on her thigh, feeling like a tart. Next day it seemed something that had happened to someone else, except for the stiff crust of semen that she found on her stockings.

A week later, embarkation postponed, her solicitor's clerk sought her out in Maida Vale, and they made love on the floor of the flat. That was their last meeting. Two days afterwards he went overseas and Joyce put the episode and the guilt—there wasn't much, it still didn't feel as if it had really happened, but she did regret having made love in the flat—behind her.

A year later, Joyce found herself in an unedifying affair with a civil servant from the Ministry of Supply, who was having the time of his life in a London suddenly full of independent and abandoned—in both senses—women. When she belatedly realised that her destiny was to be numbered among the scalps of a small-time Don Juan, Joyce ditched him. He had been on the point of ditching her, which apparently provided the real orgasm of his conquests, and let himself go in a petty and spiteful tirade. Joyce grinned her big grin, gave him a few home truths in return, and kicked him out.

That was the end of 'easy' London life so far as Joyce Johnson was concerned. Both inclination and pressure of work kept her thereafter to her regular round of flat, tube, work, lunch in the park, work, tube back to Maida Vale, weary evening in the flat, solitary bed. By 1944 sex was the memory of an outgrown amusement, and though she felt vaguely uneasy about admitting the fact to herself she simply didn't miss it. Despite her two adventures she always had regarded sex as a component of love, not a thing in itself, and love was something for which, like many another in those years, she had no energy to spare any more.

Re-enter Bill. I don't know what happened that evening; remember, while I have some evidence, the rest is speculation. But over the years I've built up rather too much experience of what happens in circumstances like those in which Bill and Joyce found themselves. More experience, perhaps, than a man deserves to have.

I think, then, in fact I'm almost sure, that at first everything went right. If Joyce's face was blank for an instant, as she mentally compared the man she saw before her with the pale, unathletic youth she had said goodbye to three years before, I'm sure it was only for an instant. Then she saw the same brown eyes, the same good humour in the corner of the mouth, the same strong chin, and that wide, unpretty, lovable grin of hers which had been growing a little rusty of recent months burst out once more.

Bill would have got up when he heard her footsteps. Now he came forward, a little hesitantly at first, more confidently as that well-remembered grin appeared.

'Hello, Joyce.' He couldn't help smiling in return; he never could help it.

'Hello, Bill. It's been a long time!' What do you say after three years? They kissed, briefly, and then Joyce drew away and indicated the bag she carried over her shoulder. 'I've brought you your favourite.'

'Lovely,' he said, guessing as well as a man could do who had not lived in London for those three war years, how hard she had to look to find liver and bacon, and how much of her month's ration those two mundane items represented.

Joyce swung the bag off her shoulder and on to the table, and began to unwind her scarf and shrug off her coat, in the unconscious sequence of actions she followed every night on her return from the office. Instinctively, she reached for the kettle.

'Here—let me do that. If I'd known when to expect you, I'd have had it brewing.' Bill took the kettle into the scullery, ran the tap, and held the kettle under it. When he returned to set it on the gas Joyce had removed her outer things and was sitting at the table in the better of her two winter outfits, reaching in her bag for a cigarette. He watched her for a moment, under cover of fiddling with the gas ring, drinking in the sweep of her hair behind her ear, the unconvincing red make-up on her pale cheeks, and the heaviness of her breasts which even the thick tweed and severe cut of her jacket could not mask; and thinking, too, sadly, that she fumbled for cigarettes like a woman who smokes a good number of them in a day. She never used to.

Then there was trivial chat over a cup of tea: his journey round the Cape, hers from Baker Street; family news; his best friend who was a colonel now, and his next-best, who had lost his corporal's stripes yet again. Bill tried not to look too hungrily at the woman opposite him; at any rate, she seemed not to notice. He rather hoped that she would initiate something, at least give one of those intimate signals which showed how much she had missed him in *that* way, suggest the supper could wait... But of course, the poor girl was dead on her feet. All those hours in the office, then the weary journey home through dreary January London—and how long had she spent queuing for tonight's meal?

The business of making supper took over then. Bill put his arms round Joyce's waist as she stood over the gas stove, but her leaning back against him was no more than a token acknowledgement of his presence and not the grateful relaxation into love he had hoped for, so instead of reaching past her to turn the gas off, Bill went back to his seat; then restlessly into the bedroom to find the gifts he had brought back in his kitbag. But the jewellery from the souk in Cairo looked tawdry in the artificial light, and the cat made out of shells had got sadly battered.

'That was good,' Bill said appreciatively, wiping the last of the gravy from his plate with a piece of bread, and suppressing the thought of the plentiful helpings of army rations to which he had grown accustomed. Joyce was smoking again, leaning both elbows on the table, watching him through the spiralling smoke. He held out a hand, and she came round and sat on his knee, reaching out for the ashtray to bring it within reach. Bill nuzzled gratefully at her neck, excusing her tension and caressing her gently to soothe it, telling himself it was bound to be hard at first, to-night... but it would get better.

Joyce stubbed out her cigarette, and held Bill's head with both her hands as his own hand slipped buttons from their buttonholes and ferreted its way inside her blouse. There was no way he could reach the catch of her brassière, and after half-heartedly playing his fingers over its stiff cloth he awkwardly pulled it down so that he could at least touch her naked breast with his fingertips; but even then the thing prevented him weighing her breast in his hand, as he had dreamt of doing for so long, and moreover he could feel that it was uncomfortable for her.

Joyce, submitting to Bill's attentions and realising how much love, as well as deprivation, lay behind them, wished she didn't feel so tired, and could make herself relax. And that they didn't remind her so much of the clumsy pressing and kneading of her uncivil servant from the Ministry of Supply. Time would help: after a day or two, or a week, they would be as they had always been. Why couldn't Bill see that, and wait a day or two before pressing at her in this way? She didn't want to seem unhappy to see him.

Conscious of guilt that he had waited so long for her and she was not responding as he deserved, Joyce let her legs fall open when Bill took his hand from her blouse and slipped it under her skirt. She was still holding his head, and knew she should be doing something less passive; she could feel his erection pressing against her; but her mind was flat and empty, and her body was too tired to respond of its own ac-cord. Now Bill had managed—she lifted her weight off him instinctively—to slip her knickers down a few inches.

Suddenly Joyce felt herself back in the grimy, overgrown churchyard, her back pressed painfully against the broken stonework, Colin's Brylcreemed hair in her nostrils; and her face contorted with the disgust of the memory.

Bill was desperately frustrated when Joyce suddenly stood up and pulled her clothing together, but he bit back the hurtful remark he wanted to make. He was a humane man. And one who acknowledged in his actions, as well as his words, that men's and women's emotional needs are not identical. None the less, he couldn't stop a part of his mind telling himself bitterly that it wasn't much of a homecoming. Was *this* what he had kept faithful for, all that time? Better the moonlight couplings beside the Sphinx with giggly secretaries from the British Council.

Later, they both made an effort. Joyce told herself she was being silly; an access of guilt now would only spoil Bill's return, and how could she, who had always so much enjoyed their lovemaking, presume to feel revulsion now? When it came time for bed, she fetched out a lace nightgown from the bottom of the lingerie drawer and spent a while in the bathroom in unwonted titivation.

Bill, too, cleared his mind of unhelpful responses and resolved to start again from the beginning, being as tender and forbearing as Joyce required. After all, he reminded himself, she had always been a voracious and passionate lover; it would come back to her.

So he was delighted to find her in bed in the lace nightgown he remembered from that last holiday together, which smelt of lavender from its long lay-by. Bill undressed in the bedroom, leaving his clothes on the floor. Joyce looked at him, the tanned body with its uncanny whiteness where the shorts had been, the aggressive masculinity of him, swollen with sexual desire, and turned her head away lest he see, even in the dim light, the distaste. Suddenly her solitariness all these nights seemed inexpressibly dear to her. Since Bill's departure three years before, no one had shared this bed. It had been the one sacrosanct place: *her* place, where she had cowered with terror, where she had cried for him, where she had lain and cursed her callous civil servant. It had come to be so dear a refuge that *no one* could be admitted to it. Now that privacy was to be invaded; and then the privacy of her body.

I'm sure Bill started off in accordance with his resolutions; and I'm sure Joyce started off determined to accept him even, as he deserved, knowing that his desire was a tribute to her as well as impersonal male lust, knowing he had purposely husbanded it for this night. What I don't know is at what stage for each of them their resolution was overwhelmed, his by anger and aggression, hers by revulsion and anger. She fought him off in the end, putting her hand under his chin to try and push him away where he lay on top of her, crushing her breasts.

He had never hit her, and he didn't now; but he seized her hair and held her head down while he forced her legs apart and with his other hand made a passage for himself. Remember she was a well-built girl. A man, even one who had spent three years in the desert, could not beat her down without exerting himself. That is, in the end, what Bill did; he exerted his strength, he beat her down, he held her neck in his grasp and he—I suppose you would have to say, raped her. And when he raised himself from her suddenly unresisting body, then it was that he saw she was dead.

HER DEATH was discovered very quickly. Joyce had become such a reliable and vital member of her office that when she neither appeared nor telephoned the next morning her alarmed boss sent his secretary round to Maida Vale to find out what had happened to her. The secretary found the door unlocked, and in the living-room evidence of a visitor. She walked along the passage to the bedroom, and there was Joyce, lying in her lace nightdress in the rumpled bed, a little pink froth at her lips. The bedclothes had been pulled tenderly up to her shoulders, so that she lay as if daydreaming except that her eyes were a little too swollen and a little too bloodshot, and her skin was ice-cold.

WE WERE ON THE SPOT within the hour. It didn't take us long to establish that someone else beside Joyce had been in that bed, but the question was: who? Joyce's boss was throwing his considerable official weight around by that time, but at first it looked like just one of those wartime encounters that go wrong. There were a good many of those.

Nobody seemed to know much about Joyce's boyfriends, but eventually we got wind of the Ministry of Supply Don Juan, and somebody else mentioned the gunner, Colin, from almost three years before.

And then for the first time we heard Bill Johnson's name. Putting the flesh on the bones was a work of detection in itself. Bill Johnson was Joyce's cousin. Did you think they were man and wife? He was younger than her by almost a year—a span that mattered very much when they were in their childhood, but shrank to insignificance when, on the verge of adulthood, they found themselves lovers. But perhaps it did contribute to the fact that Bill always felt that he had a lot to prove and a lot to live up to. And Joyce retained for him something of that enigma which those older than ourselves possess when we are young.

Once I had found about about Bill—and of course I never did find out for sure that they were lovers; it is the beauty of our job that one can follow flights of fancy, *provided* one remembers to substantiate them before putting someone in the dock—the first thing I did was get on to the War Office to find where his regiment was. On its way home from the Middle East, came the reply: due back any day. Nose twitching like any pointer's, I guessed at once that they were already back. I began to home in, and learned that the troopship carrying Johnson's regiment had docked at Birkenhead forty-eight hours before. But they had all, officers and men, been taken on from the quayside by bus and lorry to Preston, to pick up new equipment from the depot and ferry it to their new base outside Blackburn. Had anyone been granted leave, I enquired? No one, the adjutant answered. That was not to say that a few had not found the means to take it, but Bill Johnson was not among them.

I had to make a bit of a nuisance of myself then, of course. I interviewed Bill himself—that was easy. I found him desolated by his cousin's death. How had he heard about it, if the regiment had been on the move all the time since the ship docked? But that was no good. He showed me the newspaper, the Manchester edition of the *Telegraph*, with the paragraph in it about the 'Maida Vale killing'.

You don't make friends by questioning a man's colleagues about his whereabouts on the night of a murder, but I did it anyway. Five men testified to having seen him in the sergeants' mess between midday on the Wednesday and midday on the Thursday, so how could he have been in London Wednesday evening strangling a girl in a Maida Vale flat? I spoke to the subaltern who was Bill's troop commander and he looked me straight in the eye and told me there was not the faintest possibility Bill had slipped away for long enough to reach Liverpool, never mind London.

Were they all lying? Probably. We never brought a case against Bill Johnson. There was nothing definite in the flat to testify to his presence there, and too many witnesses to the fact that he never left his regiment. Ted Brand was for pushing ahead anyway. Once get those lying sergeants into court, he said, and they'd change their tune. And Bill Johnson would crack, if we pushed hard enough.

I told him Bill Johnson would never crack; not now. If he did kill Joyce, that was the time he cracked. He wouldn't do so again.

We dabbled half-heartedly with a case against the philandering civil servant, but nobody really believed that one, and when we'd given him a well-deserved fright we left him alone. In the end we let the whole thing drop—the one thing one never does with a murder case. Somehow in wartime one does a good many things that previously seemed unthinkable.

Besides, I knew. I knew what had happened. I had satisfied *myself*, and it didn't much matter to me that I would never secure a conviction. In fact, the truth is, I didn't want one. If I proved Bill Johnson a murderer he would hang. That wasn't my idea of justice. It was as simple as that.

Put it into writing? No. Never. Of course I know who Bill Johnson is. I've watched his career for the best part of thirty years, since he first began to make his mark. All right, you don't have to explain. I was doing this job when your mother was still playing with dolls. For my money he'll be good at the job, and good luck to him. I've got a lot of time for people like Bill Johnson. You won't get me to help you pull him down. Positive vetting: whatever you call it, it all comes to the same thing. You want me to help you find some dirt to pull him down. All I've told you is what you already knew: he was investigated briefly in 1944 in connection with a death in Maida Vale and nothing was ever found against him. If you thought I said anything else, son, you should have been taking notes.

Oh, that was what the tape recorder was for, was it? Wonderful how they've made them so small these days, isn't it? Used to be great huge things in our day, recording on wire or something. Out of the Ark. Tell you something, though: you could see whether the thing was going round. These tiny gadgets, you need a microscope to see if it's... Careful! Now you've gone and spilt your coffee over that nice suit. Language, please! OK, son. Not your day, is it? If I were you I'd go back to your bosses and tell them there's nothing on Bill Johnson. No need to mention me turning off the mains switch when I went out for the sugar. It was an old trick back in my day, and that's going back some.

Have I anything else to add? Don't say it like that, son! Never does to get bitter in this job. Only this. I've often wondered whether the theorists have got it right. Society is to blame, and all that stuff. There was a woman the other day, in the paper, got a suspended sentence for hitting her boyfriend with an axe. Did you read that? But the way I look at it, in another sense society *is* to blame. It must be, mustn't it? Who else was responsible for Joyce Johnson's death? There was no reason for her to die, except that a bit of the killing we were all caught up in, in the war—a bit of that spilled over into her little flat in Maida Vale. *She* wasn't to blame. *Bill Johnson* wasn't to blame. Society was to blame, wasn't it? Call it original sin. Amounts to the same thing.

OK, son, let's call it a day.

# AFTERWARDS

★

## ALIDA BAXTER

---

THE HELPLESSNESS made him depressed, he understood that: the doctors had warned him. But they didn't realise, they weren't stuck here in this bedroom, ministered to by her every day.

Lying, trapped in the bed she made smooth and fresh for him, he had to see her. Had to be the victim of her ghastly patience, her false and shining brightness, her cheerfulness.

He heard her voice, but he wouldn't listen to it: the questions about which books he wanted, the suggestion that he might like to watch some television. She'd switch on the set and hand the remote control to him, and he'd snap the thing off again. He would not watch it. Nor listen to the cassettes or read the papers she brought him.

She was well and he wasn't, and he hated her.

In the respites when she went out, he acknowledged that she was, of course, beautiful. Her cheekbones, her shoulders, the line of her calves. Everything about Helen was as lovely as on the day they had married. An accident had ruined him, but she hadn't been there; she'd not been touched.

That was why he loathed her: her unchanged health, and all that went with it. Her ability to move about, to walk, to hurry. To do the things she did for him. He even hated her because she could still smile.

Lying in the dark, sleepless nights, he thought about her, about the unfairness of her unscathed beauty. The injustice of her constant, persistent good cheer. And at last he knew he would never recover, never rid himself of this foul depression, if he didn't do something about her.

'I WON'T BE MORE THAN an hour, Harry, I promise. Have you got everything?' She moved the phone, so that it was nearer his hand. She'd had it fitted with an extension lead, to make it accessible wherever he was, though he was never anywhere but in the bed. 'You don't want another drink?' Her supple figure, bending over him; her bright face.

He stared at her sourly. 'Why don't you just go?'

Helen didn't respond to the insulting tone. Her head dipped, but she said, 'Goodbye' as gently as though he'd been nice to her. And went quietly down the stairs: she was light on her slim feet.

Light. Agile. Mobile. He was bedridden! How could he do anything, get anything—how could he deal with her! He shouted at the ceiling as he heard the front door close, a jumbled explosion of rage. He struck at the coverlet, at the bedside table. If he could only move! If only! The sweat tickled his forehead as he gripped at the edge of the bed.

OVER AND AGAIN, with enormous effort, during the following hour he attempted what he'd told the doctors was impossible: he tried to get up.

And found, after forty-five minutes, and trembling with exhaustion, that he could stand. Leaning and holding, supporting himself on the wall and the bedhead, yes; but he was *standing*. And he'd got himself on his feet alone, unaided. The determination to be rid of Helen, to be free of her sickening good health and insufferable presence—the goal had driven him on.

That first day was a revelation. From then on he urged her to get out more, to leave him, since it was only when she was away that he could practise. Within weeks he was able to cross the room, lurching from one handhold to another; a grab at a chair-back, his weight against the dressing-table, a lunge to grasp the handle of a wardrobe door.

All these months he had refused, had cursed the doctors who told him that with patience, with effort, his ability to walk would return. He had been unable to move from his bed unassisted. But now with this motive, with this need, he had succeeded!

And alongside the physical progress, his mind worked as hard as his reawakening muscles. Poison? But what. An accident? But how. The hours, both of day and night, fled by. And his smiling wife told him he was looking better, so that he snapped at her for her stupidity. Once, in the distance of the kitchen, he heard her crying.

She obeyed him, though. She went out more often and stayed away longer, always coming straight back up to the bedroom, always anxious lest she might have been needed, always met with the angry remark that, as far as he was concerned, she couldn't be away long enough.

He spoke in real earnest. His leg muscles had wasted, but every passing day was producing changes. His hands and arms, too, were becoming stronger. And all this must be kept from Helen.

He began to insist that she leave him alone in the bathroom, towels and pyjamas within reach on the stool. She was terrified he might fall and be injured, but he couldn't allow her to help him, to see him naked, now that his limbs were plumping out with firm flesh.

So, she would wait within call. When he edged the door open he saw her sitting on the top stair, where it reached the landing, her back towards him. She leant against the banister, her cheerfulness vanished. She did not know he could walk. Watching her without her knowledge, he felt as though he controlled her. The feeling gave him intense pleasure.

And the image of her sitting there like that impressed itself upon him. Again and again he returned, in his mind, to the stairs. An accident could, after all, happen to anybody. One had happened to him. He might not have survived.

When he wasn't planning, or exercising, he drifted into dreams of what life could be afterwards. Without Helen.

He had the compensation money, a large sum, tucked away in a bank. There'd be a new lifestyle: travel, excitement. And he would gradually reveal that he was getting better: the shock of having to manage without her had triggered a reaction, forced him into movement, might lead one day to a complete recovery. People would talk (but not in front of him) about Fate Moving in Mysterious Ways, and Blessings in Disguise.

'Oh, Harry, how lovely to see you smiling!' She had come in, her cheeks flushed and her skin damp. She had rushed to get back home to him.

And the irony of her ignorance, her delight in his pleasure, not knowing what it was that pleased him, amused him so much that he nearly laughed out loud.

IT WAS A FINE DAY, a Friday, and the seasons were turning when he was ready. Normally she ran the bath for him, but on this day he told her it was never the right temperature; she was hopeless at judging hot and cold, he would do it himself.

He needed the noise of drumming, splashing water, had to be sure she would hear no warning. When the taps were full on, he opened the door carefully. And she was sitting on the top step, as always, her shoulder against the banister.

Not even breathing, he trod carefully towards her. The sound of the bath was loud in the quiet house. It had come at last, this perfect moment. Her relaxed legs, her bowed head. He realised, too late for hesitation, that she was holding the phone to her ear. But he was already upon her, committed to the last, fast—

He tripped, and surprise ripped a cry from him. There was something cold, stringy! Caught round his toes! Slippery beneath his bare feet! And Helen had turned, her eyes and mouth huge.

He staggered, slid, struggled to regain his balance, snatching at the wall, at the banister rail. *Pain in his ankles! He was falling!*

Falling and screaming and crashing and breaking, with the long plastic extension lead twisting and whipping, tearing the phone away from his shrieking wife.

'IT WAS MY FAULT. All my fault,' she said.

The man opposite her shook his head. 'It wasn't.'

'If I hadn't been on the phone, I'd have heard him. He must have called me, and I was listening to you.'

Helen was crying. As fast as she dried her face it was wet again, and the man reached out and held her. They were seated in their usual place, the quietest corner of a quiet wine bar. He had loved her a long time, and watched her live only to serve her bitter husband, and died a little himself when she'd refused to leave the invalid. Now he began to talk to her, reminding her of all she had done, all she had given up, that she had been a good wife to Harry.

She lifted her stained face to him, a face that he loved. And she put her hand in his while he told her that Fate Moved in Mysterious Ways, and sometimes there were such things as Blessings in Disguise.

CLEWSEY'S CLICHÉS

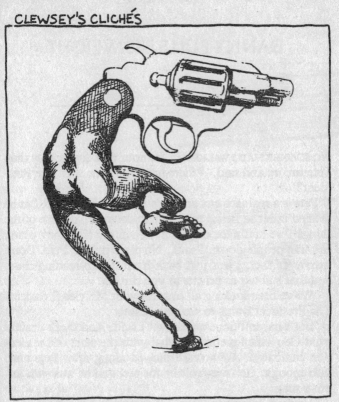

THE GUN JUMPED NEATLY INTO HIS HAND.

# DANNY PULLS HIS WEIGHT

## ★

## MICHAEL Z LEWIN

─────────────────────────

NO SOONER HAD I WALKED in the door that day in May than Pete ran up and said, 'Where have you *been*, Mr Vice President?'

Pete is a real nice guy and he's a great help to Geo, but he seemed upset so I tried to calm him down. That's one of the things I've had a lot of practice at in my first four years, calming people down. I said, 'No place public, Pete. Don't worry.' In fact, I was just back from the lip-reading class, and that's about as private as you can get.

'We've been looking all over for you, Mr Vice President. The President wants to see you, *now*!'

'But I haven't done anything,' I said. And that's exactly what Geo asked me to do, what with the start of the election campaign. Anyhow I followed along after Pete and, sure enough, Geo was waiting for me, and he was with another man.

Geo said, 'Come in, Dan. Sit down,' so I did. I try to do everything Geo says, which is an important part of my job, as I see it. That's the reason I had signed up for the lip-reading class.

'I don't think you've met Harmon Kettlemeyer,' Geo said.

'No, sir, I haven't.'

'Harmon is our nation's finest spin doctor.'

'Wow!' I said. One of the neat things about being Vice President is you get introduced to all kinds of important people. 'Pleased to meet you, Dr Kettlemeyer. But I sure hope you being here doesn't mean our nation's spin is sick.'

'We called you in,' Dr Kettlemeyer said, 'so you don't worry about a rumour you may have heard.'

'What rumour would that be, sir?'

'The rumour that the President is going to dump you and find a vice presidential candidate who would strengthen the ticket.'

'I want you to know, Dan,' Geo said, 'that I will only do that over my dead body. You can count on that. No new vice presidents.'

'In fact,' Dr Kettlemeyer said, 'to show the President's continuing confidence in you, we have a whole campaign issue we want you to handle personally.'

'A whole issue? Me?'

'Mr President, perhaps you'd care to explain what we have in mind.'

'Dan, you know that the safety aspect of life in the states of our union has gone through hell, coming off a pinnacle, you might say, of being lower. Personal safety is a little furry-feathery kind of guy who needs protecting. We've got to find a proper balance between the excesses of the regulatory movement and the excesses on the rape, pillage and plunder side. I'm not asking you to cry for Argentina, you know, or anybody else, but I'm getting sick and tired of hearing those carping little liberal Democrats jumping all over our you-know-what.'

'Me too, sir,' I said.

Dr Kettlemeyer said, 'To reiterate, Mr Vice President, we want you to be at the forefront of the fine work this administration has done to promote the issue of law and order.'

'Law and order? But that's important!'

'It sure is, Dan,' Geo said.

'This is the plan, Mr Vice President,' Dr Kettlemeyer said. 'You're going out to Indianapolis next week, I believe.'

'That's right, sir,' I said. 'They have a big car race out there and because I'm such a famous Hoosier, I get to be the Grand Marshal.'

'Perfect,' Dr Kettlemeyer said.

'And after the race there's a banquet at a hotel and somebody gives a speech there, which might be me, though I'll have to amplify on that.'

'Good,' Dr Kettlemeyer said. 'They are both big, public occasions, aren't they, Mr Vice President?'

'Yes, sir, they are.'

'Now put your thinking cap on, Mr Vice President. At these big, public occasions, how do you think that you could show the greatest possible confidence in George Bush's safer, more law-abiding America?'

'I give up, sir. How?'

'Go to Indianapolis without your bodyguards, Mr Vice President.'

THE DAY OF THE 500 Mile Race is a big day in Indianapolis—though I'd be the first to say that Indianapolis has lots and lots of big days, every single year. It's not a one-big-day town, no way.

But the 500 is such a big day that there's a parade before the race, and that's what has to have a Grand Marshal, which was me. Being a Grand Marshal is probably not the job that a person who hasn't been a vice president thinks it is. There's no badge and no gun either. However, Dr Kettlemeyer did give me a big white Stetson hat. He said it would remind everybody of law and order and of good guys. And he made me promise I'd wear it all the time I was in Indianapolis.

And I did, I wore it every minute through my Grand Marshalling which, to tell the truth, was mostly riding around in an open car and waving at everybody. Well, not *everybody* in the sense of every specific body. There were far too many bodies to wave at them individually. If I did that,

it would take much too long, probably the whole day, and
there wouldn't be time left for a race at all, which is not the
point.

It all went OK, praise the Lord, and I didn't fall out of the
car, even though it was open. Then I went to the Grand
Marshal's bulletproof box seat and that's where I got to
watch the race.

But after the race cars started their engines a surprising
thing happened, which was a knock at the door of the box.
I didn't know what it could be, but it turned out to be a man
knocking on the door. When he came in he said, 'Don't get
agitated, Mr Vice President. Harmon Kettlemeyer sent me.
He thought you might be getting bored without your bodyguards to talk to, so I'm here to make your visit more interesting.'

'If you're from Dr Kettlemeyer,' I said, 'then you'll know
I'm supposed to be proving Geo's America is safer. Are you
*sure* you're not a bodyguard?'

The man smiled and said, 'Scout's honour, Mr Vice
President. I am no bodyguard.'

To tell the truth, it does get pretty boring when you sit in
a box wearing a Stetson and waiting to see if a car that went
past a minute ago is going to come past again. I know that
was not the most diplomatic thing I could have said, but I
didn't say it loud and after all, I'm not a diplomat, I'm a
vice president.

And the man from Dr Kettlemeyer, whose name was
Euple, understood immediately. He said, 'You know, sir, I
think I could find a little action for you.'

I didn't see exactly what he was getting at, but one of the
tricks I've picked up now that I am more mature as Vice
President is not to let on right away when I don't understand something. Instead I say, 'Would you care to amplify
on that?' which is what I said to Euple.

'Oh, don't get me wrong,' Euple said. 'I'm not talking about anything that would interest the Drug Enforcement Agency.'

'I should think not,' I said. 'I'm not a senator now.'

'Or anything immoral,' Euple said.

'I never claimed that I was *completely* like John Kennedy.'

'But what I had in mind was that we could go on a ride tonight after your official engagement.'

'I can't get mixed up in any engagement either,' I said. 'I'm already married.'

Euple looked at me for a minute and then he laughed. 'They told me you didn't have any sense of humour, Mr Vice President, but they were wrong.'

'They sure were,' I said. 'I went to Arizona quite a few times when I was a kid because my grandad, Eugene, lived near there. We travelled a lot, so I think I have quite a good sense of Yuma.'

'Yup,' Euple said, 'you're a lot sharper than they say, aren't you, sir?'

'Would you care to amplify on that?'

He laughed again, and he said, 'The ride I had in mind was in a special police car.'

'You mean I might be able to get a hands-on seat-of-the-pants taste of law and order?'

'That's the idea, sir. It's what Harmon Kettlemeyer said you were here for.'

'That's a great plan, Euple,' I said. 'Because there's nothing I want more than to do my bit for Geo's re-election. If Geo isn't re-elected, boy, I'd be so upset! I just don't know what I'd do, except maybe go on to the Supreme Court!'

'Sir, what I thought was that after the big 500 Dinner tonight, I'll wink at you twice and that'll be the sign that you should follow me and we'll pretend we're going to the men's room.'

'You're not from the National Endowment for the Arts are you, Euple?''

'Me? No, sir. Not me. No way. Chill out. Uh uh.'

'Even so, do you think that we could come up with some other sign?'

'OK. I'll tug on my left ear lobe.'

'And what happens then?'

'We'll go out back and that's where we'll meet the special police car that'll take you for the ride.'

EUPLE'S GREAT PLAN almost went wrong because I nearly missed the Dinner. The first thing that happened was I spotted a neat golf course inside the oval at the race track and I probably would have succumbed to temptation except I couldn't work out a way to fly there.

Then I realised I'd left my invitation back in Washington. That was because it's Marilyn, my precious but equal wife, who looks after our invitations. What I forgot was that she wasn't with me in Indianapolis because she desperately needed some quality time at her word processor. So when I showed up at the hotel for the banquet, the guard wouldn't let me in.

'I'm sorry, sir,' he said, 'I can't let you in without your invitation. We have Vice President Quayle here tonight.'

'But I *am* Vice President Quayle.'

'That's what you say, sir, but how can I be sure without seeing your invitation? Suppose I let you in and you turn out not to be who you say you are and then you bump off who you say you are because you're not. Think of the trouble I'd be in.'

'But those two guys who got here just before I did didn't have invitations.'

'Ah,' the guard said, 'but they proved who they were.'

'How did they do that?'

'Well, the first gentleman said he was Placido Domingo and he sang me a few notes and I could tell right away he was the real Mr Domingo and I let him in. And the next guy said he was Yo-Yo Ma and he played me a few bars on his cello, and I could tell right away he was the real Mr Ma and I let him in.'

'That's not fair,' I said. 'Who *are* these Domino and Mom guys?'

'Ah!' the guard said, 'please enter, Mr Quayle!'

THE BANQUET was more fun than the Marshalling. I sat next to a man who made tyres and he told me a fact I didn't know: that in a racing car tyre they use enough rubber on the tread to make more than three hundred and fifty condoms.

When it came time for someone to speak it turned out to be me. I decided to use what I had just learned, but it seemed only right to give credit where it was due. I said, 'I am here in Indianapolis to help remind people of law and order in our kinder, safer America. And speaking of safety, did you know they use enough rubber on the tread of a tyre to make more than three hundred and fifty condoms. Of course that's in a Goodyear.'

Then the Master of Ceremonies said, 'Sounds like a *really* good year to me.'

'Would you care to amplify on that?'

And he said, 'Maybe you'll need a pocket calculator to keep track.'

'No, I won't,' I said. 'I already know how many pockets I have.'

Anyway, people seemed to get the message.

After I made my speech Euple pulled on both his ears and winked at me too and I thought, what the heck. I excused myself and went to the restroom with Euple and he let me out of the hotel by a back way. But there was no special police car waiting there, so I asked where it was.

'I'm sure it'll be here any minute,' Euple said. 'But, Mr Vice President, where's your Stetson?'

'I left it at the banquet.'

'Go and get it!' he said.

But to tell the truth, the Stetson had started chafing the tops of my ears, which is why I took it off. Besides, it wasn't as white as it was before, due to a little accident during the soup. 'It'll be all right,' I said. 'They'll save it for me.'

'But you've got to have it!' Euple said, and I was surprised at his bossy attitude, which is not what I am used to away from home.

I said, 'I'm sure Dr Kettlemeyer will understand. I'll take full responsibility.'

Just then a big, dark car turned into the alley from the street, and Euple got even more excited and he started jumping and signalling to it. Sure enough, the car slowed down when it got near us, but then it suddenly speeded up again and drove away, so it must not have been the special police car after all.

Euple was still upset, so I tried to calm him down. I said, 'Pull yourself together,' but it didn't seem to help.

We waited in the alley another fifteen minutes, but the special police car never came. By that time I was getting nervous too, and I said, 'I don't think it's smart waiting any longer, Euple. Downtown Indianapolis is a dangerous neighbourhood, you know. Guys standing around are sitting targets.'

But Euple didn't seem to comprehend what I was saying, so I said, 'You have a car, don't you? Why don't you just take me on the ride yourself?' And in the end that's what he did.

Even so Euple never relaxed. Probably it was because he wasn't used to having a vice president in his car. For the whole time his voice was husky and tense.

My voice used to get that way, but that was before I had so much experience at being the Vice President. It happened most when I had press conferences all by myself. These days, though, I am a lot stronger with the media, which is how you have to handle them. For instance I'm on record for making it clear to critics of Geo's that when there's unfair criticism going his way I will respond in kind.

EUPLE DROVE AWAY from the centre of town but he didn't drive very fast, like he was making up his mind where to go. That was understandable because Indianapolis has many, many fine sights to sightsee, even at night, and some of them as late as one-thirty or two in the morning.

But we didn't get very far at all. Just about the time Euple seemed to make a decision and start driving faster, we came to a big obstruction in the road, and it was made up of police cars. We came around a corner and there they were, and it was all Euple could do to dent only the one car just a little bit.

A lot of policemen crowded around and they were not very happy with Euple and, to be perfectly honest, some of the language they used was the worst I'd heard since I was in the National Guard.

But fair's fair, so I got out and said, 'Don't blame him. He was only trying to keep me from getting bored.'

'And who in tarnation are you?' one of them said.

'I'm Dan Quayle,' I said, and it was very exciting for them.

The police were all together because there had just been an FBI raid on some notorious interstate criminals and one of the feds had been murdered. A call had gone out on the police radios which is why there were so many police cars in the street. They'd all been in a hurry and hadn't had time to park neatly.

The corpse was in the middle of a room and a whole crowd of people were questioning each other and looking around in case the murderer was still there. I went to have a look at the body, which I have to say was not nearly as well done as on TV, because the blood was spattered all over everything and very messy. I even got some on my shoe. 'Ugh, look at that,' I said.

The policeman next to me said, 'Look at what, sir?' and he bent down. But right away he stood up again. He said, 'Tank! Come here!'

Tank, who was another policeman, came over and the first policeman said, 'Mr Quayle has spotted something red under the fed.' Tank looked and then he pulled out a red baseball cap.

The first thing that occurred to me was that maybe it would cheer Euple up if I put it on, even though it wasn't a stetson. I said, 'Can I see?' and Tank gave me the cap.

I turned it over to see if it was my size and it was, but then I saw that there was blood on the hatband. In this day and age it's not a good idea to put a hat like that on, not if your ears are chafed. But it was a real nice cap and the label said, 'J. C. Pennies,' so when I gave the cap back to Tank I said, 'I bet a nice cap like this costs more than pennies.'

Tank looked at the cap real hard, and he suddenly said, 'Well spotted, sir!'

And the rest of the story is history now.

WHEN I GOT BACK to Washington, Dr Kettlemeyer was terribly upset when I called to tell him about the murder, but he is the kind of guy who tries hard to make the best of things. Elections are won and lost from lots of issues, but I certainly think I did my bit for law and order.

It turned out that the baseball cap was part of a batch of 'J. C. Penney's' but the cap company took the order over the phone. When they delivered the order, Mr Penney wouldn't accept it because the spelling was wrong. What the company did then was sell the caps to a mail order catalogue and when police asked the mail order company how many caps they'd sold in Indianapolis, it was only the one and they had the address. Then the police drove over and picked up the killer.

The whole thing was a very great coincidence and a very handy one because, as it happened, that very same night another murder took place in Indianapolis, and almost at the very same time.

Tank drove me back to town—because we couldn't find Euple anywhere—and he told me all about this other murder on the way. It seems that a man dressed like a waiter was shot in an alley, and nobody knew why. With there being two murders the same night, it was lucky for the police that the first was an easy one. The police hadn't identified the dead man in the alley but Tank said he had a white hat and that was probably a good clue.

It seemed like another big coincidence to me. That very same night I had told Euple how dangerous it can be in an alley, even though America is a wonderful, safe place with Geo. But even a great man like Geo can't be everywhere at the same time which is another reason why it's important to have a Vice President who does everything he can to help.

# OH, WHO HATH DONE THIS DEED?

★

## SUSAN MOODY

I COULDN'T QUITE place her.

She came out of the shadows beside the old fort and walked across the palm-shaded square to stand on the jetty, looking down at the water. She had strikingly long legs, rounded hips, a face which, although hidden now by sunglasses, possessed the planes of lasting beauty. Yet, as she crossed the square, stepping in and out of the striped shadows, she was neither striking nor beautiful. Her hair was careless, her shoulders, somehow, defeated.

She had leant towards me once. She had smiled at me, her face alive with love. But when? It was a small puzzle and one which I did not dwell on longer than it took to wonder ruefully whether I had at last reached the age when any young woman reminded me of lost love.

In front of me, wind riffled the oily surface of the little harbour and the fishing boats rocked together, sending ripples towards the jetty. These were working boats; the place was too small for holiday sailors since there were no watering or petrol facilities, nowhere to stock up on whisky and tins. There was only the hotel up on the cliff, built in the thirties by an over-ambitious Frenchman who shortly afterwards went bankrupt, only the miles of empty country behind and the Roman ruins mouldering in the desert among sombre dunes of reddish sand which at sunset seemed to be made of rust-coloured cloud. And there was, of course, a beach, uncluttered, unpolluted, curling away around the coast for half a mile. For the moment, the place remained undiscovered by all but a very few, though I knew it was inevitable that sooner or later some travel writer or tourist agency would happen upon it and another paradise would be lost.

I should have realised she would be staying at the hotel—there was, after all, nowhere else. The following morning, I was sitting on the terrace which had been built out over the sea when she came hesitantly out and looked around for somewhere to sit. It wasn't difficult; at that time of year there were only half a dozen other guests, but the effort of deciding which table to occupy seemed to be too much for her. She bit her lip, frowning, moved towards one table and then thought better of it; moved irresolutely to another. Again she seemed tantalisingly familiar; curiosity made me half rise in my seat, indicating that she was welcome to join me if she wished but as soon as she caught my eye she ducked her head and scurried towards the table furthest from mine.

I shrugged. Obviously she found me a threat even though she wore a wedding ring; I could see it glinting on her finger as she picked up the glass of pineapple juice in front of her only to put it quickly down to lean her arms on the stone balustrade and gaze at the beach below. When the boy came to take her breakfast order, she shook her head and he went away.

There was something about her I recognised . . . was it the shape of her head, the line of her jaw, a sense of nostalgia I couldn't quite grasp? In the end, curiosity won. I got up and went over to her.

'Excusez-moi, madame . . .' French seemed the most obvious language to use since the port had once been part of the French colonial possessions and as far as I knew, I was the only Englishman in the place. 'Excusez-moi, mais j'ai l'impression que . . .'

She turned swiftly, her eyes wide and alarmed, as though she had not heard me approaching and was startled by my voice. 'I'm afraid I don't speak French,' she said. She had a clear, carrying voice, each word meticulously pronounced.

I smiled. 'I'm English myself,' I said. 'I saw you yesterday, down in the square.'

'Yes?' She waited, as though my remark must surely be leading on to something more significant.

'Are you here alone?' It was the crassest of questions and I realised as soon as I had made it that she would take me for some remittance man, some seasonal gigolo making a living from lonely women, giving them sex in return for a watch, a silk shirt, a cheque.

'My husband's down there,' she said pointing at the beach.

'Ah.' I peered over. The brown beach was nearly empty so early in the day though half a dozen people were cresting the long slow waves or swimming lazily in the shallows.

'That's him,' she said, pointing at a black head far out on the waves, making purposefully for the land. 'He's an actor. He likes to swim for half a mile morning and evening.' She turned to look up at me, gave a soft little laugh. I noticed that her own hair was damp. 'I don't know exactly how he judges the distance, but he seems to be able to tell.'

It was the laugh that did it. 'Desdemona,' I said.

She looked blank. For a moment I wondered if I'd got it wrong. But no... 'You were Desdemona. In the Richter film. The most marvellous Desdemona. With Bernard Peters as your Othello and Charles Everett playing Iago.'

She looked down at her clasped hands. 'It was a long time ago.'

'But unforgettable. You were so...' I sought for words, 'passionate, so innocent, so *doomed*.'

I was not the only one to admire her performance. The critics had raved, the film had been a stupendous box-office success, and the little English actress plucked from some obscure repertory company had been guaranteed an illustrious future. There'd been a second, less prestigious film, a third. In all of them her air of fragile resilience had shone through.

And then there'd been nothing. She had vanished; it was one of those Whatever-happened-to...? show-biz mysteries which occur from time to time and are eventually solved only when someone does a tragedy article or an unexpected obituary appears.

Her name was Helena Garden. I recalled that she had been married at the time *Othello* was made and the mother of a child. There was no reason why I should have remembered—except that she had been unforgettable.

For a while we talked. The boy came over and went away again. She began to watch the door out on to the terrace.

I knew when he arrived. I could tell by the way her eyes widened and then dropped. I turned. He was standing there at the door, in jeans and a white shirt with the collar turned up to frame his handsome actor's face, unable to resist making an entrance.

He caught sight of us and frowned. He came over, taking a pair of sunglasses out of his pocket and slipping them on as he walked between the tables.

I stood. 'I hope you don't think I'm intruding,' I said, my voice falsely hearty. 'I know it's some years ago now, but I recognised your wife and felt I simply had to say how wonderful I thought her Desdemona was.' I held out a hand, which he ignored. 'I'm Martin Howard.'

'Jeremy Talbot,' he said shortly. He grasped his wife's shoulder.

I smiled. I backed away, left my unfinished breakfast, went up to my room. He did not seem to remember that we had met before. But I did.

I SPENT THE DAY sailing round the coastline to Moukabi, a spectacular cluster of ruins long since abandoned to sand and wind. Time had rounded and scoured the ancient walls into a series of extraordinary shapes; they reared out of the red soil like natural growth caused by the earth's shiftings. I had been there before and never failed to find the desolation of the place somehow salutary, a reminder of the transitory nature of man. Then, too, the sound of the wind along the crumbled streets was extraordinarily soothing, mournful, resigned, striking straight at the heart.

Yet for once, I failed to respond to the place. Sitting on deck with a drink in my hand before sailing back, I watched the sun begin to lower itself behind the smooth shallow hills along the coast, and let my mind drift back ...

IT HAD BEEN years before. I'd sailed into a little harbour on the north coast of Brittany—Locquirec or Perros Guirec, I can't remember which—and tied up for the night. It was late. Most people had already gone ashore for their evening meal; those who hadn't were below—I could smell steaks grilling, and onions, hear the clink of glasses. The sun was almost down; the long lines of boats cast shadows across the dirty green water which lapped at the jetty. I was standing on the foredeck, enjoying the feel of tired muscles relaxing and the crawl of whisky down my throat, when I saw a wooden dinghy come nosing out from between two boats moored further up and make ragged progress towards me. There was a man clumsily wielding the oars; opposite him sat a boy of eight or nine, dressed in an anorak and a yachting cap which must have belonged to his father. The boy had one of those tender open faces that vanish with adolescence; his straight fair hair hung in a fringe over his eyes and

every now and then he pushed back the peak of the cap,
which was far too big. There was something touching about
him; I leant over the rail for a further look, smiling to myself. I'd been like that once: eager, happy, already in love
with the sea and boats and everything they embraced.

The man reached the point opposite which slippery steps
led up from the water to the jetty and began to manoeuvre
the dinghy towards them, between two of the moored hulls.
He said something to the boy, who stood up and put both
of his hands on the side of the nearest boat, obviously with
the intention of guiding the dinghy in to the jetty. As anyone who's ever sailed will know, it's a foolish thing to do,
and indeed, as I watched, the dinghy swung away from the
bigger boat and the boy fell, with hardly a splash, into the
widening gap. For a moment, he lay there on the water, held
up by his anorak; the yachting cap drifted slowly away and
his hair spread out around his head like a halo.

No one moved. The boy uttered no cry, the father, frozen as I was, simply watched, and I, above them, out of
sight, said nothing, assuming the man would dive in after his
son. Which, as I began to function again, calling down to
ask if he needed help, he immediately did. Once in the water, he floundered and splashed—I watched him for a few
seconds, not worried because they were no more than fifteen yards from the harbour wall, until it dawned on me that
he was in some kind of trouble.

All this took no more than a few seconds, yet already the
boy was sinking, his face under the water, his eyes closed. I
jumped in, landing almost on top of the man, who turned
a white face towards me and said, hopelessly, 'I can't swim.'

I grabbed the front of his jacket and pulled him through
the water to the dinghy, which bobbed a few yards away.
'Hang on,' I said. 'I'll get the boy.' I didn't say what I was
thinking: that only a criminally irresponsible parent would
take a child out in a boat without a lifejacket and then ask

that child to perform a potentially dangerous action when the parent himself was unable to swim.

I got hold of the boy, held his face out of the water, swam fast to the side. He weighed nothing; I got him up the steps, laid him out on the flat stones of the jetty and set to work on him. He'd swallowed about a litre of the filthy water; I got it out, banged his chest, watched his delicate eyelids flicker and open to reveal huge grey eyes. When I was sure he was conscious and breathing, I left him and went after the father, now shivering in the water, knuckles clenched over the edge of the dinghy, and pulled him too safely to land.

Having found out where they were staying, I walked them both back to their hotel and, since the father seemed unwilling or unable to do so, asked the receptionist to call a doctor to check out the boy.

For no good reason, we exchanged names. All he said as I turned to go was 'Where's the boy's cap?'

I told myself he was in shock, or terrified of what the boy's mother would say; embarrassed, even, at having put himself in a position of needing to be rescued. Nevertheless, his response both chilled and disturbed me.

As did his behaviour the following day. I met them both walking along the edge of the harbour: the boy rushed up and clung to my hand, the father followed at a slower pace and, not meeting my eyes, mumbled something about being sorry to have inconvenienced me the night before.

I neither expected—nor wanted—effusive expressions of gratitude. Anyone would have acted as I did. But... inconvenienced? It seemed a damned cold-blooded way to refer to what had happened.

That evening, I strolled up to their hotel. Since I was leaving early the next day, I bought a drink in the bar and made one last enquiry about the boy. The girl at the desk was not the one who'd been there the night before; when I explained who I was asking about, and why, she told me they had already left. She murmured something about the boy being accident prone, that it was lucky I had been on hand, that he'd already had a couple of narrow escapes. When I asked about them, she shrugged. He'd apparently tripped in the street and nearly been run over by a lorry. He'd drunk from a bottle of bleach instead of lemonade. Been treated for concussion after falling down a flight of stone steps. She didn't actually say that boys will be boys but it hung in the air between us. When I asked about the boy's mother, she told me she'd left for home two days earlier; father and son were on their back to her now.

As I walked away, I thought: there's something wrong here. But what could I do? They'd already left; I myself was sailing on the early tide. Besides, the boy hadn't seemed afraid. He was open and affectionate. And who would I have contacted if I really thought there was a serious threat to his welfare?

AROUND ME THE HILLS darkened into scarlet and orange. The crimsoned sea spread flatly towards the horizon. I shivered suddenly. Over the years, I had occasionally remembered the boy and his father, wondered how they were. Now, the thought dropped into my mind with the heaviness of a stone: if I had not spoken from above, like a controlling god, would he simply have watched his son drown? Was there a link between the boy's 'accidents' and the sudden break in Helena Garden's career?

SHE HESITATED AT THE DOOR opening on to the terrace, just as she had the previous morning. She moved towards one table, then to another, as she had yesterday. I watched her, this time making no move to rise. By then, I was pretty sure in my own mind about what had happened to her and the sick anger the whole affair roused in me made it impossible to concentrate on my coffee—or indeed, on anything else. There were two questions to which I needed the answer. If they confirmed what I suspected, then I would have to come to another decision: to tell or not to tell. I would have no real proof, only a string of circumstantial detail. Yet, if I was right, the detail itself might prove strong enough to convict a man of murder.

Eventually, I pushed back my chair and walked over to her.

She turned, startled once more. 'My husband's down there.' She pointed to the beach. 'He's an actor. He swims half a mile morning and evening. I don't know how he—'

'Yes. You told me yesterday,' I said gently. Rage filled me for what had been done to this lovely fragile creature.

'—I don't know how he knows when it's time to turn back.' She pushed her fingers through her damp hair and laughed softly.

'How long has he done this?' It was one of the questions to which I needed the answer.

She frowned. 'Years,' she said. 'Years and years.'

'Eight years? Ten years?' I had to know.

'All his life.'

I hadn't realised I'd been holding my breath. The two of us watched the dark head swimming arrow-straight for the shore below. The black-hearted bastard, I thought. There was only one more piece of information I needed.

'Your son,' I said. 'How is the boy?'

A shadow drifted across her huge grey eyes, so like those of the child I had once rescued. 'Charlie?' She moved the wedding ring up and down her knuckle. 'He died.'

I went cold. 'How? What happened?'

'He went swimming. He swam out too far. He couldn't make it back to the shore.'

I tried not to think of Charlie engulfed by some cold grey sea. 'Was he alone when the ... when this accident—'

'It wasn't an accident,' she said.

So she also knew. I wanted to say: why do you stay with him? I wanted to say: I understand the guilt and fear which keeps you tied to him, I realise you blame yourself for Charlie's death because deep down you must have known what he was trying to do and yet you did nothing to prevent it. But for your own sake, you must get away.

There were tears in her eyes now; one of them rolled down her cheek and the gesture was poignantly familiar. Just so had she faced on screen the jealous Othello; just so had she looked as the black hands closed round the white skin of her throat. She must have encountered a similar jealousy within her marriage, and the victim had been someone even more innocent than Desdemona.

Because I could see it all. Jeremy Talbot, a small-time actor, unable to cope with his wife's success, had called a halt to her career in the most subtle and terrible way. He must have guessed just how she—how any mother—would react to the shock of losing her child.

Something should be done. But what? I looked down at the swimmer below us, brown arms flashing in and out of the water as he neared the shore.

He appeared on the terrace a little later. His handsome face was frowning as he hurried towards us. His hand grasped his wife's shoulder; his expression was hostile.

'Enjoy the swim?' I asked. I couldn't keep the sardonic note from my voice.

His eyes met mine coldly. He said, 'I told you last time we met that I couldn't swim.'

So he remembered too.

Something must be done. All day the feeling nagged at me that I ought somehow to be able to release that shining talent of hers from the straitjacket in which her cold-blooded, self-centred husband had locked it. I could think of nothing.

IT WAS ABOUT twelve months later that I saw the announcement in the paper. Nothing big, a small paragraph on page 3: FORMER ACTRESS DIES.

According to the report, she'd killed herself. She'd gone out with her husband in a boat at some seaside resort on the south coast of England and thrown herself overboard. He had told the coroner he couldn't swim: weeping, he'd said that there was nothing he could do to save her. A verdict of accidental death was brought in; the coroner commiserated with him for this second tragedy coming so soon after the loss of his son. That was that. The life and death of Helena Garden, wife, rival, neatly tied up and disposed of.

Or so he thought.

THE HOUSE WAS OLD and charming, somewhere near Brighton. He answered the door himself.

'Come in,' he said quietly. 'I've been half expecting you.'

There were lines of fatigue on his face and I noticed that one of his hands trembled slightly.

'Nemesis?' I said harshly.

'I suspect you think you know what happened.'

'I worked it out,' I said, 'and if I can ever prove it...'

'You think I killed them both.' It was a statement, not a question.

'Yes.'

'She told you I could swim,' he said. 'She told you I swam half a mile morning and evening.'

'Yes.'

'I loathe the water,' he said. 'I nearly drowned when I was a child—I'm terrified of it. She was the one who went swimming every day.'

'But that evening in Brittany...' I could hear the note of uncertainty in my voice.

'Charlie was desperate to go out in a boat. And I hadn't dared let him go with his mother. It was after she'd left for home that I...' His voice trailed. After a moment, he spoke again. 'What you saw was a simple accident. And afterwards, when you'd got us both out of the water—don't you think I was embarrassed at not being able to swim, at being forced to rely on a stranger to rescue my own son?'

'But—'

'Helena—my wife—was sick.' It was exactly what I had expected him to say. 'When Charlie was born, she adored him. We both did. We were a perfectly ordinary young couple at the start of our careers, struggling to find the way up in what you must know is a precarious profession. And then they made *Othello*. Helena became a star overnight. There was the second film, and the third. And then nothing. It's always like that for actors. There'd have been something else, of course there would. But she thought it had come to an end almost before it had begun. She looked around for someone to blame and chose Charlie. Suddenly he was in her way. Things began to happen to him. It took me a while to realise they weren't accidents.'

I remembered Desdemona's voice, saying the same thing about Charlie's death. 'How did he drown?'

'It was the day after I heard I'd got the lead in *Mine Is the Glory*. My biggest break.'

I remembered it. A smash hit in the West End, with a transfer to Broadway a year or two later.

'I don't recall you being in it,' I said.

'I had to let the part go. Because the very next day, Helena took Charlie out in a boat. She said they went swimming and he got cramp when they were half a mile out. She said he panicked and was struggling so hard she couldn't get hold of him.' He looked away and swallowed. There were tears in his eyes. 'The coroner called it a terrible accident.'

'But it wasn't?'

'You know as well as I do that Charlie couldn't swim. After that business in Brittany, he was as terrified of the water as I was. I'll never know how she persuaded him to get into a boat with her.'

There was a silence. After a while, I said, 'Why did you go on living with her?'

His strong actor's voice was full of sadness. 'Because I married her for better or worse. Because I loved her. Not wisely, but too well.'

'But poor little Charlie was the one who got hurt.'

'She thought that without Charlie she'd be free, she'd become a star again. But of course she didn't. When she lost Charlie, she lost everything.'

He walked me to the door and added, not meeting my eye, 'So did I.'

DID I BELIEVE HIM? I don't know. Certainly he was convincing, but that was what, as an actor, he was trained to be. It must have been a couple of months later that I read about the new RSC production at Stratford. 'A triumph!' the papers called it. 'English theatre at its superb best!' 'Dazzling!' 'Impressively moving.'

It was *Othello*, of course. With Jeremy Talbot in the name part. 'A powerful, poignant performance,' the papers said. 'Perhaps one of the greatest actors of our generation.'

It was a part he'd been forced to turn down only a few weeks earlier because his wife, the former Helena Garden, had been diagnosed as having terminal cancer and needed full-time nursing care. There was a suggestion that she had killed herself in order not to stand in his way.

I thought how easy it would be to knock someone overboard from a small boat. How simple it would be to ward off a dying woman. How useful an oar would be in holding her under until she drowned.

I DON'T SUPPOSE I shall ever know the truth. I can only say that when I was finally able to get tickets, his performance moved me to tears.

# THE CHRISTMAS CRIMES AT 'CINDERELLA'
## PART THREE: 27 DECEMBER

★

## SIMON BRETT

---

JACK TARRANT WROTE the word that had been spelled out down the left-hand side of the song into the next point of the four-pointed star.

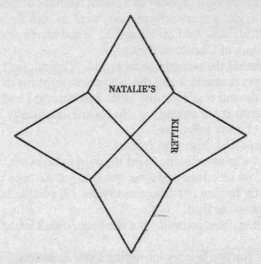

'Teasing us,' he growled. 'The "Cinderella murderer" is teasing us.'

'At least,' said Maria, 'if we're right about the initial letters, we've now got a K as well as an N. So those two are going to appear in the murderer's name.'

'Yes.' Jack Tarrant grinned sardonically. 'That narrows things down a lot, doesn't it?'


AS EXPECTED, the daily papers on 27 December were lavish with praise for Niki Grayes. Natalie Maine's murder had ensured that the dancer's transition from understudy to leading role achieved maximum publicity. At least three of the papers succumbed to the predictable 'Star is Born' headline.

As ever, murder proved good for business and the box office phone lines were jammed solid.

Jack and Maria worked separately that day. She, partly in her professional capacity as a public relations officer, and partly to glean more information, went to visit her client Ricky Sturridge, held on remand in Wandsworth since the early hours of Christmas Day.

She found the boxer in bitter mood. 'Typical, isn't it? A crime gets committed and the Bill goes straight for the first person around who's got any form. Just because I had those convictions for mugging . . .' He looked truculently up at Maria. 'I never killed her.'

'I know that. You were framed.'

'But we're never going to get the cops to believe it.'

'Yes, we are. Jack and I are going to get the cops to believe it by finding out who actually *did* kill Natalie Maine. We'll get to the truth.'

'Thanks. Sure you will.' But the boxer didn't sound convinced.

'And you can help by answering a few questions.'

'More questions.' He sighed. 'Yes sure. What do you want to know?'

'First, about your relationship with Natalie.'

'Well, I fancied her rotten, can't pretend otherwise. And I thought being seen round with someone like her wouldn't do the old image any harm. First of all she seemed like she was encouraging me, but then, last couple of days before the dress rehearsal, suddenly she turned nasty, started showing me up in front of everyone.'

'Backstage gossip said you were having a steamy affair.'

He let out a short laugh. 'I should be so lucky.'

'Do you reckon she had another boyfriend in the company?'

'Dunno. I mean, certainly she give the come-on to anything in trousers, but how far any of it went...' He shrugged. 'No, there was only one person Natalie Maine really had any time for, and that was Natalie Maine.'

'What about Wink...?'

'Back end of the pantomime horse? She certainly give him the eye, and all. Maybe he fancied his chances, dunno.'

'Did you get on with him?'

'Didn't have much in common. Bit of an intellectual, young Wink. Always wanting to play complicated word games in rehearsal breaks, that kind of stuff. Thinks he's much cleverer than anyone else—which he probably is. Not easy to get through to, anyway...you know, highly strung.'

'What do you mean?'

'Well, he...dunno. Lots of nervous energy he had...like he was always on the edge of...dunno what...'

'A nervous breakdown?'

'Yeah, suppose so.'

JACK TARRANT had more trouble than Maria in finding the person he wanted to talk to, but then Danny Kino was not in prison. He had, however, according to Scotland Yard information, served time in the less liberal forties and fifties.

Ken said that the comedian had arrived just after noon, but Jack searched right through the building and saw no sign of Danny. He even got the stage manager to put out a Tannoy call to the dressing rooms from the desk in the prompt corner, but without success. Jack had almost given up and was wandering aimlessly up the stairs to the administrative offices, when he noticed a small door.

Pushing it open, he found himself in a narrow gallery round the top of the stage area, strung with an array of ropes like the rigging of a tall ship. It was from here that scenery was flown down, and he could see parts of Prince Charming's palace, Baron Hardup's kitchen and the Ugly Sisters' boudoir—as well as the songsheet for the sing-along scene, now carrying the correct words.

Jack could also see, looking towards him in some surprise, the dimly lit figure of Danny Kino.

'Good afternoon,' said Jack. 'Spend a lot of time up here, do you?'

'Yes, I do as a matter of fact. Old habit from when I was on the halls. Always liked to get a bit of quiet before I did my act. Flying gallery's ideal.'

Jack closed the door behind him. 'I was looking for you.'

The comedian gave a humourless grin. 'I wondered how long it would take.'

'What do you mean?'

'You may think you and your girlfriend are being very subtle, Jack Tarrant, but everyone knows you're investigating the murder.'

'Well, if that's the case, I don't need any preamble, do I? I can just begin straight away asking you some questions.'

The comedian shrugged. 'Be my guest. What are you going to ask first—whether I had anything to gain by Natalie Maine's death?'

'All right. Let's start there.'

Danny Kino gave another thin smile. 'I did, actually. Quite a lot. You see, Natalie and me, coming from entirely opposite ends of show business, were actually in competition for the same job.'

'Really?'

'Odd, isn't it? There's another "romantic" television game show being planned . . . you know, like *Blind Date*. They're looking for the right presenter and, true to tradition, were considering a clapped-out comedian and an over-the-hill pop star. So—I'm absolutely delighted that Natalie Maine's out of the way.'

Jack was silent.

'Next question, of course, must be—did the job matter enough for me to kill for it? But I don't think I should do all your work for you, Jack Tarrant. I'll supply the questions. You're going to have to find out the answers on your own.'

'Let me try a question then . . .'

'OK.'

'What was—or is—your relationship with Wink Carter?'

The comedian's shoulders stiffened in the half-light. 'I don't see that's relevant.'

'Could be extremely relevant.'

'How?'

'Say, for example, you were in love with Wink and wanted to gain his affection by giving him . . . the part of Buttons?'

'If I'd wanted to do that,' Danny Kino said coldly, 'I'd have murdered Ricky Sturridge, not Natalie Maine.'

'Oh, but you've just told me you wanted Natalie out of the way. And by making it look as if Ricky had murdered her . . . you'd almost literally have killed two birds with one stone.'

After a silence, the comedian said lightly, 'Interesting theory. Pity you haven't a shred of evidence to support it.'

'Not at the moment. But I haven't asked Wink about it yet.'

Jack was amazed by the speed with which Danny Kino suddenly crossed the gallery and seized him by the shirt collar. 'You keep Wink out of this!' the comedian hissed.

'Or...?'

'Or something very nasty might happen to you.' Danny looked down and Jack's eyes followed to the hard wood of the stage far below. 'Theatres can be very dangerous places.'

For a moment they were frozen. Jack could feel the strength of Danny Kino's wiry body against his.

Then he was released. The comedian glanced at his watch before announcing, with another icy grin, 'Must go and get the frock on for the matinée.'

And he disappeared through the door.

MARIA GOT BACK in time for the matinée. She and Jack spent the rest of the day talking to other members of the 'Cinderella' company, searching out elusive clues.

It was frustrating work and took them through till nearly midnight. They were just saying goodnight to the stage doorman when a distraught Niki Grayes came rushing down the stairs.

'Ken! Ken! Have you seen Wink go out?'

'No, Miss Grayes. He definitely hasn't left the theatre.'

Her face went even paler. 'But I can't find him anywhere. Oh God, I hope he's all right.'

'Why shouldn't he be?' asked Jack.

'He's been behaving very strangely and . . . I found *this* in his dressing-room . . .' She held out a copy of the 'Cinderella' programme.

'What's so odd about that?'

Niki Grayes pointed to the back page. 'None of the others have got an advertisement for this restaurant.'

Jack and Maria exchanged glances. He took the programme. 'You go and have another look for him, Niki. I think this could be important.'

They scrutinised the advertisement.

TAKE-AWAY – DJYMBUL PREFAKH TWONG

After the panto, why not enjoy
world-beating Korean food from
our wonderful
restaurant?

NEAR BY THE THEATRE

'Is Korean one of your many languages, Maria?'

'No. Mind you, I'd be pretty surprised if that's actually Korean.'

Jack looked thoughtful. 'I've a feeling, like many puzzles, this one works by a process of elimination.'

Maria nodded. '"TAKE-AWAY"'s the clue, isn't it?'

Jack produced a pencil. They worked out the solution and filled it in in the third point of the star.

(Continued on p. 272)

# CUCKOO IN THE WOOD

★

## LESLEY GRANT-ADAMSON

A CUCKOO IN THE WOOD. When the sound of the machinery stopped Tom could hear it across the fields. Every year the same, as long as he could remember. A cuckoo sang in the wood in the month of May. It had sung when . . .

A shadow sloped across him as a fat man lumbered out of the bar and into the pub garden. Kear, it was, the one who'd been a policeman up at the town and retired to the village to be near his grandchildren.

Tom saw Kear settle himself on a stout wooden bench and put his tankard carefully on the table. Tom was a cider drinker himself. He watched as the pint was raised and flecks of foam stayed on the former sergeant's moustache. Then he slid his gaze away, up the hill beyond the elder hedge with its white parasols. Soon, when it suited him, he'd accept Kear's presence and they'd grunt a greeting. In the past, they'd had long conversations but not pleasant ones, what with Kear in uniform and paid for suspicion. Tom didn't like to think of that, it had been a bad time. Every year, though, the cuckoo brought it back to him.

Thirty-something years ago it had begun, when that girl, Mary, had come to live with her sister in the cottage by the wood. Unwelcome, the memories returned.

Tom had got ideas about Mary. Couldn't help it at all. And no wonder for Mary was always about the place, popping into the garden to the washing line or the chickens; stretching up to gather armsful of lilac, white and mauve;

crossing the fields on a short cut to the village. And he was always there too, riding the tractor or ditching or whatever task his father set him to.

Tom and Mary were always there, and her sister and brother-in-law were always out at work. Tom would sit in the shade of a May tree, open his cider jar, look down the hill to the cottage and make believe there was no other young man in the world but himself and no other girl but Mary. Occasionally she noticed him and waved, and how much he made of her distant wave! His dreams, his nonsense about her, carried him through her first season in the village. By the time the harvest was in, those dreams had grown into intention. He would have her for himself.

Tom did nothing about it, unless staring into the flames of the kitchen fire and conjuring a future can be called doing something. And then...

Another shadow fell across him, another man entered the pub garden, glass in hand. Bullman, who'd run the village shop until his retirement. Tom hadn't retired, not entirely. How did men retire on a family farm that was forever short-handed?

'Hot day, Tom,' said Bullman, wiping a hand over tanned skin.

''Tis hot enough for I.' Tom no longer noticed his accent, the quirks of grammar and dialect. There'd been a time when they'd shamed him to his tender core.

Bullman turned his head to Kear. A sheen of sweat prettified the fat man's bald head. Bullman said to him, 'Hot enough for you, Mr Kear?'

'Couldn't be better,' said Kear. 'Who needs to go to Spain when England's got weather like this?'

Bullman went on. 'The hottest May I can bring to mind. Not a time to be working out of doors, eh?' He waited for Tom's response and Tom remarked on hotter Mays, disastrous harvests, droughts, and the hills above the village alight with spontaneous fires no one could douse.

Kear attended to Tom, and Tom ignored him and spoke to Bullman. As Tom paused, the afternoon was filled with the heaviness of summer: damp grassy smells, bees fussing over yellow roses on the grey stone wall at his back, the excitement of small birds questing nest-building materials, and the call of the lonely cuckoo.

'Cuckoo. Cuckoo.'

Tom's other memories occupied the pause too. Mary, that first autumn, wide-eyed, not exactly mocking but caught off balance by him asking her—if in fact he *had* asked her. What he said was oblique, confused. Later he'd seen that and smarted at his own waste of an opportunity, not at her mild rejection. He continued to look down on her, when the field he'd reaped was stubble and when the stubble was ploughed in. Christmas, he decided, he'd ask her again at Christmas.

In November he spied her in the wood, in the arms of the salesman from the animal feed company. By spring she'd stopped walking over the farm to the village. When Tom met her in the lane one May afternoon the cuckoo punctuated their words.

'Why does it sing for just a few weeks?' she asked.

''Tis calling for a mate,' he said and felt the blood rise to his wind-browned face.

'Oh, yes.' She chanted the old rhyme. '*The cuckoo comes in April, it sings its song in May; it lays its eggs in June and then it flies away.*'

''Tis so, Mary.'

She said, 'I wonder where it flies to.'

Tom didn't know, but he knew that Mary was pregnant. He...

Bullman was speaking to him. 'Isn't that so now, Tom? A bad bend, a very bad one.'

Tom latched on. The road-widening for the village by-pass, that's what Bullman meant. Tom muttered agreement and sucked at his cider. An ant was coursing along the worn fabric of his working trousers. He brushed it aside, his hand broad and strong, a hand that heaved sheaves, steadied a ploughing team and lifted stone for walls.

Kear said, 'Forgive my saying so, Tom, but it'll be a good day for this village when the new road opens.'

Tom's family had resisted the scheme. It was robbing them of a swath of land and a greedy part of the wood. The cottage where Mary had lived, and which weekenders now owned, would survive but its outlook would be tarmac.

Tom let Kear's comment float by. He picked up Bullman's point about the dangerous bends in the lane and recited the names of the locals who'd misjudged it, not fatally but sufficiently to damage property and pride.

Bullman laughed, plucking at his throat where age had let down the skin in leathern folds. 'I'll bet you wouldn't mind a jug of cider for every time you've put the stones back in that wall.'

''Tis so,' said Tom. 'Mind, I always had a taste for walling. There be some tasks about a farm I can't abide, but walling, now there's one I do enjoy.'

'Just as well,' contributed Kear, still trying to join in. 'Remember when the cattle truck ripped a great section of it down, back in . . . oh, when was it now?'

They both knew. It was the year they had the difficult conversations, the year Mary's baby disappeared.

Tom shut his eyes against the burden of sunlight and called up a thirty-year-old picture of Kear. Slimmer, lean almost, and sweating in his regulation shirt sleeves. 'Tom, are you quite sure you didn't see anyone near the cottage?'

'Quite sure, Sergeant.'

And because no one else had seen anyone, Tom had never needed to veer from that denial. There was a search, there was repetitious questioning and there were appeals in the newspapers for information. But the baby remained missing and the village drew its own conclusions.

Sergeant Kear had put it to him: 'Tom, the mother claims the pram was in the garden. Says she put it in the shade of the laburnum tree and walked into the village. Too hot to push the pram, she says. Are you sure you didn't see anyone go near that pram?'

'Quite sure,' Tom repeated.

So Mary became known as a careless, ignorant mother who left her baby unattended in the shade of a poisonous tree, who delayed reporting him missing for two whole hours because she feared the wrath of authority and because she bred the wild hope that her sister had come home from work early and taken the baby somewhere with her. In days, rumour hardened against her: Mary had killed her own son and was concealing the body and the truth.

'Tom, you're the only one who doesn't accuse me,' she blurted out when he met her crying in the lane while he was repairing the ravages of the cattle truck. Usually vehicles toppled a few stones at the apex of the bend but the truck had flattened yards of it. Tom, always slow, was taking his time, making a good strong job of it, making sure it didn't all come down again.

'What do folks say to ee, Mary?'

She scrubbed a balled handkerchief over her eyes. 'Oh, it isn't what they say. They don't *say* much but they look. It's the way they look at me.'

He touched her then, for the first time. His fingers marked her bare arm with stone dust. 'Don't ee cry, Mary. That's the way folks do be. It don't mean nothing.'

She pulled away, slightly, exactly enough for his hand to fall free. 'Oh, Tom!' And she bowed over the broken wall and cried, not a delicate weeping that he might have attempted to console but passionately, with all the rawness of her anger and her loss.

Tom stepped away from her. Her grief put her beyond reach. He understood then that she had always been out of his reach. Firelit dreams and nonsensical plans evaporated before her intensity. Tom stared as she wailed, oblivious of him. Then he stretched out a roughened hand and took up a jagged hunk of grey stone which he added to his wall.

Bullman cocked an ear. 'A short break they gave themselves.'

The machinery had started up again, drowning out the cuckoo and the murmurous wood pigeons. Out of sight, round the flank of the hill, men were destroying the landscape in preparation for the new road.

Kear said, 'The sooner they get it done the better.'

'Won't be long, the speed they're going,' said Bullman. 'They're up to the copse field already. Could finish that stretch today, maybe.'

Tom didn't think they would. He sensed Kear peering at him. The fat man used to watch people while pretending to be doing no such thing, but since leaving the force he'd abandoned pretence. Kear had used his special way of watching when Tom was made to point out the places on the farm where a baby might have been hidden. The pond in the bottom field, the brook, the clamps. But the weed on the pond was unbroken, the nettles by the brook untrampled, the clamps undisturbed. In a day or two Kear's superiors had other work for him and he went away, not necessarily satisfied.

Tom breathed the spiciness of the pub's honeysuckle that was just breaking into flower. A reddish flower, it was. The one at the cottage was a golden tumble from the porch to the stone seat by the old-fashioned pump. If the bird annually conjured Mary for him, then it was honeysuckle that revived the day the baby vanished.

The pram hadn't been visible from where Tom was working. The porch cut off his view. He ate his lunch in the field, the combination of sun and cider spurring him to call on Mary again. Several times he'd done so and several times she'd said no, the baby took all her time.

Kear was wrong about the pram being in the shade. No doubt it was when Mary left it but the protection had crept away. The handle burned Tom's palm as he swung it round to wheel it into the lee of the house, once he realised Mary was out.

The jerk woke the baby. It cried, screamed. Tom lifted it, to pacify. The baby stiffened itself over his arm, resisting him with all its puny strength. Its bawling frightened him. He shook it. Silenced it. Killed it.

Thirty years he'd lived with the secret. For thirty years...

The silence he was expecting came. Sun scorched his cheeks and a bee brushed his ear. He stirred, opened his eyes.

Bullman was looking into his glass as he drank. Kear had his eye on Tom. Tom squirmed to rub his shoulders against the stone behind him and made a show of relaxing.

'Cuckoo. Cuckoo.'

Presently a car droned along the lane to the village, right up to the pub. Through the door to the bar they heard one of the men from the roadworks asking for a telephone. He tagged on an explanation. 'We've found something up there, under a wall.' The landlord took him to a back room where there was a pay-phone.

Tom drank the last of his cider. Bullman was admiring swallows slicing the sky. Kear and Tom studied each other.

Kear said softly, 'I wonder what they've found.' He said it like a man who wasn't wondering at all.

Some fragments of bone, some shreds of rag, thought Tom. Nothing to show who hid the tiny body there. He met Kear's eyes with a look that said nothing. Then, as the church clock struck two, he said goodbye to Bullman, took his glass into the bar and began the slow trudge down the lane and up to the top field where his brothers were turning hay.

# MRS CRAGGS
# HEARS THE NIGHTINGALE

★

## HRF KEATING

POM POM POM-POM pom-pom-pom pom, and a nightingale sang in Berkeley Squaaare.

'I dare say it did, dear,' Mrs Craggs said from down on her knees swabbing the kitchen floor of the prestige offices of the Zinc Development Association, Berkeley Square, London W1, where she and Mrs Milhorne were beginning their afternoon tasks. 'I dare say it did, but it never made no noise like you.'

Mrs Milhorne abruptly halted the sweeping slow foxtrot she had been performing in accompaniment to the music still in her head.

'I got a very nice voice,' she said. 'My rendition o' that song was what first drew Milhorne's attention. A lovely voice, he told me. Small, but lovely.'

Mrs Craggs forbore to ask whether it was that voice remaining small but ceasing to be lovely which had been responsible for any of the never-mentioned departures of Mr Milhorne. After all, she and Mrs Milhorne were friends, had been for years, and it wasn't fair to try friendship too far, truth or no truth.

Instead she gave a final swish of the cloth to her floor, rose to her feet, swilled out the cloth in the sink and began to take out of the big cupboard all the teacups and saucers which at half-past three exactly two pretty tea-girls would take round to the various offices in the building together with two chocolate digestive biscuits, just as at eleven in the morning precisely they had taken round coffee, together with two plain Petit Beurre biscuits.

Mrs Milhorne did not give Mrs Craggs any help. She was instead standing by the narrow window of the kitchen, looking down on the big tree-shaded expanse of Berkeley Square itself.

'Yaiss,' she said after a little. 'Yaiss, he's edging nearer. He's edging nearer. I said he would, and he has. He's edged a whole lot nearer.'

'Who's edged nearer what?' Mrs Craggs said. 'Half-past three's edging a whole lot nearer us, I do know. An' them old Zincs'll be wanting their teas.'

Mrs Milhorne ignored the second part of Mrs Craggs's remark and leant her bony frame a few inches further out of the window.

'Oh,' she said dreamily, 'I do like to see it. I do like to see young love.'

'That,' said Mrs Craggs. 'I might have guessed it.'

'Well, what's wrong with young love?' Mrs. Milhorne demanded, withdrawing from the window.

'Oh, there's nothing wrong with a bit o' love,' Mrs Craggs said. 'Provided it's at the right time an' in the right place. But Berkeley Square coming up to tea time ain't the right place and it ain't the right time.'

'You and your teacups,' Mrs Milhorne answered, making a vague move in the direction of the chocolate digestives which she was accustomed to place on the cups' saucers in a way that she clearly considered showed great artistic skill.

'Anyhow,' she said, 'I think it's her lunch hour. I think she gets her lunch hour late. I seen her before.'

'Oh, yes,' Mrs Craggs said, 'an' she don't eat a speck o' lunch either, but goes moonin' about with some young feller, I know.'

'No, you don't. First time she's met him.'

Mrs. Milhorne thrust yoke-thin shoulders out of the window once more.

'Oh, yaiss,' she said. 'They're talking now. Talking and sitting ever so close.'

She manoeuvred herself back in and gave a long deep sigh, mostly over the packet of chocolate digestives she had just opened.

'The first meeting,' she said. 'I remember it was just the same meself. Edging.'

'I thought he come up and said you'd got a lovely voice, but small.'

'That was Milhorne. That was later. Milhorne weren't the first. I was the belle o' many a ball, I was. In my day.'

Mrs Craggs, carrying a tower of cups round to the second tea trolley, glanced out of the open window. She had no difficulty in seeing the young man and the girl Mrs Milhorne had been giving her running commentary on. They were sitting on a bench inside the square underneath one of the huge spreading plane trees whose branches cascaded delicately down in the soft spring air. She was pretty, no doubt about that. Pretty as a picture, Mrs Craggs thought, with her neat head of swinging blonde hair and her crisp pink-and-white candy-stripe dress with the white cardigan just thrown across her shoulders. Just the way I was meself once upon a time.

Or, no, she acknowledged, the lass down there's something out of the ordinary. Prettier than a picture. He's a lucky lad if he's getting off with her.

She paused a moment longer to give the young man a rigorous inspection. And was not altogether sure whether he came out of it well or not. He looked all right. In some ways. He was tall and had a good pair of shoulders on him. Too much hair, of course. But most of them had that nowadays. Still, he looked nice and clean, and bursting with health too.

But those clothes. A pair of jeans all ragged at the bottoms. A pullover with frayed sleeve-ends. And, if she wasn't mistaken, a shirt collar that was as worn as her old piece of swabbing rag.

A girl as pretty as that deserved something better. And what was that he had on the bench beside him? A violin case, it looked like. A battered old violin case. What was a young man doing carrying round a violin case? Full of bombs, likely as not.

'Ain't they a lovely pair?' Mrs Milhorne's voice came from behind her, '*Pom* pom *Pom*-pom *Pom*-pom-pom *Pom*, and a nightingale sang in Berkeley Square.'

Mrs Craggs put down her tower of teacups with a sharp clatter.

'Be some o' those Zincs singing another tune altogether in Berkeley Square in a minute,' she said.

Mrs Milhorne hurriedly dabbed chocolate digestives by the pair on saucer after saucer.

'Yeah,' she said. 'It's a pity though that nightingales don't sing in the day, otherwise one might sing for the two o' them now. Lovely, it'd be.'

Mrs Craggs snorted.

'Nightingales not sing in the day,' she said. 'Lot o' nonsense. If you'd been brought up in the country like what I was, you'd know better. Nightingales sing just when they wants, an' good luck to 'em. Though I don't suppose it's very likely as you'd get one singing here in Berkeley Square no more, not now.'

'No,' Mrs Milhorne agreed. 'All this environment. They've all gone, the birds have. All gone.'

''Cept the pigeons,' said Mrs Craggs. 'Dirty beasts.'

IN THE DAYS AND WEEKS that followed, Mrs Craggs and Mrs Milhorne saw a good deal of the two young people who had met under the big plane tree in the square that time. Even the very next day it was clear that the talk the young man with the battered violin case had succeeded in having with the more than pretty girl with the neatly swinging blonde hair had been the beginning of something. For one thing, Mrs Milhorne spotted him waiting for her long before her lunch hour was due. 'I expect she's a secretary kept late,' Mrs Milhorne said. 'Managing director's secretary, that's what she'll be, pretty as that.' And for another thing, as soon as the girl did appear she made straight for the very same bench under the delicately cascading plane tree, and the smile she gave when she realised he was there was plain to see from right across the busy roadway.

The day afterwards when the two of them sat together on the bench it was with his arm round her shoulders straight away, and you could see, despite all the roar and racket of the traffic, that they were talking together and laughing together nineteen to the dozen.

Some time during the second week of it Mrs Craggs made a small discovery, one which she did not lose much time in passing on to her fellow worker.

'Secretary you said, managing director's secretary, weren't it?' she murmured over Mrs Milhorne's bony shoulder as the latter leant out of the window to look at the pair of them once more, her long pale face moony as if a nightingale really was singing out there instead of the traffic jostling and snarling.

'Yaiss,' Mrs Milhorne answered absently. 'Bound to be a top secretary. When you're as pretty as that, you get the job to go with it. I was thinking o' being a secretary once. Only I couldn't learn the shorthand, not with me nerves the way they've always been.'

'Saw her coming out o' her place o' work this morning,' Mrs Craggs said.

'Oooh, did you? Where was it? That big car showroom over the way? Or was it the posh flower shop? She might be an assistant there instead. Assistant going on to be manageress when she's a bit older. Yaiss, I like that. A pretty face among all them pretty flowers.'

'Chambermaid,' said Mrs Craggs.

Mrs Milhorne dropped a chocolate digestive and it shattered to fragments on the floor.

'Yes,' said Mrs Craggs. 'I was passing that big hotel just down beyond the far corner of the square there this morning and out she come.'

'Well, that don't mean nothing. I expect she's the manager's secretary there. All among them rich guests an' all.'

'Come out talking to another girl,' said Mrs Craggs. 'Talking about making beds and cleaning baths they was. Her name's Patty by the way. Patty.'

Mrs Milhorne put some more chocolate digestives on saucers with less than her customary artistic finesse.

'Well,' she said, after a while, 'it don't make him any less keen on Patty, her being that.'

'Being what?' Mrs Craggs asked, a little wickedly.

'Being what you said.'

IT WAS TRUE ENOUGH. If the boy with the violin case did know what Patty did for a living—and from the way they talked to each other all the time when they met, talked and talked and laughed and laughed, it was pretty well certain to Mrs Craggs and Mrs Milhorne that she had told him everything about herself from the day she was born onwards—it clearly made no difference to him. Even Mrs Craggs had to acknowledge that she had never seen two such lovebirds as the pair of them every day as they sat there under the big plane tree.

She wondered sometimes, however, about how much to do with himself he might have told Patty. It was the violin case that chiefly worried her. The boy always had it with him, but he never opened it. And Mrs Craggs couldn't quite get out of her mind the thought of bombs or something else nasty every time she saw it.

Until one day.

It was an afternoon that was, for some reason, rather quieter than usual on the roads round the square. The traffic, for once, was not racketing and jostling but flowed smoothly and easily. There was even a fashion photographer at work in the spring sunshine just outside the square's railings there, making a tall statuesque model walk up and down the pavement and snapping her time and again against the background of the peaceful gardens. ('I was going in for a model once,' Mrs Milhorne remarked.)

And suddenly, as Mrs Craggs and Mrs Milhorne watched, the boy did open the battered old case, and in it there wasn't the trace of a bomb or of anything else but what a violin case should have in it, a violin. The boy lifted the instrument out of the old case with delicate care and put it to his shoulder. And then he began to play. To play to Patty.

The sound of the melody—it was a love song, clearly a love song even if neither Mrs Craggs nor Mrs Milhorne could put a single word to it—floated up to them above the quiet whirring of the cars and taxis circling the square, sweet and rounded and true, and before very many moments had passed Mrs Milhorne was wiping the tears from her long pale face and even Mrs Craggs was constrained to give a quiet sniff.

'I know what he is now,' Mrs Milhorne said. 'He's one o' them great violinists. I bet he plays every day at that Wigmore Hall place on the other side of Oxford Street. I bet he does.'

But that afternoon, going home by tube for a change, Mrs Craggs discovered that once more her friend was labouring under a misapprehension. She decided next morning, when they arrived to do their early office-cleaning stint, that it would be kinder to break the news before Mrs Milhorne found out for herself. 'He's no great violinist, I'm afraid,' she said.

Mrs Milhorne bridled.

'Well, what is he then?' she demanded. 'I s'pose you're going to say he's a hotel waiter next.'

'Worse,' said Mrs Craggs. 'Hotel waiter's a steady job. And respectable.'

'Well, what's he do that's not respectable? An' Patty so pretty she deserves a hotel manager, never mind waiter.'

'Busker,' said Mrs Craggs. 'There he was just inside the tunnel into Bond Street tube. Playing away on that old fiddle of his. What they call "country" now, I think, though it's not the country I was brought up in. Silly American stuff.'

'Perhaps he was just practising there,' Mrs Milhorne suggested.

Mrs Craggs gave a rich snort.

'With a cap full o' pennies, an' ten pences too, there in front of him? Be your age.'

That afternoon the traffic round the square was back to its normal grinding and jerking racket and the boy's violin did not come out of its battered old case to sing its strangely sweet love song. Mrs Craggs was quite glad of that: she felt it would be a bit cruel on her friend to be reminded of that shattered dream of the concert violinist and the humble chambermaid.

And a day or two later she got to learn that Mrs Milhorne was not the only one to be disappointed over what the boy did in order to make ends meet. The first sign of trouble came during her own lunch break. She had gone out with

Mrs Milhorne and taken sandwiches and the evening paper into the square gardens because it was an even nicer sunny day. Suddenly Mrs Milhorne, who had been chatting away loudly enough about her nerves, broke off and thrust her face close to Mrs Craggs's ear.

'It's her,' she whispered, in a draught like the back end of a vacuum cleaner. 'It's her, Patty.'

Mrs Craggs looked round.

Patty had evidently been away from the hotel just past the far corner of the square on some quick errand or other, and she was now hurrying back. But on that wonderfully pretty face beneath the swing of neat blonde hair there was something more than a look of simple intent to get back to work as rapidly as possible. There was an expression of puzzlement. And more than a hint of anger, too. Had she passed by the side entrance to Bond Street underground station and seen someone there, someone making a living by busking?

Mrs Craggs made a point of getting well ahead with her preparations for tea for 'them Zincs' when they got back so as to be able to devote more than her usual time to looking down at the lovebirds under the big spreading plane tree. She had a feeling that all was not going to be as full of laughter and sweet looks as it generally was.

She was right, too.

No sooner had Patty arrived at the bench where the boy with the battered old violin case was waiting for her than she exploded. Up above and with all the noisy cars in between, Mrs Craggs and Mrs Milhorne could not of course hear a word that was said. But they hardly needed to. It was perfectly plain that Patty was bawling the boy out, up hill and down dale. And from the way her finger darted out and pointed like a shaft of fury at the violin case it was clear that this was indeed the seat of trouble.

The boy plainly tried protesting, but it was clear that he must in fact have been deceiving Patty all along about what it was that he did. And she was not going to put up with it.

'Quite right, too,' said Mrs Craggs.

'But they were so much in love,' wailed Mrs Milhorne.

'Well, if he really loves her, he'll do something about it still. He'll get himself a proper job and let her know he has. Why, he could go down the street to that hotel and get himself taken on there. Kitchen porter. Anything. But some respectable way of earning a living. And then he'd be sure to bump into her there, and things'd be as right as rain in two twos.'

Mrs Milhorne sighed.

'Oh, it'd be lovely. Lovely.'

But it quite soon began to look as if it never would be lovely at all. First, Patty wheeled round and marched off back towards the hotel—'an' she's not had a bite of their rolls,' Mrs Milhorne moaned—and then something altogether worse happened. Two police constables, who had been parading slowly past the square railings, suddenly began to hurry, almost ran round to the gate, went in and went straight across to the plane tree where the boy with the violin case was sitting stupefied on the bench. At once they began to question him, and soon it was clear that they were not being too polite about it.

'What's he done?' asked Mrs Milhorne. 'Whatever has he done?'

'I know what they think he's done,' Mrs Craggs said.

And she pulled from her sagging shopping bag her evening paper and pointed a lean finger at its banner headlines.

THE STOLEN STRAD. *Wigmore Hall Theft from Maestro*

A moment later it looked as though her guess was right. The policemen made the boy open his old violin case and then, despite his evident protests, they lifted the instrument from it and pointed out eagerly to each other some marks on the back.

'But he had that violin before the Strad was stolen,' Mrs Milhorne said. 'Or... or... oh, dear.'

A look of complete dismay came on to her face.

'Yaiss,' she said at last. 'Yaiss, that'll be it. He stole the Strad from the Wigmore Hall, threw away his own rotten old fiddle and put the stolen one in the case instead. Why, the dirty devil. I always knew he wasn't what he seemed. Said it a hundred times, didn't I?'

'No,' said Mrs Craggs, 'you didn't.'

Down below in the square the two policemen were hustling the boy away.

Mrs Craggs looked at them. And before they had quite got out of sight, heading in the direction of the police station at Vine Street, a look of determination came on to her creased and lined nut-brown face.

'Yeh,' she said. 'Yeh.'

She snatched her hat from the peg on the kitchen door and crammed it back on to her head.

'You'll have to see to them Zincs' tea on your own today,' she said to Mrs Milhorne. 'I got business to attend to.'

And, without another word, she hurried down to the ground floor of the glittering prestige office building and out into the square.

MRS MILHORNE WAS LATE for work next morning. Almost an hour late.

'It was the News,' she explained to Mrs Craggs when at last she did arrive. 'I kept waiting to hear the News to see if they'd got anything on it about the boy and the violin. There wasn't nothing in the paper, and you'd of thought there would be after all the fuss they made yesterday. I mean "Stolen Strad Arrest", that'd be news, wouldn't it?'

'It would be,' said Mrs Craggs. 'If there'd been any arrest.'

'What you mean? We saw 'em, didn't we? Saw them two coppers with our own eyes.'

'But that weren't all we saw with our own eyes,' Mrs Craggs replied.

'What you mean?'

'Well, didn't we see that boy—his name's Alan, by the way, Alan Lambert, and he's the son o' that millionaire Sir Peter Lambert, only he quarrelled with him and left home—well, didn't we both see him take his violin out of his case days before that Strad was stolen. An' didn't we both hear him play it, sweet as a nightingale?'

'Well, what if we did?'

'This is what. It was plain as a pikestaff to me that the boy had got a top-notch violin in his case all along. Busking at Bond Street tube he may have been, but that was no tuppenny-ha'penny fiddle he had, not by the way he took it so gentle from its case and not by the sound he got out of it when he played.'

Mrs Milhorne did some thinking.

'So you went along to Vine Street an' told them,' she said. 'An' they believed you.'

'Not a bit of it. That's why I never came back all afternoon.'

'But what then? They've let him go, haven't they? Young Alan.'

'They let him go. When we traced that photographer.'

'What photographer? I don't remember no photographer.'

'The one taking fashion pictures that day. Just when Alan was playing to Patty. Colour pictures they were, and they showed his own violin a treat. Wasn't no arguing about it after that.'

'Cor,' said Mrs Milhorne. 'So it all ends happily after all.

Mrs Craggs smiled then, a great big broad grin cracking her old nut of a face.

'It does end happy,' she said. 'But more than you thought. You ought to have been here at six this morning, like I was. You really did ought.'

'But why ever?'

'Because at six this morning, when it was quiet as quiet outside an' might have been right in the middle of the country, I heard the sound o' violin music. Music as sweet as any you ever listened to, right out there in the square.'

'It was him? It was Alan?'

'It was. And something more.'

'What? What ever?'

'You look out o' the window here. Look right across the square, and what do you see at the far end, past the big block o' posh flats?'

Mrs Milhorne thrust her scraggy neck as far out of the window as she could.

'Only the top of some tall building,' she said.

'A top with little windows in it?'

'Yes. There's windows.'

'Them's the windows right at the top of the big hotel there. The windows of the rooms where the maids an' that sleep. And one o' them windows opened a bit after the music started. It opened wide and someone leant out and waved. Waved and waved.'

'Patty. It was Patty.'

'Course it was. An' something more.'

'What more? There couldn't be no more, not after that.'

'There was. After the music had been going a little, I heard another sound. I swear I did.'

'What was that? What ever was that?'

Mrs Craggs looked at her friend. There was a tear in the corner of her eye.

'I heard it,' she said. 'I did. A nightingale sang in Berkeley Square.'

# IN THOSE DAYS

★

## LIZA CODY

11, Dock Road,
London

DEAR MR HARVEST,

I am writing to you on the very sad occasion of your sister's death because it may be a comfort for you to understand what actually happened. I know that in my own case, when my poor Arthur went with his kidneys, I could not really lay him to rest until I had found out exactly what went amiss. Afterwards I felt better. I don't know why. But in those days there were people to talk to, especially the Kings next door. You can get things out of your system if there's someone to talk to. Don't you agree? I hope you have someone. A death in the family is hard to bear when you are on your own.

I know you are Selina's brother because of that postcard I took to the letter-box two weeks ago, the one with the old-fashioned picture of bathing beauties with paper bags over their heads which said, 'Shame about the face' on the back. I shouldn't have read it, I know, but I was struck by the picture and wondered who your sister could be sending it to. Someone with a sense of humour, I decided. Anyway, people don't write secrets on postcards, do they? I wasn't entitled, but I wasn't really prying either.

Anyway, as you know, Selina came to live in my house four months ago. Well, you know she came to live at this address, but you probably don't know that it is my house. It was all my poor Arthur had to leave me and I have hung on to it through thick and thin ever since. Your sister must have told you a lot about it, and I can't imagine what you must think of me. But I would like you to know that it has only recently become the sort of house it is now.

You see, the neighbourhood has come down from what it was. A few years ago there were still business gentlemen staying here and one or two engineering students and a dental nurse. Respectable people, all of them. But times change and, what with container transport and everything, the area isn't what it was. I couldn't afford to sell the house even if I wanted to, not with the property market the way it is.

Beggars can't be choosers, I always say. The government doesn't look after old people the way it used to when this country was a welfare state. In those days, a pension was a pension. Not any more. I would be out on the streets if I didn't take rent from whoever is willing to pay it. I can't be as fussy as I'd like. I don't approve of what goes on here but I suppose it is a service of sorts. The only thing a person like me can do is maintain some small standards in the way of cleanliness, safety and hygiene.

It always puzzled me why Selina chose to come here. I know she said that photographers needed authenticity. But wouldn't it have been safer for her to stay closer to her home and take nice pictures of the people she knew? Then she wouldn't have had to come so far out of her way to find authenticity, and what happened wouldn't have happened. Really, a well-educated, nicely spoken young lady like herself has no place in Dock Road. I know, because I do not really belong here myself any more even though I have lived here for over seventy years. I should have moved out when Mr and Mrs King left for their son's place in Slough. They were the writing on the wall, if you get my drift. But I didn't

move and now it is too late. Maybe if I hang on long enough
the district will come up again. They have started developing about a mile down the river and built some lovely little
flats and shops. But they seemed to have missed out Dock
Road, which is a pity.

Your sister used to say that this area was 'the real thing'.
Although why it is any more real than Slough or Theydon
Bois I honestly couldn't say. It seemed real enough to me
when the only girl staying in one of the rooms was a dental
nurse. I mean, things don't have to be dirty to be real, do
they? Or girls, for that matter. I have always been respectable and I'm not less real for that.

I hope you don't think I'm criticising. I enjoyed having
Selina here. She raised the tone, and heaven knows it needed
raising. And she never talked down to the girls, although to
be honest most of them won't understand you if you don't
talk down. But of course, as her brother, you know Selina
better than I did, so it won't surprise you to learn that some
of her conversations were over people's heads. I myself was
never quite sure what she meant at any given moment and,
though I say it as shouldn't, I regard myself as being quite
well read—by Dock Road standards, anyway. Certainly I
was one of the few who knew where to find the public library in the days when there was one. The girls these days
leave school scarcely able to read the names of their lip-
sticks let alone a newspaper or a magazine. No wonder the
poor little things are reduced to what they are reduced to.

All they ever care about is money. I honestly don't think
your sister ever realised how much. They do what they do
for money and that's the be-all and end-all of it. They aren't
interested in their customers. They aren't even interested in
the job. They just want to do it as quickly as possible, get
paid and on to the next. You can't blame them, can you?
Not when you see the sort of customers they get in Dock
Road. What on earth is the point, I often ask myself, of

paying good money for whatever it is they pay for when they are so drunk they throw up all over my stair carpet? I wouldn't have allowed my poor Arthur inside the house in that condition, let alone my bed. And who has to clean up after them, I ask you? Well it isn't the girls. They wouldn't even know how.

I mustn't judge. Girls these days aren't brought up the way they were in my youth. We were taught how to polish a stair rail and how to turn a mattress. These girls don't even think it's necessary.

But I do think the old ways are the best so please don't think I've let things go completely at 11 Dock Road. As I said to Selina when she first came, I said, 'I can't vouch for what has gone on in this room but I can say, hand on heart, that the sheets were fresh on this morning. And you won't find dust balls under any of my beds.' I always scrub the baths out with Flash every day because you never know, do you? A person with a superior education, like your sister, will have appreciated that. Even if her clothes and shoes left something to be desired, she kept her books beautifully. There was never a speck of dust on them. But you can't get nasty diseases from books, can you? Whereas sharing a bathroom with a dirty person might give you something catching.

I am returning the books under separate cover. No one touched those. They are intact and just the way she left them. I can't answer for the clothes and toiletries though. There seems to be a shortfall somewhere in spite of the police locking the door.

What really worries me is your sister's camera. I know it was very valuable, and I can't seem to put my hands on it at all. If you ask me that camera went walking long before the police arrived. None of the girls will admit to even seeing it, but you can't trust what they say. I know for a fact they all had their pictures taken. And got paid for it too. To tell you the truth, those pictures weren't the sort you'd want to frame and put on your mantelshelf, I'm afraid.

I like a nice photograph. It was lovely when photos stopped being black-and-white and you could see the colour of the hats and frocks. I always wore a hat for any picture taken of me. Young ladies wore hats then. Now all my old hats are on top of the wardrobe in plastic bags, but no one wants to take my picture any more, not even Selina, so I suppose it makes no odds. When the time comes I'd like to be buried in a hat—the lavender one with the feather which I wore to Mrs King's eldest's wedding. I used to love a good wedding but you don't get them in Dock Road any more, and I can't see any of the girls at No. 11 getting wed. I mean, who would want to marry them after what they've done?

But you can't tell them anything. They think of me as a silly old woman, as if I was always the age I am now and as if No. 11 was always the sort of house it has become. And sometimes I ache for someone my own age to talk to. Yet, when I think of the shame of it I'm glad there's no one left. You see, I remember Mrs King—Susan Brown as she was then—I remember how we sat in the stalls of the old Majestic and watched Bing Crosby and Grace Kelly sing 'True Love' in the moonlight. We were young women then and nothing much had happened to us, but we sat in the dark with tears in our eyes for the romance of it all. I knew she had tears in her eyes because of the way she took her handkerchief out of her sleeve. That's another thing you don't see any more—a lady's handkerchief. And gloves. I sometimes ask myself where all those little white gloves and hankies went to. Hats, gloves, hankies and romance all disappeared from Dock Road years ago, and I wish I knew where they went.

I did try to explain to Selina once. She kept photos pinned to a cork board in her room where she could see them. I was in there with the vacuum one day, and I said, 'How can you bear to look at these awful things all day?'

And she said, 'They aren't awful. This is the most fundamental transaction in the world.' Or something like that. We were always talking at cross-purposes.

But they *were* awful. They were of the girls and their boyfriends and the customers. There was one photograph I particularly hated. She must have taken it from her window because it showed the derelict house opposite. One of the girls was leaning against the wall smoking a cigarette. And the man had just got out of his car and was sort of looming over her, talking to her. You could see from the way he stood and from the expression on her face just what they were talking about. It's funny, isn't it, how a picture can be disgusting without being actually rude.

So I said, 'Why don't you take pictures of nice, pretty things?' Because I suppose I was thinking of Bing Crosby and Grace Kelly, and how in the old days you used to see pictures that made you want to weep they were so lovely: things like brides and waterfalls and swans. Your sister's photos had the opposite effect, I'm sorry to say. It wasn't as if they were bad photos: you could see every detail, even the brand name on the cigarette packet and the number plate on the car. But you felt miserable and not quite clean just from looking at it.

She said, 'This is reality, Mrs B. Reality isn't nice or pretty.'

'It used to be,' I said and I finished vacuuming her room. I was wondering if your sister ever suffered a personal tragedy in her life to make her so bitter against reality. Because Selina was a well-spoken young lady with lovely manners, and she should have been married with a family, and not taking photos about the terrible things that happen in Dock Road. I mean, she had the chance, didn't she? She had all the advantages. She wasn't like the girls here who, I sometimes think, were born for trouble.

I'm afraid I won't be able to send the photographs with the rest of her things. It's just as well really because I'm sure they would have depressed you as much as they did me. That cork board disappeared before the police came, and when I asked about it the girls all said none of them had seen it. It was such a muddle that night. Everyone shouting and screaming and running every which way. And when the police and ambulance finally arrived, a good twenty-five minutes after I phoned, I was the only one left to talk to them. The girls and their customers had scattered to the four winds and left me to cope on my own.

They don't want the police in Dock Road any more. It isn't like the old days when people wanted to see the constable walking down late at night to try the warehouse doors at the end of the road. People used to say hello then, and many's the time we saw him chatting to customers outside the Prince of Wales of a warm evening. Nowadays nobody wants to know. It's the same with the ambulance men, although what on earth the ambulance men could have done to harm them I'll never know. Maybe they are allergic to uniforms.

I called the ambulance myself. As soon as I saw Selina at the bottom of the stairs I went back in my room and phoned. There used to be a phone in the hall, but I had it taken out for obvious reasons. You can't trust these girls even with a telephone, and I can't tell you the awful things I overheard in my very own hall.

I must confess that it was only the ambulance I called. The police came on their own. I may be a silly old woman, but I am not senile and I know the trouble I would be in if I had called the police to this house. My life wouldn't have been worth living. The girls and their boyfriends can be quite vindictive if they think anyone is getting at them. Es-

pecially the boyfriends. You might think I am a coward. But
you don't have to live here. I do. Which is why I never mentioned the missing camera or the photos. I do hope you understand and that you don't think I am keeping them from
you. I am an old woman, and I'm not very brave any more.
In the old days I would have had my poor Arthur to turn to.
But now I'm by myself in a house I can barely call my own.
Things go on here which I can't alter. I should be able to,
seeing as it's my house, but I can't.

I would have liked to send you everything Selina left, no
matter how depressing. After all, her property should be
yours by right. I would also like to be able to vouch for the
honesty of all my lodgers, but I can't do that either.

I am very careful with my own things, and I always keep
my door locked even during the day whether I am in my
room or not. I advised Selina to do the same but I don't
think she listened to me. I am not often listened to in my
own house.

Nowadays I am especially careful on the stairs. I mean if
a healthy young lady like your sister can have an accident
then think what could happen to an old woman like myself.
It is quite dark on the landing and anyone could miss their
footing. There used to be a light there, but I got so tired of
replacing the bulb.

I hate to think what you must be imagining about me and
my house, but you must understand what I mean by not
being able to vouch for the honesty of the lodgers. Fancy
stealing light bulbs! If you can't trust a girl with a light bulb,
what chance has a camera got, I ask you?

You see, in a way your sister died for the want of a light
bulb. I do feel bad about it, very bad, but at the same time
I can't really blame myself. No sooner did I put one in than
it went missing again. How many times can an old lady
climb a stepladder on a gloomy landing at the top of a long
flight of stairs? I wouldn't want to fall and break my neck

the way Selina did. In the old days I would have asked one
of my lodgers to do it for me. Some of them were ever so
obliging. But I couldn't ask those girls to do it. The stepladder might go missing too and I need that stepladder to
dust around the top of the wardrobe where I keep my old
hats. I know they are in plastic bags, but even so, nice things
get ruined no matter how hard you try to protect them.

But I mustn't go on about my hats, must I, when this is
supposed to be a letter of condolence. I am most awfully
sorry about your sister. I miss her too. And as I said at the
outset, I do hope you have someone to talk to about it. It
will make your loss much easier to bear.

Yours faithfully,
Rose Bratby (Mrs)

# SISTER BRONA AND
# THE PORNOGRAPHIC DIARY

★

## ALEX AUSWAKS

SISTER URSULA, who enjoyed shocking the others, poured herself a cup of well-stewed tea and made herself comfortable in the only armchair in the kitchen. 'I'll read you bits of what you all get up to when Mother Superior isn't prowling the corridors.' She already had her finger marking a particularly choice passage, which she delivered with due emphasis.

One or two of the kitchen nuns present made faces to indicate, 'We've heard this before.' From time to time material of this sort was left by accident or design. Besides, Sister Ursula was a notorious scavenger.

Sister Ursula looked round with the sort of smug look that indicated she still had something more shocking to deliver.

'This,' she said dramatically, 'happens to be a genuine diary by, shall I say, a genuine nun? Or a former genuine nun. It's the diary of our own dear ex-Sister Clare.'

'It was kind of her to leave it behind,' murmured one of the nuns, 'but surely it's for Mother Superior's manuscript collection.'

'It's only a photocopy,' said Sister Ursula.

'You mean a xerox,' said Sister Brona. 'Technically you must keep up with the times.' She enjoyed these mildly ambiguous constructions, which the others ascribed to her Irish upbringing.

'Where did you get it?' asked one of the nuns uneasily.

'Oh, it's all right,' said Sister Ursula. 'Mother Superior threw it away. You should have seen her face while she was reading it. I usually go through her room like a dose of salts, but I took my time with the dusting and all. You could tell which bit she was reading by the look on her face... or, rather, the looks that crossed her face.'

'It wasn't very kind of Sister Clare,' said another nun. 'Fancy sending Mother Superior such a thing, after everything she put her through.'

'Oh Sister Clare didn't send it. There was a letter attached.' Sister Ursula smoothed out the crumpled paper on the kitchen table. 'You see, our Sister Clare sold it to one of the posher Sundays. The editor sent Mother Superior what I would call a photostat or a photocopy or a photosomething. As a matter of courtesy before publication, he says, to assure herself that the diary was genuine and by the aforementioned Sister Clare. Hence a copy of the original.'

'And is there any doubt?' asked one of the nuns. Sister Clare had left under a cloud, casting imprecations at Mother Superior and all who prayed beneath her.

'The diary is in the school's special exercise books for exams,' said Sister Ursula in a voice of doom.

'There are dozens of schools that must use the same supplier as we do!'

'But ours are stamped all the way through with the school's name,' said Sister Ursula triumphantly, 'as suggested by our very own Sister Brona. Her father being in the gardai, it was her advice, to prevent pilfering.'

'Oh, Lord, she'll never forgive me,' said Sister Brona.

'Indeed she won't,' said Sister Ursula. 'Mother Superior has already given orders that nothing is to be stamped with the school's name in future. I think she prefers a bit of petty pilfering to "Revelations of a Nun" that can be traced back here.'

'And what's she doing about the diary?' asked one nun.

'Our Mother Superior?' said Sister Ursula, 'is no politician, as she often tells us. She is here to uphold the faith. She threw the diary into the wastepaper basket and telephoned Mr Simpkins not to handle this Sunday paper in his shop, starting this Sunday. Presumably, she'll let him know when the ban is to be lifted.'

'I think someone had better see Sister Marguerite,' said one of the older kitchen nuns.

EVERY WELL-RULED STATE eschews excess. And so, the presence of just one trait to excess (such as wisdom, charity, understanding, perception) precludes one from being its ruler. Sister Marguerite had more than one of these to excess.

Mother Superior neither liked nor disliked Sister Marguerite. She was insistent on treating everyone equally, was Mother Superior. (Perhaps those who are not politicians tend to be bureaucrats.) There was no reason why Sister Marguerite was to be listened to more than anyone else.

There were, however, certain nuns Mother Superior relied on should she need information to aid her in coming to a decision. One of those was Sister Berenice. Sister Berenice claimed it was only to make Sister Marguerite's ideas available to Mother Superior that she ingratiated herself. And so, when a crisis brewed up, nuns went to Sister Marguerite first, then to Sister Berenice who now had just that little bit of information she was sure Mother Superior would wish to be reminded of before coming to a final, final decision.

Sister Marguerite suggested that Mother Superior should be given the afternoon and evening to work out for herself (since she was no politician, but merely there to uphold the faith) the implications of such a scandal as the publication of the diary on the unfaithful. It did not require anyone with

Sister Marguerite's perception to work out that Mother Superior was not likely to go in person to inspect the original of the offending diary. Therefore, it was up to Sister Berenice to suggest to Mother Superior that it might be an idea to send Sister Brona to view the offensive diary. After all, it was due to her that the diary could undeniably be shown to have emanated from the school. After Sister Brona had viewed the diary and reported to Mother Superior, Mother Superior could ask for the time to study it in the light of the report. It would give time and room for manoeuvre. Mother Superior pounced on the advice. Yes, Sister Brona must be shown the consequences of her ill-considered advice; Sister Brona must go first thing in the morning.

In the meantime, Sister Marguerite thought Sister Brona ought to examine the xeroxes of the diary, to see whether there was any hope of it not being the real thing. To everybody's surprise, Sister Brona sat down to copying the diary. Well, she was Irish, and the Irish hardly ever did things in a straightforward manner.

TO SISTER BRONA'S surprise, the editor had a small office and a small desk. The diary now lay on it, the familiar exercise books with the school's name stamped on the covers and on random pages. There was no doubt of their authenticity.

The editor was disappointed in his visitor. He had been hoping to attract a bigger fish than this young nun. Secretly he had hoped Mother Superior would come in person. Well, the photographers stationed outside the building would have to make do with this one. The art department would have to touch up the pictures to show chagrin on the defeated face of this nun who would have to admit the diary was genuine.

'And do you use a word processor yourself?' asked Sister Brona, looking round her.

The editor was one of those Englishmen who could not take an Irish accent seriously. To him it belonged on the stage, the variety stage. He thought she was trying to impress him with her worldliness. He placed his Mont Blanc pen on the table. 'I'm afraid I'm old-fashioned,' he said.

Sister Brona looked at it enviously. How her father would have loved such a one. 'Indeed, and I prefer a pen, too. Of course, Sister Clare, that is, Sister Clare that was, she used a Biro.'

'Yes,' said the editor, wondering where all this was leading. 'These *are* your school exercise books,' he said.

'Actually, they're the ones we use for examinations. Internal examinations, of course. We bring them out twice a year, and that's the only time these particular ones are available.'

'You're not going to be petty, are you?' said the editor. 'What are you going to do, accuse her of stealing exercise books intended for exams? Or is that a breach of schoolroom security?' he added.

'Oh, but that's not it at all! You see, all of us sisters take turns invigilating, whether we are teaching nuns or whatever. It's a very boring thing to have to do, and you have to think of something to while away the time. Now I had a go at copying the diary from the xeroxes you were good enough to send Mother Superior. Oh, I mustn't forget to thank you for your courtesy. Much neglected, courtesy is these days. My Dad, he reckons country folk have more time for it than city folk. And, therefore, the more welcome when it comes from an important person like yourself. My Dad, incidentally, he's with the gardai, that's our police. He got sent to Dublin one time to do a crime prevention course. Very keen on crime prevention. It was my idea to stamp them, these books, so I feel a little responsible, seeing as you were able to identify our school because of that.'

It took all the editor's willpower not to break into a massive guffaw. The best they could muster was an Irish nun, whose old man was a country copper whose one and only perk had been a few days in Dublin, under the guise of a crime prevention course. Well, just to show the paper wasn't anti-Catholic in an ecumenical age they'd run a series on the unworldliness of the church in this day and age. Could it do justice to the challenges of modernity? Mustn't forget! His fingers curled round the Mont Blanc to make a quick note.

'You said something about copying...' he said. 'But why?'

'Oh, yes, with a Biro. Adds verisimilitude.'

'To what, for heaven's sake?'

'To my investigations, as my Dad would say,' said Sister Brona. 'Now what would you say if I were to tell you...' She leaned over and picked up two of the examination booklets from different places on the pile. 'Virtually the same Biros throughout, just as I thought. Same thickness, but only two, no, three shades in all that time. Must have come from the same supply. She couldn't have been using them for anything else, and her a teaching nun! But that's not all. Each exercise book carries a week in the life of this nun, who seems to have managed such a promiscuous existence. Now when you were sitting your exams, and a man in your position must have passed many an exam, did you notice that your last answer was always a little shorter as you ran out of time? Struck me last night, when I did my copying, that the last day for each week always had a shorter entry. And by the way, I was working in the kitchen. We've got one of those battery clocks, you know. Look awful, but keep time well. And would you believe it, every week in the diary took me roughly the same time to copy as one invigilation period.'

'I don't believe it!'

'I suppose it's hard to believe a former nun would do a thing like that, isn't it? But you know, if you've kept a diary yourself, have you noticed how in a diary you never cross out or alter? After all, nobody else is going to read it. But if you ever did a bit of creative writing, you go over and over and cross out and make corrections... Look at her crossings out and changes. There was a bit of creative writing going on there! That was no diary!'

'You're very clever, but you'll have to do better than that!'

'No, it's Sister Clare that will have to do better. I've brought out invigilation roster. If you're a betting man, you might like to put a bet on the number of booklets before you. Sister Clare always thought there was too much invigilation duty.'

He looked at the clear, wide innocent blue eyes. They had large arches and long fair lashes. Her cheeks were slightly flushed. If he had enough time, he'd break her down, break down the elaborate façade of evidence, all clearly circumstantial, that she had built up. There'd be no mercy on his part.

Her lips quivered slightly, as if she had read his intention. When she had taken her name, she had been warned, there was no saint of that name to appeal to for help.

'You've said yourself you're an old-fashioned person,' she said. 'Perhaps you're not a married man. Sister Clare is highly strung. You'd expect this to show periodically' (she pronounced the word slowly) 'now, wouldn't you? And yet there's no difference in style. Even the pen pressure on the paper is the same throughout, except as the invigilation period is ending and she hastily finishes off the last entry.'

The editor flushed as it came to him what she was driving at. A nun was teaching him what a woman could be like if she had difficult periods. If it got out of this room... He'd never be able to show his face wherever newspapermen forgathered.

'Now you mustn't be embarrassed,' said Sister Brona, suddenly overcome with shyness. 'Mother Superior wouldn't have liked one of her sisters to mislead a newspaper, especially a Sunday one. My Dad, he reckons RC stands for Renegade Catholic, but even so, Mother Superior would feel responsible for her.'

'I think you've got a bloody hide,' burst out the editor. 'My paper wanted to do the decent thing by you and give you a right of reply even before publication...'

Sister Brona rose. Sometimes she wished there had never been a Vatican Two, as it was called. At heart she was a romantic. She would have liked to sweep out, long skirts swishing, crucifix and tassel flying round her waist. And, oh, for a swan-like hat, large and white like Sydney Opera House. But then, with Vatican Two there were things a young nun could now say.

'No doubt you've an arrangement with a publishing house. Or a magazine. You could serialise that sort of thing in one of those. It would go down as fiction. So if you've paid for it, it's not irretrievably lost, the money.'

MR SIMPKINS DASHED OUT of his shop and intercepted her on her way back. 'Sister Brona, Sister Brona, Mother Superior says I'm not to handle...'

'Oh, I think it'll be all right. They were going to publish something she's just that little bit touchy about. I think they'll agree not to, and you can go ahead and sell it.'

Mr Simpkins was visibly impressed. It was no disrespect to the Holy Father to state that he was too far away to be a power in the land. But Mother Superior... 'Let me give you a little box of something for the sisters in the kitchen,' he said. 'You know, Sister Clare, that is, Sister Clare that was, always refused. Said it was bad for her. Took a packet of

Biros, instead. Said she wrote poetry. My daughter says she was always scribbling during exams. Not that our girls would take advantage and cheat when teacher wasn't looking.'

'Indeed not, Mr Simpkins, not our girls. And yes, thank you, Sister Ursula does have a sweet tooth.'

SOME CONSIDERABLE time later, Sister Ursula arrived in the kitchen and poured herself (as was her usual habit) some well-stewed tea. 'You can always depend on confiscating some light reading from the Simpkins girl. I wonder her father doesn't notice what she takes out of the shop.'

'You haven't been rifling the girls' desks?' asked one of the nuns.

Sister Ursula looked at her as if she scorned such activity. 'Nice cover. Lots of colour. Emphasis on *nun* and *diary* rather than author's name, which means the author hasn't quite made it yet. Obviously a first-time effort. Based on personal experience, there's the caveat.'

'What are you on about?' asked a nun.

'Sister Clare is in print,' said Sister Ursula. 'Not exactly upmarket. Magazine serialisation. I suppose it'll be hard covers next and then paperback.'

'Read us a bit, then,' said one of the nuns. 'Are we missing anything?'

'Oh, only the chance to fantasise. These teaching nuns need a spell in the kitchen. "What a nun dreams of"! Really! Anyway, why ask me to read it to you? Ask Sister Brona. We all know she was so taken with it in the days when it was still purely factual, she spent hours copying chunks of it on this very kitchen table.'

And she winked a big wink at Sister Brona.

# GIFTS FROM THE BRIDEGROOM

★

## MARGARET YORKE

ONLY TEN MORE DAYS to go!

'Are you nervous?' Wendy asked, meeting him by chance in the lunch hour. He had gone into town to buy tooth-paste; there never seemed to be time at weekends for such mundane shopping, for every moment had to be spent buying the things Hazel decreed essential to their future married life.

'Why should I be?' Alan answered. He'd known Hazel for over two years; they'd been to Torremolinos together, and had often made love in his bed-sitter. Once, when her parents were away, he'd even stayed overnight at The Elms, giggling with Hazel as they clung together in her narrow bed in the room where a row of stuffed teddy bears gazed down at their transports.

'It's going to be quite a do, isn't it?' Wendy said. 'How many bridesmaids are you having?'

'Three. Hazel's niece, and her friends Linda and Maeve.' He sighed. All three had to be given presents. He'd thought of gold bracelets, but it seemed Maeve wanted a pearl on a chain, and Linda favoured dangly earrings. This problem had yet to be resolved and the gifts purchased.

'Well, I'm sure it will be a great production,' said Wendy. 'Best of luck,' she added. 'I'll be thinking of you on the big day,' and she hurried off to her office.

Her words echoed in his head as he returned to his own office, where a pile of papers waited for his attention. If he worked hard and was never made redundant, in forty-two years' time—nearly twice as long as he had lived already—he might be head of a department and retiring with his graduated pension.

Retiring to what?

Why, to Hazel of course.

Through Alan's mind ran images of Hazel as she was now: small, pert and pretty, a bank clerk with the Midland. He saw also a mental picture of her mother, hair rinsed brassy gold, figure trimly girdled, neat ankles twinkly as, high-heeled on short legs, she stepped about her day, ordaining the lives of her family. Her husband was a civil servant employed by the local authority and they moved in ever rising circles. Hazel's mother had planned the wedding to the last detail; she had vetted the guest list, not permitting him to include Wendy, with whom he had been at school, because her father ran a betting shop.

A production, Wendy had called the wedding, and it was: like some sort of pageant, Alan thought.

Would Hazel choose his future friends? Alan's mind ranged over the years ahead, past the freedom to make love at will and the honeymoon in Corfu. At first, due to a hold-up in arrangements over the small first-time buyer's home for which they were negotiating, they would be living in his bed-sitter, to Hazel's mother's great chagrin; but later there would be the house, then a bigger one when their finances improved. One day there would be children. He foresaw their regimented lives, their freshly laundered, spotless white socks and shirts, their well-scrubbed faces, their diligently completed homework, all firmly supervised by Hazel. He thought of the comforts he would enjoy: the well-cooked food, the tastefully furnished home for which even now he was committed to paying by instalments. The previous weekend they had chosen an expensive three-piece suite. The salesman at Fisher's Furnishings had said it had been made by one of the foremost firms in the world. Testing its suedette comfort, Alan had wondered; he had wondered, too, about the cooker Hazel had selected, split-level hob and all, which would take up so much space in their tiny kitchen. He thought of the money in his building society account, all pledged in advance for coping with the down payment on the house, and with an effort he turned his mind's eye to Hazel in her bikini, spread out on a Corfiote beach. As he stood, eyes closed, on the marble flooring of the town's new shopping arcade, he felt her soft, responsive body in his arms. All that would be wonderful, he knew; it already was when they had the chance.

But first there was the wedding, that performance which must be enacted to please Hazel and her mother. There would be Hazel's progress on her father's arm up the aisle of the local church, which Hazel herself had visited only once to hear the banns read, and her mother on the other two occasions to show willing to the vicar. There had been half an hour's talk in his study with the vicar himself, when Alan and Hazel were advised to show tolerance to one another throughout their lives, expect from each other not perfection, but simply kindness, and adjured not to give up at the first sign of trouble but to work through storms into harbour.

Standing there while the shoppers eddied about him, Alan knew panic. What had he done in his twenty-three years? Where had he been? What could he look forward to, except routine?

He'd gone straight from school into his first job with the firm which still employed him. He had been to Spain and Ibiza. He had spent a day in Boulogne.

There was a whole world beyond this town—a world beyond Spain and Corfu. There were Australia, Thailand and India. There was China, too, and he'd see none of them, for

Hazel and their children would have to be fed and the mortgage must be paid.

As he went back to his office, Alan knew that Wendy's words had changed his life for ever.

Five days later—it took him that long to work out a plan—Mrs Doreen Groves, whose husband managed the bank where Hazel worked, was just washing up the breakfast things when the telephone rang.

'Mrs Groves?' asked a voice, male, and carefully articulating.

Mrs Groves owned to her identity.

'I'm afraid I have bad news for you,' said the caller, and went on to tell her that Mr Groves, driving to the bank earlier that morning, had had a serious accident and was on his way to hospital by ambulance. Because of the grave nature of his injuries he was being taken, not to the local hospital, but to the regional one twenty miles away where all facilities were to hand. There was no answer when she asked for more details.

For some seconds Mrs Groves was made immobile by shock. Then she attempted to dial the bank to find out if the assistant manager could give her more details, but the telephone was dead.

Alan had not cut the line. In the nearby call box, from which he had rung Mrs Groves, he had inserted enough coins to keep the connection for several minutes, and he left the receiver off the hook while he hurried round to the Groves' house. He slipped into the garden through the fence, and under cover of the shrubbery went up to the side of the building where, on an earlier reconnaissance, he had observed that the telephone line was attached, and snipped the cable neatly. He waited, hidden behind some laurels, while Mrs Groves reversed her Mini out of the garage and sped off. Then he returned to the telephone box, replaced the receiver, and made a call to the bank.

He asked to speak to the manager. It was an urgent matter, he said, concerning Mrs Groves. To the girl answering the telephone he said he was a police officer, and gave his name as Sergeant Thomas from the local headquarters.

When Mr Groves came on the line, sounding worried as he asked what was wrong, Alan held a scarf to his mouth and spoke in a false voice. His heart beat fast with excitement as he told the manager, 'We've got your wife. Bring fifty thousand pounds in used notes, fives and tens, to Heathrow Airport by twelve noon. More instructions will wait for you at the information desk in Terminal Two.' Alan had intended to ask for twenty thousand; he was quite surprised to hear himself name the larger sum. 'And don't get in touch with the police or it will be the worse for your wife,' he remembered to add, in menacing tones.

He rang off before Mr Groves could reply. Would it work? He'd read somewhere that bank managers were instructed to pay up at such times—to risk no one's life—although certain alarm routines had to be followed. It was a pity he'd never asked Hazel more about security measures; he knew that she was not meant to disclose what precautions were operated and until now he hadn't been interested. He had tried to turn the conversation that way at the weekend, but she'd wanted to talk only about the wedding.

Alan had already telephoned his own firm to say he wouldn't be coming in, pleading a stomach upset. There were jokes and quips about first-night nerves.

After making the call, Alan got straight into his ramshackle old Fiat, which Hazel had long since condemned, and drove to Heathrow. He left the car in the short-stay park and crossed to Terminal Two, where he noticed a boy wandering around without apparent purpose. Alan said he was late for his flight and asked the lad to deliver a note to the information desk. He gave the boy a pound and, skulking among the shifting people, watched to see his commission executed. Inside an envelope addressed in capital letters to Mr Groves were instructions to place the bag beside the nearest newspaper stand. Alan intended to walk rapidly by, collecting it as he passed and vanishing into the crowd before he could be detected. He felt sure that by now the police would have been alerted in some manner. As soon as she reached the hospital, Mrs Groves would have discovered that her husband had not been admitted, but she was sure to be confused. She might telephone the bank, but by then Mr Groves would have left with the ransom if he were to reach the airport by noon. He would have had no problem in finding the actual cash; now Alan wondered with misgiving whether there might not be some bugging device attached to its container. If Mrs Groves was known to be safe, the police might be close behind her husband, wanting to pounce when Alan claimed the ransom.

He began to feel uneasy. What had seemed a perfect plan now revealed flaws.

Mr Groves was, in fact, almost at Heathrow before his wife learned that the call to her had been a hoax. She spent some time telephoning other hospitals before she rang the bank, and in the interval Mr Groves had parked his car in the short-stay park near a small, shabby Fiat which looked very like one he had seen outside his own house that morning.

Awaiting his prey, but with waning confidence, Alan tapped his pocket. The previous day, he had withdrawn all the money that stood to his credit with the building society. It was not fifty thousand pounds, but it was enough to keep him for some time and it was all rightfully his own. He had his passport, and a small case in which he had planned to transport his booty out of the country.

As suddenly as Wendy's words had earlier opened his eyes to the future, Alan saw that if he went ahead with his plan he would never be free from fear of detection. Here was another moment of decision, and there was no need for any theft; he could simply walk away from the rendezvous and disappear. No one would connect him with a dumped case of banknotes.

Alan went to the Air France desk, where he bought a ticket to Paris. His original plan had been to drive to Dover, sell his car there for whatever it would fetch, and catch the ferry to Calais. He had been afraid, if he flew, that the security inspection at the airport would reveal the wads of money in the case, but now he had nothing to dread.

He'd spend a few days in Paris, then hitch south, maybe to Rome. Perhaps he could pick up some work as he went along. He'd stay away at least while his money lasted, possibly for good, depending on what opportunities arose.

At the airport post office Alan mailed, second-class, a package to Hazel. It contained the tickets for the honeymoon in Corfu; she could still use them, taking Linda or Maeve with her. He attempted no explanation beyond a note saying he was sorry to upset her but he wasn't ready to settle down just yet and it was better to find that out now rather than when it was too late. Luckily, he hadn't bought the bridesmaids' presents.

Alan sat in the plane waiting for take-off. To the other passengers he was just a young man on a business trip with the minimal luggage of a small bag and his raincoat; only he knew that at last he was starting to live. He could always come back one day; even if the hoax telephone calls were attributed to him, such a minor offence wouldn't merit much of a punishment. At the moment he felt that a journey to freedom now was worth a few months in jail later on.

In another area of the same plane sat an older man on his way to adventure.

Mr Groves was six months short of retiring. He did not look forward to spending more time with his wife, who was one of life's cosseters and would fuss over him much too tenderly, making him old before his time. She had turned down his suggestion that they should go on a trip to Australia; even a cruise did not appeal to her. A stay-at-home girl was Doreen, and their holidays, apart from a weekend in Venice, had been spent in either Scotland or Cornwall. She'd made him into her child, perhaps because they had none of their own.

If they had, he couldn't have done what he was doing now. On the way to Heathrow he had called in at his home. The cleaning woman did not come today, and it had been odd to find the breakfast dishes still in the sink. There were, however, no signs of struggle.

Poor Doreen! How terrified she must have been, he had thought, and, on impulse, collected his passport from his desk; who knew where the trail might lead?

On the way to the information desk in the main concourse at Terminal Two, another impulse had turned Mr Groves towards a telephone, from which he had called the bank. They might as well know he had arrived. The police might have some instructions for him—if they were shadowing him they could not come forward now, just as he was about to 'make the drop', wasn't it called?

Mr Groves had been told that his wife had telephoned and, though distressed, was unharmed. She had been to look for him at the hospital as the result of a hoax telephone call; the whole thing was some prank.

Mr Groves had replaced the receiver, relieved beyond measure to know that Doreen was safe. Then he realised that here he was, as a result of someone's idea of a joke, with fifty thousand pounds of the bank's money.

What a chance! But the police would be watching him and he mustn't waste time.

He had collected the envelope left for him at the desk— there had been one; the hoaxer had clearly meant business—opened it and read the message. Then he had turned and gone, as if instructed, to the Air France counter where he had bought a ticket to Paris. The police would reason that, having discovered his wife was safe, he intended to lead them to the perpetrator of the hoax kidnap. It would be some time before they would suspect him of having fled himself. Interpol might have to be invoked, and by then he would be on his way to Australia. If he were to be traced, he could be extradited from there but there might be time, before he was apprehended, to move on to Spain, where barons of crime still lived in safety, although he thought plans were afoot to end that.

Mr Groves mingled confidently with the other travellers at Charles de Gaulle airport. He noticed a pretty woman, perhaps thirty-five years old, walking ahead towards passport control. The world was full of pretty young women with broader views than those of his wife. Hitherto a strictly moral man, Mr Groves's thoughts dwelt happily on the delights that might lie ahead.

Thus enjoying his future, he saw a young man who seemed vaguely familiar going through customs. He carried only a case and a raincoat, and he looked eagerly confident, the world at his feet. Ah youth, reflected Mr Groves, and his mind turned to Doreen. She would be very upset and she would never forgive him. No matter what happened now, he could not go home because he had stolen the bank's money. Well, at his age it was easy to resolve that he would not be caught alive. He would seek present pleasure, and if capture threatened he would take the final escape.

HAZEL WEPT when the holiday tickets arrived. How dreadful of Alan to behave like this! She could not understand what had got into him; it was all so humiliating.

Her mother was furious, but it seemed that Hazel had, in the nick of time, been saved from wrecking her life. To think that that quiet young man could be so deceitful!

She drew comfort from the troubles of others, however, when she learned that Mr Groves at the bank had apparently set up a fake kidnap to lure his wife from home, then pretended to receive a ransom demand so that he could obtain a large sum of money and flee the country. The police had found his car at Heathrow. Oddly enough, Alan's car was found there too, in the very next bay. It was almost as though the two had conspired.

# THE CHRISTMAS CRIMES AT 'CINDERELLA'
## PART FOUR: 28 DECEMBER

★

### SIMON BRETT

THE TWO INVESTIGATORS looked at the tiny word revealed by 'taking away' the letters of 'DJYMBUL PREFAKH TWONG' from the restaurant advertisement. 'Just games!' Jack Tarrant snorted. 'Delaying tactics.'

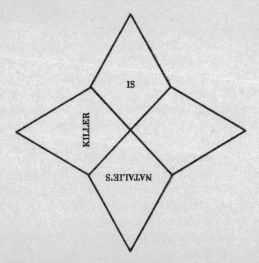

'So now we've got three-quarters of the murderer's name,' Maria mused. 'An N, a K, and an I . . .'

'So who do you fancy?' Jack asked wryly. 'Freddie *Link*? *Niki* Grayes? *Wink* Carter? Danny *Kino*?'

'Don't know yet. But it's someone with that kind of mind. Ricky Sturridge said Wink Carter was very into word games.'

'And Danny Kino has a reputation as a practical joker. Mind you, now I come to think of it, I've seen Niki Grayes doing the *Times* crossword...'

'Yes, but she's eliminated because she was with Freddie Link at the time of Natalie's murder, wasn't she?'

At that moment the actor in question stumbled out of his dressing-room by the stage door. Clearly, since the curtain went down, he had been playing his favourite game with a whisky bottle.

'Freddie,' said Jack, 'just talking about you...'

'Flattered, old boy,' the actor mumbled.

'Niki Grayes was definitely in your dressing-room at the time Natalie Maine was killed, wasn't she?'

'No question about it.' A shrewdness came into Baron Hardup's bleary eyes. 'Still investigating the murder, are you? Still trying to get Ricky Sturridge off?'

They didn't deny it.

'Everyone knows what you're up to,' Freddie went on. 'I wonder if that's what was worrying young Wink this evening...?'

'What do you mean?' asked Maria.

'Well, he seemed all over the place, didn't you notice? Dreadful in our sing-along scene. Clearly got something on his mind. Probably knows you're on to him.'

'But we aren't necessarily on to him.'

'He thinks you are. Because of what Danny Kino said.'

'What was that?'

'Heard them in the wings, just when we were about to go on for the kitchen scene this evening. Danny sidled up to

Wink and said, 'Watch your back. Jack Tarrant and Maria Lethbury are getting very close to the truth.'

'Oh,' said Jack.

'Ah,' said Maria.

'And certainly,' Freddie went on, 'the boy's performance fell apart from that moment.'

Jack nodded. 'You're right. Something like that could really panic someone as unstable as Wink. I wonder if he's got—'

He was interrupted by a terrible sound. A cry, only just recognisable as human—a cry that was suddenly cut off by a booming impact which seemed to shake the whole theatre.

'It came from the stage!' Jack shouted, as he and Maria hurtled towards the pass-door.

The scene they witnessed from the wings was a grim one. A solitary working light illuminated the stage, in the middle of which, crumpled and misshapen, lay a human form, from which a feeble moaning escaped.

'Oh no!' Maria murmured. 'It's Wink.'

'He must've fallen from the flying gallery.'

The boy, still dressed in Buttons' walkdown suit, was unconscious but alive. Just.

While Maria hurried to summon the emergency services, Jack Tarrant leant down over the body. He found what he was looking for pinned on to its silver lamé chest.

A Christmas card, bearing a picture of a snow-covered Maltese cross. Deftly Jack detached it and read the nonsense message inside. Recognising the clue in the cross, he quickly worked out the answer to the last of the 'Cinderella' murderer's puzzles.

*What larks what fuss what a to-do*

🎗

*But at last you have a final clue*

🎗

*Wish you a wonderful New Year too*

*

'AMBULANCE ON ITS WAY.'

Jack looked up at Maria's approach and indicated the answer he'd written in the final point of the star. 'Confirms it. The puzzles were just games. This boy has a very sick mind.'

'Still, the anagram works.'

'Oh yes. It was definitely Wink who killed Natalie Maine. Thought he was clever enough to run circles round everyone—hence the puzzles. Then he panicked and...this is the result.'

'Do you think he'll survive?'

Jack pursed his lips. 'Pretty unlikely. I'll go in the ambulance with him . . . just in case he comes round.'

They heard a slight sound. In the wings on either side stood Niki Grayes and Danny Kino. As they looked at the crumpled heap of silver lamé, both of them wept uncontrollably.

But then, of course, they were both very good actors.

JACK HAD GONE to the hospital with little hope of witnessing more than Wink Carter's death. Maria agreed to wait till he came back.

There weren't many people in the theatre. Ken was dozing in his cubbyhole. Niki Grayes and Danny Kino were in their dressing-rooms, nursing their grief.

Maria climbed purposefully up to the flying gallery. She took out a pencil torch, as she moved along the narrow catwalk amid stalactites of dangling ropes. The torch beamed on to the wooden protective rail and she saw what she half feared, half hoped she would find. A section of the rail was broken and hung crazily over the void.

Perhaps it had given way under the weight of Wink Carter's suicidal body. But Maria's probing torch beam found another explanation. The break in the rail was clean and bore the marks of a saw. Maria Lethbury breathed deeply in the stillness as she planned her next move.

Decisions made, she went swiftly back down to the stage. At the stage manager's desk she put the first part of her plan into action. Then she woke Ken and gave him his instructions.

As she stood outside Danny Kino and Niki Grayes's dressing-rooms, her heartbeat accelerated.

She knocked on one door, went inside and spoke briefly to the occupant. Emerging, she knocked on the adjacent door, and asked the person inside to come down to the stage with her 'just to check something out.'

The two of them stood by the stage manager's desk. Still, just the one working light was switched on. It caught the dull gleam of congealing blood where Wink Carter had fallen.

'What's this about?' asked the suspect.

'About how you killed Wink,' Maria replied evenly.

'What? He killed himself. He realised he was going to get caught for Natalie's murder, and couldn't stand the pressure.'

'I don't think that's what happened.'

'You mean you don't think he killed Natalie?'

'Oh, no. He did that all right, but you made him do it.'

'Why would I do a thing like that?'

'Because there was a job you wanted and Natalie Maine stood in your way.'

'Supposing that was true, why would Wink do as I asked?'

'Because you have a very strong personality and are very single-minded in pursuit of what you want. Wink was a confused and suggestible young man. He thought you loved him. By doing your bidding, he thought you'd...maybe give yourself to him...maybe leave him alone...?'

'I thought, according to your friend Jack Tarrant, Wink had confessed. In some puzzle or something.'

'Oh yes. You set those up brilliantly. Just as you set up the framing of Ricky Sturridge. It was all very carefully worked out.'

'Thank you.' For a moment, in the face of this flattery, the murderer's guard slipped. 'This is all very interesting, but do you actually have a shred of evidence to support your theory?'

'Some one sawed through the railing in the flying gallery.'

'Difficult to pin that on me. I was extremely careful.'

Maria seized on the lapse. 'So you admit you did do it!'

Her reward was a patronising smile. 'Yes, I admit I did it, but I know you can't prove that I did. The police like nice open-and-shut cases. Wink murdered Natalie and then killed himself when the investigation was getting too close for comfort. Very neat. They won't look further than that. So I'll be in the clear.'

'But you've just confessed!'

'Nobody else heard my confession. It's your word against mine.'

Maria grinned. 'Really?' She turned to the desk. 'You know this is where the stage manager sends calls out over the Tannoy...?'

'Yes. Of course.'

Maria pointed to the Tannoy key, switched to its 'on' position. 'Everything you've just said has been heard by the person in the dressing-room next to yours.'

She was amazed by the savagery of the attack as the murderer leapt at her. She saw the flash of a knife and grasped at the descending wrist.

It was very fortunate that the police, alerted by Ken, and the witness from the dressing-room upstairs burst on to the stage at that moment.

AFTER THE MURDERER'S arrest, Maria Lethbury felt profoundly relieved, but also at something of a loose end. To pass the time, she sat in Ken's cubbyhole, writing.

She was there when Jack Tarrant returned from the hospital. 'Poor kid never regained consciousness,' he said grimly.

Maria was downcast for a moment. 'Well, at least his death has not gone unrevenged.'

'What do you mean?'

And she told Jack what had happened during his absence.

'So who was it, Maria? Which one?'

She smiled and pushed across the piece of paper on which she had just been writing. 'The answer's in this puzzle, Jack. Just what everyone needs at this time of year.'

MARIA LETHBURY's PATENT HANGOVER CURE
Ingredients:
    1 pint of lemonade
    ¼ pint of ginger ale
    4 measures of gin
    4 measures of rye
    2 measures of saki
    1 clove of garlic
    the juice of 4 lemons
    2 tablespoonfuls of demerara sugar

Method: Mix the alcohol together and that will be the end of all your headaches.

(Solution on p.311)

# STONESTAR

★

## REGINALD HILL

---

I WAS BORN IN A HOUSE called Stonestar, so that's what I say when they ask my name.

IT WAS SET on a rocky shelf above a northern river. Behind it, a hanger of pines trapped whatever of the evening sun might have slid over the western fells, so that it was always early dark at Stonestar which made the locals say the house was haunted. But in the morning it drew in all the golden light from the east, and seemed to store it in the very granite, so that even in the greyest dawns the old house woke up glowing.

'STONESTAR?' says the smaller man, opening up a scruffy notebook. 'Spell it.'

The bigger man is twisting my arm further up my back in case I need encouragement. But I rejoice to see the letters painfully penned into the book. That gives them substance, that gives them life.

THE LOCALS WERE RIGHT though they didn't know it. The house was haunted, but not by any shades of night.

There was a big golden cat used to carry its litter one by one out of the stable into the sunlit yard, and lay them on the warm cobbles, and wash them with her rough tongue till the little ones yowled in protest and pushed beneath their mother in search of her teats. But if you went towards them with hand stretched out to stroke, then cat and kittens vanished in a trice.

And there was a horse that would whinny in the empty stable and often you would hear its hooves beating across the paddock and feel a rush of air as it galloped past you, full of joy in its own raw strength.

And there was a baby that would cry upstairs in the little nursery room, not a distressful cry but just the noise a baby makes when it wakes up hungry, and very soon it would change to a contented gurgling, as if its mother had picked it up and put it to her breast.

'STONESTAR! Wake up! You'll get no sleep till you tell us the truth. Where did you hide the body, Stonestar? How did you kill her, Stonestar?'

And the light burns in my eyes, the hands twist in my hair, the fists drive into groin and belly. And I scream and weep and vomit, and inside I am laughing because the fools do not know what a healing, protecting magic I have put into their mouths, do not realise how every time they snarl and spit my name, I draw strength from simply hearing it.

STONESTAR. It was what I always whispered to myself in time of trouble. It was often all I had in the world to comfort me, and it never failed. Stonestar. A house haunted by happiness. Sometimes you would smell the sweet crumbling odour of baking bread though you knew the kitchen was empty and the great oven cold. Often you could hear fiddlers playing a jolly jig in the old gallery though the boards were rat-gnawed and rotten. Always I heard the laughing voices of merry companions as I ran naked down the sloping meadow to plunge deep into the shining river.

I was an only child but never a lonely child at Stonestar.

'STONESTAR, this silence will get you nowhere. No use denying anything. The servants have identified you. You were seen carrying her through the streets. What have you done with her, Stonestar? Speak, man. It will go easier with you if you tell us.'

EASIER! I know their *easier*. It would have been easier for my father to give up Stonestar when they first approached him. All the valley from the first bubblings of the newborn river to the deceitful wastes of the sandy estuary belonged to Milady, all save the broad meadows and proud old grange of Stonestar. These she wanted too, for though young in years, she was old in arrogance and saw no reason why her riotous guests should not range at their will in pursuit of deer and otter, hare and partridge. Not that my father, true to the tradition of country sport, ever put obstacle in their way. All he asked was to be told in advance so that he could fold his sheep and byre his beasts out of harm's way.

But this smacked too much of asking leave, and Milady did not care for such demeaning.

Instead she sent her factor with a bag of gold and a contract to purchase.

My father refused courteously.

The man returned with more gold and something of menace in his tone.

My father rejected the new offer with less courtesy.

The following week, the hunt drove through Stonestar's meadows without warning, frightening a dozen lambing ewes into the river, where they drowned. When my father went down to the Castle to complain, he found the gates barred against him and the dogs loose.

Now he looked to the law for compensation and found as many before that once you set foot on that road, you face a long and wearisome journey, and uphill all the way.

Meantime, the hunt passed over his fields again and again, terrifying stock and ruining crops. Mysterious fires broke out in his coppices and stacks. Streams were damned and diverted. And just below the boundary of Stonestar land, a barrier was set up across the valley track and a toll-bar established.

Here was more material for the law. Milady's factor produced old parchments which he claimed gave the owner of the Castle the right to levy tolls to subsidise the upkeep of the track. The lawyers settled down to another long and for them profitable debate, while the toll-bar remained and the assaults on Stonestar land and stock continued without bate.

All this was before I was born, yet I did not escape its effects even in the womb. My mother, a delicate lady, saw her pet spaniel pursued and torn to pieces by a pack of hounds. The shock sent her into labour early. The doctor was sent for, but had not arrived when the final contractions began, and I was brought into the world by my father and an old half-blind maidservant.

An hour later the doctor arrived. Seeing that both mother and child were in perilous straits, he wasted no time on apology or explanation, but set about his work.

Me he was able to preserve, but for my mother it was too late. She held me in her arms a little while, then he took me from her, and she died.

Now the doctor spoke.

'I set out as soon as I got your message,' he told my father. 'But I was held for more than two hours at the toll-bar. They said that no one could pass after dark without Milady's permission, and neither she nor her factor could be found.'

So ill-auspiciously my childhood began.

My father was quite overthrown by my mother's death. Almost bankrupted by his pursuit of justice through the courts, he turned off his staff one by one and was eventu-

ally reduced to the status of smallholder, keeping only that
stock and growing only those crops necessary for his own
and his child's needs. Nor was there money for the upkeep
and repair of the house. Dust lay thick on the unswept floor
and rats ran free through the empty barns.

Yet I was never neglected. Though to the inhabitants of
the district my father must have appeared a strange, un-
couth man, driven half mad by misfortune, to me he was
everything—father, mother, nurse, teacher, friend. It was
his words that conjured up those happy ghosts, it was his
love that wrapped me in the golden world of Stonestar.

'STONESTAR, why did you do it? Were there others in the
plot with you? Give us their names and you may yet go free.
Believe us, Stonestar. We are your friends. Every man needs
friends, and none more than you, Stonestar!'

FRIENDS? I had friends, and not just my ghostly companions either. My father had laboured mightily to build his
boundary fences high and thorny, to lay traps of briar and
mire across all the tracks that led on to our land, to deepen
streams and heighten walls. The hunters still came but often at greater cost to themselves than their prey, and the wild
things took note that here was sanctuary. Soon the Stonestar woods were full of deer who treated me as their own,
and on the bare fellside, I danced with the ungainly hares to
the tune of a thousand singing birds.

And still the mills of the law ground on, till as I neared my
tenth year, rumours spread north of a new spirit of democ-
racy in the great cities, and though there was still much
grinding to do, it was no longer so certain as in the old days
that Milady would get the pure flour and leave my father
with the chaff.

These rumours it probably was that broke the uneasy
truce which had come to exist between the Castle and

Stonestar. Milady was now a mature woman at the height of her powers and beauty. She kept her court in the capital and rarely came north to visit what was merely one among her many estates. That a broken old man and his half-wild child should eventually be annihilated by her lawyers was enough for her. But when, on a visit of inspection to the Castle, she caught a whisper of the possibility that the law might find some merit in my father's case, she gave the signal for action.

They came in the dark and took us in our nightclothes with hardly a struggle. They put torches to Stonestar, bound us together on a single horse, and led us away down the valley. I was facing backwards. I saw flames painting the sky and heard the crash of falling masonry as the great roof beam collapsed in a wave of golden ashes.

The men who took us did not bother to muffle their faces, but I was too young to grasp the significance of this indifference to recognition.

My father however knew what it meant.

'Son,' he whispered as we bounced along, 'if you get the chance to run, run! Think not of me. Run till you are far from here. Then when you are rested, run again. Forget this place, forget your name, forget your father. They will put a mark upon you which will mean your death, so ask for no man's help for you can trust no one. Run. All the days of your life, you must run!'

They took us right down the valley. We passed the Castle at a little distance and heard music and laughter on the soft night air, but we never paused, still following the course of the river till it began to broaden as it neared the sea.

Then at last we came to a halt on a long level plain of sand, gleaming in the starlight and trembling gently beneath the horses' tread. Away before us it stretched, its damp gleam broken by the sparkle of pools and rivulets, and eventually by a broader fillet of dim light. This was the river, diffused now into a shallow estuary more than a mile wide and crossable at low tide by a fast-moving man guided by an expert sand-pilot.

But tonight there was no pilot; between us and the cottage lights twinkling on the further shore were pools and creeks and quicksands; and away to the west could be heard the passionate groaning of the sea as the tide came rushing in to embrace the reluctant river.

They cut our bonds and pushed us off the horse's back. I flung my arms around my father's waist and hung there trembling from fear and from cold for I was naked apart from my loose cotton nightshirt. There we remained till a coach came bowling along the level sands, drawn by four grey horses. We did not need the arms on the door to tell us who sat behind the curtained window.

My father strained forward and cried, 'Have you come to see your minions murder us, Milady? Or is that work you wish to reserve to your own dainty hands?'

Despite his near nakedness he was no figure of pathos and his bravely spoken words gave me courage too. I was able to look up to see the curtain drawn back. A palely beautiful woman's face looked out and a gentle voice, said 'Murder? Who speak of murder? No man of mine will raise a hand against you. You and your child are free to go.'

My father said nothing but began to urge me forward towards the nearer shore.

'No,' said that gentle voice. 'There lies your path.'

And a slender bare arm reached from the coach window and a long white finger with a blood-red nail pointed south across the estuary.

Now the factor urged his horse forward, his hand resting on the pistol butt protruding from his waistband. But there was no need. My father did not stay to argue. Already he was thinking of me. Each moment we spent here brought the tide snuffling and snorting further up the sands. For a grown man, even one rendered so thin by deprivation as my father, there was little hope. Before we were out of sight of our tormentors, strung out along the shore to prevent us cutting back, his feet were sinking deep in the saturated sand.

But for me there was still a chance.

'Run, run!' he urged. 'Feel wings on your heels, skim the surface, don't stop for a moment, never look back!'

And so I ran, alongside my father at first, but soon I drew ahead of him, my slight frame not heavy enough to do more than break the sand's surface while his weight was already sinking him calf deep.

'Run, run!' he still screamed at me. 'I command you, boy. Run!'

Soon I too was beginning to flounder. Once I looked back and saw his torso rearing out of the sand with the first fingers of the tide already floating his nightshirt around his waist.

'Run!' he shouted still. 'Run for your life, for all of your life.'

I heard his words in my ears long after I must have been out of earshot; long after the waters must have closed over his head.

I heard them still as I nimbled my way like a sea bird up the opposing shore. I heard them in my sleep at night and when I woke in the grey dawn. And I heard them every day of the rest of my life till twenty-five years later, ragged and penniless, I came ashore in this great capital city and, loitering aimlessly through its unwelcoming streets, was brushed aside by a coach pulled by four grey horses and with an unforgettable coat of arms on its door.

I ran after it for two miles or more, ran as I hadn't run since that night on the sands, and when I saw it turn through the gates of a great town mansion, I collapsed gasping against a wall; and as I recovered my breath, I realised my father's voice was still.

'STONESTAR, were you paid to kill her? Is that it? You have the look of a sailor, Stonestar. Were you suborned by foreigners? Or did you rape her, Stonestar? Had you been at sea too long and couldn't wait? Speak, man. We're men of the world, we understand. But first, tell us where the body lies, Stonestar. Tell us that, and you may rest.'

MY FATHER'S BODY lies deep beneath those greedy northern sands which never give up their dead. No obsequies were spoken over his coffin; no friends wept, no faithful dog scratched the sealing soil; no obelisk was raised to record the excellence of his life and the sorrow of his son; no flowers in season shed their fragrant dew.

It was not enough for me simply to kill this woman who trembled before me in her nightgown. Wealth and cunning doctors had kept her beautiful, as want and harsh neglect had dilapidated me, so that now she probably looked the younger; yet death would come to her soon enough, and I did not want merely to steal from her a few useless years. I wanted her to remember.

'What does Stonestar mean to you, Milady?' I demanded.

'I don't understand you. What do you mean? What do you want?'

'Stonestar!' I snarled, pressing the knife close against her throat.

Fear sharpened her memory.

'There's a ruin on my northern estate,' she quavered. 'Isn't that the name the peasants use...?'

*A ruin on my northern estate...*

With those words she killed a drunken dream I sometimes had of returning to Stonestar and mending my fractured life there. It no longer existed except in my memory. Its reality was a pile of weed-grown rubble on my father's murderer's estate.

She saw my abstraction and made a sudden grab at a bell-pull.

I hit her on the temple with the haft on my dagger and she collapsed across the bed. I rolled her up in the silk coverlet and threw her across my shoulder. She weighed very little. Vanity had kept her from indulging that appetite at least.

In the wide vestibule at the foot of the stairs, two maids were kneeling by the footman I had knocked unconscious when he opened the door. They screamed when they saw me. I nodded at them and smiled and walked by them into the night.

The hunt must have been up very quickly yet I neither saw nor heard anything of it. Perhaps no one surmised that I would simply walk through the streets with my unlikely burden over my shoulder. And once I entered the alleys of dockland which was my goal, I knew I was unlikely to be interfered with there, even if I walked with a severed head in either hand.

By the time I reached the river, she was beginning to revive. I saw that my timing was perfect. The tide was out, leaving a smooth margin of mud, plated with silver by a rising moon, between the harbour steps and the deep central channel where ships lay anchored with bow and stern lanterns rocking gently as the sleeping monsters pulled against their chains.

I pushed her before me down the steps till we reached the level of the mud. She was fully awake now.

'What do you want from me?' she cried. 'I'll give you money...jewels...my body...anything! There'll be no prosecution...I'll sign a paper...'

'I want nothing,' I cut across her rising pleas. 'You're free to go.'

She looked at me in disbelief, then tried to take a faltering step upwards.

I shook my head. Out in the channel the red and white lanterns were rocking to a different rhythm as the tide turned.

'No, Milady,' I said, pointing to the sleeping ships. 'There lies your path.'

Now I think she understood. Certainly something stirred in that evil old mind for she made no further effort to plead with me, but, gathering up her nightgown, she turned and began to run across the shining mud.

'WE DON'T NEED a body to try you, Stonestar. You do understand that? Not telling us where she is won't stop you being hanged. Why don't you co-operate? Who knows? A family able to express its grief could be that much more susceptible to a plea for clemency...'

But finally they give up, and having abandoned both threats and promises, they now impose upon me without forethought the one deprivation that can cause me pain. For now I am shut away without the daily visits of my interrogators, my guards never speak to me, and though I talk to myself constantly, from my own lips the word no longer has its healing magic.

Stonestar...Stonestar...Stonestar...

All I can see is a pile of charred rubble on a dead woman's estate.

Time passes. Soon there will be no time. I fall silent myself. I have forgotten my name. I have forgotten all names. I am like a man who has had nothing in his life except a dream, and now he is waking to forget it.

Dawn. Light weeping through the bars. Then footsteps in the corridor, keys in the locks, stern faces in the doorway. And my arms pinioned behind me, a hood pulled roughly over my head.

They hustle me forward. It isn't far. Will no one speak? A few steps up. The rope against my throat.

Please God, let someone speak!

A harsh, jeering voice close to my ear.

'Goodbye, Stonestar!'

AND A SHEPHERD driving his sheep through the vapours drawn up by the rising sun was surprised by the laughter of children; and looking across to the fire-blackened ruin, he saw a slim and naked boy run down the sloping meadow and dive like an arrow into the shining river.

# THE LAST SARA

★

## SUSAN KELLY

I'M STEPHANIE LAWLESS; my friends call me Steve. I was with the City of London Police until a year ago and I was good at it. I was all set to take my sergeant's exams when I upped and quit.

It was the name. I was sick of taking suspects into the interview room; putting on my toughest expression; switching on my tape recorder; saying, 'I'm Detective Constable Lawless'—and recording their mindless sniggering.

So I resigned, just like that; ignored the protests of my long-time boyfriend Detective Sergeant Jim Smith—who even offered me the marital protection of his own anonymous surname—and went freelance. I became the boss and sole employee of the Lawless Detective Agency.

The name brought people in: they still thought it was a joke. Well, most of them did. Some of them thought it meant I'd do things that shaded into the area of the criminal. They were quickly shown the door, as were would-be clients who insisted offensively that anyone called Steve Lawless had to be a man and a big one at that.

Lately I'd begun to specialise. It was a sad sign of the times—a trend which, like Mutant Hero Turtles and Madonna, had flown supersonically across the Atlantic. My clients were young women: stockbrokers, merchant bankers, barristers. They came to me by word of mouth, through the City Women's Network where it was whispered over the coffee and brandy that Ms Lawless was efficient, discreet and fairly cheap.

This young woman—I thought of her generically as 'Sara'—had a good address although she was reluctant to give it at first. She lived in Docklands if she was trendy or in Islington if more conservative. She had a car with electric windows and real leather seats. She owned shares—not just in British Telecom or London Electricity but a carefully balanced portfolio built up over the years. She had PEPs and a TESSA and a pension scheme.

She was in her early thirties and single, having spent the last dozen years building her career. Just lately she'd found herself peering into prams and thinking how lovely the cribs in John Lewis were with their stencilled sides and floating draperies. Then Mr Possible came along. Sometimes he was Mr Wonderful but mostly he was just Mr Might-Be-Right. She was ready to take the plunge.

Except... that she had so much to lose.

There *was* usually something. She was bright, Sara, often brilliant. And then there was her woman's intuition which had brought her to that back street in the fashionable part of Wandsworth in the first place. Bisexuality, maybe, or promiscuity—so risky these days. More usually it was just petty fraud, bad credit records, debts. In one case it was a woman in Stockwell with a prior claim: she was his wife.

Sara would come back at the end of a week: full of hope, a little nervous, looking for reassurance. She would examine the photos or the credit references without comment; pay her bill without quibble; and leave without pride. She never seemed very *grateful* for all my hard work—for the cold nights outside his flat, for the boring hours spent in St Catherine's House or the Land Registry.

I longed to tell her how very far from unique she was: how many other lonely Saras there were in this city. But I knew that Sara hated to be pitied.

But to get to the Last Sara.

One morning about two weeks ago, I'd just put the kettle on and happened to glance out of the window to the street two floors below. A taxi had drawn up outside the Midland bank opposite and a Sara got out and looked around. I knew she was a Sara—it was something in the suit and the briefcase and the look of disbelief that such slums still existed in South London in 1991.

I rinsed the spare mug at the corner sink. Sometimes, browsing in the remnant china shops, I considered buying a mug with the name 'Sara' on it for occasions like these. I put a bit more water in the kettle and waited for the knock at the door.

'AND THEN THERE'S AIDS, of course.' The Last Sara reddened slightly as she reached the end of her confused but brief justification ten minutes later. 'Not that...I mean, of course, no one knows...'

'It's seventy-five a day plus expenses,' I said. 'You should allow a week to ten days, average. Two hundred and fifty deposit. I'll take a cheque. Is that all right?'

Sara nodded. 'Money's not a problem.' She began to write out a cheque. I noticed that she wore a rather nice diamond and sapphire engagement ring. So we were playing for high stakes here.

'More coffee?'

'No thanks.' I suspected she had been about to say 'No fear.' That cheap powdered stuff from Budgens was false economy. Definitely.

'I need a name and address for him, his place of work, car registration would be helpful otherwise make and colour. If you have a photo that would be great, otherwise I'll take a full description.'

My businesslike attitude seemed to relax Sara. We were talking the same language: money and facts. It made checking up that the man you loved wasn't a gold-digging, pox-ridden bigamist that much more bearable.

TWO YEARS EARLIER I could not have said for certain what Future Options were. Now half the men I investigated claimed to be in them. I knew it was the sharp end of the City—the one where you were a paper millionaire on Monday and looking at the wrong end of a bankruptcy court on Friday. Future options traders were, by definition, gambling men. It always boded ill for Sara.

My heart sank as I followed Adam Scott and another muscular Adonis to the nearest wine bar. There was always a moment at the start of a case when I wanted to pack it in; to retreat into the waiting arms of Sergeant Jim Smith who had shared my Surrey childhood. There was nothing unknown in Jim's past; nothing sinister beyond a little innocent trespass in the grounds of the local manor house on the night of my sixteenth birthday.

I can still remember the texture of the lawn beneath my naked—and shivering—body.

Adam Scott was a golden boy—his photograph didn't do him justice. At twenty-nine he had to be some years younger than Sara. He was also in another sexual league: Sara was smartly turned out, even elegant; she had intelligent eyes, neat features, nice figure. But her best friend wouldn't have called her beautiful. Adam Scott was beautiful. Every female eye followed him round the room and the assistant in the Golden Grape flirted with him relentlessly.

No, there had to be something although it wasn't, on the face of it, money. Adam had a BMW and a penthouse on New Crane Wharf which was, according to the Land Registry, not only legitimately his but unencumbered by any mortgage. A painstaking afternoon at St Catherine's House had not turned up a wife hidden in the wardrobe. It looked like being a long, hard case.

Occasionally I would find nothing. Even then it didn't mean that there was nothing to find, just that I maybe hadn't been smart enough to find it. Besides, once the seeds of doubt were sown in Sara's mind, once she'd climbed the thirty steep steps up to my office and fished in her briefcase for her cheque book...you might as well write the relationship off.

BY THE WEEKEND, it was beginning to look as if Sara had decided to give him...whatever the opposite of the benefit of the doubt was, anyway. I had yet to see the lovers together—rather a low-key social life, I thought, before remembering that I myself had been too busy with this case to see Jim all week.

City fraud was Jim's and my area of expertise back in the days when we made a cracking team working out of Wood Street police station. I remember the day I handed in my notice. I can still hear the grief in Superintendent Talbot's voice:

'You've got a nose for it, Stevie. You could catch Mother Teresa out fiddling her tax returns. You always know when people are lying to you.'

It was the best unsolicited testimonial I was ever likely to get and Bill Talbot was right, of course. I could smell an insider dealer, could smell the cockiness mixed with fear in the sweat on his Armani suit. Steve, the sniffer dog.

And Adam Scott smelt like last week's kipper.

I'll get you, I thought. I was sitting in a dark corner at Tramps, nursing a coke, wondering how soon I could leave and watching him jiggling about with a mammiferous redhead. I'd get him for the sake of all the poor, deceived Saras.

'I'M SO VERY GRATEFUL,' the Last Sara said, to my amazement. We were sitting in the Wadsworth office again ten days after her first visit. 'Now, how much do I owe you?' I did some rough sums on the back of an envelope and told her. As Sara began to write out the cheque, I said, 'You realise I have to take it to the police?'

'I'll go to them myself.' She ripped out the cheque with a satisfactory tearing noise and handed it across the table.

'I dunno,' I said. She might warn him, give him a chance to do a bunk. 'If you still feel . . . you know.'

'I assure you I don't feel the least bit "you know" about him any more,' Sara said crisply. 'Let me shop him. It'll be my way of getting my own back.'

I hesitated but said at last, 'I'll give you twenty-four hours.' I trusted her. I always knew when people were lying to me.

BUSINESS HAD TAILED OFF again and I was on my way home to my flat in Battersea the following lunchtime when the first edition of the *Standard* caught my eye.

### INSIDER DEALING ON FUTURE OPTIONS—DAWN ARREST

I bought a copy and found myself staring at an unflattering front-page picture of Adam Scott, looking a good deal more dishevelled and a lot paler than he had at Tramps. But Adam didn't keep my attention for long. A smaller picture at the bottom of the page grabbed at my eyes as did another headline:

### PERSONAL TRIUMPH FOR CITY FRAUD SQUAD INSPECTOR

Grimly, I read on.

'Senior police officers were full of praise today for Detective Inspector Sara Crook of the Wood Street

Fraud Squad. Weeks of painstaking undercover work by vivacious Inspector Crook, 34, resulted in the arrest of insider dealer, Adam Scott, in the early hours of this morning. Mr Scott is being held on charges believed to involve millions of pounds.

'''She's only been with us six months but she's got a real nose for it,'' said Superintendent William Talbot, who heads the square. ''She could catch Mother Teresa out fiddling her tax returns. She always knows when people are lying to her.''

'Inspector Crook was assisted in her undercover operation by her colleague and fiancé Detective Sergeant Jim Smith, pictured with her here.'

I held the pictures up in the early spring sunlight. There was Jim—dear dependable Jim Smith, my childhood sweetheart—with his arm tightly round Sara Crook, who, unlike me, had not let her name get in the way of her ambition.

Unlike me, the Last Sara was not a quitter.

'''We've been after Scott for ages,'' Superintendent Talbot said. ''But he'd covered his tracks well. Then just yesterday Sara and Jim came up with the crucial bit of evidence we needed.''

'''I suppose we could become a sort of sleuthing couple,'' said Inspector Crook, displaying her diamond and sapphire engagement ring for the camera, ''like Peter Wimsey and Harriet Vane, or Tommy and Tuppence Beresford.''''

I turned to the back of the paper and began to leaf through the Situations Vacant.

I told you: I'm a quitter.

# THE RAPE OF KINGDOM HILL

★

## DICK FRANCIS

THURSDAY AFTERNOON, Tricksy Wilcox scratched his armpit absentmindedly and decided Claypits wasn't worth backing in the 2.30. Tricksy Wilcox sprawled in the sagging armchair with a half-drunk can of beer within comforting reach and a huge colour television bringing him the blow by blow from the opening race of the three-day meeting at Kingdom Hill. Only mugs, he reflected complacently, would be putting in a nine to five stint in the sort of July heat wave that would have done justice to the Sahara. Sensible guys like himself sat around at home with the windows open and their shirts off, letting their beards grow while the sticky afternoon waned towards opening time.

In winter Tricksy was of the opinion that only mugs struggled to travel to work through snow and sleet, while sensible guys stayed warm in front of the TV, betting on the jumpers; and in spring there was rain, and in the autumn, fog. Tricksy at thirty-four had brought unemployment to a fine art and considered the idea of a full honest day's work to be a joke. It was Tricksy's wife who went out in all weathers to her job in the supermarket, Tricksy's wife who paid the rent on the council flat and left the exact money for the milkman. Eleven years of Tricksy had left her cheerful, unresentful, and practical. She had waited without emotion through his two nine-month spells in prison and accepted that one day would find him back there. Her dad had been in and out all her childhood. She felt at home with the minor criminal mind.

Tricksy watched Claypits win the 2.30 with insulting ease and drank down his dented self-esteem with the last of the beer. Nothing he bloody touched, he thought gloomily, was any bloody good these days. He was distinctly short of the readies and had once or twice had to cut down on necessities like drinks and fags. What he wanted, now, was a nice little wheeze, a nice little tickle, to con a lot of unsuspecting mugs into opening their wallets. The scarce ticket racket, now, that had done him proud for years, until the coppers nicked him with a stack of forged duplicates in his pocket at Wimbledon. And tourists were too sly by half these days, you couldn't sell them subscriptions to non-existent porn magazines, let alone London Bridge.

He could never afterwards work out exactly what gave him the great Bandwagon idea. One minute he was peacefully watching the 3 o'clock at Kingdom Hill, and the next he was flooded with a breathtaking, wild, and unholy glee.

He laughed aloud. He slapped his thigh. He stood up and jigged about, unable to bear the audacity of his thoughts sitting down. 'Oh Moses,' he said, gulping for air. 'Money for old rope. Kingdom Hill, here I come.'

Tricksy Wilcox was not the most intelligent of men.


FRIDAY MORNING, Major Kevin Cawdor-Jones, manager of Kingdom Hill racecourse, took his briefcase to the routine meeting of the executive committee, most of whom detested each other. Owned and run by a small private company constantly engaged in boardroom wars, the racecourse suffered from the results of spiteful internecine decisions and never made the profit it could have done.

The appointment of Cawdor-Jones was typical of the mismanagement. Third on the list of possibles, and far less able than one and two, he had been chosen solely to sidestep the bitter deadlock between the pro one line-up and the pro two. Kingdom Hill in consequence had acquired a mediocre administrator; and the squabbling executives usually managed to thwart his more sensible suggestions.

As a soldier Cawdor-Jones had been impulsive, rashly courageous, and easygoing, qualities which had ensured that he had not been given the essential promotion to colonel. As a man he was lazy and likeable, and as a manager, soft.

The Friday meeting as usual wasted little time in coming to blows.

'Massive step-up of security,' repeated Bellamy positively. 'Number one priority. Starting at once. Today.'

Thin and sharp featured, Bellamy glared aggressively round the table, and Roskin as usual with the drawling voice opposed him.

'Security costs money, my dear Bellamy.'

Roskin spoke patronisingly, knowing that nothing infuriated Bellamy more. Bellamy's face darkened with fury, and the security of the racecourse, like so much else, was left to the outcome of a personal quarrel.

Bellamy insisted, 'We need bigger barriers, specialised extra locks on all internal doors and double the number of police. Work must start at once.'

'Race crowds are not hooligans, my dear Bellamy.'

Cawdor-Jones inwardly groaned. He found it tedious enough already, on non-race days, to make his tours of inspection, and he was inclined anyway not to stick punctiliously to the safeguards that already existed. Bigger barriers between enclosures would mean he could no longer climb over or through, but would have to walk the long way round. More locks meant more keys, more time-wasting, more nuisance. And all presumably for the sake of frustrating the very few scroungers who tried to cross from a cheaper to a dearer enclosure without paying. He thought he would very much prefer the status quo.

The tempers rose around him, and the voices also. He waited resignedly for a gap. 'Er...' he said, clearing his throat.

The heated pro-Bellamy faction and the sneering pro-Roskin clique both turned towards him hopefully. Cawdor-Jones was their mutual letout; except, that was, when his solution was genuinely constructive, when they both ve-toed it because they wished they had thought of it them-selves.

'A lot of extra security would mean more work for our staff,' he said diffidently. 'We might have to take on an ex-tra man or two to cope with it ... and after the big initial outlay there would always be maintenance ... and ... er ... well, what real harm can anyone do to a racecourse?'

This weak oil stilled the waters enough for both sides to begin their retreat with their positions and opinions intact.

'You have a point about the staff,' Bellamy conceded grudgingly, knowing that two extra men would cost a great deal more than locks, and that the racecourse couldn't af-ford them. 'But I still maintain that tighter security is es-sential and very much overdue.'

Cawdor-Jones, in his easygoing way, privately disagreed. Nothing had ever happened to date. Why should anything ever happen in future?

The discussion grumbled on for half an hour, and noth-ing at all was done.

FRIDAY AFTERNOON, Tricksy Wilcox went to the races hav-ing pinched a tenner from his wife's holiday fund in the best teapot. The trip was a recce to spy out the land, and Tricksy, walking around with his greedy eyes wide open, couldn't stop himself chuckling. It did occur to him once or twice that his light-hearted, single-handed approach was a waste: the big boys would have had it all planned to a second and would have set their sights high in their humourless way. But Tricksy was a loner who avoided gang life on the grounds that it was too much like hard work; bossed around all the time, and with no pension rights into the bargain.

He downed half-pints of beer at various bars and wagered smallish amounts on the tote. He looked at the horses in the parade ring and identified those jockeys whose faces he knew from TV, and he attentively watched the races. At the end of the afternoon, with modest winnings keeping him solvent, he chuckled his way home.

Friday afternoon Mrs Angelisa Ludville sold two £1 tote tickets to Tricksy Wilcox, and hundreds to other people whom she knew as little. Her mind was not on her job, but on the worrying pile of unpaid bills on her bookshelf at home. Life had treated her unkindly since her fiftieth birthday, robbing her of her looks, because of worry, and her husband, because of a blonde. Deserted, divorced and childless, she could nevertheless have adapted contentedly to life alone had it not been for the drastic drop in comfort. Natural optimism and good humour were gradually draining away in the constant grinding struggle to make shortening ends meet.

Angelisa Ludville eyed longingly the money she took through her tote window. Wads of the stuff passed through her hands each working day, and only a fraction of what the public wasted on gambling would, she felt, solve all her problems handsomely. But honesty was a lifetime habit; and besides, stealing from the tote was impossible. The takings for each race were collected and checked immediately. Theft would be instantly revealed. Angelisa sighed and tried to resign herself to the imminent cutting off of her telephone.

SATURDAY MORNING, Tricksy Wilcox dressed himself carefully for the job in hand. His wife, had she not been stacking baked beans in the supermarket, would have advised against the fluorescent orange socks. Tricksy, seeing his image in the bedroom mirror only as far down as the knees, was confident that the dark suit, dim tie and bowler hat gave him the look of a proper race-going gent. He had even, without reluctance, cut two inches off his hair, and removed a flourishing moustache. Complete with outsize binoculars case slung over his shoulder, he smirked at his transformation with approval and set out with a light step to catch the train to Kingdom Hill.

On the racecourse Major Kevin Cawdor-Jones made his raceday round of inspection with his usual lack of thoroughness. Slipshod holes in his management also resulted in the police contingent arriving half an hour late and understrength; and not enough racecards had been ordered from the printers.

'Not to worry,' said Cawdor-Jones, shrugging it all off easily.

Mrs Angelisa Ludville travelled to the course in the tote's own coach, along with fifty colleagues. She looked out of the window at the passing suburbs and thought gloomily about the price of electricity.

Saturday afternoon at 2.30 she was immersed in the routine of issuing tickets and taking money, concentrating on her work and feeling reasonably happy. She arranged before her the fresh batch of tickets, those for the 3 o'clock, the biggest race of the day. The extra-long queues would soon be forming outside, and speed and efficiency in serving the punters was not only her job but, indeed, her pride.

At 2.55 Cawdor-Jones was in his office next to the weighing room trying to sort out the muddle over the casual workers' pay. At 2.57 the telephone at his elbow rang for about the twentieth time in the past two hours and he picked up the receiver with his mind still on the disputed hourly rates due to the stickers-back of kicked-up chunks of turf.

'Cawdor-Jones,' he said automatically.

A man with an Irish accent began speaking quietly.

'What?' said Cawdor-Jones. 'Speak up, can't you. There's too much noise here . . . I can't hear you.'

The man with the Irish accent repeated his message with the same soft half-whisper.

'*What?*' said Cawdor-Jones. But his caller had rung off.

'Oh my God,' said Cawdor-Jones, and stretched a hand to the switch that connected him to the internal broadcasting system. He glanced urgently at the clock. Its hands clicked round to 2.59, and at that moment the fourteen runners for the 3 o'clock were being led into the starting stalls.

'Ladies and gentlemen,' said Cawdor-Jones, his voice reverberating from every loudspeaker on the racecourse. 'We have been warned that a bomb has been planted somewhere in the stands. Would you please all leave at once and go over into the centre of the course while the police arrange a search.'

The moment of general shock lasted less than a second: then the huge race crowd streamed like a river down from the steps, up from the tunnels, out of the doors, running, pelting, elbowing towards the safety of the open spaces on the far side of the track.

Bars emptied dramatically with half-full glasses overturned and smashed in the panic. The tote queues melted instantaneously and the ticket sellers followed them helter-skelter. The stewards vacated their high box at a dignified downhill rush and the racing press pell-melled to the exit without hanging round to alert their papers. City editors could wait half an hour. Bombs wouldn't.

The scrambling thousands deserted all the racecourse buildings within a space of two minutes. Only a few stayed behind, and chief of these was Kevin Cawdor-Jones, who had never lacked for personal courage and now saw it as his duty as a soldier to remain at his post.

The under-strength band of policemen collected bit by bit outside the weighing room, each man hiding his natural apprehension under a reassuring front. Probably another bloody hoax, they told each other. It was always a hoax. Or nearly always. Their officer took charge of organising the search and told the civilian Cawdor-Jones to remove himself to safety.

'No, no,' said Cawdor-Jones. 'While you look for the bomb I'll make quite sure that everyone's out.' He smiled a little anxiously and dived purposefully into the weighing room.

All clear here, he thought, peering rapidly round the jockey's washroom. All clear in the judges' box, the photo-finish developing room, the kitchens, the boiler-room, the tote, the offices, the stores ... He bustled from building to building, knowing all the back rooms, the nooks and crannies where some deaf member of the staff, some drunk member of the public, might be sitting unawares.

He saw no people. He saw no bomb. He returned a little breathlessly to the open space outside the weighing room and waited for a report from the slower police.

Around the stands Tricksy Wilcox was putting the great Bandwagon idea into sloppy execution. Chuckling away internally over the memory of an Irish impersonation good enough for entry to Equity, he bustled speedily from bar to bar and in and out of the other doors, filling his large empty binoculars case with provender. It was amazing, he thought, giggling, how careless people were in a panic.

Twice, he came face to face with policemen.

'All clear in there, officer,' he said purposefully, each time pointing back to where he had been. Each time the police gaze flickered unsuspectingly over the bowler hat, the dark suit, dim tie and took him for one of the racecourse staff.

Only the orange socks stopped him getting clean away. One policeman, watching his receding back view, frowned uncertainly at the brilliant segments between trouser-leg and shoe and started slowly after him.

'Hey...' he said.

Tricksy turned his head, saw the law advancing, lost his nerve, and bolted. Tricksy was never the most intelligent of men.

SATURDAY AFTERNOON at 4 o'clock, Cawdor-Jones made another announcement.

'It appears the bomb warning was just another hoax. It is now safe for everyone to return to the stands.'

The crowd streamed back in reverse and made for the bars. The barmaids returned to their posts and immediately raised hands and voices in a screeching sharp chorus of affronted horror.

'Someone's pinched all the takings!'

'The cheek of it! Taken our tips, and all!'

In the various tote buildings, the ticket sellers stood appalled. Most of the huge intake for the biggest race of the meeting had simply vanished.

Angelisa Ludville looked with utter disbelief at her own plundered cashbox. White, shaking, she joined the clamour of voices. 'The money's gone.'

Cawdor-Jones received report after report into a face of anxious despair. He knew no doors had been locked after the stampede to the exit. He knew no security measures whatever had been taken. The racecourse wasn't equipped to deal with such a situation. The committee would undoubtedly blame him. Might even give him the sack.

At 4.30 he listened with astounded relief to news from the police that a man had been apprehended and was now helping to explain how his binoculars case came to be crammed to overflowing with used Treasury notes, many of them bearing a fresh watermark resulting from the use of a wet beer glass as a paperweight.

MONDAY MORNING Tricksy Wilcox appeared gloomily before a magistrate and was remanded in custody for seven days. The great Bandwagon idea hadn't been so hot after all, and they would undoubtedly send him down for more than nine months, this time.

Only one thought brightened his future. The police had tried all weekend to get information out of him, and he had kept his mouth tight shut. Where, they wanted to know, had he hidden the biggest part of his loot?

Tricksy said nothing.

There had only been room in the binoculars case for one-tenth of the stolen money. Where had he put the bulk?

Tricksy wasn't telling.

He would get off more lightly they said, if he surrendered the rest.

Tricksy didn't believe it. He grinned sardonically and shook his head. Tricksy knew from past experience that he would have a much easier time inside as the owner of a larger hidden cache. He'd be respected. Treated with proper awe. He'd have status. Nothing on earth would have persuaded him to spill the beans.

Monday morning Major Cawdor-Jones took his red face to an emergency meeting of his executive committee and agreed helplessly with Bellamy's sharply reiterated opinion that the racecourse security was a disgrace.

'I warned you,' Bellamy repeated for the tenth self-righteous time. 'I warned you all. We need more locks. There are some excellent slam-shut devices available for the cashboxes in the tote. I'm told that all money can be secured in five seconds. I propose that these devices be installed immediately throughout the racecourse.'

He glared belligerently round the table. Roskin kept his eyes down and merely pursed his mouth, and Kingdom Hill voted to bolt its doors now that the horse was gone.

Monday evening Angelisa Ludville poured a double gin, switched on the television and put her feet up. Beside her lay a pile of stamped and addressed envelopes, each containing one of the dreaded bills. She sighed contentedly. Never, she thought, would she forget the shock of seeing her empty till. Never would she get over the fright it had given her. Never would she forget the rush of relief when she realised that everyone had been robbed, not just herself. Because she knew perfectly well that it was one of the £5 windows whose take she had scooped up on the scramble to the door. It would have been plain stupid to have lifted the money from her own place. She couldn't know that there would have been another, more ambitious thief. And besides, there was far more cash at the £5 window.

Monday evening Kevin Cawdor-Jones sat in his bachelor flat thinking about the second search of Kingdom Hill. All day Sunday the police had repeated the nook and cranny inspection, but slowly, without fear, looking not for a bang but a bank. Cawdor-Jones had given his willing assistance, but nothing at all had been found.

'Tricksy must have had a partner,' said the officer morosely. 'But we won't get a dicky bird out of him.'

Cawdor-Jones, unsacked from his managership, smiled gently at the memory of the past few days. Cawdor-Jones, impulsive and rashly courageous, had made the most of the opportunity Tricksy had provided. Cawdor-Jones, whose nerve could never be doubted, had driven away on Saturday evening with the jackpot from the tote.

He leaned over the arm of his chair and fondly patted his bulging briefcase.

THE CLEWSEY CLASSICS

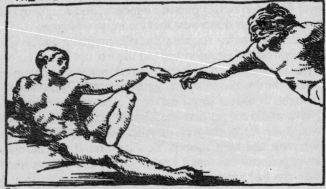

"SO YOU SEE, SIR EUSTACE, THE GAME IS UP."

# THE CRIME WRITERS' ASSOCIATION

The CWA was founded in 1953 by John Creasey to 'raise the prestige and fortunes of mystery, detective story and crime writers, and writers generally'.

Membership is open to professionally published crime writers, of fiction or non-fiction, and associate membership to others working within the genre. Our monthly newsletter, *Red Herrings*, keeps everyone in touch, for we now have a worldwide membership.

In London and in 'chapters' around the country we meet both to exchange views and hear features from experts dealing with every aspect of crime.

Our coveted awards include the CWA Gold Dagger for the best crime novel, the Silver dagger for the runner-up and the John Creasey Award for the best first crime novel.

The prestigious CWA/Cartier Diamond Dagger, also awarded annually, goes to an author who has made an outstanding contribution to crime-writing. Recipients so far include: Eric Ambler, P. D. James, John le Carré, Dick Francis, Julian Symons, Ruth Rendell and Leslie Charteris. We believe John Creasey would approve.

NANCY LIVINGSTON

*Solution to 'The Christmas Crimes At "Cinderella":*
*Nita Grayes.*

# BIOGRAPHICAL NOTES

The contributors to *1st CULPRIT* were invited to describe themselves and their recent work in about forty words.

**Catherine Aird**'s most recently published book is *The Body Politic*. Three of her earlier works are to be published in a one-volume paperback in 1993, and she is presently working on a book called *A Going Concern*.

**Alex Auswaks** is the author of *A Trick of Diamonds* and a number of short stories involving politics and the occult in Russia.

**Robert Barnard** spent much of his adult life teaching English in universities in Australia and Norway. He is now a full-time crime writer, and lives in Leeds. His most recent books are *A Fatal Attachment* and *A Scandal in Belgravia*.

**Alida Baxter** is probably best known for a series of humorous autobiographies which started with *Flat on My Back*. Currently she concentrates on short stories and serials with a mystery element for international magazines.

**Simon Brett** has written fourteen crime novels featuring actor Charles Paris and four about the the elderly widow Mrs Pargeter, the latest of which is entitled *Mrs Pargeter's Pound Of Flesh*. He also wrote the radio and television series 'After Henry'.

**Clewsey**'s cartoons appear regularly in the CWA's monthly newsletter, *Red Herrings*.

Born in London, **Liza Cody** is the author of six Anna Lee mysteries, most recently *Backhand*, and a new novel, *Bucket Nut*.

**Celia Dale**'s latest novel, *Sheep's Clothing*, her collection of short stories, *A Personal Call*, and an earlier novel, *A Helping Hand*, are available in Penguin. Many of the short stories have been broadcast by the BBC. She lives in London.

**Terence Faherty** is the author of two novels, *Deadstick*, Edgar nominated in 1991, and *Live To Regret*. He lives with his wife, Jan, in Indianapolis, Indiana.

In 1989 **Dick Francis** received the CWA's Cartier Diamond Dagger, in recognition of his outstanding contribution to the crime genre. In 1991 Tufts University of Boston awarded him an honorary Doctorate of Humane Letters. His latest novel, *Driving Force*, is published by Michael Joseph.

**Antonia Fraser** has had two collections of short stories published, *Jemima Shore's First Case* and *Jemima Shore At The Sunny Grave* which appeared in paperback in June. She has written seven full-length mysteries, the most recent being *The Cavalier Case*.

**Lesley Grant-Adamson's** *A Life Of Adventure* was published in spring 1992. Her earlier novels, *Patterns In The Dust*, *The Face Of Death*, *Guilty Knowledge*, *Wild Justice*, *Threatening Eye*, *Curse The Darkness* and *Flynn*, are all available in paperback from Faber and Faber.

**Reginald Hill** lives in Cumbria. His latest D. L. Pascoe novel, *Recalled To Life*, was published recently by Harper Collins.

**HRF Keating's** most recent Inspector Ghote novel is *Cheating Death*, with *The Iciest Sun* the newest Ghote paperback. *A Remarkable Case Of Burglary*, a Victorian thriller, has recently been reissued.

**Susan Kelly's** novels, *Hope Against Hope*, *Time Of Hope*, and *Hope Will Answer* are published by Piatkus books in the UK and Scribner's in the US. She lives in London with her solicitor husband and a black cat called Hope.

**Michael Z Lewin's** latest Albert Samson mystery, *Called By A Panther*, is now in paperback.

**James Melville** has written thirteen novels set in Japan and featuring Superintendent Tetsuo Otani. The most recent is *The Body Wore Brocade*.

**Susan Moody,** a former Chairman of the CWA, lives in Bedford. Her latest book, *Hush-A-Bye*, was published in September 1992.

**Stephen Murray** has been a full-time writer for six years. He has published five crime novels (the latest is *Fatal Opinions*) and also the biography of a medical missionary. He lives in Wales with his wife and young son.

Although his thirty-fourth crime novel, *Third Time Fatal*, is due for publication in the autumn, 'A Distant Affray' is **Roger Ormerod**'s first short story. He is an ex-civil servant, his other retirement interest being photography.

**Sara Paretsky**'s newest novel is *Guardian Angel*. Her sequence of novels, featuring Chicago detective V. I. Warshawski, began with *Indemnity Only*, and *Toxic Shock* won the CWA's Silver Dagger award. She was a founder member of Sisters in Crime. She lives in Chicago.

**Ian Rankin** is currently in the USA as winner of the Raymond Chandler Prize. His latest Rebus books are *Wolfman*, *A Good Hanging And Other Stories* and *Strip Jack* (all 1992.)

**Ruth Rendell** is the author of many novels in her own name and as Barbara Vine. Her latest is an Inspector Wexford detective story, *Kissing The Gunner's Daughter*, which was published in February 1992.

**Penelope Wallace** prefers writing short stories but she had four books published in Germany and one, *A Clutch of Bastards*, is currently in print in the UK from Tallis Press.

**Margaret Yorke**'s thirty-fourth novel, *Criminal Damage*, was published by Hutchinson in April 1992.

# ACKNOWLEDGEMENTS

Previously unpublished stories in this collection are: 'Steady As She Goes' by Catherine Aird; 'Sister Brona and the Pornographic Diary' by Alex Auswaks; 'Soldier, from the Wars Returning' by Robert Barnard; 'The Christmas Crimes at "Cinderella"' by Simon Brett; 'In Those Days' by Liza Cody; 'Cuckoo in the Wood' by Lesley Grant-Adamson; 'Stonestar' by Reginald Hill; 'The Last Sara' by Susan Kelly (broadcast on Woman's Hour, 1991); 'Danny Pulls His Weight' by Michael Z Lewin; 'Programmed for Murder' by James Melville; 'Oh, Who Hath Done This Deed?' by Susan Moody; 'Positive Vetting' by Stephen Murray; 'A Distant Affray' by Roger Ormerod; 'Freud at Thirty Paces' by Sara Paretsky; 'Trip Trap' by Ian Rankin.

Acknowledgements are due for first publication to: *Woman's Day* (Australia) and *Woman* (UK) for 'Afterwards' by Alida Baxter; *Winter's Crimes 15* (Macmillan) for 'Faery Tale' by Celia Dale; *The Arts Indiana Literary Supplement 1991* for 'As My Wimsey Takes Me' by Terence Faherty; *The Times* for 'The Rape of Kingdom Hill' by Dick Francis; *The Fiction Magazine* for 'Boots' by Antonia Fraser; *Mrs Craggs: Crimes Cleaned Up* (Buchan and Enright) for 'Mrs Craggs Hears the Nightingale' by HRF Keating; *Esquire Magazine* for 'The Mouse in the Corner' by Ruth Rendell; *Police Review* for 'Goodbye Jenny' by Penelope Wallace; *Winter Crimes 18* (Macmillan) for 'Gifts from the Bridegroom' by Margaret Yorke.

# CANCELLATION

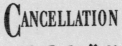

BY *DEATH*

## DORIAN YEAGER

### A Victoria Bowering Mystery

First Time in Paperback

## IT'S A WRAP

While ever anticipating her big break, New York actress Victoria Bowering lands a stint on the hot soap opera, "Raging Passions."

Vic handles the role with her usual aplomb, never dreaming that when the heartthrob star of the soap is murdered, her many talents would be called into action.

Accused are the victim's flaky widow, as well as Vic's almost ex-husband. Small world—she's also dating the investigating cop. The combination can't miss: megalomaniacal producer, blackmail, embezzling, illicit affairs and musical beds. And Vic is up for a cameo...as a corpse.

"...this first novel is pleasantly breezy...."
—*Kirkus Reviews*

**Available in January at your favorite retail stores.**

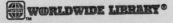
WORLDWIDE LIBRARY®

# THE PRINCE OF DARKNESS

# P. C. Doherty

*First Time in Paperback*

**A Medieval Mystery featuring Hugh Corbett**

HOLY TERRORS

The beautiful Lady Eleanor, mistress of the feckless
Prince of Wales, is banished to Godstow Priory by
King Edward, eager to be rid of an embarrassment
while negotiating his son's betrothal.

Whispers of murder echo through the hallowed halls
when Eleanor dies mysteriously. Hugh Corbett, Edward's
chief clerk and master spy, is dispatched to solve the
riddle. Suspicion falls upon the malicious and cunning
new royal favorite, Piers Gaveston. But others also
wanted Lady Eleanor dead.

"...this novel is well-plotted." —*Mystery News*

**Available in March at your favorite retail stores.**

**WORLDWIDE LIBRARY**®

PRINCE

# DATE WITH A PLUMMETING PUBLISHER
## Toni Brill

*First Time In Paperback*

### A Midge Cohen Mystery

## FROM RUSSIA WITH LOVE

Normally when Midge Cohen's mother calls from her dental receptionist job with the latest gingivitis-cursed dream date, Midge runs for cover. But Simon Waterhouse, the premiere publisher of Russian literature? Now, *that's a* date.

Sadly, the man is a pompous cheapskate, but Midge gets to meet former Russian hooker and literary sensation Polina Volkova, whose juicy Kremlin tell-all is a book to kill for. And die for, apparently, when Waterhouse plunges from a high rise.

"A warm, observant, breezy talent."

—*Kirkus Reviews*

### Available in February at your favorite retail stores.

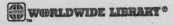 **WORLDWIDE LIBRARY®**

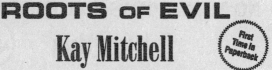

# NO MARDI GRAS FOR THE DEAD

# D. J. Donaldson

### An Andy Broussard/Kit Franklyn Mystery

## NO BED OF ROSES...

Criminal psychologist Kit Franklyn has had experience with skeletons in the closet—but not in her own backyard. The discovery of a body's remains leads her boss, New Orleans chief medical examiner Andy Broussard, to some interesting facts: female, twenty-five, twenty years dead, a prostitute...and brutally murdered.

Two more violent deaths soon follow: an aquarium shark consumes the limbs of one individual; someone else takes a messy plunge at one of the city's classiest hotels. The trail leads back two decades to a night of violent passion in the French Quarter among a group of medical students...and to a present-day killer with more than just secrets buried in his own backyard.

"...keeps you coming back for more." —*Booklist*

**Available in March at your favorite retail stores.**